The MARGARET CATCHPOLE COUNTRY

Scale of Miles

0   1   2   4   6

Main Roads ——— Other Roads ——

Wickham Market

Saxmundham

Lowestoft

Eyke

Tunstall

Snape

ed re lk

gham est

Butley

River Alde

Capel St Andrew

River

Butley

Sudbourne

Boyton

Orford

Aldeburgh

Slaughden

River Ore

Havergate Is.

Lantern Marshes

ley

Bay

Orford Ness

To Darling. Anne.
wishing. you a
Happy Xmas. 1949.

From. Granny. & Grandpa

MARGARET CATCHPOLE

The Girl from Wolfkettel

Autobiography
LOOMING LIGHTS

Novels
THE SMACKSMEN
ABLE SEAMAN

George Goldsmith Carter

Margaret Catchpole
THE GIRL FROM WOLFKETTEL

Constable & Co Ltd

LONDON

PUBLISHED BY

CONSTABLE AND COMPANY LTD

10–12 ORANGE STREET W.C.2

INDIA *and* PAKISTAN

ORIENT LONGMANS LTD

BOMBAY   CALCUTTA   MADRAS

•

CANADA

LONGMANS, GREEN AND COMPANY

TORONTO

First published 1949

Printed in Great Britain by Butler & Tanner Ltd., Frome and London

ACKNOWLEDGEMENTS

To my wife, in the difficult days of flat life, when she was so forbearing.

To Richard Sadler for his share in this book.

To the Reverend Richard Cobbold for his book *The History of Margaret Catchpole, a Suffolk Girl*.

To Miss Dorothy White, Librarian, Ipswich Public Library, for much about Margaret Catchpole herself.

To the Librarian and staff of the National Maritime Museum, Greenwich, for details of " The Glorious First of June."

SMUGGLER'S SONG

On through the ground sea shove!
Light on the larboard bow!
There's a nine knot breeze above,
And a sucking tide below.

Hush! for the beacon fails,
The skulking gauger's by;
Down with your studding sails.
Let jib and foresail fly. . . .

R. S. HAWKER, *c.* 1804–1875.

CHAPTER ONE

I T was an unpleasant October night. Clouds were scudding past a moon as small and watery as a pig's eye. Somewhere down to the nor'rard a gale was gathering, pushing the bulk of the shallow North Sea into sullen, foam-skeined unease.

The visibility was poor. There was no horizon: it merged into the thin moonlit mist in a sheet of dull silver. A watcher straining his eyes might have seen the dark, towering masts of two ships ghosting through the night. In spite of the gathering force of the wind both vessels had every stitch of canvas drawing. The pursuer, H.M. Preventive cutter *Rattlesnake*, was a craft built for speed. Her low hull had a bold sheer, and her lofty tapering masts carried an almost unbelievable spread of canvas. There was a loose footed mains'l, a huge squares'l above which bellied a square tops'l on a tiny yard. In addition she carried a large heads'l, studding sails, topmast stays'l and a reaching jib. She roared along in a smother of white water, the wind strumming her rigging like some great æolean harp.

Frequently a sea would boil up and tower high above her stern, giving the impression that the *Rattlesnake* was about to be pooped. Faster than the wind, faster than the swiftly following sea the Revenue cutter hurtled into the night, sometimes heaving her low counter aloft as if she were about to dive headlong to the sea-bed. A flag fluttered from her yard-arm. It was the Preventive Pennant, a golden castle with a portcullis and two ports, one shut, one open, on a background of dark blue.

On the drenched flush foredeck of the cutter stood a group of men around the long barrel of an eighteen-pounder gun. One of the men was holding a piece of tarpaulin over the vent to protect it from the flying spray. A tall young officer in the blue (and somewhat tarnished) silver of the Preventive Service stood narrowly eyeing the fleeing shape of the brig they were chasing.

This was the *Alde*, fastest brig and most notorious free trader on the whole of the east coast. With the wind abeam she was even faster than the speedy *Rattlesnake*. With the wind aft the cutter had the heels of the brig. The cutter had the wind aft now and was gradually overhauling the brig.

As the *Rattlesnake* lifted to a hissing wave the commanding officer lifted his hand and brought it down with a sharp gesture. " Fire ! "

The long gun belched a dagger-thrust of red flame into the night and the air was suddenly foul with the stench of black powder, instantly purged by the wind. The men at the side-tackles eased the strain as the ball struck a wave-top in a cloud of spray and whirred across the bows of the brig. The officer aboard the cutter snatched up a speaking trumpet. " Heave-to in the King's name ! " he thundered into the night.

The brig *Alde* also carried a mountain of canvas. She was the fastest vessel of her class between the Thames mouth and the Humber. Specially built for smuggling, although ostensibly trading between the east coast and the continent, she possessed a peculiar and rather sinister beauty all of her own. She had a slender hull with little free-board and an unusual tumble-home. Her entry into the water was clean and her stern had none of the usual clumsiness of a brig. It was built to give as little " drag " as possible. Her tall raking masts carried one more sail than was usual for a brig ; and in addition she bore main stays'l and studding sails. Notwithstanding her disreputable business it was instantly obvious to the eyes of a seaman that she was a vessel well cared for, even loved by those aboard her.

Her brasswork, usually as bright as gold, was now hidden beneath a coating of tallow. All her hand-rails were served round with canvas scrubbed to the whiteness of a hound's tooth and decorated with seven stranded turk's-heads. Her deck planking was as white as scouring sand, salt water and brawny arms could make it. On deck she carried six long-barrelled eighteen-pounders.

On the after deck stood two men. They were at the breech of one of the guns, and both of them were dressed in the plain blue and white of merchant officers of the day.

William Laud, master of the *Alde*, was no more than twenty-seven years old, powerfully built and about five feet ten inches in height. His features were aquiline and dark, tanned by exposure to salt winds and sunlight. His eyes, beneath clean-cut brows, were a bright, mischievous, reckless blue, and his thick, black wavy hair was swept back into a small pigtail.

The other man, John Luff, ostensibly mate, but in reality the true master of the brig, was a man of about forty. He wore a disreputable " Brown George " wig askew on his thick, coarse black hair which sprouted untidily from the sides of his massive head. He was no more than five feet eight inches tall but so immensely broad he looked even shorter.

To look into Luff's eyes was to recoil, for they were not the eyes of a man completely sane. There was a touch of madness in their strange, tawny depths.

An ex-naval officer, John Luff was the finest seaman on the whole coast of East Anglia, and one of the most detested. There was a predatory look about him as he stood, massive shoulders hunched, nursing the cascabel of the long gun snouting over the stern.

He turned his strange eyes and fixed them on Laud. When he spoke his voice was barely audible, for a flying splinter had once injured his throat so that he spoke ever after in a hoarse whisper.

" Shall I gi' 'em a blast o' case-shot, Will ? "

The younger man eyed the tall masts and the drum-taut canvas of the brig. His voice was pleasantly bantering with a moderate Suffolk accent.

" You-together are too fond of the trigger lanyard, John," he said. " I think I know a trick worth two o' that." He glanced swiftly at the gaining Preventive craft. " We're not far off Bawdsey Bank according to my reckoning, John."

Luff looked askance. " Be Christ, you aren't thinking o' crossing the Bald Head, are you, Will ? There's not enough water there to float a shallop. The whole place is a-feather white wi' surf. You'll rip the bottom clean out on us." He put his arm affectionately round Laud's shoulders. " Give them there bastards a blast, lad," he whispered.

Laud laughed. " Don't you fret, John, old pardner," he said. " There's a swatchway through the Bald Head I'll lay this fellow won't care to follow us through." He turned to the helmsman. " Keep her a couple of points off, Ezra."

Ezra Coffin, bos'un and helmsman extraordinary of the

Alde, glanced aloft with his expressionless, light blue eyes. " Two points off it is, Will ! "

Luff peered astern at the dark hull of the gaining *Rattle-snake*. " Best we fire, lad. The sod is gaining on us."

" Hold your hand, John. There's the Bald Head on the weather bow. This is where we get rid of master *Rattlesnake* and nobody'll get hurt. Steady your hellum, Ezra, nothing to larboard."

The helmsman's voice was tense when he answered.

" Nothing to larboard, Will."

The black hull of the brig surged forward into a smother of white water and what appeared to be certain destruction ; surf thundered all about her, bursting inboard in clouds of drenching spray. Luff, in spite of himself, tensed for the shock of the brig striking, watched for the masts to topple and crash in a confusion of shredded canvas and tangled rigging.

The *Alde* swept forward, stern high in the air, surf boiling at her bow. Then she was in deep water and safety.

The *Rattlesnake*, thrown into confusion by this daring action, hastily luffed up and lay on the edge of the surf, her sails aback. Laud, his hands on his hips, threw back his head and roared with laughter at the confusion he had caused.

" Better luck next time, old pardner," he shouted.

Luff nodded non-committally. " You were lucky, Will."

Nevertheless, Luff was impressed. He knew that few would have dared run the gauntlet of the Bald Head, especially with a falling tide. He himself would have much preferred to have fought it out with the cutter.

Laud nodded easily to the helmsman. " All's right, Ezra. Down hellum. We'll drop between Bawdsey Bank and the Kettle Bottom. Keep your eye lifted for the light on Languard Point."

When the *Alde* had crossed the Sledway, Laud turned to Luff. " There's a light in Ramsholt Church, John," he said. " So far so good. Now we sail up the Orwell as far as Wool-verstone Park. If the old white cat is waiting in the window at the Cat House we're to drop down river to the ' Butt and Oyster ' at Pinmill. Cap'n Bargood will be waiting there for us."

The *Alde* sailed across Felixstowe Ledge, around Languard Point and into the Orwell. Leaving Bloody Point to port she crept slowly up Lower Reach, past Jill's Point and Pinmill. As they went Laud gave orders for the tops'ls to be brailed up so that the vessel's silhouette might not be so conspicuous.

A little later Luff put his hairy hand on Laud's sleeve. Ahead of them on the left bank of the river, on a small mound, stood the Cat House, a strange, isolated, box-like dwelling with gothic windows and a crenellated roof.

The Cat House was the residence of a gamekeeper in the pay of Captain Bargood. This gamekeeper had once owned a large white cat which had come to an untimely end in a rabbit snare. Its owner had had it stuffed and now kept it sitting in a life-like posture, looking across the river.

Even in death the white cat served a purpose, for if it were not to be seen in its accustomed position it meant that preventive craft were in the river.

Luff gave his almost soundless chuckle. " Pussy is there, Will."

The *Alde* went swiftly and quietly about and dropped down abreast of Pinmill. A little later a light flickered briefly from the shore, and not long after the brig had dropped anchor a boat with muffled oars crept out and made fast alongside. Then Captain Bargood, owner of the *Alde*, came aboard.

Anything less like the popular conception of a smuggler than Captain Bargood would be hard to imagine. He was a smallish old gentleman with a benign expression and a fringe of snow-white hair round a yellowish, bald cranium. He was mild mannered and bespectacled, the very picture of a quietly successful doctor or solicitor.

Captain Bargood was also a very careful man. Each of his vessels was skippered by a man of his own choice, a man who, although he had not been aware of it, had previously been under the minutest observation for a long period. So well paid were Bargood's captains, that even if caught red-handed they took all responsibility and breathed not a word about their employer.

True, in the past there had been one or two broken reeds who might have betrayed their master, but quite unaccountably they had been lost at sea in wild weather. Strangely enough, on each occasion John Luff had been mate aboard the vessel concerned.

To those who served him faithfully Bargood was a good master. If through no fault of their own, they became known to the customs, they were quietly pensioned off, to live in small but comfortable cottages, Bargood's property, in desolate spots along the coast of Suffolk—such places as Trimley,

Ramsholt, Shottisham, Hollesley Bay, Boyton, Bawdsey, Butley, Eyke and Orford—where they still served Bargood as spies.

Aboard the *Alde*, Bargood, in spite of his age, climbed nimbly down the companion to the cabin. Below decks Luff was standing by with a bottle of gin from which he had just drawn the cork. He handed a glass of gin to Bargood and one to Laud. Then he told Bargood of Laud's daring evasion of the *Rattlesnake*.

Bargood patted Laud's shoulder. " Good work, lad, good work. In three years' time you'll have made enough money to settle down and get married if you want to."

Laud poured himself another glass of neat gin and as he did so a slight shadow crossed his face. Bargood noticed it and was about to say something when Luff shook his head almost imperceptibly. He then handed some papers across the cabin table to the owner of the *Alde*. " The manifest, cap'n," he said.

Bargood scanned them closely and short-sightedly. " Potatoes, manilla rope, flour. H'm, a mixed cargo, John."

Luff gave his ghost of a laugh. " Mixed is right, cap'n. Do you want to check the cargo now ? " As Bargood nodded, Luff turned to Laud. " You'll be wanting a run ashore, Will, no doubt." There was a smile around Luff's mouth as he added, " There's a pile o' fripperies baled up in the forepeak."

When the young skipper of the brig had gone, Luff and Bargood went below. Down in the dim hold, illuminated by the smoky light of horn lanterns, Bargood asked, " How's he shaping, John ? "

Luff's yellow eyes were half closed when he answered. " Will's a rare fine sailor, sir. Daring, too. He made me cross the Bald Head wi' a falling tide, spite o' myself. I wanted to stay and gi' that bloody cutter a bellyful."

" Yes, and maybe got a bellyful yourself, John, to say nothing of killing, which you know I don't like if it can be avoided."

Luff nodded slowly. " Yes, sir, that's so. But with regard to young Laud, he's a promising youngster. The men like him and he knows this coast blindfold. There's only one thing amiss."

" Well, what's that, man ? "

" That black-haired mawther o' his. He worries about her,

y'see. 'Tween ourselves, he told me that she thinks he's skipper of a respectable trader."

"Respectable, John?" There was reproof in Bargood's voice. "Why, none more so. If it wasn't for the free trade half of the poor of this country would go short of a drop of gin to warm their bellies in winter. None of them would know the joys of a pipe of bacca or a pinch o' snuff—to say nothing of parsons and—ahem—magistrates encouraging—ah—trade." His voice became almost as soft as Luff's. "Ever since I saw Will as a lad sailing his small boat on the Alde at Slaughden near his uncle's boat-building yard, I knew I should one day have him as one of my men. Look you, John, he's to be kept under your lee, d'ye follow?"

There was something sinister in Bargood's tones and something equally menacing in Luff's barely audible reply. "I follow, Cap'n Bargood." He walked over to a corner of the hold containing sacks, picked something out of one and thrust it into his employer's hand. "Fine taters these, sir."

Bargood looked at it briefly and without much interest. "Yes, yes, but business, John, business," he said testily.

Luff smiled. "Business it is, sir. Watch now." He knocked the clay from the big potato and gave it back to Bargood, whose interest quickened as he looked closer.

"Tobacco, John! By God, man, that's clever. I've been in the trade a few years now and that's the first time I've ever seen bacca made to look like a potato."

Luff grinned, showing long, pointed teeth which heightened his wolfish appearance. "Got the idea from a Dutch billy-boy, skipper. Yares ago when I was master of a barquentine trading up the Scheldt. We met him off the Broad Four-teens. 'T was a calm night I mind, not a breath of wind out of the heavens. We went aboard for a noggin. The skipper got foxed and fell overboard—lost, poor devil. We up sail and started for home and blast, when we looked back if that billyboy warn't alight from truck to waterline. Some-body must ha' knocked a lamp over!" Luff went across to a bag marked 'Flour.' "How'd you like a cake made with this, cap'n?"

Bargood tasted it. "Starch, eh!" (There was a heavy duty on starch.) He closed the neck of the sack. "By the by, what's this doxie of Will's like, John?"

"Like, sir? Why, a pretty enough little mutton. Margaret Catchpole har name is. A dark-haired mawther.

Only a sarvant though. Damned if I know whay our Will should be so crazy over har."

Bargood nodded slowly. "There's many a good man's career been spoilt by apron-strings." He ran his hand over his bald head, which was suddenly glistening with sweat. "About that billyboy, John, a sad accident, but accidents are a blessing in disguise sometimes, if you follow my drift?"

A significant glance passed between the two men. Luff nodded and smiled as he went up on deck to give orders for unloading operations to commence.

CHAPTER TWO

WILL LAUD, clad in the sober blue, white and brass of a merchant captain, jumped out of the small boat as it touched the wooded banks of Levington Creek. One of his boat's crew handed him a large bundle done up in a sack.

"Here you are, skipper. When shall we come back for you?" Laud paused. "See you at midnight, lads." He put his hand in his pocket and pulled out a coin. "Here's a crown. Pull you across to the 'Butt and Oyster' and drink my health. But don't get foxed and talk too much, do Luff'll tear your hearts and livers out and eat 'em raw." He tramped up the grassy slope in the direction of the Nacton road.

When he was gone one of the men remarked softly, "Pity to see a fine youngster like that in harness wi' one like Luff. I'd sooner see our Will back boat-building at Aldebro' with his uncle, Nick."

Nick Segel, foretopman of the *Alde*, gave a soft chuckle. "Boat-building be damned, Sam. Our Will is too bright a blade for a life o' that sort. Lookit how he slipped across the Bald Head, that fare scared the chitterling out o' me. That took guts, that did. He's a free trader born and bred."

Sam Nye nodded gloomily. "Ah, so were them six what I see hanging in chains on Selsey Bill when I made a passage round them parts."

Nick got out the oars. "Ah come on, old pardner. You've got a touch o' the megrims or suthin'. Best we get across the river; a glass o' bumbo'll put you right."

The small boat slipped quietly out of the creek and headed for the opposite bank of the Orwell in the direction of Pinmill.

Nacton Heath, across which Laud made his way, was one of the most desolate stretches of land in a desolate county— a wild wind-swept waste of coarse grass and heather, thickly

9

studded with trees and gorse bushes. His destination was the tiny parish of Wolfkettel to the north of Nacton.

In the year 1010 this lonely spot was the scene of a bloody battle between the Danes and the Earl of Ulfkettel—hence its name. The parish commenced at Seven Hills, and ended on the south side of ancient Alneshbourne Priory Farm. In a small, cramped cottage at the southern extremity of the parish lived Jonathan Catchpole, a widower, with his three sons, Robert, James and Edward and their sister Margaret.

The night wind from the river was cold against Laud's cheek as he shouldered his bundle across the heath. He saw no one, for few people crossed it at night. It was the haunt of footpads : and some of the more fearful and imaginative travellers who passed that way in the darkness had told strange tales of spectral figures in horned helmets, brandishing huge double-bladed axes, swirling and intermingling like smoke.

Laud did not suffer from the superstitions of the locals ; and having heard the stories gave no credence to them. As for footpads and cutpurses—well, he had a brace of heavy pistols in his pockets and a razor-edged cutlass at his side.

But tonight his thoughts were neither with ghosts nor criminals. Like any other young man on a similar mission, his mind was full of his girl and her sweetness, and he was intent on constructing the probable course of events in the near future.

Soon he would see the light of the cottage. He would knock on the door. There would be a moment of silence and then the sound of light footsteps across the flagstones of the floor. The door would open and she would be there outlined against the light from within. Then she would be in his arms, the softness and warmth of her young body against his, the fragrance of her hair in his nostrils.

Ah, there was the light now, just ahead through the trees. He quickened his footsteps, and was soon knocking at the door of a small cottage.

Inside the tiny dwelling-room a young woman of about eighteen years was clearing the remains of a meal from the table. She was as unlike a farm labourer's daughter as it was possible to be. Margaret Catchpole was small—a mere five feet two—and her waist so slender that a man could encompass it with his hands. Her father had frequently pondered about her, wondering to what ancestor she owed her slender bones and delicate bearing. But notwithstanding her seeming fragility, she was strong and possessed untold energy.

She had beautifully rounded arms and a well-formed figure, and the rise of her breasts was accentuated by the lacing on the bodice of her dress. Her forehead was low and broad, and across it hung three little kiss curls ; the rest of her thick, dark hair was caught up behind with a scarlet ribbon. Her mouth was vivid with a full lower lip and a small upper one.

But it was her eyes that had held Laud from the start. They were large, and of a velvety, pansy brown, alive with small lights flickering in their depths. Laud had looked into her eyes and had caught his breath. Once he had been swept overboard and nearly drowned. He remembered the first bitter struggle and then the deep content which comes to drowning men. Each time he looked into Margaret's eyes he suffered a sensation akin to that last moment.

Edward Catchpole was nearest to the door when Laud knocked and his face lit up in a smile of more than ordinary welcome when he saw who the visitor was.

" Ha, come in, Will. We heard the *Alde* was up, and Peggy has been expecting you."

Margaret had indeed been expecting him. She had been in a state of excited anticipation all the evening : and when the knock had sounded on the door colour had flooded to her face and a little hard core of fear that it might not be Will had settled in her stomach. She stood clutching the wooden bowl, head bent down until she heard her brother's greeting : then she dropped the bowl on the trestle table, and the next moment she was in Laud's arms, knowing once again the feel of his cool, freshly-shaven cheek against hers, the salty flavour of his kiss and the clean tang of the sea about him.

" Oh, Will," she said presently, pushing him away with a gasp, " you'll crush my ribs ! "

Robert Catchpole, a heavily-built man of about thirty, gazed at Will in admiration. " That's the way to buss your mawther," he grinned. " No sneaking around behind hedges for our Will."

Jonathan Catchpole, Margaret's father, a thick-set quiet man with eyes the same colour as his daughter's, reached up to a circular iron pipe cradle near the fire and took down a long-stemmed clay pipe.

" Our Peggy is suthin' different now to when she used to race all over the farm bareback on the Master's hosses."

Margaret, flushed from the ardour of Laud's embrace, blushed even more.

"Oh, father, I wish you wouldn't bring those things to mind. I was only a child then," she said with all the mature dignity of a woman of eighteen.

Will gave Margaret another affectionate squeeze and then went across to where he had dropped his bundle. He picked it up, slung it on the table and proceeded to undo it. Inside was a handsome double-barrelled fowling piece complete with powder horn. He handed it across to Edward Catchpole, the youngest of the brothers. "Here you are, Ned. There's plenty of fowl on the Orwell. Go out and knock over some widgeon for the larder."

Edward's mouth fell open. "Why, Will, this here piece must ha' cost you a whole heap o' money. It's—it's got a silver inlaid stock! I can't take it, man!"

Laud thrust it into his hands with a laugh. "That's a'right, lad. Maybe your master'll let you have a shot at a coney or two on the farm as well."

He tossed a leather case and a package into Jonathan's lap. The case contained a beautiful meerschaum pipe, and the package enough fine-quality tobacco to last him a year. Catchpole senior was knocked speechless by the splendour of the gift. Had he saved his meagre earnings for a year he could not have purchased its like. He put aside the clay pipe he had been smoking and studied the new one in silence. Then there was a silver-mounted whip for Robert and a silver inlaid clasp-knife for James—and the bundle was empty.

Laud looked around in comical dismay, shaking the empty sack. "Why, there's nothing for our little Peggy." He dived a hand inside his pocket. "Oh, here, wait a minute, what was it that old Dutchman in Amsterdam gave me?"

Laud pulled a flat case out of his pocket. When he opened it its contents flung back a hundred little multi-coloured flames from the light of the oil-lamp. He clasped the object around Margaret's neck.

Margaret flushed with excitement and then grew pale as she realized only a part of the value of the gift. "Oh, Will," she said, and her voice was scarcely audible, "where did you get it?"

"Never you fret, girl, it's yours for a kiss. If you don't want it, why then, give it back. I think I know someone who'll wear it." He pretended to take it from her.

Laughing and evading his hands she ran into her tiny

bedroom, lit a candle with trembling hands, picked up a little hand mirror and admired a diamond and sapphire necklace worthy of a lady of the land.

Her father and brothers sat in stunned silence, dazzled by the jewels, until Margaret broke the spell by running out of her room and flinging her arms around Laud's neck, thanked him with kisses. " Will, what lovely, lovely, presents," she said breathlessly.

Jonathan Catchpole glanced at his pipe and then back at Laud. " I dun't know what to say, Will. You must ha' spent all your money on these things."

Laud shrugged carelessly, a shade too carelessly. " Never mind about that, father. Things are cheap across the water and I'm not doing so badly."

He sat down to a meal that Margaret was preparing for him. When he had finished, Margaret cleared the table and then threw a shawl around her shoulders.

" We're going for a stroll, father. Don't wait up, Will'll see me home."

Will rose and put on his hat. Arm in arm the couple set off across Nacton Heath, now illuminated by a bright moon. When they had gone, Jonathan still sat examining his new pipe. Then he spoke in his quiet voice. " These here things "—he waved his hands at the gifts Laud had brought— " must be wuth more'n we've ever seen. I wonder how the cap'n of a little brig like the *Alde* can afford to buy 'em ? "

Edward Catchpole looked up indignantly from the flint of his new gun. " You don't think Will stole 'em, do you, father ? There's nothin' of a cutpurse about our Will."

The old man shook his head. " No, I don't think they're stole," he said, and there was a worried expression on his face. " If he bought 'em over the water, how did he get 'em past the Excise. This bacca now—there'd be heavy duty to pay. What if it's all smuggled stuff ? "

Edward shook his head. " Oh come, dad, our Will's a lively lad, but he's never mixed up wi' a bunch o' bloody cut-throats like the gentry."

But in spite of Edward's reassuring words, father and sons exchanged uneasy glances.

The smugglers operating on the Suffolk coast had the worst name of any on the British seaboard. They were desperadoes who would stop at nothing. Murder and atrocity were being laid at their door. And to make matters worse, no one knew who the smugglers were. Neighbour was beginning to eye neighbour with suspicion, and it was whispered in hedge taverns and like places that even magistrates and clergy were in collusion with the free traders.

Edward got to his feet and put the fowling-piece away in a cupboard and went out. Robert and James went to their room up the tiny stairs without even their usual " good-night " to their father.

When they had gone, Jonathan Catchpole sat staring broodingly into the fire, worried by the thoughts that had sprung unbidden into his mind.

He recalled the ugly story of a farmer at Snape, a little village farther up the coast. He, unlike the others, had refused to leave his stable doors open and his horses at the disposal of the smuggler's carriers. This farmer had gone even further and had laid information to the embarrassed and frightened magistrate. A few nights later the farmer was dragged naked from his bed by a gang of armed, masked men who had burst into his house. He was gagged, tied to a tree in his own orchard and flogged until he died.

Early the next morning Will Laud was ashore again and away up to the cottage on Nacton Heath to say good-bye to Margaret.

When he had taken leave of the family, old Jonathan put his hands on his shoulders and looked at him with troubled eyes. His voice was troubled too. " Will, lad, I'm getting on in yares now. Peggy means a deal to me—dun't gi' her no cause for hurt." He paused for a moment. " And, Will, dun't think me ongrateful, but I wish you-together wouldn't bring such gifts as ye do. We're only humble folk—an'—an' not used to the likes o' such."

Laud put a powerful arm round the old man's shoulders. His tones were cheery when he answered. " Never you fret, father. Never you fret." And he turned and went outside to where Margaret was waiting for him.

Together they walked slowly down to the river's edge. The woods were still and the wintry sunshine picked out a branch here and a twig there. Pigeons circled uneasily over-head. Suddenly a breath of cold wind set the trees shudder-ing. Showers of golden-brown leaves swirled earthwards to join the brown carpet of the woods. The force of the wind increased and, damp from the sea, it twisted and tormented the sere yellow tops of the oaks. Across the heath a lonely hawk perched on the blackened skeleton of a lightning-blasted tree. Grey clouds were scudding up with the wind and as it increased in force the showers of yellow and brown leaves became thicker.

Suddenly Laud turned to the girl at his side.

"Tell me, Peggy," he asked. "Why doesn't your father like me?"

"It's not that, Will," she answered. "You see, ever since mother died father has relied on me to look after the cottage for him. He knows that I must leave some time and he fares anxious about things." She hugged his arm tighter. "He got the idea into his silly old head that you're working with the free traders." She stopped and looked earnestly at her lover. "You aren't, are you Will?"

Laud hesitated. Many times he had been on the point of telling her, and each time, frightened of losing her, he had kept silent, preferring she should believe him to be a respectable merchant captain. Now she had driven him into a corner with her deliberate question. If he denied it now and she found out later, she would never forgive him the deception.

Margaret noticed his hesitation. "Are you, Will?" she asked more urgently.

Laud, his face pale and his mouth twitching, swung his sweetheart round and drew her into his arms.

"Look, my little dunlin," he said hoarsely, "supposing I were in with the gentry. Would it make any difference to us—would it?"

Margaret stood appalled as realization came to her. Her eyes widened and her natural pallor deepened.

"Oh God, Will," she cried in horror, "you are in with those devils. All those splendid things—father was right!"

She gave a violent sob and, putting both hands to his chest, thrust herself away. "Don't touch me—don't!" Sobbing and gasping, she turned like a hare at the jaws of a hound and vanished among the trees.

Laud ran forward a few steps. "Peggy—MARGARET!" There was no answer other than the rustling of the leaves. He shrugged his shoulders and, with a bleak face and a world of misery in his eyes, made his way slowly to the creek where Nick and Sam were waiting for him in the small boat.

Margaret ran blindly through the woods until she thought her lungs would burst. Then at last, exhausted by grief and physical effort, threw herself headlong into a pile of dry bracken and sobbed as if her heart would break.

Overhead, dark grey clouds blotted out the watery sun.

Margaret felt a splatter of rain on her cheek. She sat up, dried her eyes and did her best to wipe away the tear marks. Then she got to her feet, tidied her hair, smoothed her rumpled clothes and made her way slowly back to her father's cottage.

Jonathan Catchpole was on his way back to work when he met his daughter. He mistook her subdued silence for grief at the departure of Laud.

"Never you mind, Peggy mor'. If there worn't no partings there'd be none o' the joys o' meeting agen. He'll soon be back."

CHAPTER THREE

1

WHEN Laud and his men went alongside the *Alde*, Luff was already weighing anchor. He was leaning over the bow watching the muddy cable come up. Suddenly he gestured and spoke in his hoarse whisper. " Buckets and swabs for'rard here. We don't want the cable locker stinking like a pig sty." The work proceeding to his satisfaction he lurched along the deck to where Will Laud stood. " Anchor's broke out, cap'n."

Laud, his mind full of Margaret, nodded abstractedly as he went below.

Luff turned back to his men. " Hands alorft. Shake out your torps'ls, ease your weather braces."

The *Alde* slid through the water under topsails and flying jib only.

2

In the Coast Guard station at Shingle Street Lieutenant Edward Barry of the Preventive Service was talking to his men. He was a tall, spare man of thirty-five, with red hair and blue-grey eyes. He was dressed in a blue cut-away coat with silver buttons and silver-laced button-holes. A three-cornered hat, white breeches, sword, white stockings and silver buckled shoes completed his dress.

" You know article eighteen of the Coast Guard Regulations, men," he was saying earnestly. " It quotes ' A more special regard to be had herein for such vessels whose construction bespeaks them as fit for the purposes of smuggling and not for the foreign trade such as they often pretend to be employed.' That's what I wish to draw your attention to. This brig, the *Alde* ; I'm not satisfied with her condition. As you know she is very fast and is handled by one who is

17

above the usual small coaster's captain both in ability and daring. Several times she has been seen backing and filling off the coast between here and Yarmouth after dark, in the most suspicious circumstances."

Barry turned to the Chief Commissioned Boatman who, as his second in command, was standing nearby.

"There's been a lot of covert talk about a ' run ' at Sizewell Gap hasn't there, Last ? "

The man nodded his fair, curly head. "That there has, sir, and not so covert eether."

Barry fumbled with the gilded hilt of his sword. "A trifle too obvious, I fancy. I think the run will take place elsewhere." He glanced around. "And I wouldn't mind wagering that it will be around here. They're trying to draw us off. Boatmen Stevens and Reynolds, what's to report from the old Beach House ? "

Two men stood forward and saluted. Reynolds, the senior, gave his report.

"The place is full of workmen, sir, stone-masons, bricklayers and carpenters who are building the Martello towers. Me and my mate has been yarning with them. They seem a fair enough lot, sir."

Barry nodded slowly.

"Nobody who acted suspiciously ? "

"No, sir, not a soul, all just ordinary workmen as far as we could judge." Reynolds paused as if waiting permission to go on. Barry gestured to him to continue. "If you ask me, sir, it's not strangers we've got to watch but local folk. Stevens and I ha' seen some lot o' sheep tracks along the foreshore and saltings o' late. There's precious little fodder for a beast there. Them there sheep are driven along the strand to cover up footmarks, sir. There's an old shepherd living in the cottage on Havergate Island, sir, a rare hard-featured cove for one of his calling. He's allus driving sheep up and down the North Weir."

"Yes, I agree with you about the local folk," Barry said. "And I don't think we'll have to worry about Sizewell Gap. Call the muster, Last."

Last read out the names of the men and, when each man had answered, Barry gave his orders.

"Last, take the men to the store and see that each man gets a carbine, a brace of pistols, cutlass and twenty rounds of ball. See they get a double ration of rum, too. I fancy we're in for a discomfortable night.

"Each man is to bury himself in the shingle up to his neck, fifty yards from his neighbour. Keep a strict watch to seaward. After dark we'll patrol the beach. If you see a landing each man is to pick up his neighbour and report to me. Last and I will be abreast of the spot where the last Martello Tower is under construction. The password is 'King George for ever' and the countersign 'Hurrah.' Now is everything clear? No questions? Very well, Last, dismiss the men.'"

"You know, sir," said Last, when the men had gone, "this business fare sickens me to the stomach sometimes. I've fought agen them bloody-minded French. Ah, and joyed in it. But this fare different. It's Englishman cutting down and shooting Englishman and whatever way you look at it it's a poor how-d'ye-do. Some o' them smugglers took at Covehythe not long ago were old schoolmates o' mine."

Barry nodded sombrely.

"I know that, Jim, I know. But you've got to look at it this way too: quite a number of those fellows are deserters from the Navy. Others are poachers, cutpurses, horse thieves—all manner of rakings and scrapings of hell. Gallows meat in the long run anyway. It's a cleaner, quicker way to die, hot lead or cold steel. And another thing: there's a lot of good lads in the Coast Guard die too."

"Ah, that's the part I don't like, sir," Last said. "We should be fighting the Frogs instead of slitting each other's gizzards."

3

It was a deadly task the Coast Guard had, waiting buried in the cold wet shingle. For two nights they waited fruitlessly at Shingle Street, the last and most desolate hamlet on England's most desolate coastline. It was a place of a few lonely cottages, a Coast Guard station and an old wooden inn, built on an immense bank of shingle which formed an inadequate rampart against the winds which bellowed in from the North Sea, winter and summer alike. Behind the village the country was almost as desolate. A vast tract of marshland swept to the skyline, uninhabited but for the will-o'-the-wisp, the huge, dark-furred marsh hare, the dagger-beaked heron, and the curlew.

A little way along the coast was the mouth of the sullen dangerous River Ore, winding its way clear of the desert of

shingle and thundering out into the North Sea at North Weir
Point in a turmoil of yellowish-white surf. The whole place
was one vast confusion of shingle, rushing muddy water, clots
of yellow oleaginous sea spume whirling in the wind, and
desolate marsh land.

Such was the appalling environment in which Barry and his
men waited for the *Alde* to land her contraband.

On the third night of the vigil Barry and Last were crouched
in the lee of the half-completed Martello tower. Barry drew
up the collar of his cloak.

" Look at that roke [1] rolling in. Just the night for a run."

As he spoke footsteps crunching hurriedly along the shingle
brought both men to the alert with their hands on pistol butts.
One of the Coast Guard doubled out of the rapidly gathering
cold and clammy sea-fog.

" A light flashed from Hollesley Church, sir. It wor
answered from a point a little to the south of the Kettle
Bottom. We got a glass on the spot, sir. There's a brig
there right enough, but the roke came down and we lost sight
on it."

Together Barry and Last went along the top of the beach
making contact with each man and telling them to stand-to.
The scene was eerie in the extreme. The low-lying roke
swirled wetly over the shingle, whilst overhead sounded the
puckish whistle of invisible teal flighting in from the sea.

Barry mustered his men and gave them final instructions
in a natural hollow in the shingle.

" Each man back to his post. If you hear a boat land, do
nothing until you are certain all the goods are unloaded.
Then creep along the back of the bank to Last and myself.
We'll stay here. Tell the others as you come. We'll attack
when they have discharged their goods. Shoot to kill—it's
them or us."

As the Coast Guard returned to their stations to wait, the
fog swirled in even wetter and denser, so that the men had
only taken a few paces before they were hidden from sight.

Barry held up a masked lantern and peered at his Commissioned Boatman in the feeble, woolly yellow radiance.

" What's amiss, Jim ? "

Last's face was pale and drops of sweat were on his forehead
in spite of the cold.

" I don't like this business, sir, English lads murdering each
other over a few ankers o' brandy and cases o' bacca. I wish

[1] Sea-fog.

to Christ it was the Mounseers coming ashore now. I'd be doing this job with a far better heart, sir."

Barry patted his aide's shoulder.

"Judging by the news, it could happen, lad. Villaret Joyeuse is at sea with the finest fleet o' men-o'-war ever seen afloat ! "

Last shook his head. A few fair curls had escaped from under his hat and the fog had condensed on them in little drops. "I feel right queer, sir. I never felt like this afore."

Despite himself Barry felt a superstitious pang. Jim Last was the best man he had ever had under him. He was as courageous as a lion and intelligent far above the average.

To ease the tension, Barry flicked open the priming pans of both his pistols to make sure the fog had not dampened the powder. Last also checked his weapons and loosened the cutlass at his side. The sea-fog eddied wetly about them.

4

Aboard the *Alde* the fog was swirling wetly too. Wisps of it were reaching wraith-like over the combings of the open hatches. The decks were laden with barrels, cases and packages, while still more were being hoisted up from below. Two men were working a windlass that had been carefully greased, as had every block and fairlead aboard the whole vessel. The *Alde's* sheer, raking hull and her towering masts had merged into the sea-fog, and her crew were working as silently as a company of phantoms. Even the light bales and casks were being lowered on to sword-matting as they swung up from the hold.

Down in the cabin Laud was checking over the lists of receivers, his face tense with concentration. In another part of the cabin John Luff was checking over the arms. He had just finished testing the edges of cutlasses and examining the locks of pistols, muskets and carbines, and when Laud looked across he was in the act of testing some gunpowder. He had a small heap of it on a piece of clean white paper. He touched it with a red hot wire. There was an orange flash, a hiss, and a puff of stinking smoke. The result seemed to please Luff. He held up the almost unmarked paper.

"It's good powder that leaves paper unmarked, Will ! "

Ezra Coffin started to measure the powder into flasks as Luff rolled across to Laud. Tonight his whisper was even more sibilant than usual.

" That's about it, Will. I've got the feeling it'll be sharp work tonight."

Laud glanced up. Luff's face repelled him, for it was plain that at the thought of possible bloodshed the man's evil nature was uppermost. His wolfish features were pale and the flecks of his deep-set eyes were pinpoints of flame. A tiny nerve twitched in each temple.

Laud shivered slightly when he saw Luff's long black-haired fingers, which could bend a musket barrel into a horseshoe, fondling the haft of his Corsican knife.

" How do you know it will be, John ? "

Luff looked straight into his captain's eyes, and the impact of that strange, evil personality was like a blow.

" The Kiss has been singing these two nights past, lad. She allus does when she's thirsty."

Laud made a gesture, part irritation, part distaste.

" I wish to heaven you wouldn't have such wild notions, man. There's work enough in the offing without that ! "

Luff seemed to come to earth. " Come on then, Ezra, serve out the arms and we'll get ashore with the first boatload."

Coffin called softly along the deck. " All right, lads, muster aft for your arms."

The crew of the *Alde* were a wild lot, which was the reason for Laud keeping the arms under lock and key in the cabin and only distributing them as the occasion warranted.

Ezra Coffin, whose home was at Aldeburgh, dared not be seen ashore, as he was known to have killed Coast Guards in various mêlées along the coast from Yarmouth to Felixstowe. He passed the arms over a table drawn across the cabin door. In addition to the weapons he issued a half-pint of neat rum to each man. His shallow blue eyes, set in a round bland face, blinked like an owl's as he spoke to the men.

" Come along, m'hearties, drink up. It'll be cold wet work tonight."

As each man came up to draw his weapons and his rum the feeble light from the *Alde's* cabin fell briefly on his face. There was fat and jolly-seeming Jabez Tagg, from Dunwich, deserter from H.M. Navy. The equally fat Sam Nye, sailor and smuggler from Southwold, who had been coasting all his life and knew every creek and backwater of the East coast. Squat, swarthy, scar-faced Jacques Coulthard was a French smuggler from Dunkirk. Coulthard did not dare show his face in his own country. At one time he had been working aboard a French smuggling vessel and, dissatisfied with his share, had betrayed his companions to the customs, thereafter collecting the substantial reward offered for the capture of his shipmates. Being a Frenchman Coulthard was not popular, but he was useful as a liaison with French smugglers. His life was not worth a button anywhere on the French coast and Laud, who knew the man's story, kept him to heel with the simple threat of landing him on one of his own beaches.

There was little Jesse Legget, driven to sea because his poaching proclivities had brought him under the threat of transportation. Legget had no desire for Van Diemen's Land, so he had joined the elect company of the *Alde*. His shipmates voted him a lubberly fellow but as he had cat's eyes and could hear the grass grow, or so they said, he was useful to the small community.

Nick Segel, tall, dark and lantern jawed, had been a master rigger, pressed into the navy whence he had deserted. He could repair shot-torn rigging whilst most were thinking of it, and was a fine sailor in every sense of the word. He was the bosom friend of fat, slow-thinking Sam Nye.

Perhaps the most incongruous member of the crew was smart and dapper Jacob Ludin, a highwayman sheltering from the grim trunk of Tyburn Tree. He was in no way a sailor, but he could handle horses and was therefore useful to the *Alde*, as Laud always resorted to horseflesh to carry the contraband once it was landed. Ludin was dark and almost as unpopular as Coulthard. He despised most of the brig's crew and showed it on every possible occasion. The dislike was mutual, for Ludin's fastidious ways did not fit in with the uncouth men with whom he associated.

Nevertheless, the sailors of the *Alde* did not go too far with Ludin, for he was a dead shot and very handy with his fists, as he had demonstrated on several occasions. He was afraid of nothing on earth, with the possible exception of John Luff. The rest of the crew were plain unlettered men, sailors and fishermen who had left the ill-paid hazards of fishing for the more lucrative hazards of the free trade.

When each man had received his arms and his rum Laud and Luff mustered them under the *Alde's* tall mainmast. The wind had freshened in from the sea and it was as much as the men could do to recognize each other even in the close confines of the brig's deck. There was a nasty short sea and the vessel was scending [1] uneasily.

" I'm going ashore with John and the lads, Ezra," Laud

[1] Pitching.

told his bos'un. "Make bold o' the land and if you hear the sound of an onfall on the strand, stand off for the open sea and keep hull down until tomorrow night. Stand in after dark, and if it's safe to put a boat ashore someone will send up a blue light. Oh, and keep clear o' the *Rattlesnake*. I fancy she's got our measure. If you have to, put the remainder of those ankers o' brandy in the collar [1], but don't do it unless you ha' to. We don't want a lot of stinkibus [2] on our hands."

Laud turned back to the men going ashore with him.

"Well, lads, all set?"

He climbed over the brig's low rail and Luff followed him. The rest of the men going ashore climbed over bales, casks, barrels and boxes and took their places at the oars.

Luff gave the whispered command: "Let go for'rard there, bear her off," and when the boat was clear of the ship's side he ordered, "Give way together, lads."

"You're quiet, lad," he said to Laud. "Anything amiss?"

"This bloody roke frets me, John."

"Don't be fretting over the roke; it's good cover for us!"

"Ah, and for the Excise, John. English lads all, don't forget. It goes against my guts fighting my own countrymen when the face o' the sea's alive with bloody-minded Frenchmen."

Laud did not see the flash of hatred in Jacques Coulthard's eyes, Luff noticed it, however, although he made no sign.

"Howsoever, Will, a good fight is a good fight, say I."

Laud shook his head. "Wish I felt the same about it, John. Give us your flask; my guts are wambling with the cold."

He took a draught, rubbed the back of his mouth and spat overboard.

"Christ, man, what've you done to that rum?"

"Put a pinch o' gunpowder in it, lad; gives it body!"

Luff stood up in the boat.

"Easy all on your oars," he whispered.

He stood for a moment in an attitude of listening.

"We're not far off the breakers. As soon as we ground, every man out, and as the breakers hit the boat, heave it up the beach. The carriers'll be waiting wi' the cattle.[3] There's a nasty hob-gob[4] alongshore, so get the stuff un-

[1] Sink them on an anchored line to be grappled later.
[2] Barrels of spirit impregnated with salt water.
[3] Horses.   [4] Sea.

loaded as quick as you can—and wi' no brustle.[1] Noise carries a long way on these beaches."

The boat grounded in a cloud of spray. As Luff had remarked, there was a nasty sea running and the men hove the boat clear little by little as each succeeding breaker hit her broadside up the beach.

When the boat was clear of the immediate danger of the breakers a figure came out of the mist and strode down the beach, to be covered instantly by a dozen pistols. Luff advanced, a pistol in each hand. " The password ! "

Without hesitation it came : " Orford ! "

Luff made a gesture of reassurance to the indistinct figures grouped about the boat.

" Get to work, men. This is Abe Horsenell, chief o' the carriers from Orford."

In a short time the men were standing in a line passing the goods from hand to hand to the carriers, who swiftly and silently lashed them to waiting horses, animals which had been " borrowed " from outlying farms. The coastal farmers left their stable doors unlocked at night for two reasons. If the free traders wanted a horse they took it, whether the stable doors were locked or not : and it was a much pleasanter affair merely to leave a door unlocked and find your horse returned in the morning together with a chest of tea or maybe an anker of brandy, than leaving a door locked and finding it burst in with the horse gone for ever and perhaps a circle of smouldering ashes where a corn-stack had once been.

So the doors were left without locks, and the farmers went to bed and slept soundly. Some of the farmers went further and gave food and sanctuary to the gentry, knowing it was well worth their while : others even gave strict orders to their labourers to keep their mouths closed and to ignore whatever they might see.

[1] Commotion.

CHAPTER FOUR

L IEUTENANT BARRY and Commissioned Boatman Last were lying in a hollow in the shingle not fifty yards from where the *Alde's* boat had landed. They had heard it strike the beach and could hear the crunch of footsteps in the pebbles, and the gasps of the men lifting heavy loads. But the smugglers themselves were hidden by the eddying roke.

Barry put his mouth to Last's ear. " We're too close to walk back to muster the others," he whispered. " Give the emergency call."

Last loosened his cutlass and then, putting his hands to his mouth, sent the quavering cry of a curlew echoing through the night. Curlews were common enough in that part and the men working around the boat took no notice—except for Jesse Legget, whose ear detected a false note to the sound. He seized Luff's arm.

" That's no curlew, cap'n ! "

Luff's whisper had a savage urgency to it.

" Down with your tubs, men. Stand-to ! "

There was a pause, and then Barry and Last, with the others not far from their heels, came over the shingle bank, the fog billowing mistily about them, its dankness in their nostrils.

The Coast Guard advanced steadily with about the space of two men between them. The free traders went to meet them in a compact mass. Red flashes lanced through the swirling mist and the smell of burnt powder hung heavily on the wet air. But apart from the fog-muffled reports of the fire-arms the battle was fought in a deadly silence. After the first exchange of shots, men falling on both sides, the battle resolved itself into a series of single combats. Barry found himself engaged with Laud, whilst Luff, his face demoniac in the fog, was at it in furious cut and thrust with three of the Excise men. He fought like a devil from hell. When his edge fell it was like a falling axe. Nothing could stay the strength of the iron arm behind it. One coastguard lay dead at Luff's feet, his head almost severed from his body; another sat stupidly on the shingle nearby, his hat clapped over the spouting stump where his hand had once been. The hand, still grasping a cutlass, lay down the beach. Now, concentrating on his third adversary, Luff made a lightning feint with his edge, then neatly slid the point of his weapon under his opponent's guard so that the blade stood out a foot behind the man's back. Then he turned to meet two more men.

Barry and Laud had their blades locked. There was little to choose between them. Barry was the better swordsman, Laud the stronger man.

Both of them were fumbling for pistols. Barry had his out first but Laud kicked it from his hand, freed his blade with a sudden movement and then caught Barry a heavy blow on the head with its steel hand-guard. Barry went momentarily to his knees and Last, seeing his commander in such dire straights, sprang at Laud, to be engaged immediately by two of the smugglers. Brief as was the interlude, Barry had managed to clear his head, and he and Laud were left to it again, the superb swordsmanship of Barry gradually giving way to the whirling, tireless blade and strength of Laud. The other combatants were lost to sight in the fog, from which came an occasional groan or the scream of a wounded man. The carriers were not fighting men, and had fled, leaving their horses behind.

Fighting on the defensive, Barry backed up the steep beach, followed closely by Laud who, abandoning edge for point, made a savage thrust at Barry's heart. Barry parried it and from his vantage point gave Laud a lightning back-hand cut across the face. Blinded by a sudden torrent of blood, Laud toppled face downwards, senseless, into the shingle. There was a savage roar and Luff burst like a demon through the fog. Barry, his head laid open to the bone by Laud's blow, knew that he was no match for Luff and called loudly to where some of the Coast Guard were doubling in his direction. Luff broke off the fight and vanished in the fog. He made his way back to where Laud lay, and turning his young captain over, hissed to himself when he saw the hideous injury.

The edge of Barry's sword had gone clean through Laud's

skull, completely severing one eyeball in half, the gash extending vertically from forehead to corner of mouth.

As Luff leaned over his captain to pick him up he heard a step in the shingle and, looking up, saw Last, the Commissioned Boatman. He was poised on tiptoe, sighting along his cutlass blade. Luff's hand blurred to his sea-boot and even in the fog there was a lucent quality to the foot-long Corsican blade as it whispered through the air.

It seemed as if a red and silver blossom had suddenly sprung from the throat of the Commissioned Boatman. Already on tiptoe, he teetered even higher for a moment, then, dropping his cutlass, he wheeled and staggered down the beach, collapsing in the breakers like a marionette with its strings cut. Luff was after him in two leaps and drawing his knife from the throat of the dying man, deliberately and with fiendish malice mutilated him.

" That's for my young captain, you Excise bastard," he hissed. There was the sound of approaching footsteps as Luff leapt up the beach, swung Laud across his back as if he were a child, and vanished into the fog in the direction of the deserted horses which were snorting uneasily at the scent of fresh blood.

CHAPTER FIVE

MARGARET sat quietly over her mending. Ever since she had learnt that Laud was a smuggler she had tried to put him out of her mind, had tried to obliterate from her memory the sight of his laughing eyes and the tingles that the mere touch or sound of him would send running, like mice, up and down her spine. She could not shut her mind's ear to the sound of his last words. " Would it make any difference to us ? Would it ? " And from her heart came the answer, " No. No. No ! " Smuggler or honest man, Will was just—Will. He had the same white teeth, the same strength, the same gay, reckless laugh, the same way of sweeping her up to his own level to kiss her, the same rough hands that could be so surprisingly gentle— hands that made her senses reel . . .

Suddenly there was a thunderous knocking at the door of the cottage, so loud and urgent that Jonathan and Edward jumped hastily to their feet and Margaret almost dropped her work. Of late she had been going about in fear. It had hung over her and her thoughts like a cloud and now, despite the fact that she deliberately walked leisurely to the door, her eyes were dilated and her heart hammered loudly.

Edward Catchpole stood at her back as she opened the door. Outside there was a blowing horse and in the doorway stood the powerful figure of a man, his clothes saturated with blood.

After Luff had picked Laud up, he had thrown him across one of the horses and had galloped as hard as he could drive the horse to one of Bargood's many cottages by the coast, situated not far from the mouth of Woodbridge Haven. Leaving Laud in the temporary care of a crone named Moggy Mitchell, who was the housekeeper, Luff had then ridden headlong to Wolfkettel and the Catchpole cottage. When he had left, Laud had been in a raging fever, calling loudly for Margaret and fighting with such violence that Luff had lashed him to the bed.

Luff came to the point quickly.

" Does Margaret Catchpole live hereabouts ? "

Margaret nodded fearfully.

Jonathan had come to the door and saw the blood on Luff's coat.

" Come inside, man," he urged. " You're hurt."

Luff shook his head impatiently. " No, not me ; it's Will. He's . . . had an accident. Fell off his horse and got kicked in the face. Hurt bad and calling for Margaret ! "

At the mention of Will's name a cold tide of fear had surged round Margaret's heart. Will was hurt and needed her. But borne on the tide came a tiny ripple of hope, hope that in tending him she might be able to lead him away from the free trade. And then the hope was gone because in her heart there was no room for hope, only fear for Will's safety : and she ran to get her cloak.

" Oh, where is he ? " she cried, wrapping the cloak round her shoulders. " For God's sake take me to him." Her voice shook with anxiety.

" Never mind about where he is," said Luff roughly. " Can you get a horse ? If you don't hurry, he'll be dead ! "

Edward jumped into the breach. " I'll get a pony and trap from Mr. Denton. He'll lend us one, I know."

A few minutes later he came back to the cottage with a pony and trap borrowed from his employer, and soon they were clattering away along Nacton Heath Road. Luff, having left his almost foundering horse to be taken care of by the Catchpoles, lashed the fresh pony into a wild, headlong gallop until the trap was swaying crazily from side to side.

When they got to the cottage Luff spoke to Margaret and her brother. His whisper was barely audible.

" What you see and hear in this cottage tonight you want to forget as if you've never seen or heard it. For your own sakes and those of your folks. Understand ? "

" That's all right. We shan't say anything, don't worry," Edward answered gruffly, trying to hide the shake in his voice. He had never met Luff before but he sensed here a tiger in human shape.

Luff grinned. " It's you that'll have to worry if you don't clap a stopper on your tongues. Get inside, the pair of you ! "

Inside Will Laud lay on the bed, his head and face half

hidden by a dirty, blood-soaked bandage. He was delirious, twisting and turning from side to side and muttering to himself. His legs were drawn up and he was making motions as if he were running. There was a white scum at the corner of his dry, cracked lips. He turned his head and a sobbing cry burst from him.

" Peggy ! Peggy . . . for God's sake, girl . . . don't run away ! "

On one side of the bed sat old Stephen Laud, the Government Ferryman at Languard Point, Will's father. On the other was old Dame Mitchell, a wrinkled hag whose wispy hair was a dirty yellowish grey and whose toothless gums mumbled revoltingly upon a crust of bread.

Margaret stepped slowly up to Will and drew the rag aside. She gasped at the hideousness of the injury. She could see that Laud was blinded permanently in one eye and that he would most likely die. Her eyes blazed as she swung on Luff.

" Why didn't you get a surgeon ? He'll die ! "

Her breast rose and fell violently with the intensity of her anger.

Luff lurched up to her and grasped her arms in his iron fingers so that she almost screamed. The glare in his eyes struck terror to her heart and she felt her anger drain from her. She stood there white and shaking.

" You bloody little lorette [1]," Luff whispered to her, " d'ye want to stick all our heads in a halter ? Will got this from the Coast Guard. Ay, he's one o' the gentry and after tonight's work there'll be a price on his head. What's to be done you and the old crone'll have to do."

He went over to a cupboard in the wall and opened a door. Inside was a fully stocked medicine chest, such as was carried aboard a man-o'-war. Luff smiled at Margaret's look of enquiry.

" Don't fret. You won't be kept short o' medicines and such."

He turned savagely on the old woman.

" Get and wash your hands, you bloody old slut. Will's in bad enough case wi'out being mauled by your dirty paws ! "

Stephen Laud put a trembling hand on Luff's sleeve.

" Can't I stay with my boy, Cap'n Luff ? "

Luff shook his head. " No, get back to your ferry, do

[1] A useless strumpet.

people'll start to talk. And keep a still tongue in your head."
He turned back to Margaret. "Don't go out in daylight.
I'll send a man up here after dark with food and what not."
He switched the glance of his strange eyes back to Edward
Catchpole. "Your sister'll be all right here. Go you back
to Nacton and if anyone asks you where your sister is, tell 'em
she's nursing a sick friend." He eyed briefly each person in
the cottage. "And don't forget what I said about keeping
a still tongue." He drew two heavy pistols from his pockets,
examined the priming, thrust the weapons back and, whirling
swiftly, opened the door and was gone.

Edward went back to his sister, who was bending over
Laud.

"He's right, Peggy, there's nothing I can do stopping here.
If I get back I can at least make up some tale or the other."
He turned to Stephen Laud, who was sitting with his head
in his hands. "Don't take on too badly, dad," he said
gently, "Will's in good hands. Let me give you a lift as far
as the ferry."

Edward kissed his sister. "I'll come over after dark tomorrow, Peggy," he said as he went out with Laud's father.
Margaret heard the clatter of the departing trap, and then
she was alone with a hideously wounded man and a frightening
old hag.

Calling to Moggy Mitchell to bring hot water and clean
rags, Margaret cleansed the wound and re-dressed it with
clean bandages. In the box was a small phial of opium
pills. She gave Laud two and was relieved to see that they
quietened his ravings so that he lay with nothing much more
than an occasional mutter.

When she had done all she could for her lover, reaction
set in and she laid her head on her arms and wept. Since
the day she had learnt that Will was in the free trade she
had been frightened—frightened that Will might get hurt,
frightened that he might get involved in something larger
than himself before she could persuade him to quit that
perilous occupation. And now her fears had been justified.
She did not know how serious the fight with the Coast Guards
had been, but that terrible man who had summoned her had
said there was a price on Will's head. A price on the head
of the man she loved, and he likely to die ! Even if he did
recover, the merry good looks he had once possessed would
be gone. He would be blind in one eye and would carry a
terrible scar from brow to jaw for the rest of his days.

The old woman, who had done nothing else but fetch and carry, sat crooning and rocking in her chair at the bedside, mumbling on her sodden brown crust and shooting sharp glances, first at the unconscious man on the bed and then at Margaret, who was making valiant efforts to subdue her sobs.

Margaret dried her eyes and took stock of her surroundings. The cottage was in an appalling state. Laud's stained and dirty clothes were scattered about the floor, together with dirty, bloody bandages. There were countless muddy footmarks, and the remains of a meal lay pushed to one side on the table. A big bowl of bloody water stood on a small table by the bed.

Margaret's sense of orderliness was outraged, and the strain of the night's events was telling on her. She swung on the old woman in no uncertain fashion.

" Why don't you get to work and clean this place up. It's not fit for a pig to be in, much less a man wounded near to death ! "

The hag cackled and did not move.

" Don't you start bettying about the place, mawther. If you want it cleaned then do it your ownself ! "

Margaret was round the table like an outraged wild cat. She dragged the old crone out of her chair into the room behind the one where Laud was lying. Here she shook her with such a will that had the old woman had any teeth they would have chattered like castanets. Margaret's huge eyes were blazing.

" If you don't do as I tell you," she cried, " I'll beat you half to death, you old trollop ! "

Dame Mitchell realized that this young fury could and would put her threat into execution.

" All right, m'dear, all right, m'dear," she snuffled. " Don't be hurting an old woman aged enough to be your grand-mother."

Despite the whining appeal in the old harridan's voice, she shot Margaret a look of such bitter hatred that the younger woman realized instantly she would have to be wary in the future. With the realization came the sudden awareness that the old hag was an accomplice of the free traders and would carry reports to them regarding Will and herself. At that moment too she realized the magnitude of her task if she were going to win Will away from the smugglers.

One evening several nights later, Moggy Mitchell suddenly

got up from her seat by the fire, whence Margaret had shifted her from Laud's bedside.

She went over to Laud, who was sleeping heavily, still under the sedatives Margaret was giving him, and stood looking down at him. There was so much unction in Dame Mitchell's voice that Margaret longed to pull her hair.

" We must get the poor lad well as soon as we can," she said.

" Get him well so that he can go back to his old ways, you mean," Margaret flared. " I'd sooner see him dead."

" Don't talk like that, m'dear. He's a fine young man ; a fine young man."

Margaret went across to the fire, where she was stewing a piece of beef. Whilst she was stirring the pot a double knock at the door startled her. She cautiously slid the door open without removing it from its chain.

It was her brother Edward. He glanced nervously over his shoulder. " Let me in quick, Peggy ! "

Margaret undid the chain. Inside, Edward looked uneasily at the old woman, then at his sister.

" Go into the other room," Margaret ordered Moggy Mitchell curtly. " My brother has some news he wants to tell me in private ! "

The old woman shrugged her shoulders. " Cunning little bitch cat," she muttered to herself as she left the room.

When she had gone Edward put a basket on the table.

" There's some food, Peggy. A capon, eggs, milk, butter and vegetables. I've got some serious news. There was a rum set-to on the beach at Shingle Street. That's where Will took his hurt the other night. But before he did he gave Lieutenant Barry a funny knock. He's had to take to his bed too." Young Catchpole shuddered. " They say that devil Luff killed two o' the Excise and others are like to die. He stabbed the Commissioned Boatman through the throat and then . . ."

Margaret looked up.

" Go on, Ned, what then . . . ? "

" I can't tell you, Peggy, but there's a price on the heads of both Will and Luff. For God's sake leave this place and come home, sister." Edward nodded towards the bed. " He's in this thing too far to ever come out alive now. He'll have us all in the dock. And besides, what that fiend Luff did to that poor devil of a dying boatman has got the whole countryside shaking in their shoes. The magistrates'll never rest until the free trade is stamped out in these parts. They'll turn the dragoons out to help the Excise. Come you on home before it's too late ! "

A weak voice from the bed interrupted them. " Why don't you do as your brother says, Margaret."

She turned wide-eyed to the figure with the bandaged face on the bed.

" Will ! How long have you been listening ? "

" Long enough, my girl. Now do as Edward says and get off home before that's too late ! "

Margaret swung on her brother.

" You didn't think of this when Will was bringing all those fine presents, did you ? Shame on you, Ned ! " She turned back to Laud. " I've some nice broth here, Will. Do you have a few spoonfuls now."

Laud turned his marred face to the wall.

" When's this damned bandage coming off, Peggy ? " he asked.

She dreaded that day and was determined to put it off as long as possible.

" Plenty of time for that, Will. The wound isn't healed yet. Here, take some of this broth. It'll give you strength ! "

" Better you let me die, girl. Easier that way for everyone."

Margaret nodded hurriedly to the door and Edward, with a shamefaced expression, slipped quietly out. " I'll be coming over again directly, Peggy," he said as he went, but Margaret barely heard him. She was humouring the sick man like a child and gently forcing spoonfuls of beef broth between his teeth.

CHAPTER SIX

Next morning, when Margaret was busily cleaning up, a gentle knock sounded on the door. She opened it with her usual caution. It was Captain Bargood.

He raised his hat. " Have I the pleasure to address Margaret Catchpole ? "

She nodded. " Yes. But who are you ? " she enquired cautiously.

" A good friend of Will Laud's, m'dear. Would you mind telling him that Captain Bargood is here ? "

She turned towards the bandaged face on the bed.

" There's a Captain Bargood to see you, Will. Shall I let him in ? "

Laud nodded urgently. " Ah, quick as you can, girl. Then you and Moggy leave us alone for a bit."

She clasped her hands. " Oh, Will, can't I stay ? " she pleaded.

There was an impatient rasp in Laud's voice. " Do as I say, girl, and leave us alone ! "

The tears started into Margaret's eyes but she did as she was bid and left the room.

Bargood pulled a chair up to the bedside, put a box of tobacco and pipes on the table and then squeezed Laud's shoulder.

" How goes it, Will ? "

Laud lifted up the bandage on his face. " Look at this, Cap'n Bargood. I'll never see again in that eye, but by Christ I've got one good one left and God help Barry or any of his kin if I ever get to see them over a musket barrel with it ! "

" Time to think of that, lad," said Bargood soothingly, " plenty of time. We've got to get you about again." He paused for a moment. " John keeps to the open sea these days, only lands after dark. That senseless piece of cruelty at Shingle Street the other evening . . ."

Laud raised his eyebrows. " Cruelty ? "

Bargood told him briefly of Luff's atrocity.

" You'll have to lay quiet too, lad. Folks think you're dead —a good thing in its way."

Bargood looked silently at Laud's disfigurement. It would be a perfect disguise.

" As soon as you get about again I'll put you aboard one of my ships. You'll be all right, Will." Bargood pulled something out of his capacious pocket. " By the by, John sent this for you. He's a strange creature, with the soul of a shark, as bloody and remorseless. And yet I feel what he did the other night was done because in his way he cares for you more than any living thing."

Bargood unwrapped the gift from Luff. It was an Italian pistol of exquisite workmanship. Bargood pressed a catch and a six-inch slender steel blade shot from beneath the pistol muzzle. On it a piece of paper was impaled ; on the paper the words : " From your shipmate, John Luff. For Edrd. Barry."

Bargood read it and shook his head.

" Ah well, Will, if there's anything you want, let me know ! "

When he had gone Laud hid the pistol dagger beneath his pillow.

Margaret came into the room a little while after.

" Who was it, Will ? What did he want ? "

" Oh, just an old friend, Peggy," he said casually. " He's giving me a berth on one of his ships when this has blown over."

As Laud was speaking the girl was changing his bandage. She was about to re-dress the wound when he stopped her. " Fetch me a mirror, my maid," he said.

Margaret looked with horror at the wound. It was ugly, red, puckered, distorting the whole side of his face. The ruined eye was obscene, filmed and hideous.

" It's not healed yet, Will," she said hurriedly. " Best you leave it for a while."

Laud knew she was evading the issue and there was a quality in his voice that was new to her.

" Give me a glass, I say ! "

Unwillingly she did as she was bid. Laud's one bright blue eye glared at the ruin that had once been a handsome face. Margaret heard a long shuddering breath that was almost a sob. Then Laud swung to face her. She was shocked at his appearance. Every semblance of the laughing, happy-go-lucky young sailor she had once known was gone. It was not merely the wound. There was madness flooding his face. A white-hot quality, giving him a terrifying, demoniac look.

" Do you want to stay with a man with half a face ? " he asked chokingly. " Best you get back to your clod-hopping menfolk."

He climbed out of bed and stumbled over to the lattice window. Margaret could see his hands with their whitened knuckles clenched on the woodwork.

She went after him and, leading him gently back to the bed, tucked him in and then held the ruined face close to her breast, whilst he sobbed like a broken-hearted child.

2

As Will Laud's convalescence progressed and he gained strength, he became more and more restless, more and more fretful of the restraints of his present existence. At last he could bear it no longer, and one evening he said to Margaret, " Give me hold of my cloak, Peggy. I'm going out for a bit."

She looked at him questioningly. He was not really fit even yet, and it was dangerous for him to go out in case he was seen. She had known the moment would come when he would say he was going out, and that nothing would then stop him : but now the time had arrived she wanted desperately to put it off, to delay it, to hold him a little while longer until, perhaps, the danger to him had passed, or until her heart as well as her head was convinced that he would not return to his previous calling. Captain Bargood's visit had allayed her fears on this score ; but deep within her there was still the tightness of a doubt. Had Will's wound made him bitter ? Had revenge grown like a disease in the pain he had suffered ? She did not know. But now he wanted to go out and she knew she could not stop him.

" Oh, not tonight, Will dearest," she pleaded without hope.

He shook his head irritably. " When else can I go, mewed up here all day ? It'll drive me light." [1]

She gave him his cloak and then took down her shawl.

[1] Mad.

"I'd sooner go by my ownself, my dunlin," he said.

She slowly drew off the shawl, and whilst her back was turned he whipped the pistol dagger, now loaded, from beneath his mattress and thrust it into his pocket.

"Don't worry about me, Peggy," he said. "Don't sit up. The old woman'll let me in."

"Where are you going, Will?"

"To see Captain Bargood about a berth."

"Be careful, won't you, darling?"

But Margaret found herself talking to a shut door.

Through the lattice she watched him striding in the direction of Bawdsey Cliff. It was a fine night with a gentle drift of scud across the face of the moon.

3

In Bawdsey Cliff there was a cave. An underground stream had once formed a hollow ravine in the earth and, swirling round and round through the years, had gouged out a perfectly round chamber. This had been found quite by accident by a man sinking a well. He had continued boring right through the cave until he had struck water, and the place had been forgotten until some smugglers, before Laud's time, surprised by the Excise, had thrown their contraband down the well. Going back for it later they had found the cave.

Laud and his gang had rediscovered it and had furnished it with chairs, tables, hammocks, rugs—everything, in fact, to make the place a comfortable hide-out. Besides furnishings, they had stocked the place with food and weapons until it was a secret arsenal. They had even bored a shaft up from the cave through the chimney of a nearby cottage, so that in cold weather the occupants of the cave could have a fire without betraying themselves.

The only entrance to the cave was by means of the well-rope which, although the smugglers kept it renewed, was kept well blackened with soot.

The only other person aware of the cave other than themselves was the old fisherman who lived in the nearby cottage. He was in their pay and saw to it that no strangers came too close.

It was to this cottage that Laud made his way on leaving Margaret. When he arrived there he knocked on the door

—three short taps, three long ones. It was opened by the old fisherman, who did not recognize his visitor.

"What d'you-together want at this time o' night, my master?"

He was closing the door when Laud thrust his foot in it.

"Don't you know me, David man?"

The fisherman instantly recognized his voice.

"Why, Cap'n Laud, sir, come in. I didn't hardly . . ." The old man broke off in confusion.

Will laughed bitterly. "Go on, say it, man. You didn't recognize me. I may as well get used to it. It'll be useful from now on." His fingers strayed unconsciously to his face. "Are the lads down below, David?"

"That they are, sir. Been expecting you this several night. They'll be glad to see you."

Laud pressed a coin into the old man's hand. Going out, he looked carefully around and then swung himself over the coping of the well and slid down the rope.

Luff, pistol in hand, met him at the bottom. As soon as he saw who it was he put the pistol back in his pocket and advanced, both hands outstretched. His evil features creased in the nearest thing to a smile of welcome they could assume.

"Well met, Will, well met, lad. How are you?"

Inside the cave most of the crew of the *Alde* were assembled. Laud glanced around and saw there were faces missing.

"Where's the rest, John? Aboard?"

"Ah, all but Legget. He's dead; so is Ludin. Shot at Shingle Street. Coulthard was caught."

Laud nodded sombrely, unaware of the embarrassed silence of the rest of the men who were looking at his ruined face.

Nick Segel stepped forward and coughed awkwardly.

"Sorry about your hurt, Cap'n Laud, sir."

Will laughed, this time without bitterness. Then crossing over to the table he picked up a bottle and poured himself a generous measure of spirits. He sat down on the edge of the table and turned to Luff.

"John, that was a foolish thing you did to Last at Shingle Street."

Luff gestured to Laud's sightless eye and scarred face.

"Fair enough payment for that, Will."

Laud did not speak, but twirled the stem of his glass in his fingers, realizing at that moment what a dangerous creature Luff really was.

Luff was weighing up his young captain at the same moment. Laud was no longer the careless lad playing at smugglers.

The injury had transformed him into a dangerous man.

The two men looked at each other with a new and mutual respect.

The silent men, too, sensed a change in their once gay young captain.

Laud motioned to the bottles on the table.

" Fill your glasses, lads. I've a toast to drink."

When the glasses were filled, Laud held his up.

" To Will Laud," he announced, " who died on the shingle."

He drank, and hurled his empty glass to the floor and ground it to a powder beneath his heel.

John Luff handed him another full one, then held up his own. His whisper penetrated to the utmost corners of the roomy cavern.

" To our new captain, lads. Captain . . . Hudson ! "

Laud smiled as he drank. " As good a name as any, John."

Luff handed Laud a shade for his sightless eye and helped him to adjust it.

He passed Laud a small mirror.

" Your own mother wouldn't know you now, Will."

Laud peered critically at himself.

" You're right. My own mother, God rest her soul, wouldn't know me now." He put the mirror down and turned back to Luff. " Well, what's passed since we last met, John ? "

Luff drew a chair up to the table for his captain and then sat down himself.

" Whilst you were abed the *Rattlesnake* lay a Frenchman by the heels. Sailed her up to Aldeborough, discharged her, and now her stuff is all in the old custom house at the bottom end o' the thoroughfare. The froggy is a fine vessel. Torps'l schooner. Moored alongside Slaughden Quay wi' only a ship's husband aboard." Luff paused and looked across at Laud, who nodded.

" What have you in mind, John ? " he asked.

Luff interlaced his black-haired fingers. " Well, I figure it out this way . . ."

The rest of the men closed in round the table.

CHAPTER SEVEN

A FEW days later, Margaret, realizing that Laud was as well as he ever would be and also realizing that his heart was set on getting back to sea, made preparations to return to her father's house at Nacton, sending word to her brother Edward to come and fetch her. When the trap rattled up to the door she flung her arms round Laud's neck and kissed him.

" Good-bye, Will. You'll send me word, won't you ? "

He swung her up in his arms.

" Of course I will, Peggy." He lowered his voice. " And say nothing to anyone about . . . us, will you ? "

He waved a friendly hand to Edward Catchpole sitting in the trap. Edward nodded coolly and did not speak. Laud made a laughing grimace in his direction.

" Something fallen athwart brother Ned's hawse, I fancy."

Margaret looked at her brother's gloomy face. " Anything wrong at home, Ned ? "

" Time enough to tell you on the way home, Peggy," he shrugged.

When his sister was seated he whipped the pony into a trot. Margaret turned and waved until Laud was lost from sight, then she spoke to her brother.

" What's the matter, Ned. You need not have been so short with Will ! "

" How could I help it, Peggy. You 'ont be so happy when you hear what I've got to say. Father's lost his place wi' the Dentons : so have Robert and James. Laud was recognized that night at Shingle Street. The Dentons knew he used to visit us."

Edward eased the pony to a walk.

" When father asked Denton what was wrong, Denton just looked awkward and says he can't have folk working for him who associate with free traders. Father's taken it some hard, I might tell you."

Margaret's face had grown pale.

"Does anyone know where I've been," she asked, "and that Will is at Bawdsey?"

"Not that I know of. Not yet anyhow."

Margaret said no more, but as soon as she got home she went straight to the Dentons. Mrs. Denton was a placid, kindly soul and her face was red with confusion when she saw Margaret.

"I know what you've come about, my dear. I'm sorry that this has happened, but it's more than my husband dare do, employ folk who associate with the gentry. We're tenants of Sir Philip Broke, the Squire of Nacton. You know he's sworn to stamp out the free trade in these parts. He'd turn us out if he knew we kept you working here."

Margaret's cheeks were white with passion, and it was with an effort that she kept her temper.

"It's not my father and brothers who're at fault. It was I that Will used to visit."

"I'm sorry, m'dear, but I've put in a good word for you with Mr. Wake at Alneshbourne Priory Farm. He owns the farm and the land and can employ whom he likes."

Margaret was about to throw the offer back in Mrs. Denton's face but suddenly she remembered that her father and brothers would be out of a place. She thanked Mrs. Denton briefly and went back to the cottage on Nacton Heath.

Indoors Robert was reviling the Dentons most bitterly.

"That's the thanks you get for years o' faithful service. I've heard Denton say wi' my own ears that father was the best all round man with animals he'd ever had and the best horseman in the district. That's how he treats good service —dismissal at a moment's notice, 'cos Laud came up to see our Peggy once or twice. These small farmers make me sick to the guts with their lickspittle ways : the Squire this, Sir Philip that. He's more'n God a'mighty to most of them!"

"Don't talk like that, my boy," said Jonathan Catchpole, quietly but with disapproval. "That 'ont help matters. Denton only did what thousands would have done."

Robert Catchpole's quick temper was up.

"That be damned, father. It's true what I say. What chance have little folks like us got, wi' our faces ground into the soil? We live from hand to mouth, up to our chins in mud and dung all our lives. From the time we leave the cradle until we go to the grave our eyes are fixed on the soil.

Someone else's soil. If we lift our hand for a bit o' game that belongs to the squire it's transportation. Look at that poor little sod, Johnny Cracknell—a boy of thirteen, mind. Snared a rabbit and got a birching that put him to bed for a week and that cruel old hell of a magistrate telling him he was lucky to ha' escaped the hulks. My God, all for a rabbit. I tell you, father, I'm sick of the land and everything that goes with it. I'm going out ! "

James Catchpole, who up to that moment had remained silent, also got to his feet.

" What Bob says," he announced, " goes for me too, father. He and I ha' worked on this farm ever since we were old enough to lift a two-tined fork."

He stalked out after Robert, who up to that moment had always been the leader of the three brothers. But now Edward declared himself. He went across to his father and put his arm round the old man's shoulders.

" Never you mind, Dad," he said, " you'll soon get another place, with your skill with horses. I know suthin' of sheep too."

The two other Catchpoles went striding along the road that led down to the banks of the Orwell. Both of them were coarser masculine editions of their sister, with the same luxuriant dark hair and the same brown eyes. Robert was the heavier and stronger of the two, whilst James was as fleet of foot as a hare.

" I'm glad we've finished along with farm work, Jimmy," Robert said, as they went towards the river. " All I could see was working all our days for a crust and as like as not ending up with a parish burial."

James looked doubtfully at his brother. " Well, what now, Bob ? We've got to do sorthen for a crust and that's a fact ! "

Robert's eyes narrowed as he gazed towards the towering masts swaying gently off Pinmill.

" Be damned to a landsman's life, Jim," he said fiercely. " I'd go to sea for two pins."

James looked enquiringly at his brother. " What do a couple of clod-hoppers like us know o' the sea, Bob ? Who's going to give us a berth ? "

" Well, whose fault is it that we are where we are now, wi'out a place ? "

" Laud's, I s'pose."

Suddenly the realization of what was in his brother's mind dawned on James Catchpole. He looked uneasily at Robert.

" You don't mean for us to join with the free traders ? How would you find Laud ? And think of the risk, man. I don't fancy transportation or the execution dock at Wapping myself."

" Look a'here, Jim, don't you think I hev thought of the risk ? All smugglers don't get caught. Lookit some o' them things Will used to bring us. We'd never a seen things like that in our whole lives, much less had 'em, if it hadn't been for the free trade. It's worth a bit of risk anyhow."

James Catchpole shrugged his shoulders in silence and followed his brother down the road.

CHAPTER EIGHT

Alneshbourne Priory Farm on the North bank of the River Orwell, where Margaret took her place as maid of all work, was as lovely a spot as could be found in the whole of the Eastern Counties.

The farmhouse itself, its front timbered and whitewashed, was the shape of a letter L. It had high dormer windows ; and at one end a quaint old gable, sagging with its enormous age, supported a towering chimney. There was a similar chimney at the other end of the house.

The road leading to the farm was not much more than a deep, tree-lined rut, sticky with mud in winter, whilst in summer warm winds dried the mud into an ankle-deep, choking mass of dust of the consistency of flour.

The small clearing in which the farm stood was shut in on three sides by a thick grove of tall elm trees, and on the side of the farm that faced the river towered an ancient sycamore tree. The river side of the farm ran down in a gentle slope to the Orwell, a slope of turf as ancient as time and as smooth as soft green velvet. Centuries before the farm had been owned by a body of Augustine monks. The old barn nearby had once been the original monastery. The lofty rafters which had echoed the chanting of the Agnus Dei and had harboured the scent of the smoke of incense, echoed to nothing now, except the scuttling of rats and the almost inaudible chirrup of bats, and harboured nothing but cobwebs, spiders and the dust of centuries.

Next to this mouldering stone and thatch edifice stood the cemetery of the monks, which from time to time gave up the bones and the simple possessions of the holy men buried there centuries before.

As Margaret trudged down the lane to Priory Farm, her spirits fell. Everything was so utterly lonely. Used as she

46

was to dwelling in isolated places this spot had such an atmosphere of eeriness and remoteness that it seemed almost as if the ancient owners of the Priory objected to the intrusion of this young girl, so full of life and vitality.

Margaret went round to the back and knocked upon the kitchen door. It was opened by a large red-faced woman, sweating from the heat of the kitchen fire. Despite her disarray Ellen Grimshaw, cook of Priory farm, had a kindly face, which in some measure comforted Margaret's uncertain spirit.

" Come in, m'dear, come in. Mis' Wake has been telling me about the new maid. You'll be har n' doubt ? "

Margaret nodded and looked about her with misgiving. In all her life she had never seen a kitchen like that of Priory Farm. It was larger than the total area of any cottage she had lived in. There was no ceiling, but a lattice work of blackened oaken rafters and beams towered into the soot-shrouded apex of the roof. In addition to the large oven there was an open stone fireplace as big as a cottage living-room. In it was an iron turnspit, operated by a chain and capable of roasting a whole bullock. Down the middle of the stone-flagged floor ran a long trestle table on which Ellen had been making the weekly batch of bread and pastry. In the corner near the fire, flanking a pot-bellied red earthenware bread crock, stood a large wooden cheese press. On the other side of the kitchen stood an enormous Welsh dresser on which was an orderly array of spotless wooden bowls and yellow and brown " combed-ware " dishes. On another side of the room was a glass-fronted cabinet containing a variety of small household items—wrought iron ember tongs, used to convey hot coals to pipes : silver candle snuffers, clay wig curlers, and sharp-bladed sugar cutters : and surrounding a large charcoal box-iron were tinder pistols, a candle mould, a taper holder and a gingerbread press.

Beneath the long table with the dough still clinging to it stood a wooden kneading trough ; and beside it, a large wooden cream bowl and a lidded wooden butter tub.

Ellen Grimshaw wiped her big, capable floury hands on a piece of clean sacking, blew a stray wisp of auburn hair out of her jolly grey eyes and nodded to a chair.

" Sit you down, mawther."

She went to an earthenware bowl and ladled out a bowl of milk and gave it to Margaret with a slice of freshly-baked cake.

" Here's a bite and a sup," she said. " It's tiring thirsty work tramping down Gainsbro' Lane."

As she was eating and drinking Margaret was aware of the cook's appraising scrutiny. Presently, when Margaret had nearly finished, Ellen Grimshaw nodded her head.

" So you're Margaret Catchpole," she remarked, " who was Will Laud the smuggler's girl, eh ! "

Margaret flushed and looked appealingly at Ellen who nodded in a kindly way. " You'd rather not talk of it, maw ? Well, I don't blame you. Howsomever there's some sharp eyes and sharp tongues here as you'll presently find out. But never you mind. Do as you're told, tend to your work and you 'ont come to n' harm ! "

After a day or two in which she found her way about, Margaret settled down to work at the Priory. She soon became popular with most of the house servants and with the men who worked the farm. Ellen Grimshaw found her a willing and hard worker and, like many another, was surprised at the strength and endurance in her tiny, perfect body.

The days went by, and Margaret did not know when she would hear from Will again ; much less when she would see him. It was, she was certain, merely a question of time— no doubt of that. It all depended, of course, on what ship Will was aboard. It might mean a long trip, or possibly just across to the Continent. Will would never think of letting her know : he was like that. She would merely get a message to say that he was on his way to see her and then he would turn up and the fact that she had been without news of him for weeks no longer mattered and all the worries and anxieties and doubts that may have crept into her mind were swept away.

But, if traces of anxiety over his wound still lingered in her mind, Margaret no longer feared for him beyond the normal fears of any girl whose lover was a sailor. He was safe in some merchant vessel owned by Captain Bargood—or so she supposed, for Will had said he was going to find him a berth when he had recovered from his wound. And so Margaret, with little to worry her as she went about her work in the kitchen of the farm, was happy.

There was, however, a fly in the ointment. This was Milly Drewitt the dairymaid. Milly was a buxom, handsome, red-headed shrew who, instantly becoming aware of Margaret and her background, proceeded to make life as miserable as possible for her.

As Margaret's duties often led her to the dairy she frequently fell foul of Milly. The first day that Margaret had to go to the dairy for milk Milly humiliated her by telling her to stand outside and wait as she didn't want the floor dirtied. At meal-times, when the servants sat down at the trestle table in the huge kitchen, Milly usually managed to turn the talk to the free trade, much to Margaret's embarrassment. Nevertheless, Margaret did all she could to keep her naturally quick temper under control, aware that she was a newcomer and not wishing to cause a disturbance so soon.

One dinner-time Milly came out with some startling news. "Old Coulson came up with a basket of fish from the river this morning," she announced. "He says a day or two ago a gang o' the gentry broke open the custom house at Ald'bro', took all the goods, then went down to Slaughden Quay where there was a French craft taken by the Excise for smuggling. They threw the ship's husband into the river and sailed off wi' the goods they'd taken. They say the captain of the gang is a man named Hudson!" Milly turned her malicious green eyes on Margaret. "It must have been lovely to ha' had a daring smuggler for your man!"

The thrust was too pointed for Margaret to ignore. She pushed her plate leisurely away from her.

"Yes," she replied composedly, "something more exciting than huggling on top of a hayrick wi' the second cowman, Milly!"

One moonlit night Margaret had been making her way along Gainsbro' Lane to her father's cottage and had seen Milly and the second cowman, a somewhat dull-witted youth from Seven Hills, together atop a hayrick. They were in circumstances which could only be described as embarrassing. The titter of laughter which went round the table caused Milly's cheeks to match her hair. She flew round the table at Margaret.

"You smuggler's whore!" she screamed.

Then the two girls were rolling on the floor, their hands locked in each other's hair.

Despite her smaller build, Margaret had given Milly's red head several sharp raps on the stone flags before Ellen Grimshaw, outraged at this violation of her own little kingdom, dropped heavy-handedly upon them both and pulled them apart with arms and hands as strong as a man's. "None o' that old Bolsom in my kitchen. You, Milly," she gave the dairymaid a hearty shake. "Keep a still tongue in your head in future about Margaret's affairs." She also shook Margaret, not quite so violently as she had Milly. "And you-together mind your business about what Milly do on top o' hayricks." She glanced down the long table with a significant gleam in her eyes. "I dun't doubt but what we've all had our fancy men at one time or another."

When peace had been restored, the others gone about their tasks and Margaret was clearing the dishes, Ellen spoke softly to her. "I'm glad you gave that little bitch Milly a soling, my girl," she said. "She's been crowing over the others plenty long enough now. Ah, and she's a hot little mare into the bargain.

"Now don't you-together fret, m'dear. What you said was true. Better have a free trader for a man than an addle-pated dung-heeled cowman. But there, that dratted mawther 'ud bed down in a haystack wi' anything in trousers."

2

One afternoon Margaret had been to the dairy and was coming back with a heavy wooden bucket, full of milk. Suddenly a big brown hand closed over the handle of the bucket.

"Better you let me carry that, my maid."

Margaret, whose thoughts had been a long way off, gave a startled gasp and looked up. By her side was a tall, sun-burnt young man of magnificent physique. He was hatless, and his auburn hair was lightly coated with dust from the granary where he had been working. His shirt, open at the neck, showed a vast expanse of chest, thickly coated with curling black hair. His sleeves were rolled back, exposing herculean arms. The sunlight played in his warm brown eyes, reminding Margaret of the crystal clear, iron-tinted "pulks" or little marsh ponds when the rays of the sun struck slantwise down into them.

"Who are you?" Margaret gasped rather breathlessly.

The young man laughed, exposing crooked, but white and attractive teeth.

"Why, Margaret, surely you've been at the Priory long enough to know me. I'm John Barry, the foreman. I know all about you." Barry paused and then went on a little uncertainly. "You . . . you see, Edward Barry is my brother."

Margaret's face went white and she leant against the side of the dairy.

"John Barry, Edward Barry's . . . brother ? "

But Barry had picked up the milk bucket and had taken it into the kitchen.

Ellen Grimshaw noticed the little act and nodded to herself with complete approval. "A pity she couldn't a kept company with a nice, hard-working youngster like that instead of thet wild rake-hell Laud," she muttered. Then she sighed and shrugged as if admitting the pattern of human behaviour was beyond her understanding.

As John Barry had told Margaret, he had known all about her. He had in fact hardly taken his eyes off her since she had been at the Priory. And although Barry did not realize it, he was falling in love with her day by day, hour by hour. He watched her and as far as was possible used to time his visits to the dairy so that they coincided with hers.

The red-headed Milly was very much put out of countenance by this. She had long set her cap at Barry, for his parents were well-to-do farmers at Levington and he would have been a fine catch for her. She was well aware of Barry's increasing infatuation for Margaret and remarked spitefully to one of the other dairy maids, " I don't see what John sees in her, the little whipper snapper, with her great black eyes covering half her face ! "

Had Milly known it, it was just those great, dark, pansy velvet eyes that were drawing John Barry's soul right out of his body.

He would lie in his bedroom night after night unable to sleep. He would blow out his candle and then lie awake, getting up at last to stare from his window at the bright moonlit reaches of the Orwell. Lacking the opportunity of telling Margaret that he loved her, he fell back on the scheme of giving her every possible attention. When his work on the farm was done he personally saw to it that logs and kindling were ready to hand for her each morning. Early one evening, however, the chance offered itself.

He was returning from work along Gainsbro' Lane when he met Margaret, who was off on an errand for her mistress. He realized in a flash that this was just the chance he had been waiting for. He caught hold of Margaret's arm.

"Don't be in too much of a hurry, Margaret. I . . . I want to talk to you ! "

Margaret stopped and looked up at Barry and the impact of her eyes caused his heart to jump like a crazy thing.

He put his arm gently round her tiny waist.

" Margaret, I've loved you ever since the first day I saw you. I . . ."

She reached up and put her fingers over his mouth and he saw that her lovely eyes were flooding with tears.

" Oh, John, please don't say it, please ! " she beseeched, and the tears were trickling down her face as she spoke.

" Why are you crying, sweetheart ? I love you with every part of me, body, soul and mind. All I want is the chance to make you happy for the rest of your life."

" Dear John, you're too good to me. Apart from Ellen you are the only one on the Priory Farm who has been kind to me. But . . . but you see I can't love you ! "

" Why not, girl ? I'm not dashing like . . . Laud, and couldn't make you such fine gifts, but I know I could make you happier than he could have done, if you'd only give me the chance. You can't live and die an old maid just because Laud is dead ! "

Margaret staggered back against a nearby tree, her huge eyes even larger, her hand over her mouth and her face ashen.

" Will . . . dead ? " she cried wildly. "Oh no, no ! that's not true."

Barry looked puzzled. " Yes, my brother told me. He . . . killed Laud in the fight at Shingle Street that night. But I thought you knew that ? "

A relief so vast that she nearly fainted flooded through her. At the same time she realized how, unwittingly, Barry had caused her to betray herself. She leant back against the tree-trunk for a moment with her eyes closed and her brain working furiously.

There was only one thing she could do now and that was to take Barry into her confidence.

" John, you said you loved me just now. Did you mean that ? "

" With all my heart, girl."

" Then you wouldn't betray me, would you ? "

" My God, Margaret, need you ask that ? "

Barry's thoughts were not travelling in the same direction as Margaret's and he was due for as great a shock as she had just received.

Margaret's voice had dropped almost to a whisper.

" I know for a fact that Will isn't dead, John."

For a moment Barry did not grasp the portent of her words. Then he seized her by the arms so fiercely that she cried with the pain of it.

" Laud not dead ? " he cried. " My own brother killed him, girl. Have you taken leave of your senses ? "

" No," she said quietly. " After the fight at Shingle Street I nursed Will myself. Don't ask me how or why or where. He came near to death but he recovered and is now serving aboard a respectable trader."

Speechless at this unexpected news and the way he had been tricked into keeping silent, Barry stood as if turned to stone, his fists clenched and his head sunk on his chest.

Margaret turned and ran along the lane.

CHAPTER NINE

I

THE dark bulk of Butley Priory was only a little blacker than the night. A cold wind was whispering in from the sea, causing the man sheltering beneath the vast Priory gate, with its five armorial bearings, to curse and draw his cloak about his ears. Suddenly the sound of footsteps on the grass caught his ears and he drew back into a corner of the wall, cocking a pistol as he did so.

A soft whisper came out of the darkness.

" All's right, Will. Take your finger off the trigger ! "

John Luff, heavily bearded and with a Monmouth cap pulled down over his eyes, lurched out of the surrounding darkness. Laud carefully eased the hammer of his pistol down to half cock and slid the weapon from sight in the depths of a deep pocket.

" John, man," he said, savage with discontent, " I'm sick unto death of this life ; never able to come out except after dark, creeping from pillar to post. I'm going to leave the trade and marry Margaret and settle down ashore ! "

" And get a halter for your trouble ? How long d'ye think it 'ud be afore someone puffed the gaff that Cap'n Hudson and Will Laud, who's s'posed to be dead, were one and the same man. If you're so riled about marrying that little mutton, then why not get her aboard out o' harm's way for a bit ! "

Just how much she would have been out of " harm's way " aboard the brig only Luff knew.

Laud was not convinced. " How in hell can I do that, John ? She fancies me aboard an honest trader."

" Blast it, Will, let her think so still. As soon as the *Alde* comes out o' dock we'll get the mawther aboard and make a quick passage to Amsterdam. The two on you could get spliced there ! "

Laud did not answer for a while, but when he did it was in the tones of a man who had made up his mind.

" You know, John, the more I think on it the better I like the notion. If we can get Peggy aboard then you shall have my share in the next run . . . and there's my hand on't ! "

It was as well that Laud was unable to see his mate's face in the darkness as they shook hands on the bargain.

After leaving Laud, Luff pulled his cap further over his eyes and set off in the direction of Orford village. Pausing outside the low windows of the " Jolly Sailor " inn on the quayside, Luff peered through for a moment, then opened the door and went in, calling for rum. The interior of the " Jolly Sailor " was warm and snug. Around the walls in glass cases was almost every species of bird and beast that bred in the district. There were small marsh owls, herons, snipe, wild duck, bittern, loon, hawks and harriers, pheasants and partridges. In a large glass case over the fireplace was a tableau of foxes, stoats, weasels and rabbits, all in lifelike if somewhat glassy-eyed postures : and on either side there were cases of stuffed miniature dogs, brought from the far East by some forgotten wanderer many years ago.

There was the usual gathering of watermen, sailors and mud pilots inside, and Luff knew them all, with the exception of two men in the corner. The larger one, obviously drunk, was talking in a loud boasting voice, much to the concern of his companion who was as obviously sober. They were Robert and James Catchpole.

As Luff entered, the landlord of the " Jolly Sailor " gave him a significant glance, and with a barely perceptible nod of the head indicated Robert Catchpole, who was addressing an interested company over the top of a beer mug.

" Tell you I knew 'm well. Didn't he court our sister ? Will Laud was a fine young feller. A fine young feller. If I could see 'm now I'd shake 'm by the hand for old time's sake."

James Catchpole, sober and uneasy, gave his brother a nudge, but he might as well have nudged the wall for all the effect it had.

" Yes," Robert went on, " Will used to bring us presents ; fine presents, the like o' which would a cost us a year's wages an' more." His face took on a cunning leer. " You-together think Laud's dead, don't you ? But we know diffrunt, don't we, Jim ? Laud's no more dead than we are. My sister . . . ! "

Luff seemed to stumble against the drunken man and

Catchpole's tankard went to the floor with a crash. He turned with his face flaring with rage and his fist lifted. Luff shrank away.

"Sorry, shipmet," he mumbled. "Don't hit a poor old sailor that didn't mean no harm. Here, let me buy you another drink!"

Luff retrieved the pot and the landlord refilled it. He then finished his drink, climbed the three stone steps leading to the street and the quayside and vanished.

Some time later Robert Catchpole staggered out into the cool night air, assisted by his brother. About a mile along the road to Sudbourne they were overtaken by a man in a pony and trap. The driver slowed down when he came up with the two brothers making slow and painful progress along the road. Robert's hulk was as much as the slighter James could cope with. The driver of the trap gestured, offering the two brothers a lift. Between them he and James hoisted Robert into the trap. After a while the driver handed the reins to James.

"Here, old brother, gi' us a spell. My daddles are something cramped!"

When they had changed seats and the trap was jolting on its way the driver of the trap spoke again. The menace in the low tones startled James Catchpole.

"That's right. Do you drive now until I tell you to stop. I've a pair of pops here and there's nothing better I'd like than to blow both you and that loose-mouthed fool to hell and gone!"

Luff dropped one of the pistols into his pocket and, taking the whip, gave the pony a cruel cut, holding the second heavy calibre, short-barrelled pistol in the other hand.

Presently they came to Butley village. "Slow down here," he ordered, "and sing. Sing like the drunken bumpkins you are."

Luff thrust his pistol in James Catchpole's back. James did as he was bid, singing in a somewhat uncertain voice, whilst Robert snored pig-like in the bottom of the trap.

Luff glanced downwards.

"Drunken swine!" he hissed, and kicked Robert Catchpole heavily in the ribs.

As they passed through the villages of Capel St. Andrew, Hollesley and Alderton on their way to Bawdsey Cliff Luff ordered James to slow the trap down to a jog trot and sing like a drunken farmer. As soon as they were through the villages he whipped the pony so that the trap swayed crazily from side to side and it was all James could do to prevent the pony from going down on its knees.

When at last they came to the old fisherman's cottage on Bawdsey Cliff, Luff leaped down, drew the other pistol and turned back to James, pointing to the drunken and still snoring Robert.

" Get him out ! "

James bundled his brother out of the trap, while Luff went up to the cottage door and tapped with the butt of his pistol, three short taps and three long. Old David the fisherman opened it, and shrank back when he saw the visitor.

" What . . . what d'ye want, Cap'n Luff, sir ? "

Luff pushed James, who was half carrying, half dragging his brother, inside the cottage and thrust one of the heavy pistols into the trembling hand of the old man.

" Do you watch these two for a while." He nodded to the pistol. "And use that if you have to ! "

He went out to the well and for all his tremendous bulk went down the well rope like a monkey.

Laud was in the cave with several of the crew of the *Alde*. He sat apart from them these days. The men were rolling dice in a desultory fashion at one end of the table ; while Laud, glass in hand, sat staring morosely into nothing, his long legs stretched out before him. At intervals his hand would stray to the black patch over his eye, stroking it gently.

Luff came straight to the point.

" I've got a pair of prize pigeons up top, Will. Maybe you'd better see 'em." He told Laud of the occurrence in the " Jolly Sailor." Laud got up, belted on his hanger, thrust two pistols into his pockets and climbed up the well rope, followed by Luff.

As soon as he saw the brothers he assumed a friendly attitude—more because there would be news of Margaret than from any interest he had on their behalf. Robert had come out of his drunken slumber and was looking blearily around trying to get his bearings. He peered up at Laud and then got to his feet.

" Hullo, Will man," he said, " I hardly knew you."

" No, I've Barry to thank for that. Luff here tells me you were having a lot to say for yourself in the ' Jolly Sailor ' at Orford. Foolish, wasn't it ? "

Robert Catchpole glanced down at the floor of the cottage. " Ah, I reckon I'd had a drop too much. Things haven't been too good wi' us since . . ." He went on to tell Laud of all that had happened since their dismissal from Denton's farm. He also mentioned the fact that Margaret was working at the Priory Farm on Downham Reach.

" So Margaret is at Priory Farm ! " Laud turned to James. " Perhaps you'd take a message to Peggy for me ! "

James Catchpole shook his head.

" Not me. You-together have brought enough misery to us Catchpoles a'ready."

Luff took a step forward but Laud laid a hand on his arm : he could not help admiring James's courage.

Robert, his head rapidly clearing, broke in. " I'm glad we've found you, Will. We've been living like dogs. Jobbing labourers, sleeping in barns o' nights. Have you got a place for us ? "

" D'ye mean the free trade, Bob ? "

" Why not ? I'm sick o' working for a pittance."

Laud gently touched his black patch and looked at James. " And you ? "

James shrugged his shoulders. " Might as well be killed for a sheep as a lamb. We've gone too far to back out now ! "

He glanced at Luff as he spoke and was chilled by what he saw.

2

Whilst the *Alde* was fitting out at Ipswich some of her crew dispersed to their homes at Aldeburgh, Orford, Butley, Eyke, Boyton, Hollesley and other small coastal villages. Laud, Luff and the rest, including the two Catchpole brothers, spent their time at the cave on Bawdsey Cliff, sometimes staying at the Green Cottage, one of Captain Bargood's houses at Butley. The Green Cottage was not so much a cottage as a small mansion.

One of the favourite pastimes of the free traders when they were ashore was to go poaching on the extensive preserves of the Marquis of Hertford. While they poached principally for food they also did it for the thrill of a possible brush with the army of gamekeepers who patrolled the estate.

One evening in the Green Cottage Laud and Luff were alone, Laud reading and Luff sprawled back in a deep chair, a long clay pipe in one hand, whilst with the other he fingered his long, cleft chin—so deeply cleft that there was always a small tuft of black hair which persistently irritated him. He had divided his beard into two forks, one each side, whilst he scratched the sensitive spot absentmindedly.

"The long tails[1] in the larder are running low, Will," he said suddenly. "How about a drag across the stubble?"

Laud looked up. "Where d'ye fancy a drag, John?"

"We could do worse'n a beat around the fields between Orford and Iken. The partridges are thicker'n fleas on a dog."

Laud nodded thoughtfully. "They tell me his lordship has got spring guns, man-traps and man-killing mastiffs all over the place."

Luff made a gesture of unconcern.

"I know where the traps and guns are, Will," he said. "As to the dogs, they're turned loose after dark till sunrise, so we'll have to take a chance along o' them." Luff gave a grin. "The lads are getting stale, they need suthin' to liven 'em up. There's a full moon tomorrow night. We'd get a rare bargain o' game wi' a drag-net."

The next night seven men met at the entrance of the lane leading to Iken wood—Laud, Luff, Ezra Coffin, Nick Segel, Sam Nye and the two Catchpoles. Luff had a bulky sack across his shoulders, containing the draw-net. He dumped it down and whispered the last instructions.

"Jim here and myself will take one end of the net, Nick and Sam there t'other. Ezra will follow up after the game. He's an expert at wringing necks. Will and Bob there can spell us wi' the net. In the meantime Will is going to take the check string and if he hears anything he'll jerk the line. If he does, drop the net and make for cover. If you run into a keeper or dog use a knife—a pistol is too noisy. Look out for man-traps and spring guns."

The net was shaken from the sack, spread out and every man took up his station. There was a grim business-like atmosphere about everything. If the poachers met up with the gamekeepers it would be a battle with no quarter given. Frequently a kicking in the net would tell of a victim : then Ezra would swiftly and silently wring the neck of rabbit, partridge or hare, dropping the still twitching carcase into a bag. They were half-way across the second field when a blood-chilling, full-throated baying crashed through the moonlight.

Laud jerked hard on the check string. The others dropped the net and took to the bushes and trees.

"We're down wind o' those cursed killers," Luff whispered

[1] Pheasants.

urgently to James Catchpole. Taking his arm, he led him to a narrow clearing in the trees. " Go you down there between the trees. It's a beater's path leading to Iken. When you get back on the road make for Orford. Most on 'em'll be in the ' Jolly Sailor ' or the ' Mariner's Compass.'"

Luff broke off in another direction and vanished into the shadows.

James Catchpole suddenly felt the terror of those man-killers baying behind him in the darkness. He could hear their heavy bodies crashing through the undergrowth and the sweat suddenly burst out on his forehead. He sped off down the dark leafy corridor like a startled hare. Suddenly he heard a click : iron jaws clashed about his ankle, and inch-long, needle-sharp teeth bit into the bone.

The heavy bodies and the slaverings were closer now. In agony and terror, James Catchpole screamed.

Robert Catchpole paused for a moment in his headlong flight and stared wild-eyed into the darkness : then with a sobbing breath, he turned and took to his heels as if the pit had opened at his very feet.

CHAPTER TEN

P RIORY FARM was noted far and wide for the pure cold quality of its water. It was quite a common thing for sailors who knew the district to row ashore at this point on a hot day and ask for a drink.

Margaret had grown quite used to this, so that when a knock sounded at the door her actions were unhurried as she put down a pair of butter-pats she had been using. She went to a huge red earthenware crock and ladled out a dipper of water in a wooden ladle.

The sailor at the door knuckled an eyebrow and asked in English but with a strong foreign accent if he were at Priory Farm.

Margaret nodded.

" Yes, this is Priory Farm. What do you want? What country are you from? "

" Hamsterdam, mevrow. I left my vessel in der river. Mynheer the captain tell me stop at Priory Farm and tell wan Margaret Catchpole that he will be here at nine o'clock tomorrow in the evening."

" What's your captain's name? "

" Villiam Laud."

Margaret's face flushed and her eyes sparkled. " Oh! is Will in port? " she gasped excitedly, clasping her hands together. The sailor grinned and nodded. " Yah, mevrow. Do not forget the time. Nine of the clock tomorrow night."

He took a deep draught of water from the proffered dipper, thanked her and was off up the deep, narrow dusty lane that led to the high road and Ipswich.

It was a hot, dry, late September day. The corn stooks in the fields were a warm bronze against a greeny-yellow stubble across which the long shadows of evening were creeping. There was a slight wind stirring the dust, a wind already infinitesimally cool with the promise of autumn. It rustled

61

through the stubble and stirred the thinner branches of trees and bushes.

Margaret went outside and looked across the Orwell, shimmering in the late sun like a stretch of molten gold. Outside the kitchen door tall red hollyhocks nodded gently with brilliant yellow evening primroses in a blaze of colour. The air was swamped with the perfume of mignonette, heliotrope and tobacco plants. Lazy bees, yellow with pollen, blundered clumsily from flower to flower. Margaret saw none of these things, nor was she even conscious of the perfume : her eyes were fixed on the shimmering river. That was the way *he* would come.

She thought of his poor scarred face, and a tight little knot of compassion grew in her throat. God !—how she loved him. More than ever now, because of his injury. There was nothing of passion in her thoughts at that moment, only the upthrust of pure love, a maternal longing to draw that beloved, scarred cheek and sightless eye comfortingly to her breast, and to hold it there.

With a deep sigh she entered the house and went about her work late into the night, hardly noticing the rapidly passing hours, lost in a dream. It was midnight and past when she climbed the stairs to her tiny attic bedroom.

After she had plaited her long, black hair she undressed and let her drab, shapeless clothing fall in a heap by the bed. For a moment she stood mother-naked by the window, letting the gentle wind touch her. The thick black plaits fell over her firm pointed breasts. She ran her hands down velvety smooth flanks, over her buttocks and thighs, feeling a sudden voluptuous pride in herself. Out on the river a huge burnished moon was bathing the water and the surrounding woods in liquid silver. She gazed at the river again ; then suddenly ashamed of her thoughts she quickly drew on a coarse flannel nightgown, jumped into her narrow bed and blew out the stump of candle.

She was up early the next morning, for this day the last of the harvest was coming in with its traditional garland of green boughs together with the merry shouting of the labourers and the blowing of harvest horns. Later in the evening all the farm workers with their wives and children would assemble in the old kitchen for the Harvest Home Feast.

It was part of Margaret's duties to help Ellen the cook prepare the food.

It was a gigantic task. It entailed the cooking of huge

dishes of boiled puddings, both plain and plum ; dishes of boiled and baked potatoes, boiled cabbage, turnips and carrots ; huge roast sides of beef, done on the turn-spit ; roast and boiled ribs and haunches of mutton and legs of pork. There were apple tarts to bake and custards to prepare for over forty people, most of whom had enormous appetites bred of fifteen hours' hard work in the open air. The mere laying of the long trestle table was no small task.

When the feast was over it was the custom of the men to retire for an evening of song, story and drinking. Tradition demanded that on this one night of the year Mr. Wake, the owner of the farm, should wait on his men. He handed a large can to the boy who assisted him. " Here, lad, take this can to Margaret and ask her to fill it with ale."

When she had filled the can Margaret looked anxiously at the clock. It was past eight and she made up her mind that when the can had been emptied and re-filled she would be off. With this in mind she ran up the back stairs and got her shawl, leaving it on a hook behind the staircase door.

Ellen was sharp-tongued to anyone who left a dish out of place in the kitchen, so Margaret made sure that each plate was in its rack, the cutlery in the proper drawers, and the roasting-spit clean of grease and polished and put away, the skewers polished and strung along their cord ; boilers, sauce-pans and grid irons washed and hung up.

She was just finishing this work when suddenly amongst the general talk and singing she heard somebody shout, " The can's empty. Here, boy, take it out to Margaret to fill ! "

She filled the can with shaking hands ; then, as soon as the boy had taken it to the revellers, she put her shawl over her head and stepped out into the light of the rising moon.

Inside the farm-house one of the labourers named Will Riches, his bovine face flushed with heat and drink, turned to the man who had been elected Lord of the feast, an elderly harvester named Tom Keeble.

" Hey there, Tom, we've all sung a song bar Jack Barry."

The rest of the company chimed in.

" Ay there, Tom, call on Jack, call on Jack ! "

The penalty for refusing to sing a song was that the person who refused had to declare the name of his favourite girl. Now Tom Keeble was well aware that Barry could not sing a note, but he had his obligations as Lord of the Harvest Home.

He took his long-stemmed clay pipe from his lips, blew out a cloud of smoke and rose a trifle unsteadily to his feet.

"John Barry, what are you-together going to sing?"

"Sorry, master, I can't sing a note," replied Barry.

"Then a toast to your favourite lass!"

A roar went up from the assembly. "Ay, come on, Jack bor, a toast to your favourite lass!"

Barry's open face reddened. How could he tell them his lass was Margaret Catchpole, when out of her own mouth he had heard that Will Laud was still alive and that Margaret loved him?

Keeble took another puff at his pipe and after that a long draught of ale. He could see that Barry was confused and, whilst Keeble did not have an inkling of the truth, he had a certain delicacy of feeling.

"Come you on, Jack bor," he encouraged gently. "Surely you-together've got a maid?"

But Will Riches had had just enough drink to make him belligerent. "I've sung my song and so have t'others," he said, appealing for popular support. "A song, or your mawther's name—do no more ale for anyone." And he grabbed the ale can and held it out of reach.

Jack knew the feeling of the company was against him. They had indeed all sung their songs, and were now in the beer-happy, contented frame of mind when, having done their duty, they could not at all see why Jack should not do his. If he couldn't sing, they said, why shouldn't he tell them the name of his girl?

"Well, if you really must know," he said in a low voice, "it's because the girl I love doesn't love me."

This remark set up a buzz of conversation and speculation. "Wonder who the mawther is?" they asked one another, astonished that any girl should refuse good-looking Jack Barry with his promising prospects. Some whispered that it was the Master's daughter. Married men thought of their wives with misgivings.

Did they all know her? Will Riches asked. Yes, they all knew her. One man, more kindly disposed, reckoned it best not to press him for the name. "Press him be damned," shouted Riches angrily. "It's the law of the Harvest Home, 'int it?" And tempers began to rise.

Keeble thought the matter had gone far enough and, knowing Will Riches was overproud of his voice, called on him for a song. "Time you've sung it," he said, "no doubt Jack will be ready to tell the name of his mawther."

Riches, vanity overpowering the bully in him, lifted up his

full baritone voice and sang the ancient Suffolk song, " Hullo
Largesse " :

> " *Now the ripened corn*
> *In sheaves is borne,*
> *And the loaded wain*
> *Brings home the grain.*"

Then the chorus roared through the huge old room in time
to the banging of beer mugs.

> " *The merry merry reaper sings again*
> *And jocund shouts the happy harvest swain ;*
> *Hullo Large, hullo Large, hullo LARGESSE.*"

On the " Largesse " the beer mugs came down in a concerted thump which shook the room.

Riches caught up the next verse :

> " *Now the harvest's o'er*
> *The grain we store,*
> *And the stacks we pull,*
> *And the barn is full.*"

Then the chorus roared through the room again.

Riches came to the third verse.

> " *Now our toil is done,*
> *And the feast is won,*
> *And we meet once more,*
> *As we did of yore.*"

Then the red-faced laughing men waved their clay pipes
and beer mugs, and bellowed :

> " *The merry merry reapers sing with glee*
> *And jocund shout their happy harvest spree,*
> *Hullo Large ! Hullo Large ! ! Hullo LARGESSE ! ! !*"

This song, old as the hills, was founded on the practice of
the headman of each farm requesting a small sum of money
as " Largesse " from all who might enter the harvest field or
stop to watch the men at work.   Even the master of the farm
and his friends were expected to give a coin, as were tradesmen
visiting the farm on business.   At the end of the harvest the
money so collected was doled out amongst the men and their
families on the night of the Harvest Home Feast.

When Riches had finished his song and Keeble had proposed his health, the money was shared out.

Then Keeble turned to Barry and begged him not to spoil the evening by withholding his sweetheart's name.

The unhappy man, sensing the antagonism in the room, the animosity, even, which Riches had developed with a quantity of liquor inside him, realized that a continued refusal would see the festivities breaking up in a fight. And after all, why not tell them? For Margaret's sake? But she didn't love him, he thought in a burst of anger against her. Let them gloat, he thought fiercely, let them laugh and gossip.

" All right then, Will, and the rest of you," he capitulated. " I'll toast a health to the girl I love but who doesn't love me. Here's to Margaret Catchpole ! "

Barry drained his mug and with a violent gesture shattered it in the wide old fireplace.

There was a concerted roar of " Margaret Catchpole ! " and every mug in the room was tossed aloft. Then John Barry was outside and striding across the bridge of the moat of Priory Farm, from whence he could still hear the uproar of the merriment he had caused.

Suddenly he was stopped by the sharp challenge, " Who goes there? "

" John Barry. Who is that? "

It was green corduroy-clad John Gooden, head keeper to Sir Phillip Broke, the Squire of Nacton, hero of the fight between the *Chesapeake* and H.M.S. *Shannon*.

Gooden had a long, double-barrelled flint-lock fowling-piece across his shoulder.

" Hullo, Jack bor, where are you off to this time o' night? "

" Oh hullo, Mr. Gooden. I'm just off for a walk. Has the tide dropped enough for me to get along the shore to Levington? "

" Ay, the tide has dropped enough for you to get round. If you take the wood path to Nacton you can keep to the shore along Orwell park and pass the hall to Levington. But what makes you leave the Harvest Home? Good company there tonight."

" That there is, Mr. Gooden, and there'll be some thick heads come dawn. Mine is thick enough a'ready. I'm just having a blow to clear it."

The old keeper shifted his long gun and nodded his grey head.

"If it'd been anyone else but you, John, I'd have suspicioned 'em as poachers. I think I'll go up to the Priory and give the lads a look. Good-night."

"Good-night, Mr. Gooden."

CHAPTER ELEVEN

MARGARET CATCHPOLE stood on the bank of the Orwell, the huge orange moon giving her a strange glamour. Her eyes were shadowed pools and the moonglow cast a deep shadow between her breasts, half revealed by her low-cut bodice.

She gazed across the river to where the moon reflected in the many windows of Freston Tower. Her heart leapt as she saw a sail in the direction of Woolverstone Park, and then sank again, for she recognized the sail to be that of the crazy boat of an equally crazy owner, old Coulson, the mad fisherman who fancied himself hag-ridden. As a protection against the phantasies which pursued him Coulson wore numerous charms about his person.

As the girl watched his sail another boat, smaller and skimming like a racing gull, passed Coulson. In it were Will Laud and John Luff, and as they passed the fishing-boat Luff pointed to it.

" Who is that, Will ? "

" Only old Coulson, John. They call him Robinson Crusoe round these parts. He's light. You could talk all day along o' him and still get n' sense."

Coulson looked across at them. There was an intent, peering look in his mad, brilliant eyes and the night wind tugged at his long grey hair and matted beard. It rattled the bone charms slung around his neck. Then he called across to the others in a powerful voice, " Ahoy there, Laud, you've got the foul fiend aboard ! "

Luff scowled. " The fiend take *him* : he's recognized you, Will ! "

Laud grinned. " He's a'right if you humour him, John." Then he shouted across to Coulson. " If you've got a good haul, better you hurry, Robin : do you 'ont make the Grove tonight. The ebb's dropping away fast."

The old man's voice was eerie and matched his appearance

as he stood up in the boat looking like a tall marine scare-crow in his flapping rags.

"I'll be there afore you, Will. You've lightened my cargo. I can see my black fiend at your masthead. Take care he dun't drive you aground. He sticks hully close to the sail."

The old man gave an eldritch cackle of laughter as the other boat sped past.

Luff shook his head uneasily. "Poor talk that, Will ; talking of fiends and such at a time like this."

A little later they passed the crenellated Cat House on its mound. The white cat was in the window. Above the Cat House shone the lighted windows of the manor of Mr. Berners, owner of the estate.

Laud altered course to meet a slight change of wind brought about by the turn of the river. Luff nodded with satisfaction. "We're dart afore the wind now, Will," he said.

"I'll be happy when this night's work is over, John. You'll be welcome to my share of the next run."

"Never you fear, Will. The task is an easy one."

"Shows what little you know of Margaret, man ! "

"Pah ! We'll cut her cable quick enough, never fear about that, Will. Then we'll be back aboard the *Alde* afore you can say Jack Robinson. Then there's not a boat on the east coast that'll catch us. Since she's been in dock and had her bottom cleaned there's nothing of a drabble tail about her." Luff trailed off into a little whispered song.

> "*Here am I, poor Jack,*
> *Just come home from sea.*
> *Shiners in my sack,*
> *What d'ye think o' me ?*
> *Five long years I've been cruising*
> *The world over,*
> *And many a strange sight*
> *I've seen, but wish*
> *The wars were over.*"

As they got nearer the shore, Laud said softly, "John, I want to handle this thing m'self."

"And so you shall, Will lad, and so you shall. But here, take this bos'un's whistle. Blow it if you want me to bear a hand, do I'll lay like a log in the boat's bottom."

Laud took the curved whistle and peered towards the rapidly approaching shore.

"There she is, John, I see her. Take you hold o' the

tiller a bit, ease your mains'l : I'll ease the fores'l. Bear
up on your hellum a bit, bear up ! "

Margaret stood watching the sails of the small boat,
ghostly in the moonlight. She held her hand against her
heart as if she feared it would hammer its way out of her
bosom.

The boat grounded and a small wave eddied around
Margaret's feet, but she did not notice it, for Will was ashore,
and their lips and pounding hearts were together.

Presently Laud had breath enough to speak softly.

" My little dunlin—my love." He kissed her again so
that she sagged in his arms and he, fearing that she might
have fainted, strove to make his voice matter-of-fact.

" Peggy, I've seen Robert and James, they told me of your
troubles. For God's sake give up this place you're in ;
you're too fine a metal to mar those pretty hands in dish
water. There's our boat and my vessel is waiting off Pinmill. There's as snug a cabin aboard her as any you've
ever seen. I dare swear you'll find more hearts and hands
to serve you there than ever you've had in your life before."
Laud was tense with emotion and his face was eager.

Margaret looked up at him. " But where would I go,
dearest ? What would your owner say to a woman aboard
his vessel ? I thought you wanted to marry me from father's
house."

" Peggy, I can't stay here long. Say you love me and
we'll cross to Holland and be married before the week is out."

" Will ! I can't leave father. Who would look after him ?
Get permission from your master to stay a while and we'll
be married here in Nacton."

" I can't get leave, sweetheart. I'll pay someone to look
after your father. What does it matter where we're married ?
Marriage is marriage whatever the country."

" That may be, Will. But I've learned that marriage in
some countries don't hold good in others. And whether
it does or not, I'd like father's consent. He'll give it I know,
now that you've finished with the free trade. I shouldn't
be happy leaving him like this. He was grieved enough
when Robert and James left home."

" It won't matter if he doesn't know until we get back."

Laud paused as a sudden thought struck him.

" You haven't found anyone that you care for more than
me, have you, girl ? "

" What makes you think that, Will ? "

"You don't seem over eager to come. I thought you would ha' been."

"All right, then," she flared, seized with a sudden desire to hurt him, goaded by his selfishness. "There is someone. He loves me, Will." And as suddenly she relented. "But it's not my fault. I've told him I still love you."

There was a sudden glitter in Laud's single eye.

"Ye little fool, ye've given me away. Folk think me dead !"

Margaret looked at him reproachfully.

"No, my heart, I haven't betrayed you. He was so sincere that it was only right I told him I loved you and that you still lived."

There was an ugly quality to Laud's voice. "Well, you must have some feeling for him, do you wouldn't have told him as much as you did. Anyway, who the devil is he ?"

Margaret thought furiously. She knew that it would be dangerous even to mention the name of the man whom she had refused, but she was being driven into a corner.

"He's a sincere young man, Will, and comes from decent folk. I see him every day at the Priory and surely I'm woman enough to know if he'd betray anyone or not !"

Laud sneered. "A pretty tale, b'God. Maybe you'd like him to be bride's man at our wedding ?"

"You could do worse than that, Will !" she cried, her temper rising. What right had he to question her like this ?

"What's his name ?" he asked impatiently.

It was out before she realized what she had done.

"John Barry !"

Laud recoiled and his hand instinctively flew to the black patch over his eye.

"Barry . . . of Levington !" he hissed with such ferocity that Margaret shrank back from him.

Laud went on speaking softly, almost as if to himself. He seemed completely unaware of Margaret.

"John Barry ; brother to that —— Lieutenant Barry of Shingle Street !"

He ripped the black patch from his face and, seizing Margaret, thrust his disfigured features into hers.

"Remember this, mawther ? You should do, you helped heal it. But it seems you've damned soon forgotten who gave it."

He thrust her savagely away from him and stood head on chest and hand on the pistol-butt at his belt.

Margaret went up to him and put her hand on his arm.

"It won't help to bear malice, Will," she said gently. "There were things done on both sides that night, things best forgotten. And John Barry has been kind to me. He's the only one on the whole farm who hasn't at one time or another mentioned that I've been a smuggler's mistress."

Laud's tanned features were white and drawn in the moonlight, the scar remaining an angry crimson.

"You'll never forget the injury that Barry did to you that night, will you, my dear," went on Margaret quietly. "You would've killed him if you could. And what did John Luff do to James Last?"

Laud's lip lifted in a snarl like an angry dog's. He too felt the stigma of Luff's atrocity, but his strange perverse nature refused to admit it, even to Margaret.

"Luff, is it? Well, let me tell you this, my girl: he's loyal at least, whatever else. He doesn't go mixing up with the Barrys from Levington."

He shivered violently and sat down on a nearby tree-stump.

Despite the angry tone of his words Margaret felt a sudden rush of concern.

"Will, you aren't well!" she cried.

Laud wiped the sweat from his face. "I'm a'right. Don't start bettying about now. There's a drop o' rum in the boat. I'll get it directly."

Margaret started towards the boat. "I'll go and get it for you . . ."

Laud started up.

"No, don't go to the boat, Peggy. . . . Hold a minute. They've been reproaching you with being a smuggler's mistress, eh! Well, the smuggler is here to marry you. Do you think those damned busybodies would believe that I was ever anything else but a smuggler. I've gone too far now, too far. . . ."

Margaret buried her face in the folds of his jacket. She felt the pistol-butt grinding into her breast. Oh, why was he so obstinate, she thought?

"I know you were a smuggler once, Will," she said in a muffled voice. "But now they say the fleets of France are sweeping the seas. Smugglers are being given pardon if they volunteer to go. I . . . I wish you'd go, Will. You'd feel happier and so would I. Folk could say what they liked, it wouldn't matter then."

" You could persuade me, my little dunlin, do you sail to Holland with me."

She drew back. " Oh, Will, my dearest," she beseeched, " don't urge it more. I've already stolen away from my work and they may have missed me. Just tell me that you'll come back soon and marry me at home and I'll be happy."

Laud was silent for a while and when he spoke there was a sombre quality of despair in his voice.

" I can't do it, Peggy."

" Why, Will ? Why ? "

" Don't ask me, girl. For God's sake come on down to the boat. Come and share my life. There's nothing I couldn't do with you at my side."

" How can I leave father ? He'd think I'd fallen into the river."

" Peggy, I can't live without you," he pleaded. He put his arms round her and kissed her ardently. " But I can't come here the way you want me to." He moved her gently in the direction of the boat.

" Come away, my love," he urged. " You'll never regret it."

She struggled against the gentle but insistent pressure of his arm.

" No, Will, not this way, not this way ! "

" Then we'll never marry ! "

" Why not, Will ? Oh, why do you say that ? "

" Because I'm a smuggler, lass ! "

Margaret did not grasp the significance of his words.

" You have been, I know, but you aren't now. Most folk think you are dead. The memory of Will Laud the smuggler will soon vanish from people's minds. Why, already there's a new name becoming notorious round the Suffolk coast. A daring, dangerous fellow by the name of Hudson ! "

" I tell you," cried Laud desperately, " I'm a smuggler still ! "

" Oh no, Will, you're the master of a trading vessel ! "

Laud in hopeless despair threw all caution to the winds.

" For Christ's sake stand and face realities, girl ! I *am* Hudson. Every moment I stand here I'm in danger ! " He hustled Margaret towards the waiting boat.

At his brutal words Margaret was suddenly overcome with a faintness of both mind and body. Her dreams and hopes were shattered and lay broken all around her. Will, her own Will in whom she had put so much faith, was still a

smuggler. Those days of dreaming of him safe in the service
of some law-abiding merchant, had they been days in a fool's
paradise? Will *had* been a smuggler, of course, but there
had been none of the ugly stories about him that there were
about Hudson. And now he said he *was* Hudson. Could it
be true? Could it? And yet surely he would not be so
cruel as to mock her love for him by telling her this if it were
not true.

Like one in a trance she found herself being impelled
towards the boat, all volition driven from her by the weight
of her grief and despair. She was dimly aware that at
that moment she would have been very happy to have
died.

She came to herself just before they reached the boat and
started to struggle, quietly at first, and then violently against
the iron arm that held her.

" Will, Will, you don't mean . . . to force . . . me to
go ! " she cried breathlessly.

" I will if I have to, Margaret ! "

" And you . . . told me . . . that you loved me. Don't
do it ; let me go ! "

She pushed both her hands against his chest. Laud swung
her off her feet.

Panic flooded her then and she fought like a wild cat.
Laud, realizing that he could not get her to the boat without
knocking her senseless, drew his bos'un's pipe and gave a
long, shrill, single blast.

It went echoing away down the Orwell, startling roosting
duck and curlew : it brought Luff from the bottom of the
boat in an instant. There was a frightening grin of triumph
on his face in the moonlight as he ran up.

" Suthin' late blowing that whistle, weren't you, Will ?
But better late than never ! "

With a flash of intuition Margaret realized the trap into
which she had been decoyed. But it was too late. With a
single leap Luff was on her like a leopard on to a lamb, and
in an instant she was slung like an old sack across his huge
shoulders. She had breath enough for one piercing shriek
before Laud clapped his hand over her mouth. She uttered
it with all the power of her lungs. It went reverberating
through the woods of Downham Reach and echoing away
through the woods of Woolverstone Park on the other bank
of the Orwell.

The festive ones at the Priory Farm heard it and their

merry-making stopped as if they had suddenly been stricken dumb.

Will Riches looked across at Tom Keeble.

" Blast ! Did you-together hear that, Tom ? "

An Irish labourer by the name of Fagan stood with a glass of ale half-way to his lips. " The Banshee ! " he whispered.

Tom Keeble came out of his amazement.

" Banshee be damned. That's some poor mawther in trouble. Get lanterns and sticks you-together. Hurry now ! "

John Barry was just entering the wood by the gamekeeper's cottage when he heard the shriek.

Without stopping to think he leaped across the paling of the wood and saw two men, one with a girl across his shoulders, the other trying to stifle her cries.

When Laud had first clapped his hand over Margaret's mouth she had immediately bitten it to the bone. He had whipped off his kerchief and wrapping it round his hand, partly to stop the bleeding and partly as a gag, thrust it into her mouth to stifle her cries.

Barry looked hastily around for some weapon, and seeing a stout pole sticking out of the mud left by the receding tide, drew it out with a jerk and rushed to the rescue. Swinging it round his head he hamstrung Luff so that, despite his strength, he dropped Margaret and rolled cursing into the muddy waters of the Orwell. Laud rushed in and caught Margaret, picked her up, turned one arm about her and with the other drew a pistol. There was a click as he cocked the weapon. Luff had got to his feet and had also drawn a pistol. Barry, determined not to give them a chance, flew at them.

" Damn you, let the girl go ! " he shouted.

Margaret recognized the voice, and cried out to him. " Oh, John, John Barry, help, for God's sake help ! "

Luff raised his weapon but Barry knocked it from his hand. This interlude gave Laud the time he wanted and, raising his pistol, he sighted along the barrel with his single eye, as coolly as if he had been firing at a contest. He squeezed the trigger gently and Barry went reeling away from the thundering report, clutching his left arm. The ball had ploughed the full length of his arm, lodging in his shoulder. Then Laud flew into the attack with his cutlass.

" Barry is it ? Damn you to hell, I'll ruin your looks as your brother did mine ! "

Barry's left arm hung useless and saturated with blood, but he parried the blow with his stick and smashed Laud's cutlass from his hand and into the river.

By this time Barry was beginning to feel the effects of the wound. He staggered slightly as the two men, who had had no time to reload, leaped in with their weapons reversed. The noise of the fight had attracted attention and luckily for Barry, old Coulson, the mad fisherman, who had landed not far away, came striding to his aid. He looked a fearsome figure in the moonlight. His long beard parted by the night breeze had blown back along each side of his bony jaw. His rags flapped like tiny pennants, whilst his thick hair stood upright and his mad eyes blazed like lamps. In his great, gnarled hands he had a long-handled gaff.

"Ye damned cowardly whelps," he shouted. "The foul fiend'll drag ye to hell yit!"

There was no stopping the strange being with the string of bones and other gruesome relics around his neck. He had the strength of ten men and his whirling, glittering gaff was everywhere at once. Evading the deadly hook as best they could, Laud and Luff were driven back to their boat.

As they pushed off and jumped in, Laud seized a long-barrelled musket laying in the boat's bottom. There was a double click as the hammer came back to full cock.

"Make us a rest wi' your back, John," Laud said coolly to Luff.

The little boat heeled slightly to the recoil as the heavy report of the musket went crashing away in echo after flat echo down the reaches of the Orwell.

Barry threw his arms wide, spun in a half circle and crashed forward on his face.

In the meantime Margaret, frantic with fear and confusion, had run into the men from Priory Farm. With no knowledge that old Coulson had gone to Barry's help, she threw herself into Tom Keeble's arms.

"Hurry, for God's sake, do they'll murder John!"

Then she collapsed.

John Gooden had heard the uproar of the conflict and the reports of the pistols, followed later by the crash of the musket that went thundering away down the river. He arrived on the shore about the same time as the men from the farm, and found old Coulson supporting the head of Barry, who was unconscious and bleeding profusely from two gunshot wounds.

The men formed a double row and lifted him as gently as

they could. Even so the movement brought a retching groan from the wounded man.

As old Coulson stood shaking his fist at the smuggler's boat rapidly vanishing downstream, Laud's voice came back thin with fury.

" Take that back to your brother and be damned to all Barrys ! "

The mad fisherman held both his hands above his head in a terrifying gesture.

" The foul fiend be with you. He'll consume ye yet, you bloody cowards ! "

A jeering laugh came back from the tiny craft as it merged into a moonlit patch of water and was gone.

CHAPTER TWELVE

I

MARGARET lay face downwards on the settle in the kitchen of Priory Farm, overwhelmed by fear, grief and disappointment. For a while she had lain without even conscious thought, her mind stunned. Then, as feeling had gradually flowed back, she had given a shuddering sob.

" Oh, Will, Will, why did you lie to me ! "

A murmur of voices came to her as the men returned with John Barry. Margaret shut her eyes and clasped her hands over her ears in an agony of remorse. But for her John Barry would not have been killed, for she thought that he was dead. Even at this moment her anxiety was less for Barry's actual death than for the fact that Laud was his murderer.

A hand shook her, not over gently.

" Margaret, better up and get bandages and water. It 'ont do you n' good lying there, n' John either ! "

It was Tom Keeble who had spoken and there was the coolness of blame in his tones and in his honest countryman's face.

Margaret caught a glimpse of Barry, white and bloody, his clothes foul with river mud. She heard him groan and an acute spasm of relief stabbed her. He was not dead ! Will was not his murderer after all !

On her way out to the pump she ran into her mistress. Mrs. Wake's face was marked with tears and she had just sent one of the farm hands off at full gallop for the surgeon. She passed Margaret without speaking and in her silence the girl felt condemnation.

A bed had been prepared for Barry, and his companions carried him up as gently as they could. Riches, who felt some blame for baiting Barry to the extent of causing him to leave the gathering, turned on Margaret.

" It's all your fault," he said, " you damned little smuggler's slut ! Barry is like to die all on account of you."

Tom Keeble jerked his head at Riches.

" Steady there, Will ; she's suffered enough a'ready, I fancy ! "

Riches turned away without speaking.

The jolly atmosphere of Harvest Home had vanished from the spacious, ancient rooms of Priory Farm. The laughing happy faces had vanished too and were replaced by anxious and grave and tearful ones. The children had been packed off home to bed and the men and their wives stood about talking softly.

Old Coulson, the fisherman, sat in the kitchen, his right hand doubled into a huge, gnarled brown fist and his left on his forehead.

After Barry had been made as comfortable as possible pending the arrival of the surgeon, one of the men turned to the old fisherman.

" Who was it fired that last shot, Robin ? "

The old man looked up vacantly. " Who else but the foul fiend. I saw him in the boat."

Riches made a significant gesture to his forehead. Tom Keeble, however, thought otherwise. He put a restraining hand on Riches' arm.

" Hold you on, Will," he said, and turned to Coulson. " What manner o' fiend, Robin ? Was he devil or man ? "

" He wor a demon. He left me a while to torment others. I knew there'd be mischief as soon as he left me. He's allus stirring up strife and he'd bring his hellish comrades agin me but for this here charm ! " He held up a piece of perforated bone from amongst his collection of gruesome relics. Then he sidled up to the men with a cunning leer. " Do you-together know what this is ? I'll tell ye. 'Tis a rib o' Margery Beddingfield who wor gibbeted on Rushmere Heath for the murder o' her husband. Heh ! Heh ! Heh ! When I show the fiend this he'll soon be off."

Coulson looked fearfully over one shoulder and suddenly pointed to the door with one long, black-nailed finger. " There he stands. There ! "

The men of Priory Farm glanced fearfully in the direction the mad old creature was indicating, fully expecting to see the murderer in the doorway. The old man held up his perforated rib.

" Ay, look at this, thou false fiend. Dost remember

whispering to Margery and Richard Ring her lover to murder John Beddingfield her old husband of Saxmundham? Thou knewest that the old man was of little use to the hot-blooded Margery. Off. Off, I say! Heh! Heh! Heh! He's gone."

The old man stuck the bone back in his rags.

Will Riches shrugged. "You-together 'ont get n' sense out o' him!"

Then turning impatiently to Coulson, he pointed to Margaret who had just come back into the kitchen.

"Tell us, old man," he enquired, "what did Margaret here have to do wi' the fight?"

"Ask her yeself. The fiend allus find a woman easy."

Coulson turned to Margaret. "Tell them who wor fighting, girl."

The men crowded round her.

"Yes, come you on, Margaret, tell us who wor fighting."

She backed away white-faced, knowing that if she told she would betray Laud.

At that moment the voice of her mistress calling from the parlour saved her. As she fled from the room old Coulson cackled, "Heh! Heh! Heh! that's a clever girl. Which o' you-together want to wed har?"

"Ask Jack Barry," said Riches. "My belief is that a rival for Margaret shot'm."

Coulson looked cunningly at the speaker.

"Do *you* know of any rival that'd do it, Will?"

"That I don't! But I do know who it would be if he wor alive."

"Well, who is that man, Will?"

"Who else but Will Laud. But he was killed at Shingle Street. Did you-together know him, Robin?"

"That I did, but I never knew he wor dead. If so the foul fiend ha' brought him back to life. I spoke to him this very night and he to me. Laud, is it? I know him well and wish the fiend had dragged'm to hell afore he give that gallant lad his death!"

There was an immediate uproar amongst the men. Keeble seized Coulson by the arm.

"Are you telling us you saw Laud on the river tonight, Robin?"

The look of cunning spread over the old man's face again.

"Do you ask Margaret. She can tell you as much as I, if not more."

Margaret had just entered the room for a bowl of warm water. Will Riches went up to her. There was little love lost between them. At one period he had been importunate until a saucepan alongside his head had convinced him that Margaret was no admirer of his bucolic good looks. He had neither forgiven nor forgotten and delighted in the opportunity to bait her.

" Who did you go out to meet tonight, Margaret ? "

Despite her grief, anxiety and disappointment Margaret's fighting spirit asserted itself at the impudent question and attitude of Riches.

" Do you mind your own affairs. He's a better man than you'll ever be."

" Ay," Riches sneered, " and a better ' Will ' too, mebbe. One whose had his will o' you a few times, I don't doubt."

Margaret's face was pale but her head was up and her huge eyes flashed lightning.

" If he has it's something you'll never do, even if you do come creeping into the kitchen when I'm alone. He'll make a will-o'-the-wisp of you one of these days."

Riches' face was beetroot in its fury.

" He'll be hanged fust, mawther, don't fret y'self. Take my word for that. He 'ont be shot or drowned. He's born for the gibbet ! "

" And what do you think you're born for, you cowardly whelp. Quarrelling wi' me at a time like this ? "

" I'll tell you what I'm born for. I'm born to be Laud's informer. And before long I'll have the pair on you up before the Squire for this night's work ! "

The men looked uneasily at each other. Riches' mouth was running away with him. It wasn't healthy even to be associated with informers against the gentry.

Margaret eased the tension by deliberately turning away and speaking to Robin.

" The master wants to know if you'd like some supper, Robin ? "

Coulson shook his uncouth head. " Thank you, mawther. All I want is to hear what the surgeon thinks o' young Barry upstairs."

Riches broke in again.

" Well, Margaret, if you 'ont say who you met tonight, I'll tell you. You met one who old Robin says the fiend has brought back to life. Will Laud ! "

Margaret's pale face was even paler as Riches continued.

" You've got a guilty face, girl.   Where have you-together hidden Laud all this time ? "

As the others started to crowd round, Margaret broke through them with a violent sob and rushed into the parlour and flung herself at Mrs. Wake's feet.

The good lady mistook her actions.

" Come, Margaret, John's not dead ! "

Margaret looked up with the tears streaming down her face. " Oh, mam, they 'ont let me be," she wept.   " They say it's all my fault.   They're blaming me for what happened."

Mrs. Wake smoothed her dark hair.   " There, there, Margaret.   Sit you down quiet for a while.   I'll speak to the master."

The men were still grouped about Riches and talking in low tones when the master of Priory Farm came in.   Anger edged his voice as he spoke.   He did not like the thought of all these robust men baiting one girl who had enough trouble already.

" What've you been saying to that unfortunate girl ? Whatever she has or hasn't done, it's poor talk, a crowd of hulking men baiting a girl who has already been scared half out of her wits.   Best thing you can all do is get off home. And do I hear any more of this squit some of you'll be looking for new places."   His eyes lingered on the red face of Riches.

2

When Dr. Stebbing entered the room where Barry was lying one of the maids was wiping his face, while others were removing the blood and grime from other parts of his body. He was in pain and every now and then shudders would run over his big frame.

" All right," Stebbing said quietly to the frightened-faced women, " leave us alone for a while.   I'll call you when I need you."

" Will he get over this, Doctor Stebbing ? " asked Wake anxiously.

" I can't tell you yet," the doctor replied.   " The boy is in a bad way.   He's lost a lot of blood and his arm is broken. We'd better get his clothes off first.   All I hope is that those two balls didn't carry any cloth into the wounds."

Between them Dr. Stebbing and Mr. Wake carefully stripped Barry.   It took a long time and they had to work slowly, for, besides being heavy, Barry groaned in heartrending fashion when they moved him, gentle as they were. At last his clothes were removed and he was laid on his face.

Stebbing shook his head when he saw the wound. The heavy musket-ball had traversed diagonally across Barry's back, piercing the dorsal muscle and lodging against the spine.

Stebbing rolled up his sleeves, took a probe and looked at the ugly, purple-lipped hole.

" If it were anyone else but a clean-living youngster like him I wouldn't give a groat for their chance. Hold him now, I'm going to probe and it will hurt ! "

The sweat was pouring down the faces of both the men when at last Stebbing gave a cry of triumph.

" Hah, I've got it ! "

Carefully withdrawing the probe he held up a lump of shapeless lead with the cloth still adhering to it. When the wound had been washed and bandaged Stebbing and Wake turned Barry over and the doctor got to work on the wound in the arm.

It was ugly, but not nearly so dangerous as the other had been. Running the whole length of the fore-arm the ball had broken the humerus and lodged in the trapezian muscle, just below the surface of the skin. It was easily extracted, and the broken shoulder was carefully reset and splinted. When the work was done, Stebbing called the maids to bring warm blankets and carefully wash Barry with warm water and vinegar.

As Margaret came into the room with warm flannel for Barry's feet, he opened his eyes and looked vaguely round the room. His gaze first lit on Wake, then on the doctor, then it fell on Margaret. When he saw her he gave a faint smile, as if relieved to see her safe, and closed his eyes.

Stebbing gently patted the injured man's face.

" There you are, John, you'll be better now. If he suffers overmuch," he added, leaving a sedative on a table at the bedside, " give him two of those pills."

Stebbing noticed that tears were running down Margaret's face as she left the room.

When she had gone Wake grasped Stebbing's hand.

" I can't thank you enough for all you've done, Doctor . . . your attention to that poor lad. I'll be glad when we can get to the bottom of this night's work. Is there anything I can give you before you leave ? "

" Ay, a little nutmeg in a glass o' warm brandy and water, and a nice big slice of your famous harvest cake."

When the tall rubicund-featured doctor was seated, balancing a plate loaded with a huge slice of the rich, fruity harvest cake on his knee and holding a glass of nutmeg, brandy and water in his hand, Wake asked, " What is your honest opinion about John Barry ? "

The doctor answered through a mouthful of cake, which he was obviously enjoying.

" A nasty wound, a nasty wound. Take months to heal, but he'll get over it. Don't move him for six or seven weeks at least. By the by, where do his parents live ? "

" Levington Creek. His father's a well-to-do farmer over that way, has a large family. John came here to learn the business so that he can take over later on—from his father, I mean. A fine lad that. Quiet, sober and a grand worker to boot."

Stebbing nodded absently, cramming the last of the cake into his mouth.

" Tell me, what's that crazy old fisherman doing in the kitchen ? I've been told that he would never enter any house, whatever the reason."

" He's waiting to see you, Doctor. From what I gather he helped John in the fight. But don't expect to get any sense out of him."

Stebbing got to his feet and wiped his mouth in a voluminous handkerchief.

" Sense or not, if he stood by John against those desperadoes, whoever they were, he deserves credit. I'd like to speak to him."

Wake went into the kitchen, came back with Coulson and retired, leaving them together.

Stebbing laughed at the old fisherman.

" What an odd fish you are, Robin. I can never get you into my kitchen on any pretext, yet here you are hob-nobbing with Wake's men at the Harvest Home. Damme if I don't tell my daughter and get her to set some of those fiends of yours on to you."

The old man shook his shaggy head dismally.

" The fiends ha' done enough this night, Doctor, less I'm wofully mistook and there'll be more jookery [1] afore long."

Stebbing knew how to humour Coulson.

" Well, who did the fiend work on tonight, Robin ? "

[1] Roguery.

" He left my boat and went aboard Will Laud's."

There was a look of eager interest on Stebbing's face as he moved forward on to the edge of his chair.

" What ! " he cried, " Will Laud the smuggler ? I thought he was dead long since."

" Ay, so did a tidy few others, sir. But not me. I saw him t'night, ay, and that bloody-minded John Luff. They wor sailing up-river, and when the fiend left me and sat mowing at their masthead I knew he wor up to mischief."

" What mischief, Robin, what mischief ? "

" Blast, sir, 'int you just dressed young Barry's wounds ? "

" Ay, but what had your pet fiend to do wi' that ? "

" Don't ask me, don't ask me. Do you ask Margaret."

Stebbing was persistent. " Was the fight because of a love-affair ? "

" Don't know about that, sir. All I can tell you is this . . ." and Coulson told the doctor of the fracas on the river bank.

When he had finished, Stebbing patted him on the shoulder.

" Well done, old man, well done. But for you a damned fine lad would have lost his life. Here, take this ! "

Stebbing tried to thrust a guinea into the old man's knotted fingers.

Coulson drew back indignantly.

" What, take money for what any man would a' done ? No, sir, that I 'ont. Pay me for my fish if you like. I'll bring some up in the morning." Coulson looked fearfully over his shoulder. " The fiends would be at me if I took money for saving life. Do you tell me the boy'll do well. That'll be payment enough."

Stebbing pondered on a way of rewarding the old man. Suddenly he hit upon an idea.

" Well, Robin, if you won't take money, come up to my house any time you fancy and I'll give you any charm you like to ask for."

A delighted smile spread over the old man's eagle features.

" That I will, sir, that I will," he said. " And now would you be kind enough to ask the master of the house if I could have some help to get my boat afloat ? She's high and dry."

When Coulson had left with some of the men who lived on the farm to refloat his crazy boat, Stebbing called to Margaret, " Come here a moment, girl."

He felt her pulse and looked at her tongue.

" Better you get to bed, my girl, you're something feverish."

Margaret had a high colour and her eyes were yet more brilliant than usual. Even her voice was quick and feverish.

"Oh, thank you, sir. I'm all right, I really am." She paused. "I . . . I'm sorry for what happened."

"Not your fault, girl, not your fault," said the doctor brusquely.

"I don't know, sir . . . I . . . I . . ."

Stebbing eyed her keenly. "You're trying to shield someone. You don't like to blame anyone else, is that it?"

Margaret looked even more confused.

"Yes . . . yes, sir, that's right, but . . . well, he was to blame."

"D'ye mean young Barry?"

"No, no. I mean he who shot him."

"A damned cowardly act whoever done it. What in God's name induced him to do it? Barry never hurt a soul in his life."

"It was because John's brother marked him for life. It was done in revenge, sir."

"Still a cowardly act, Margaret."

"Yes, sir, but I still feel to blame."

"How so?"

"Because I told *him* that John loved me."

"Jealousy, eh!"

"Yes, Doctor, I suppose so. You see, I thought that he knew I loved him." Margaret's tones grew slightly bitter. "He should know by now. I pray to God that John will get better, sir!"

Stebbing's gaze was sombre. "Barry's in a bad way, girl. A lesser man would have died. There's already a price on Laud's head. This affair is like to drop a noose over it!"

Margaret sank on her knees at the doctor's feet and threw her arms around his legs.

"Then you know, sir! Oh, for pity's sake save him!"

"D'ye mean John Barry?"

"Yes, oh yes!"

"Look here, my girl, d'ye love that poor boy?"

Margaret hung her head and a tear fell sparkling to the floor.

"No, sir, oh yes, don't let him die for his parents' sake."

"Then you don't really love him, eh?"

The doctor bent and lifted the weeping girl to her feet. There was no deceiving the astute Dr. Stebbing. Margaret looked straight into his eyes.

"I'll always feel grateful to John for his kindness to me, sir. He was the only man on the farm who didn't jeer at me. But, oh, sir, for God's sake don't let him die, do Will'll hang."

Stebbing nodded thoughtfully. The girl's heart was still with Laud, attempted murderer, smuggler and desperado that he was. What strange creatures women are, he thought.

A little later he saw Wake, advised him to send for Barry's parents as soon as possible, then climbed into his trap and drove up Gainsbro' Lane and across the fields to Ipswich.

3

The next day Barry's parents arrived and took up residence at Priory Farm.

Some days later John's father was allowed to go in and talk to his son.

John Barry's big body was wasted by the wounds which, as Stebbing had remarked, would have killed a lesser man. His face was white and his auburn hair was curling up at the nape of his neck and round his ears, giving him an unworldly look. His father felt a pang of pity and love as he went up to the bed and gently took his son's hand in his own.

"This is a fine way to greet your old dad, John bor," he said gruffly.

Barry smiled faintly. "Hullo, Dad."

His father sat gazing thoughtfully at him for a while. Then he said, "Out wi' it, son. There's something more than your hurts troubling you. What is it?"

John turned his head to the wall so that his father should not see the tears of weakness in his eyes.

"Dad, I . . . I wish I could die."

His father kept his voice gruff and hearty only with the utmost effort of will. "That's poor talk, John. Who'll run our farm? Why, I hope I'll be laid to rest long afore then."

John's father had been told the whole story of his son and Margaret and after a while he went on speaking in a gentle voice. "Look a'here, John. I know how you-together must feel. I wor disappointed in love once. Long ever afore I met your mother. Thought about throwing myself in the Orwell. But it passed. They say all good things come to an end, so do bad things such as sorrows. There'll be plenty of others for you, lad, right good mawthers too." Old Barry emphasized the word *good*.

John turned to face his father again.

"Father, I know I've not had the experience of life that you've had, but don't condemn Margaret before you've heard what I've got to say."

The elder man shook his head.

"Hard not to, John. How can I help not condemn a girl who's mistress to a wild rake-hell smuggler who tried to kill my own son?"

"That's not her fault, Dad. She hates the life Laud leads."

"How do you expect me to feel," his father asked, "to one who associates with a man like Laud who'll revenge himself on an innocent man, even if that man were not my own son? I've heard many tales of Laud, none of them good. Edward has told me of his connection with that human fiend Luff, the worst man on the whole coast of England. He told me of what Luff did to his boatman Jim Last, and when your brother speaks of that, even I his own father feel afraid. Edward'll never rest until he's wiped out Luff, Laud and the whole gang they work with. When your brother is at home on leave he's up early o' mornings in the field with his pistols, and he can knock sparrows off the top of corn-stacks with 'em. It's more than just smuggler and coastguard now. Laud is fore-doomed."

"Dad, I wish I could make Margaret see all this. I know she's good. As good as my own mother if only she were given the chance."

Old Barry shook his head.

"No, my son, I could no more be persuaded to believe that girl would break wi' Laud than I could persuade you to break wi' har."

He got up, squeezed his son's hand and left the bedroom.

A few weeks later John Barry's workmates on Priory Farm built a frame to fit his bed, complete with shoulder pieces for carrying; and in this contrivance they carried him back to his parents' house at Levington.

CHAPTER THIRTEEN

I

WILL LAUD sat in the darkened cabin of the *Alde*, the only illumination a guttering candle in a horn lantern. His face was set in a mould of deep gloom. Luff stood with a hand on Laud's shoulder, and it seemed that a portion of his evil essence had flowed into the sitting man, for Laud's single eye had in it something of the mad glitter which shone in Luff's.

" Never you mind, Will bor," Luff whispered consolingly. " We failed ; but when one means fails there's other to be thought on."

Suddenly a scream echoed through the vessel, a scream which although Laud had heard it before still caused the short hairs on his neck to lift like a frightened dog's.

He looked enquiringly at Luff.

" Ah, Catchpole agen," Luff nodded. " He's not drawn a sober breath since the night of the . . . er . . . accident to his brother. It wor rum, rum, rum till we had to stop his ration and now he's the horrors."

Laud got up and belted on his sword and pistols. He never left even the *Alde's* cabin these days without his arms. He strode forward to the foc'sle where Nick Segel and Sam Nye were struggling with a third man.

Robert Catchpole was hardly recognizable. His dark hair had grown long and matted. He was unshaven and filthy and his eyes glared unseeingly past the master and mate of the brig. He was struggling madly in the grip of the other men and shouting in a thick, terror-ridden voice.

" Jim, Jim, for Christ's sake, the hounds, the hounds ! "

With a superhuman heave of his big body he broke clear of the powerful men who were holding him, and as he did so the phantoms of his dead brother and the man-killing hounds vanished. He looked at Laud and grinned vacuously.

"Sorry, Will. I . . . I . . ." He broke off and stared in horrified fascination at the opposite bulkhead.

"Ah God, the hounds, the hounds!" He screamed like a burning horse and backed away, his dirty hands guarding his throat, his eyes bolting from his head and a froth gathering at the corners of his mouth.

Suddenly he went down with such force that it seemed to the watchers it was beneath the slavering jaws of one of the rum-inspired phantoms of his deranged mind. Then he was struggling furiously on the deck with an invisible dog which appeared to be trying to tear out his throat. All the time hoarse worrying sounds were coming from his own foam-flecked lips. He squeezed a phantom throat and then went through the motions of pushing a heavy body to one side. Slowly raising himself to his knees and then to his feet, he backed away with his fingers crooked like talons, ready for the next attack.

"Come on, ye man-killing sods, I'll throttle the lot on you!"

As the phantom hounds closed in, Catchpole backed against Luff, who drew a brass pistol from his pocket and brought the heavy cannon-barrel crashing down on the deranged man's head. He thrust the pistol back in his pocket and gestured at the man lying on the deck.

"Tie him up and no more rum until he stops raving. Understand?"

Sam Nye went down on to one knee and turned the prostrate figure over. Catchpole's head sagged grotesquely : his eyes were wide and staring, and there was no fear of anything in them now, only an inhuman blankness. A trickle of blood ran from the corner of his mouth. Nye lowered him hurriedly.

"Why . . . why he's dead, Cap'n Laud, sir!"

Luff pulled his beard.

"I must 'a tapped him a mite too hard on the noggin," he said casually. "And all that rum, too. Ah well, get him overboard then."

Luff's inhumanity shocked even Nick Segel's hardy soul. "Can I have an old hammock," he asked, "to sew him in, sir?"

Luff shot him a swift glance.

"Hammock be damned," he said roughly. "Don't waste good canvas on carrion like that. Get it roped up wi' a lump o' ballast."

Master and mate of the *Alde* strode out of the cabin in silence.

When they had gone, Segel drew his sheath-knife and slowly sawed through the clews of his own hammock.

" Don't seem fitten to cast the poor sod overboard like that," he said somewhat shamefacedly to Sam Nye.

Nye nodded. His face too was shocked, as he whispered, " Ah, there's sorthen about Luff o' late that fair turns my guts to water. And Will too, he's hully altered."

He nodded to where his hammock was swinging.

" My hammock is plenty big enough for two, Nick, if you didn't mind like ? "

Nick got up from the long canvas bundle on the deck.

" You're a good shipmet, Sam," he said, " but don't you fret. It 'ont take me long to sew a new hammock."

A little later two dark figures climbed on deck carrying a long bulky object between them. They staggered to the rail and paused as Sam Nye whispered in the darkness, " Do you-together know any prayers, Nick ? "

" The only prayers ever I knew my old mother taught me s'long since I've forgotten 'em . . . God rest her soul, and his." The canvas-shrouded body of Robert Catchpole slid over the side with a deadened splash, leaving rings of fire in the phosphorescent water. As it slid beneath the surface bubbles streamed upward for a while, vanishing astern as the *Alde* thrust her black hulk uncaringly on into the darkness.

2

Some time later the look-out at the fore-topmasthead shot swiftly down the ratlines, ran aft to the cabin and knocked urgently on the door.

" Cap'n Laud, sir, there's a light in Ramsholt church tower."

Laud went on deck and peered into the darkness. He then returned to the cabin. " Bring her to, John," he said to Luff, " then get the boat away. I'm going ashore."

It was not long before the brig lay with her topsails aback and the small boat alongside. There were six men in it and Laud was at the tiller. He called softly up to Luff who was leaning over the rail.

" Keep your eye lifted, John, and if you see me fire a pistol stand off for the open sea. Give way together, lads."

The little boat crept silently off with muffled oars. As it neared the sandy foreshore and low cliffs a light blinked briefly from the beach. A little later the moderate swell cast the boat broadside up the beach. The boat's crew, drenched to the waist, jumped out, weapons in hand.

Laud and Coffin stood waiting tensely. Presently a figure stepped out of the darkness, and was covered instantly by four pistols.

" Cap'n Laud, sir ? "

" Ay, what is it ? There's no time to waste."

" Cap'n Bargood sent me, sir. He said to tell you that information has been laid agen you. That night at Priory Farm, you and Cap'n Luff were recognized and Sir Philip Broke has been informed."

Laud drew a long hissing breath. " Who was it ? The name, man, the name ? "

" One of the men fr'n the Priory, sir, a Will Riches. Cap'n Bargood says keep away fr'n the Orwell."

The figure faded into the darkness as the boat's crew fought their way back through the surf to the *Alde*.

On the way back Laud remarked softly, partly to himself and partly to Ezra Coffin, " So the Commodore wants us to keep clear o' the Orwell, eh ! Well, this is one time we're not taking orders."

Back aboard the *Alde* Laud and Luff were in conference for an hour before Laud came out on deck and gave orders to make a passage for Downham Reach. His experienced eye watched the vessel's stern come past the wind.

" Flatten aft your mainsheet, aft on your foresheet."

He eyed the sweeping yards.

" Check your foretops'l weather brace ; check mains'l weather brace."

The wind billowed the big sails and then filled them and the *Alde* slid lithely through the water, gathering speed every yard. Laud stood, head thrust forward, gazing morosely along the deck.

" Break out your main stays'l ! " he called.

The brig's mighty main stays'l broke clear like a giant wing and for an instant the air was filled with its flapping thunder.

" Flatten aft on your stays'l sheet ! "

As he gave the order, Laud leapt like a tiger to bear on the rope. When the stays'l sheet was belayed he glanced aloft and then nodded to Luff.

" All a-taut aloft and alow, John. See a good look-out is kept." He turned and entered the cabin.

With the soft thunder of wind-taut canvas the brig surged forward into the night.

3

Supper at Priory Farm was over and the men pushed back from the table with satisfied expressions on their faces. The fight on the foreshore was still the main topic of conversation, more so now that Riches had been to the squire about Laud. Sir Philip had been as surprised as any to hear that Laud was still living. He had listened to Riches' somewhat garbled story, had given him five guineas and sent him away, saying that in the near future he would send for him to make a statement in front of the magistrates.

Riches was something of a hero amongst his own workmates, for it required an intrepid spirit to lay information against a man like Laud, especially as he was associated with Luff. Nevertheless, their admiration was somewhat tinged with uneasiness. Riches laughed at their fears. Stretching his legs, he filled a long clay pipe, lit it, thrust his hands into his pockets and closed his eyes.

" How much did you say there was on Laud's head, Will ? " Tom Keeble called across the table.

Riches coughed somewhat pompously. " Sir Philip told me that there was two hundred guineas on Laud's and two-fifty on Luff's, dead or alive, the pair on 'em."

Keeble whistled. " Four hun'ned and fifty Jimmy o' goblins, man. What ud you-together do wi' all that much rhino ? "

" Do ? What in hell d'ye think I'd do. Buy a small farm and marry our Margaret."

A laugh went round the long table at this, and Keeble shook his head.

" Don't fret yourself about har, bor. She 'ont look at you. She hates your guts ! "

" That might be, Tom, but she 'ont hate being mistress o' a snug little farm."

Keeble laughed. " Why, I didn't know that a man could be so bloody fulish, Will. She 'ont marry you if you owned Priory Farm itself. That mawther's a fiery 'un an' . . ."

A knock outside on the kitchen door interrupted them. One of the labourers opened it. Outside stood two figures in the green corduroy of gamekeepers. They both had long-barrelled fowling-pieces over their shoulders.

At that period poaching was so prevalent and poachers under the threat of transportation so desperate, that no keeper walked unarmed through the woods day or night. Many bloody battles had been fought, with fatal casualties on both sides. Keepers had died, blasted from ambush, poachers had been killed by cunningly concealed spring-guns.

"Master Will Riches here?" asked the taller of the two keepers.

"Ay, that he is."

"Well, tell him Sir Philip wants to see him at the Hall."

Riches' red face flushed even deeper and his prominent blue eyes sparkled. He winked at his friends as he got up from the table.

The two keepers led the way up to the top of Gainsbro' Lane.

The shorter of them gestured to an opening in the woods.

There was surprise in Riches' face and in his voice as he turned to the keepers. "That's not the way to Sir Philip's house!" he said.

Suddenly the shorter keeper's long gun leapt into line with Riches' stomach.

"Mebbe not, but that's the way you're going, Master Will." There was a movement of the long gun. "Turn you round and walk quietly, do I'll blast you all over the wood!"

The colour drained from Riches' face and his breath came short.

"Who . . . who're you? You're not keepers!"

There was a soft laugh from the taller "keeper."

"Will Laud and John Luff at your service, Master Will. You've heard of us I don't doubt?"

"Laud . . . Luff . . . My God!"

Riches' knees gave way beneath him and he crouched on the ground, his mouth agape and eyes staring upward like a stoat-stricken rabbit.

Luff prodded him to his feet with the long gun. In spite of the mildness of his words there was something in his whisper like the sweep of steel from a sheath.

"What! The brave informer chicken-livered? Shame on you, Will man!"

With a sob Riches went stumbling down the narrow path ahead of Luff.

There was a little knot of men around the small boat drawn up on the banks of the Orwell as the two "keepers"

and their victim broke clear of the woods.   Luff gave Riches
another prod with his gun.

"Turn round, Will!"

The wretched man did as he was bid ; then grovelled in
the mud of the receding tide as he heard the hammers of the
gun go from half to full cock.

"For God's sake don't, don't, don't!" he whimpered.

Slowly the long barrels lifted, and Riches' bulging eyes
gazed into the gaping muzzles.

Suddenly Luff pulled both triggers and Riches fell back
with a scream.   The only sound from the gun was two loud
clicks.

Luff looked in comical astonishment at the piece.

"Well, blast if I didn't forget to charge it!"

He put the gun in the boat and booted the grovelling form
of Riches.   "Get him into the boat, then."

The men around the boat hove in the terrified, half-fainting
man and pushed off towards the unlighted brig lying in
mid-stream.

4

Down below, Laud sat at the crescent-shaped oak table,
curved to fit the shape of the cabin.   Before him, Ezra Coffin
on one side and Nick Segel on the other, stood Riches, slack-
mouthed with terror.   "There's the gallant lad, Will," said
Luff, as he entered the cabin.

Laud, chin on fist, looked across at Riches.   "Why did
you inform, Will?" he asked, his voice soft and impersonal.

Riches gulped and said nothing.   Luff prodded him.
"The cap'n talking to you, Will.   Tell him it was greed that
made you go up to Sir Philip, greed for blood money on the
heads of men who have never done you any harm.   Greed,
wasn't it, Will?"

He prodded the shivering wretch harder.

"Yes . . . Yes . . ." Riches choked in an almost inaudible voice.

Laud gestured briefly.   "Take him away and lash him
up."

When the men and the prisoner had gone, Luff looked
enquiringly at the master of the *Alde*.   "What d'ye suggest
doing wi' him, Will?"

"Give him a keelhauling and let him go."

Luff shook his gigantic shaggy head.   "He's dangerous,

Will. Snivelling cowardly whelps like that allus are. We ought to get rid on him."

There was a gentle smile round Luff's mouth and a rapt faraway look in his strange, flecked eyes.

Laud shook his head. " No need to kill him, John. He'll be so scared he 'ont speak. A keelhauling'll meet the case."

" Keelhaulin' it is, Will."

5

Riches was stripped, and hauled ashen-faced and shivering on deck. Tackles had been rigged at the opposite ends of the mainyard. A broad canvas belt was strapped round the wretched man's waist and in an eye at the back of the belt the slack of the tackle was hitched ; he was then hoisted, struggling and screaming, on to the rail of the *Alde*.

" For God's sake don't throw me over. I'll drown, I'll drown ! " he shrieked.

Luff gave his whispering laugh. " You should ha' thought o' that afore you went to Sir Philip, lad. You 'ont drown, Will m' hearty, I promise you that "—he gave a heave on the tackle that sent Riches over the side—" but by the time we've keelhauled you a few times you'll wish to God you had."

There was a laugh from the rest of the crew.

Riches gave a thin scream as he hit the water and the bight of the rope allowed him to trail astern, bouncing from wave to wave as the *Alde* swept on.

Luff let him bounce for a time or two, enjoying the gull-like screams which were periodically cut short as Riches went beneath the surface. Then the mate of the *Alde* turned to the men at the hauling parts of the tackle.

" Heave away, lads."

Muscles tautened and sinews stretched as they hove Riches beneath the keel of the brig.

Luff was an expert in the art of keelhauling and flogging, knowing to the second how long a man could be kept under before drowning or lashed before dying. He signalled to the men at the opposite yard.

" Heave away ! "

Riches was hove almost up to the rail, blue-faced and vomiting sea-water. He looked up, his eyes bulging, lungs pumping for air, whilst blood and water mixed ran down his body from the multitude of lacerations where the barnacles on the ship's bottom had bitten into his flesh.

"Not again, not again, for God's sake!"

Luff, knowing that another dose too soon would bring merciful unconsciousness, put his elbows on the rail and looked into the blue-white, agonized features.

"Why, Will lad, can't you take your medicine? It seems informers ain't the hardy coves I fancied."

He covered Riches' face with his broad palm and shoved, at the same instant signalling the men at the yardarm to slack away.

Riches, with a scream that was quickly choked in salt water, vanished beneath the brig's keel a second time. The men at the other yardarm hove on their tackle leisurely until the wretched man appeared on the opposite side of the vessel. The procedure was repeated, until the third time up Riches was unconscious, his head hanging on his chest, his whole body a mass of shallow gashes.

Luff signalled to the men to heave him inboard. There was no point in keelhauling a man who felt nothing. When Riches slumped on deck Luff booted him into the scuppers. At that moment Laud came out on to the deck.

"I fancy he's had enough, John," he said, eyeing the limp form sombrely. "Get'm below. It'll be a long time afore he informs agen any other free trader, I'll lay."

"What are ye going to do with'm, Will?" enquired Luff.

"We'll put him ashore just below Aldeburgh. You can see him safely as far as the lime-kilns at Slaughden."

Luff turned and ordered two of the crew to take Riches below.

6

Some hours later the *Alde* lay hove-to on the north-easterly tip of Aldeburgh Ridge. Luff was on deck directing the launching of the small boat.

"Get your boat-strop fast," he ordered. "Sam, you—together overhaul that tackle and make fast." Sam hooked the tackle into the boat-strop.

Luff lifted a hand. "Heave away roundly now; over she goes."

The boat was launched broadside over the *Alde*'s low rail and settled with a gentle squelch into the water. The boat's crew took their places, followed by Luff, hustling Riches before him.

The brig lay about five hundred yards off shore, hidden

by the marsh mist which concealed the village of Slaughden. The morning was cold and there was but little sea running. The cold, wet roke hung in condensed globules of glistening moisture on the clothes of the boat's crew. It glimmered like the eyes of crouching spiders on the hafts of sheath-knives and the butts of pistols, moistened the dour, grim faces of the men and mingled with the sweat on Riches' forehead. There was a dank, earthy smell about it such as might have come from a newly-dug grave. It blended with the sour smell of the leather on the oars, and lapped over the boat's gun'le in a thousand creeping, curling, nebulous fingers.

There was a silence in the boat but for the faint grunts of the rowers and the creak of oars in worn thole pins, together with the musical tinkle of the grey water. Little swirls of yellowish bubbles and miniature whirlpools left the blades of the rhythmically dipping oars and eddied away into the fog from the thrusting bow.

The boat went forward in a series of jerks, synchronizing with the motions of the brawny, tattooed arms that urged it towards the steep, and as yet invisible, shingle beach. Riches' white face was drawn, partly from the keelhauling and partly from terror of the unknown fate that awaited him on the beach, now just visible as a low, grey cliff seen in the swirling roke. Somewhere an invisible bittern boomed and ghostly teal whistled overhead, their strange cry seeming to trail behind them like a streamer of sound in the air.

" Easy all ! " Luff's harsh whisper broke the silence.

The boat's bow grated softly on the shingle and a little wave caused by the heavy-laden boat's displacement chuckled up the beach for a few inches.

The men jumped into the breakers and, using the oars as rollers beneath the boat's keel, hove her well up the shingle.

Luff bundled Riches unceremoniously out on to the beach ; then, with a sudden movement that caused a hissing breath from the men gathered round, drew his Corsican knife and slashed the rope that bound Riches' wrists.

A wild, unbelieving look of relief flooded into Riches' face.

Luff nodded and smiled at him. " Cap'n Laud has been lenient wi' you, Will lad. Told me to bring you ashore and see you safe as far as the lime-kilns at Slaughden."

Riches gave a hysterical laugh and set to rubbing his numbed wrists.

Luff turned back to the boat's crew. " Wait here you together," he said. " I 'ont be long."

He and Riches crunched along the shingle and vanished into the fog. Side by side they plodded on until Luff stopped, lifted his head and sniffed.

" We're not far from the lime-kiln now," he said. " Do you know the lime-kilns along here, Will ? " he asked, as if making polite conversation. " They say the stuff is so dense that if you got one foot in you'd never get out. Quick-lime, lad, a fathom and a ha'f on it. Do you know, Will, these lime-kilns have allus drawed me."

He beckoned to Riches and turned up the beach. The odour of quick-lime was tart in their nostrils.

They stood on the edge of a pit of lime. Luff casually picked up a pebble and tossed it into the smoking mass. It vanished with a soft " plop."

Riches stood staring in fascination at the spot where the pebble had disappeared : then, half turning, went reeling before Luff's thrusting shoulder. He caught desperately at the edge of the pit and hung there gazing up piteously for a moment.

There was a gentle smile hovering around Luff's mouth as he drew back his heavy, iron-shod sea-boot.

7

Back at the boat Nick Segel looked across at Sam Nye. Sweat stood out on his forehead, despite the cold.

" Sam, did you hear that ? " he asked fearfully.

" Northen but a teal, Nick, northen but a teal."

A little later Luff came back along the stones. There was silence except for the crunch of the boat's keel in the shingle and the slap of her bow as it hit the little waves rolling up the beach.

CHAPTER FOURTEEN

JOHN BARRY's severe wounds gradually healed with Doctor Stebbing's skilled attention, but despite this his spirits flagged. He hardly slept at all, and although he tried to read, he could not concentrate. His sisters all did their best to amuse him but with no success.

" Father," he asked, not long after he got up from his bed, " when is Ned coming home on leave ? "

The elder Barry shook his head. " I don't know, John. Why ? "

" Oh, I . . . I'd just like to see him, that's all."

John Barry seemed so anxious to see his brother that at last his father wrote to the Coast Guard station at Shingle Street, telling Edward Barry of the true state of affairs, and suggesting that he should try to get leave as soon as possible as it would help John's somewhat tardy recovery.

One day a trap pulled up outside the Barry farm at Levington and Edward Barry jumped out. John Barry was in the garden at the back of the house, leaning against a tree and puffing slowly at a pipe. There was an abstract, brooding look on his face ; but as soon as he saw his brother his face lit up and he caught both of Edward's hands.

" Why, John," cried Edward banteringly, " you don't look your old self at all. What's amiss ? Here, let's sit down and have a yarn."

The two brothers sat side by side on an old tree-trunk whilst John told Edward the details of the night at Downham Reach. Edward listened in silence until his brother had finished.

" So Laud really is alive," he said softly, " and you've seen him ! Like many others I thought his account was paid at Shingle Street that night ! And you say that Luff is with him. . . . Laud and Luff," he went on in a preoccupied voice, " the deadliest pair on the whole of the coast between the Humber and the Thames ; dangerous as tigers, the pair of them. What devilry one doesn't think on t'other will. And yet I know that one day I'll be the death of both of them."

John Barry slowly shook his head. " I'd rather not hear you say that, Ned. It's bad having blood on your hands. Blood calls for blood, even the blood of a pair of human fiends like those. I'd be a lot happier to know that someone else had accounted for them or that they had been lost at sea."

Edward put his arm around his brother's shoulders.

" Look a'here, John bor. If that smuggling brig was wrecked, how would you know that either o' those two devils was lost. They've more lives'n a cat. That cut I gave Laud would have killed an ordinary man. There's nothing like a ball to make sure, and after what happened to you and my boatman there's nothing I'd like better than to shoot the pair of them out of hand."

" Nothing would please me more than to hear both Laud and Luff were dead, but I'd sooner someone else shot 'em, Ned."

" Don't worry about that, John. I'd think no more of it than shooting a pair of wild dogs. Apart from draining the revenue of the country, to say nothing of doing their best to kill my favourite brother "—Edward Barry's face darkened with sorrow—" look what Luff did to my poor lad Jim Last. By God, John, I loved him nigh as much as I do you. He was as brave as a lion and he'd never done a wrong thing in his life." He paused. " I think somehow Jim knew he was to die that night, but thank God he didn't know how."

" That night at Shingle Street, Ned," said John hesitatingly, " you had a bad time."

" Ay, they cut us up to hell, John ! "

Edward pointed to where Laud's cutlass guard had laid his head open to the bone. " Laud left me wi' this, and Luff killed three o' my men and maimed one for life. But it won't happen like that next time."

He hesitated momentarily, for he felt the question he was about to ask was a delicate one.

" John bor, do you truly love that . . . Margaret Catchpole ? "

" I'll never marry any other, Ned ! "

Edward sighed and turned away. John took his arm.

" Ned, you don't think badly of her too ? " he asked earnestly. " Why, man, there's not a drop of bad blood in that girl's body. She's . . . she's just unfortunate, that's all."

Edward was not convinced.

" I'm sorry to say this, John, but if she's as good as you say, why does she cling to Laud like she does ? You asked her to marry you and she turns you down for a hunk of gallow's meat. Doesn't fare sense to me, brother."

" That's just it, Ned. Margaret's that steadfast that she thinks one day she'll wean him away from his evil ways and company."

Edward laughed shortly. " Not if I see him over a pistol barrel first ! "

" Ned, I still feel that there's hopes of marrying Margaret yet, and I'd like your goodwill in the matter."

" John, whatever I do or don't think o' the mawther, if you want to marry her—good enough. I'll help you all I can and the best way I can see o' doing that is by putting either steel or lead through Laud's carcase, and here's my hand on't."

A few days later Edward's leave expired. " Take care of yourself, lad," John said earnestly as he was leaving. " If anything happened to you, God knows what I'd feel ! "

" Never you fret, John. It's been a long time, but I think I've got the measure of Laud and his gang at last."

They shook hands and Edward Barry climbed into the trap and drove away.

CHAPTER FIFTEEN

I

AT the Priory Farm Margaret's position was rapidly becoming intolerable : increasingly so since the night of Riches' disappearance. Before then she had suffered gibes and insinuations regarding Laud and Barry, but now the whole farm was convinced that she was an accomplice of the free traders, rumouring it around that she was directly responsible for Riches' vanishing.

At the meal table various members of the household would deliberately announce that a smuggler had been caught at Aldeburgh, that one had been shot at Dunwich or even captured at sea. If a casual sailor called at the Priory it was engineered so that Margaret would have to answer the door. Even Ellen the cook no longer took Margaret's side. Garbled tales of Barry's condition would reach her ears, until at last she felt that if she continued at the Priory she would lose her sanity.

The only bright spot in her whole existence was the fact that Mr. and Mrs. Wake ignored all rumours and were kindness itself. At last, however, even this could not compensate Margaret and she told Mr. Wake that she wished to leave and return to her father's cottage on Nacton Heath.

Jonathan Catchpole was earning a living as a jobbing labourer, and Margaret felt that she could justify herself by keeping house for him.

Wake nodded his head as he listened to Margaret's reasons for leaving his service.

" I think you're right, Margaret," he said. " You've been a good girl and the mistress and I have no complaints to make. But you can't stop people's tongues and I know you are not happy at the Priory."

And so Margaret left the farm and returned to her father's cottage on Nacton Heath.

2

Margaret stood gazing out of the cottage window over the snowy expanses of Nacton Heath.

Her father was away somewhere on the heath cutting faggots, whilst Edward, who had obtained employment as a shepherd, was somewhere out in the blizzard keeping a watchful eye on his sheep. A north-east gale had been bellowing out of a leaden sky for a week, bringing with it continuous snow which was over a foot deep on the level and on some of the remoter roads had blown into drifts deep enough to bury a coach and four. It had mounted up so that only by constant shovelling and brushing was Margaret able to keep the doors and windows clear.

After her father and brother had gone in the morning she lived in a silent, snow-beleaguered world. As she turned to build up the logs on the already roaring fire a tap sounded on the door. Margaret's heart jumped into her throat for the snow had deadened any sound of footsteps.

Cautiously opening the door, she peered into the whirling drift outside. Before her stood a tall figure almost invisible under the clinging snow. Suddenly she recognized it and a hot flush came to her face. It was John Barry.

Slowly Margaret took the chain off the door.

" Come in, John," she said. " Whatever brings you out in such weather ? "

He shook the snow from his coat and kicked it from his boots before entering.

Margaret dusted a chair and drew it up to the cheerful, crackling fire.

Barry looked pale, as if labouring under some excitement.

When Margaret spoke it was with some hesitation : it was the first time she had seen Barry since the night he was carried into Priory Farm kitchen.

" Sit you down, John. How . . . how are you ? "

" I'm much better, Margaret, thank you. I hear you've left the Priory. I'm sorry, lass," he sighed. Then his voice became firm with resolve. " Peggy darling, for God's sake let me take you out of all this. There's nothing to keep you here now. Your father and Edward can look after themselves. Marry me and you shall have the finest home that money can buy. You'll never regret it ; you never will ! "

Margaret turned her head away, tears in her eyes. But

for John Barry she might have been carried off that night at Downham Reach to heaven knows what fate. And yet . . .

Barry was talking urgently, almost breathlessly. " Say something, girl ; give me some hope ! "

She turned back to face him. He saw the tears on her cheeks and caught her in his arms and would have kissed her, but she pushed him away with all her might.

" Oh don't, please don't. Can't you see, John, that while Will is living I can never marry anyone else ! "

" Why not, Margaret ? If I could only break down that misplaced loyalty you have for him. Great God above, he's wanted the whole length and breadth of the coast, he and that evil genius of his, John Luff. You know as well as I do what Laud is. You know the sorrow and misery he has brought to you and your family." Barry was speaking through clenched teeth. "Laud ! Smuggler, pirate, would-be ravisher, ay, and murderer . . ."

Margaret interrupted. " Oh, not murderer, John, not murderer. You didn't die ! "

" I'm not speaking of myself, lass. But what of Will Riches, and your own brothers Jim and Robert—what happened to them ? "

Margaret's face was deathly white and she could barely whisper, " They . . . just went away, Jim . . . that was an accident. He was caught . . . poaching."

Barry laughed, a touch of hysteria in his voice. " Ay, poaching ! With Laud and his gang. Margaret, do you know the last man your brother was seen with on that night ? Shall I tell you ? It was John Luff ! "

Margaret put her hand to her mouth. " Luff ! " she said faintly.

" Ay, Luff ! And what of Will Riches ? Where's Robert ? Have you heard of him and others that *just vanish* ? Do you think you will ever hear of them again ? Do you think men just walk out of the lives of their families like that ? " Barry snapped his finger and thumb. Then his voice became soft and pleading again. " Marry me, Margaret, and let me take you right away from all this death and misery and fear ! "

" Oh, John, my dear," she sighed, " why can't you understand ? Can't you see Will needs me, needs what strength I can give him to get away from Luff and the rest ? Poor John, you have been so kind to me. But I've told you that I love Will. I must stay with him. I may fail in what I am trying to do. But I must try, don't you see, I must try." The strength of her determination shone through the words, illuminating them, transforming them into a statement of faith, a religious creed, almost. But John Barry did not see, and Margaret saw that he did not ; and his lack of understanding angered her, just as the senseless movements of sheep will anger a traveller in whose path they lie, and there rose in her quite suddenly an urgent desire to wound him.

"John," she said, "would you have me, knowing that despite everything my heart was still Will's, and always will be ? Would you have me as a whore, you making love to me and me not loving you ? Must I tell you that I have been Will's willing mistress ? Would you have me in spite of all these things ? "

Margaret saw him wince, and his face was distorted as if in pain.

"Margaret," he said slowly, " I'd still have you, knowing all that." He paused, and then went on, "You said that while Laud was living you'd never marry another." He drew a deep breath. " Well, I've come to tell you that Laud is dead."

Margaret had heard so many varied stories of Laud's death that Barry's words affected her but little.

" I've heard many tales of Will's death of late, John ; all false."

" This isn't false, girl. I saw him myself this morning. A brig was wrecked last night. My brother was on duty at Bawdsey Cliff this morning and saw a capsized boat in the breakers. It had been smashed to flinders by the surf and came ashore with four bodies. One of them was Laud's. Ned sent a fast courier to me and I went straight back to Bawdsey boathouse. The four dead men were there and one was Laud right enough. They were all badly battered but there was no mistake."

" How did you know it was Will, John ? "

" Both my brother and I recognized the scar on his face. Ned should do ; he gave it."

" I shall never believe it," said Margaret firmly, " until I see that dead man myself."

" Well, let me take you over. I'll soon get a pony and trap."

" No, my brother Edward will take me, John. I'd sooner it were like that."

" Then, Margaret, with your permission I'll wait here until

you return. But . . . well, it's wild weather to be abroad and do you think that you and Edward will get there ? "

" We'll do our best."

3

When Margaret and her brother did at last arrive at Bawdsey Cliff the snow had stopped and the sun was shining. Nevertheless, Edward had almost to lift his sister out of the trap, so numbed with cold was she.

At Bawdsey boathouse they were challenged by a coast-guard. Edward Barry came out into the snow and eyed the couple keenly for a moment. " Are you Miss Catchpole ? " he asked, raising his voice above the surf.

Margaret nodded and a small shower of snow fell from her bonnet.

Barry glanced swiftly at Edward, and Margaret explained, " This is my brother Edward, sir. You're . . . you're Lieutenant Barry ? "

" Yes," he nodded. " Come inside."

Inside the boathouse there were four stiff, tarpaulin-shrouded figures lying across hastily erected trestles. Margaret's face was almost as white as the snow on her clothes.

Barry pointed to the still figure nearest the door and his voice was completely non-committal. " You must prepare yourself. The sea has mutilated him badly." He pulled back the corner of the tarpaulin.

Margaret gave the dead man a swift glance and then, closing her eyes, leaned back against her brother. Edward put his arms around her. In his heart there was an immense relief. Now that Laud was dead perhaps their luck would change.

Margaret opened her eyes and looked at Lieutenant Barry.

" That's not Will ! " she said.

Barry put both hands on the trestle and leaned forward.

" What ! Not Laud ? Surely you are mistaken. The scar . . . ? " His voice was startled and unbelieving.

Margaret was overcome by a sense of profound weariness. The reaction was setting in and she felt that she wanted to sit down somewhere, quietly, by herself.

" He's like Will, even to the scar. But I've never seen him before in my life."

" You are certain ? The sea has . . . ! "

Margaret looked beseechingly at her brother. Edward drew her to him, and then turned and addressed Barry, who was gazing in a perplexed fashion at the covered form of the dead man.

"Thank you, sir, for allowing us to see for ourselves."

Barry seemed to come to with a start. "Perhaps you and your sister would like to wait until this squall has passed?"

Margaret looked at the stiff, sodden figure and thought of its marred face, so like that of her lover's. She shuddered. "Take me home, Ned," she said to her brother.

Together they went out into the whirling snow and the thunder of the wind and surf.

Inside the gloom of Bawdsey boathouse, amid a raffle of blocks and tackle, spare oars and sails, Edward Barry stared thoughtfully at the stiff figure nearest the door.

Outside the sky grew blacker and the rising power of the gale plucked with almost maniacal violence at the old lichened and salt-crusted tiles of the boathouse. Receding breakers left lines of yellow, clotted foam that were instantly ripped to pieces and blown high over the low sandy cliffs in balls of oleaginous spume.

4

John Barry sat in the tiny but cosy cottage on Nacton Heath staring unseeingly at the ancient black oak carved mantelpiece above the roaring log fire. Outside the snow still whirled and the wind at times threatened to tear the thatch clean away.

It was long since dark. Jonathan Catchpole had finished his meal and was sitting silently at the table.

Barry had told the old man the reason of his errand and frequently Catchpole would glance at him, wishing to himself that his daughter would get Laud from her mind and give Barry a chance.

Jonathan sighed softly, shook his head to himself and then got to his feet and started to clear away the few crude dishes on the table.

It was past one the next morning when the trap returned. Edward Catchpole, covered with snow, staggered into the kitchen with Margaret in his arms. The cold, the strain of her mission and the length of her journey had been too much for her. Her face was blue and she was unconscious. Edward took off her coat and bonnet and laid her on the bed, then he and Jonathan undressed her whilst Barry heated bricks in the fire to put at her feet.

When she had been made comfortable and a hot drink forced between her pale lips, Jonathan looked across at Barry. " Best you stay here the rest o' the night, John," he said. " It 'int fitten to turn a dog out ! "

" Well, Ned, was it him ? " John asked, when the rush of tending to Margaret was over.

Edward stared gloomily into the fire. " I'd 'a sooner Peggy told you this, John ; but it worn't Laud. Like him as his own twin, a'most, but . . ."

There was no sound in the tiny cottage, except the crackle of the logs and the hoarse rumble of the wind in the chimney.

CHAPTER SIXTEEN

I

J OHN BARRY's father stood with one gaitered leg resting on the wheel of a tumbril-load of farmyard dung. His expression was as thoughtful as his tone of voice.

" Well, John, my boy, you're old enough to know your own mind, but I do wish you'd not banish yourself so far afield. Van Diemen's Land is a life-time off."

" What matter, father." John Barry shrugged listlessly. " I shall never be happy here and I feel that a fresh start in life is the only thing for me."

" Well, if that's how you feel, son, best you go. We'll see you well furnished with money and goods. Will you see . . . her again afore you leave ? "

John nodded over his shoulder as he walked off. " I'm going up to Nacton today."

After the midday meal John Barry turned out of the farmyard and stepped at a smart pace along the path to the stable, where he threw a blanket and saddle across his horse.

His father, hearing the urgent clatter of hooves, watched his son go, shook his head and then turned back to the task of forking dung into the tumbril.

John Barry pulled his horse up outside the Catchpole cottage and knocked on the door. Margaret opened it and stood framed against the darkness behind her.

" I've come to say farewell, Margaret," John said hoarsely. " I'm leaving England for Van Diemen's Land tomorrow ! "

Margaret looked and was taken aback. " Van Diemen's Land ? But, John, isn't that the furthest place in the whole world. They say black cannibals live there."

Barry seized her hands. " For God's sake come with me, Margaret," he cried vehemently. " Forget Laud, he'll ruin you. Let's get married tomorrow before the *Kitty* sails ! I've hinted it to Captain Johnson and he says he'll marry us

110

aboard. I've got your bridal dress ready. We could have our honeymoon on the way out, away from all this. Can't you see that the shadow of the free traders is across your path? Can't you see what manner of man Laud is? He would have taken you away by force. You could never be happy with him. Your children would grow up in fear of their father's name. From the Thames to the Humber his name is one that is feared and hated."

"Don't say any more, John, please," Margaret begged. "I can't come. I'll never leave Will while he lives."

Barry laughed bitterly. "Murderer, smuggler, ravisher, and yet you say you'll never leave him. Margaret, my dear, on my knees I beg of you to come with me." Barry knelt before her, his upturned face imploring.

Margaret closed her eyes to shut out the sight of his beseeching face. Try as she might she could not prevent the tears from squeezing beneath her eyelids. Her voice was barely audible when she spoke.

"Not . . . while Will . . . lives!"

Early the next morning John Barry stood aboard the transport vessel *Kitty* watching the beloved banks of the Orwell, his Orwell, slide past. Ipswich was shut from sight. His folk were down at the creek, a group of tiny, impersonal figures, made insignificant by distance, waving, waving until the vessel rounded Jill's Point and they were gone. Lower Reach, Bloody Point, Orwell Haven and the open sea.

Barry turned and gave one last long look as if to retain the picture of those beloved shores in his mind for ever. Then, as the *Kitty* buffeted her way into the North Sea, he went below to his berth.

Across the tiny table a brocaded wedding-gown was draped. Barry slumped into a chair and, throwing his arms wide, lowered his head on to the gown. His fingers wound themselves into the rich material until the fabric shredded beneath their grasp.

2

When Barry had left, the sense of loneliness and oppression which Margaret had felt for so long became more acute. He had been her one true friend, despite his embarrassing attentions. People blamed her for his voluntary exile, and if such a thing were possible Margaret's existence became even more intolerable.

One day whilst shopping in Nacton Street Margaret saw Ellen Grimshaw. Margaret smiled tentatively, but Ellen was busy looking in a shop window. Margaret's face flushed and she bit her lip to stop its quivering, blinking her eyes to keep back the tears. Even Ellen's broad mind and generous nature had at last revolted against the hard facts of Riches' disappearance and Barry's final self-banishment.

Jonathan Catchpole said little, but his heart was uneasy.

One day he said to her gently and casually, " I met your uncle from Brandiston today, Peggy. He wor wholly put out. Since your aunt died he's had as much and more than he can rightly handle with them there seven childern of his. He say to me could I let you go over to Brandiston for a while."

Margaret turned her huge, dark-circled eyes on her father. " Who is going to do for you and Ned if I go, father ? " she asked.

" Ned tells me the old sexton's sister says she'll come and do for us. Don't worry about that."

Jonathan Catchpole was determined in his quiet way that his daughter should go to Brandiston and get away from the scandal and spitefully wagging tongues which were so manifestly undermining her health ; and in addition it would remove her from Laud's unwanted attentions.

Margaret acquiesced somewhat listlessly to her father's suggestion.

3

On the evening of the day that Margaret left for Brandiston, Jonathan had just finished his supper and was awaiting Edward who was folding his sheep down for the night. The old man was laying out a slab of cold bacon, bread and an earthenware jug of small beer for the young shepherd's supper when a soft knock sounded at the door. He opened it and felt a sudden icy shock strike straight at the pit of his stomach.

Outside stood Laud and Luff. The light from the door fell on Laud's face, emphasizing the high cheek-bones, shadowing the sunken cheeks, and accentuating the puckered scar and the black patch over the sightless eye. It fell, too, on Luff, revealing the leonine head and bearded face, reflecting in the tawny eyes, which held nothing of humanity, nothing of understanding, nothing of fear, of laughter, happiness, love or even hate. They had the fixed unblinking negation of expression one finds in the greater beasts of prey. Side by side they stood, the leopard and the lion.

Laud smiled at his sweetheart's father. The scar gave his smile a strangely lopsided, cynical appearance. Catchpole noted that both men were heavily armed with pistols and cutlasses.

It was Laud who spoke first. " Good evening, dad, can I come in ? " Without waiting for a reply he went inside, followed by Luff.

Catchpole looked at the two men sombrely. " I wonder," he said, " the pair on you 'int feared to be seen in this part o' the country. Four hun'ned and fifty guineas is a mort o' money. There's plenty about these parts 'ud be glad o' that."

Luff smiled gently, gazing at, through and beyond the speaker. " And yourself among the number, I don't doubt."

Old Catchpole's voice rose slightly. " Poor talk, Luff. D'ye fancy I'm as fond o' money as yourself ? That I'd sell my daughter's man, whatever he is ? The door you came through aren't shut yet. Do you talk like that the sooner you go back through it the better ! "

" Well spoken, father," cried Laud, clapping Catchpole on the back. " You're a man after my own heart."

" A boding welcome for men," Luff whispered, " who ha'nt seen the inside of a house for months."

Catchpole's sluggish temper was slowly being roused. " What in hell's name welcome d'ye fancy ye'll get here ? " he said fiercely. " Men like you-together who cause the death and ruin o' others ? "

Laud laughed at his henchman. " Ye've met your match, John, ye've met your match ! " Turning to Catchpole, he said, " We don't intentionally bring about anyone's death or ruin, father. We come in peace, wish to bide in peace and depart in peace."

" Depart in peace, you say ! Did my boy James depart in peace ? Where is Robert ? And mebbe you-together know suthin' o' poor Will Riches ? "

Luff's hand strayed to the Corsican knife. Catchpole did not miss the significance of the movement.

" I'm not afraid of ye, Luff, ye bloody murderer," he said. " I only let the pair on ye in because my Peggy, poor little bitch, is fare crazed over Laud. Ay, crazed enough to refuse an offer of marriage from a fine, clean-handed youngster like John Barry. He's left for Van Diemen's Land all on account o' har ! "

Laud put both hands on the old man's shoulders. " So Margaret still loves me after that other business, dad ? Where is she ? "

At this moment the door opened and Edward Catchpole came in. Like his father, he too felt a sudden cold shock of horror when he saw the two visitors.

" D'ye remember me, boy ? " Luff asked him.

Edward thought swiftly. Best not to provoke Luff. " Yes, sir, I remember you," he said. " When I was coming across the heath I met a party of coastguards led by Edward Barry. . . ."

Before he could finish, Luff was across the room with the speed of a greyhound on a hare. He seized Catchpole by the neckerchief. " Where are they ? " he demanded.

Edward Catchpole was half choked by the iron fist at his throat. There was a hiss to Luff's whisper. " Did you-together talk ? "

" Easy there, John," Laud broke in, " easy, Edward didn't know we were here."

Luff released his grip, glanced about the cottage and then turned to the elder Catchpole. " Have you any powder and ball on the place, old man ? "

Laud, however, had other ideas. " Come you on, John," he said. " This is no place for a shoot with the customs. They'd fire the place and roast us out." He turned back to Jonathan. " Where did you say Margaret was ? "

The old man remained silent.

Luff drew a pistol and cocked it. Edward Barry stepped in front of his father. " She's at Brandiston," he said.

Laud thanked him for the information and tossed a bag of money on the table. Edward threw it back, almost weeping with rage that the threat to his father had made him divulge his sister's whereabouts to Laud.

Luff swept the money up in mid-air and thrust it into Laud's hand. " This'll be more useful to us, Will. Best we move if you 'int making a fight on it. Our bloody boat'll be high and dry."

The two smugglers went quickly through the back door into the darkness.

4

Now the danger had gone, Jonathan Catchpole sat in a chair, his face buried in his shaking hands.

" Sorry I told Laud where Peggy was, father," Edward said slowly.

Old Catchpole had always been fond of his youngest son and now the bonds of affection were forged even closer. He put his arm round him. " Never mind, my boy, you did what you thought was right."

A few moments later the sound of marching feet rattled along the road. Father and son glanced fearfully at each other. From outside came the sharp command, " Halt ! "

The tramping feet stopped and a few seconds later a pistol-butt thundered on the door.

" Open in the King's name ! "

Edward opened the door. Lieutenant Barry stood outside with two customs men. Barry came straight to the point. His voice was crisp.

" We've had information that Laud and Luff called here. . ."

Edward, still hot at having betrayed his sister's whereabouts to Laud, broke in eagerly :

" Yes, sir, they forced my father to let them in. Laud came here to see Peggy. If you hurry you'll catch them : they've gone to the river."

Barry patted Edward's shoulder. " Thank you, lad," he said, and then turned to his men. " Forward, at the double ! "

When they arrived at the river's edge the small boat was already back alongside the *Alde*, which was under weigh.

Barry pointed his sword and ordered, " Independent fire ! "

The roar of musketry reverberated down the Orwell whilst musket-balls threw up small fountains all around the boat. One or two of the better-aimed balls thudded into the *Alde's* bulwarks. The breeze filled the brig's sails and she vanished into the night.

CHAPTER SEVENTEEN

I

WHEN Margaret arrived at her uncle's home at Brandiston she found things in a complete state of disorder. Mr. Leader, although a respected member of the community, was only a farm labourer and could not afford to pay for help in the house. In consequence, the older children had to tend the younger ones, with the result that the cottage was filthy and the children completely out of hand.

Margaret looked around her, wondering where to make a start. The uproar was appalling and the children grubby beyond belief. The youngest ones were playing in the ashes of a dead fire and resembled little sweeps.

Two small boys, with their noses running into their mouths, were fighting a determined battle over a crust, the grubbiness of which was in keeping with the rest of the house.

Margaret took a deep breath and turned speechlessly to her uncle, who stood with a worried look on his face.

" I'm sorry, m'dear," he said helplessly, " but, well, you see how it is. I can't work in the fields all day and look after the children too."

The first thing that Margaret did was to take off her best clothes and change into her oldest ones. Then methodically she went to work.

Cleaning out the dead fire, she re-lit it, filled the biggest kettle in the house and set it on to boil. Then to her dismay she found that there were no clean clothes in the house for the children, for they had dirtied all the shifts with the somewhat doubtful exception of their night clothes.

There was only one thing to do and Margaret did it. Despite protests, screams and howls she gave all the children a thorough tubbing in a huge tub which had once been the half of a barrel. She scrubbed them until their skins were as pink and shiny as parboiled sucking-pigs, put them into their night clothes and packed them off to bed.

She then set about washing fourteen sets of extremely grubby clothes—fifteen including her uncle's. This done, she hung the clothes out to dry, hurriedly mixed a cake and set it to bake in the now hot oven.

All mats were thrown outside and the red-brick floor scrubbed and cupboards turned out.

Attracted by a bad smell she went to the larder. There hung a brace of rabbits, forgotten by her harassed uncle and now literally creeping with maggots. Holding the decomposing rabbits at arm's length, fingers to nose, she took them outside and buried them, then thoroughly scrubbed the floor and shelves.

She finished off by dusting every ledge and shelf in the cottage.

After preparing a meal for her uncle and laying the table, she went upstairs to the children. They were all in one room, four in one bed, three in another—at least, that is how they should have been. However, Johnny and Walter, the six-year-old twins who had been fighting over the crust and should have been in bed with two-year-old Sammy, had decided to invade the girls' bed. The squealing and shouting as Margaret entered the room was deafening.

She swiftly grabbed the troublesome twins, planted a stinging slap on each bare bottom, and thrust them back into their own bed with little Sammy, who with round eyes and thumb in mouth was solemnly watching the fun.

The twins, too astonished to cry, sat open-mouthed in the bed whilst Margaret pushed a lock of hair out of her eyes and swiftly took stock of the situation. The girls in the big bed had pulled the bed-clothes over their heads. From beneath these somewhat grubby and nondescript coverings came muffled giggles.

"Now come you along," Margaret said as persuadingly as she knew how. "Get the bed-clothes off your faces. I want to talk to you."

The muffled titterings did not cease, neither did any faces emerge.

Margaret tried another means of persuasion. "Oh well, I don't suppose any of you want any of my cake for your supper. I'll go down again."

She made as if to go.

A red face, wide grey eyes and a shock of auburn hair popped from beneath the bed-clothes.

Margaret looked at the jack-in-the-box. " Who are you ? " she asked.

" I'm Mary," a somewhat breathless voice answered.

" How old are you, Mary ? "

" Ten—I think."

" Well, Mary, you are quite a big girl and should be setting your brothers and sisters a good example. I want you to help me like a good girl. Wrap something round yourself and come downstairs."

A pair of thin legs shot over the side of the bed and trotted down behind Margaret, who set out seven plates on the table and filled seven earthenware mugs with milk.

" There you are, Mary," she said, " take those up to your brothers and sisters. Then come down and have your supper along with me as you are a grown-up girl."

In that instant Margaret won a stout ally.

Jack Leader came home from work that night and it was a pleasant change that greeted him. Instead of a horde of over-tired, dirty, grizzling progeny to be dealt with, everything was quiet. The cottage sparkled and a tasty meal awaited him upon a newly-scrubbed table. He looked around, his eyes dim with gratitude and memory. " God bless you, maw'. Things hint been like this since Mary died," he said to Margaret, who was busy at the fire.

Jack Leader had always been a hard worker and an honest man. Latterly, however, he had fallen behind with his rent and there were several bills outstanding in the village. It did not take long for Margaret to find this out ; and in addition to the children and the housework she took over the finances of the Leader household.

2

From the most haphazard family in Brandiston the Leaders became one of the most regular and well-managed. Promptly every Saturday night Margaret saw to it that all bills were paid. Money for the housekeeping was set aside, and Jack Leader found himself in possession of a small but adequate sum each week for beer and tobacco.

Margaret's expert management of her uncle's affairs and children was the talk of the village.

One morning the vicar's wife stopped Margaret in Brandiston Street. " I couldn't help noticing you in church

on Sunday," she said, " with those seven children of Leader's.
They were a credit to you."

Margaret gave a small curtsey. " Thank you, mam."

The vicar's wife, a rosy buxom soul, as unlike the pre-
conceived idea of a parson's wife as anyone could be, was
silent for a moment. Then she said, " Managing that house
and seven children is a heavy task for so young a woman.
Would it help if I could find a place in the village school for
two of them, possibly the elder children ? "

" Indeed it would, mam," Margaret replied. " It would
help me, and help the children more still to be able to read and
perhaps write."

Following this meeting, Mary and the next eldest girl,
Jessie, became pupils at the village school. Mary, who had
always been a child eager to learn and had always wanted to
go to school, realized that it was through Margaret she had
attained her heart's desire, and she repaid Margaret by con-
ceiving a passionate attachment for her.

In fact, all of Leader's children adored their new " mother "
as time went on.

Through her association with Laud Margaret knew more
about boats than most and she completely won the hearts of
the hitherto unruly twins, Walter and Johnny, by carving
them little wooden boats with paper sails, which they launched
gleefully upon a nearby duck-pond.

Feeling that she was loved and that she was justifying her
existence, to say nothing of being free of the gossips of Nacton,
Margaret was happy. In fact, she was as happy at Brandiston
as she could ever remember being. To be sure, her existence
was one of hard work, and narrow too, but she was glad it was
this way. At the cottage on Nacton Heath every rap on the
door might have been the free traders or those in pursuit of
them. She had grown to catch her breath at the mere sight
of a casual sailor, whether near or far.

In Brandiston the nearest water was the narrow stream of
the Deben, far too small to admit any craft. So Margaret saw
no sailors and at last knew something of security—a security
suddenly to be shattered by the folly of her uncle.

In the village of Brandiston was a seemingly jolly widow
woman, one Blanche Pearce, rosy-cheeked, yellow-haired and
blue-eyed, and the owner of two pieces of land in Brandiston
Street.

If Jack Leader had not been so attracted by the idea of
marrying property, he might have taken a second look at

Blanche. He might have noticed that her rosy cheeks were a trifle too rosy ; that the yellow hair was a shade too yellow and that the blue eyes were too closely set.

The first week that the new Mrs. Leader was in the cottage Margaret knew that her brief period of happiness was over.

If Mrs. Leader the second had been an intelligent woman, she would have realized that Margaret was a capable ally. As it was, the ownership of a little property had given Blanche an exaggerated idea of her own importance.

Instead of wisely co-operating with Margaret, her first step was to take the household affairs clean out of her hands. So far so good, but it was her attempt to manage the children that started the trouble.

The children loved Margaret as much, if not more, than they had loved their own mother. They regarded Blanche as an intruder and treated her accordingly.

Seeing Margaret's slightest command instantly obeyed and her own flatulent instructions completely ignored, the woman's temper became inflamed.

One day at the dinner-table she turned on Margaret, who had cooked the dinner, set each child's meal before it and had just finished feeding the tiny Samuel. " I don't think it fitten that you should sit down to meals with us, Margaret," she said, with rancour in her somewhat grating voice.

" Why not, aunt ? "

" Servants don't sit down to meals with their betters in the Squire's house and I don't see why they should here."

Margaret's pale face flamed and her eyes widened and then narrowed. Jack Leader, a timid man where women were concerned, sat open-mouthed, not daring to interfere.

Margaret was more than capable of dealing with the fair, fat and forty Blanche, but as the children were present she kept her temper and her sense of proportion. " That's not a kind thing to say, aunt, and not true either," she said.

Blanche's stupid, spiteful nature was uppermost. " No, that's right enough. A servant gets wages ; all you get here is your keep, and lucky to get that. You know as well as I do that nobody 'ud give you a place. Your name is beginning to stink all over Suffolk as a smuggler's drab." Blanche spat out the last word.

Leader tried to make a belated stand on behalf of his niece.

" Blanche, m'dear . . ." he began.

Blanche turned on him. " You keep out of this, Leader," she cried contemptuously.

Without speaking Margaret left her dinner on the table and went up to her bedroom.

The children did not understand the cause of the trouble but sensed the hostility in the air and started to cry. The twins went even further. Howling at the tops of their voices, they jumped down from the table, in spite of Blanche's futile orders for them to return, and fled upstairs to Margaret.

Blanche shook her fat shoulders like an angry hen and finished the meal with a sense of triumph, convinced that she had gained a victory over Margaret.

Day by day matters got worse. Blanche foolishly indulged the children, thinking thus to win them over to her side. The astute youngsters took everything that she offered them, despised her accordingly and still worshipped Margaret.

Mary and Jessie were removed from the village school and turned out with the rest of the children to play in Brandiston Street.

Blanche took every opportunity to remind Margaret of her position in the house and it was only Margaret's love for the children that kept her at Brandiston.

Several nights after the wordy conflict at the dinner table Margaret lay sleepless in bed. She was feeling utterly depressed and wondering what was to be the end of it all. Latterly she had been assailed by a sense of doubt, doubt even about Will. It seemed that they would never marry. He was still with the free traders. She was growing older and had nowhere that she could call home. At Nacton it was the spiteful tongues : here at Brandiston it was Blanche. She had been foolish to refuse John Barry. She would have had love and security, even if she could not have returned his ardour.

Margaret fell asleep and then began to dream. In her dream it seemed that a furious hailstorm was raging and that the hailstones were lashing the window-pane. She awoke with a start. Outside the moon was shining brightly in an unclouded sky and all was quiet. She was about to lay down again when something really did rattle loudly against the glass.

The frightened girl's heart beat so loudly that it nearly stopped her breathing. Huge-eyed, and clasping her night-gown close to her, she sat up and stared at the window. A voice came softly out of the moonlit night. " Margaret, Margaret, are you there ? "

Half eagerly, half in dread she jumped out on to the cold boards, throwing a shawl around herself as she did so. Tiptoeing barefoot across the little room, she peered out. A dark figure stood beneath the window, its upturned face clear in the white moonlight. Margaret shrank back against the window-frame.

" Will," she whispered. " Will ! "

" Come you on down, girl," he hissed urgently. " I want to speak to you."

" I shan't be long, Will. Get in the shadows of those bushes."

All memory of Laud's attempt to kidnap her was gone as she hurriedly threw on her clothes ; all fear of the dread, far-reaching shadow of which he was part. He was her lover come to find her, perhaps even to take her away. She would not care now.

In her hurry Margaret was not as cautious as she might have been. Mrs. Leader, after a heavy supper, was tossing and turning unable to sleep. The rattle of the pebbles that Laud had tossed against Margaret's window roused her. Creeping softly from the side of her heavily sleeping husband, she gently drew the curtains to one side.

3

Outside the cottage Margaret flew straight into the arms of Laud, like a homing pigeon to its loft. He swept her from her feet and she lay hardly conscious beneath his kisses.

When some measure of sanity had returned to them both Margaret asked breathlessly, " How did you find me, Will ? "

" Your brother Edward told me," he replied ; but he did not mention the circumstances under which Edward Catchpole had divulged her whereabouts, and Margaret was too excited to wonder at them.

Laud locked his two hands in the small of Margaret's back and strained her to him passionately.

" My love, my love," he cried, burying his face in the soft warmth of the space between her shoulder and neck.

" I began to think you had forgotten me, Will."

" I'll never forget you as long as there's breath in my body, Peggy. Can you ever forgive me for that night at the Priory ? " Mention of the word " Priory " brought a change of thought to him. " Your father told me that John Barry had offered you marriage and a home and you refused him on account o' me." His muffled tones became clear as he lifted his face from her shoulder. There was a great tenderness in his voice. " God love you for that, my little dunlin. I've come to tell you that I've finished with the gang."

" Oh, Will," said Margaret in a choked voice, the memory of her agonized disappointment when Laud had confessed to being Hudson still fresh in her mind, " if I could only believe you."

" You can believe me, girl, as God's my judge. An amnesty has been granted to all smugglers who of their own free will volunteer to serve the country at this present time of crisis. When your father told me how you turned Barry aside for me, I . . . I . . . Well, I'm joining Lord Howe's flagship, *Queen Charlotte*, at Portsmouth within two days. See, here is my pardon and my other papers."

Margaret, her heart too full for words, pressed her face against her lover's broad chest.

Just at this moment, Mrs. Leader thought it time to interfere. She crashed open the windows. " Margaret," she shouted, " come indoors at once, creeping out o' doors like some hedge tavern drab, come in I say ! "

So loud was Blanche Leader's voice that lights in nearby cottages began to go up.

Margaret gave Laud a long kiss, then pushed him into the bushes. " Go, Will. Write to me . . ."

" I'll come for you soon, my little dunlin," he promised, and turning, vanished into the bushes.

Inside the cottage the whole Leader family was awake. Jack Leader sat shivering on the edge of the bed, his somewhat bony, unattractive shanks protruding beneath his night-shirt. The younger children were grizzling loudly. Blanche Leader, her fat body wrapped in a grey shawl, was downstairs waiting for Margaret. She was white-faced, and shivering with cold and fury. In all her life no one had tossed pebbles at *her* bedroom window. She opened the door to Margaret.

" You dirty bitch," she raved, " creeping out after men in the middle of the night. You're nothing better than a common whore. I saw who it was you were with, that no-good smuggler Laud. I'll have the magistrate on to him and in the morning you can pack your things and get out. We don't want the likes o' you in Brandiston."

Leader, like most others of that time and place, had a wholesome fear for the free traders. He tried to stop Blanche's tirade. He might as well have tried to stop the flow of the Deben.

Margaret's temper was up too.

M.C.   E

"Will is an honest man, I'll have you know, aunt," she flared. "He's joining Lord Howe's ship at Portsmouth."

"A likely tale . . ."

Blanche was interrupted.

"And as for turning me out, don't fret yourself; I won't stop here another minute." She turned to her uncle. "I've done my best for both you and the children, uncle, but there's not room here for both her and me. Good-bye!"

Margaret went straight up the stairs, collected her few things, tied them in a bundle, kissed the children good-bye and stepped outside into the early dawn.

Blanche Leader had encountered a spirit greater than her own. Expecting Margaret to beg and plead to be allowed to stay, and thwarted of the enjoyment of the girl's humiliation, she toppled back in a dead faint. He, realizing at this moment the mistake he had made by allowing this gross creature to invade the home so ably handled by his niece, stood staring at the recumbent form with rapidly growing distaste.

Blanche looked incredibly like a heap of slightly discoloured dough.

Jack sighed at the recollection of Margaret's trim figure, happy face and efficiency. He thought of his happy children, the sparkling house, good food and excellent management. Going out to a pump he filled a bucket with icy water and then went indoors and dashed it forcefully and with great relish over the prone figure of his fat spouse.

4

Out on the Woodbridge road the dawn had broken and larks were carolling so high in the air that they were not visible.

The burly, red-faced driver of Noller's Wagon, a local carrier's service between Ipswich and Woodbridge, reined in his horses and looked with pity at the figure of a slender young woman tramping doggedly along in the dust of the road.

"Hey there, missy, d'ye want a lift?" he called.

Margaret looked up gratefully. "Oh, thank you," she said, and handed her bundle up to the driver, who made room for her beside him.

"Where are you bound for?" he asked.

Margaret thought swiftly. Back to Nacton and the gossiping spiteful tongues? The wagon was bound for Ipswich. Whom did she know there? Suddenly a name came to her like the answer to a prayer. Doctor George Stebbing, he lived at Ipswich.

She turned towards the driver. " Ipswich—if you please."

The driver took a straw from his teeth and whistled. " A funny long tramp for a young woman all by herself. Good job I happened along." He put the straw back in his teeth and cracked his whip.

" Hey, giddap there."

CHAPTER EIGHTEEN

I

IT was two o'clock when Margaret arrived at Ipswich. Descending from the wagon she thanked the driver, dusted her dress and enquired from a passer-by the way to the house of Doctor George Stebbing.

She found it easily enough. It was a large, red-brick, three-storey building in Orwell Place, an opulent house truly reflecting the valuable practice of its owner.

Doctor Stebbing had on his books some of the wealthiest people in the town. This was not only due to the fact that he was a good doctor, but also to the fact that in an age of sportsmen he was an excellent shot. He had been known to bring down three brace of partridges in a few seconds with three guns. His fame with a gun had spread far and wide and he had met many of his wealthiest patients in the fields of the landed gentry.

Margaret knocked at the doctor's door and was shown into the surgery. The window of the room she was in looked down into a stone area filled with greenhouse plants and mass after mass of flaming geraniums. As she was admiring the blooms Stebbing came in.

He was tall and heavily made but carrying very little fat. His hair was dark and thinning on top. His blue eyes, set in a full and somewhat rubicund face, were friendly.

" Well, young woman," he said, " you want to see me ? What's the matter ? "

Margaret curtsied. " There's nothing wrong with me, sir. I have come to ask you to help me get a place."

Stebbing looked blank.

" Good Gad, young woman, what do you think my surgery is," he demanded. " A registry office for servants ? What in heaven's name have I got to do with ' places ' ? Who sent you ? "

" No one, sir. I came because you are the . . . only person . . . I know in Ipswich."

Black spots were dancing before Margaret's eyes and she had the odd feeling that she was looking at Stebbing through the wrong end of a telescope. Suddenly she reeled and would have fallen had Stebbing not caught her. He led her to a couch, and looked at her closely.

" When did you last have anything to eat and drink ? "

To Margaret it seemed that her voice came from an infinite distance away. " Yesterday . . . sir . . ."

Stebbing went to a decanter and poured out a glass of brandy.

" Here, girl, drink this," he said.

He pulled a bell-cord and a few seconds later a maid appeared. " Take this young woman to the kitchen, Norah, and ask cook to give her a meal." He gave Margaret an encouraging smile. " We'll talk about ' places ' and such when you've seen to the inner man, or, ah . . . um . . . shall we say woman."

An hour later, when Margaret had finished her meal, she again sat in Stebbing's surgery. He was at his desk, thoughtfully twisting a quill pen in his big, blunt, capable fingers.

" Ay, I can call you to mind now, girl," he said. " That night at Priory Farm. The fight at Downham Reach. Young Barry : he had the constitution of an ox to have recovered from those gunshot wounds. He's gone to Van Diemen's Land, you say. Lost your two brothers. Made your way from Brandiston alone. By Gad, you deserve a helping hand." He paused, and pulled a sheet of paper towards him. Then he looked awkwardly at Margaret. " Have you dropped your . . . ahem . . . unfortunate associations ? I should be sorry to bring trouble to any family I might recommend you to. You see, ah . . . rumour has even reached Ipswich about . . . well, you know who I mean, girl . . ."

Margaret's voice was soft with a hint of pride in it when she answered the doctor.

" I know you mean Will, Will Laud, sir. He has finished with his old companions . . ." and she told him everything that had happened at Brandiston, emphasizing the fact that she had seen Laud's pardon and the papers directing him to join H.M.S. *Queen Charlotte* at Portsmouth.

When she had finished Stebbing sat in silence for a while : then he put the pen back in its stand.

" I think it would be wiser," he said, " for you to stop here for the present, and later on we'll see what happens."

When Margaret had left the room he slowly tore up the paper on which he had started to write.

2

If Doctor Stebbing had any doubts about Margaret they were soon dispelled.

She went about her work willingly and with such diligence that despite the rumours Stebbing had heard of her and the gossip and scandal connected with her name he was convinced that Margaret was a girl of excellent character, more sinned against than sinning.

Accordingly, one day after lunch he sat down and wrote a note. When it was written he called Margaret in.

" Margaret, I want you to take this note up to Mrs. Cobbold who lives at Cliff House overlooking the river. You've been a good girl here and I rather fancy she'll have a place for you."

Margaret climbed the steps to the terrace upon which Cliff House was built, and found the mistress of the house sitting in the garden.

When Elizabeth Cobbold had read the note she looked up with a smile on her sweet, gentle face.

" So you are Margaret Catchpole."

She was interrupted by a fisherman climbing the steps with a basket of fish. Margaret glanced swiftly at him and her heart gave a frightened leap : it was old Coulson who had gone to Barry's aid the night that Will had tried to kidnap her.

He recognized her instantly. " Why, Peggy mawther," he cried in his strange sing-song tones, " that fare a long time since we met. Has the fiend played you any more of his tricks ? "

Margaret was speechless with confusion and, blushing a deep crimson, she curtsied to the astonished Mrs. Cobbold, but could find no words to utter to the crazy figure before her.

Coulson mistook her silence. He thought that she was too proud to speak to him. His easily inflamed temper soon got the upper hand. His eyes flashed and the wind plucked at his long grey hair and beard, making him a truly terrifying sight.

" So you're too proud to speak, maw ! " he said. " Mebbe it would 'a ben better if young Barry had let Laud carry you off that night. You'd 'a made a right fine pair, go to hell if you

wouldn't. For you couldn't find a wuss'n than Laud the hull
length and breadth o' the coast ! "

Mrs. Cobbold took Margaret's hand in her own. Not
knowing of Coulson's previous meeting with Margaret at the
Priory, the good lady mistook his words for his usual ramblings.
" There, there," she said consolingly. " Don't take old Robin
too seriously, my dear. He's got a heart of gold when you get
to know him, as you most surely will."

Coulson turned his uncouth head towards Mrs. Cobbold.
" N' so'll you, mam, afore many more tides. The fiends ha'
long dwelt wi' the Catchpoles, as you'll soon find out if she's
comen into yare sarvice. There'll be rum goin's-on at Cliff
House afore long, mark my words ! "

Margaret turned away and bit her lip to stop its quiverings.
She made a tremendous effort to stop the tears from running
into her eyes and down her face. It was the same everywhere
she went. There seemed no release from the fate that dogged
her.

The mistress of Cliff House gently pulled the distracted girl
round to face her. " Now tell me, dear," she enquired gently,
" what's this wild talk of Robin's ? What have you done to
offend him ? "

" I never did anything to offend Robin, mam. He was
good to me, saved me from . . . from . . ." She was too
distressed to continue.

Coulson saw that he had made a mistake ; saw, in one of his
singularly clear-sighted but brief spells of sanity, that he had
confused the girl's embarrassment for pride. In his rough
fashion he tried to make amends. He touched his forehead to
Mrs. Cobbold.

" Beg your pardon, mam ! " He turned to Margaret.
" And yours, Peggy maw. I see how't is. Ay, yes I do. I
mistook har. Fancied she fared too proud to speak to an old
fisherman. So the fiends made me haller at har. That they
did ! "

He made a clumsy bow to Mrs. Cobbold and patted
Margaret's shoulder : then, picking up his basket of fish, he
went down the stone steps two at a time, muttering into his
fluttering grey beard and shaking his head as he went.

3

Mrs. Cobbold turned back to Margaret.

" All right, my dear, don't fret. Robin's a queer customer,

as it seems you already know. Come back and see me tomorrow."

She watched Margaret keenly until she was lost from sight.

Some mystery hung about the slender, dark-eyed girl. Elizabeth had known Coulson for years and knew that amongst his ravings one could sometimes find a hard kernel of truth.

Early the next morning Margaret came back to Cliff House and was engaged in the dual role of under nursemaid by day and cook's helper in the evening.

Mrs. Cobbold was an unusual woman. At a period when domestics were little else than serfs, working long hours for less than a pittance with little liberty and no redress, she took an active and personal interest in every servant in Cliff House, from the scullery maid to the housekeeper.

Margaret immediately captured the heart of her mistress. Somewhere in the girl, thought Mrs. Cobbold, was breeding : the slender ankles, well-turned forearms and wrists, the carriage of the dark head, the huge brown eyes and the quiet, well-bred manner, utterly untutored though she was—these were no common heritage.

In her own quiet way the good lady of Cliff House set about bringing all the best in her new servant's character to the surface : and Margaret, sensing her mistress's goodwill, set about making herself worthy of it.

There were fourteen children at Cliff House and, like the Leader children, they very soon came to love their new nanny.

4

One of Margaret's special duties was to take the children for an airing along the back of the cliff to a place called Sawyer's Farm, and from thence along the banks of the Orwell to a place known as the Grove.

On the way she would devise all manner of small amusements for her charges, making daisy chains for the girls and whistles from hog-weed stems for the boys. Very soon she became the be-all and end-all of the young Cobbolds and the order to dress for a walk with Margaret was always a sign for an outburst of childish joy.

One afternoon Margaret had the children out for their usual stroll. Frederick and George, aged six and seven, called over to her.

" Marg'ret, Marg'ret, come over here and listen to this old rat ! "

There was a high brick wall where the two youngsters were crouching in listening attitudes. Margaret walked slowly over with the others frollicking at her heels.

" A rat, master Frederick ? Mind he doesn't jump out and grab that funny little button nose of yours ! "

Suddenly her expression changed. Her eyes dilated and her face grew pale. Without hesitating an instant she swept up the two boys, one under each arm, and hurled herself away from the wall.

A few seconds later it collapsed with a grinding rumble and a cloud of red brick-dust.

When the dust had cleared Margaret picked herself and her two charges up. They were whimpering and so were the rest of their brothers and sisters.

A pale-faced man came up to Margaret. He was the fore-man of the gang of labourers who had been working on the other side of the wall demolishing it.

" My God ! " he said, his voice hoarse with relief. " I saw it all. Too far away to done anything. We thought that side of the wall was clear."

Margaret's face was almost disguised by the layer of brick-dust but the ganger recognized her.

" Pardon me, miss, but aren't you the young lady from the Cliff? I'd better walk up with you. If anything had happened to Mr. Cobbold's children . . . ! "

Up at the Cliff House Margaret led the dirty-faced Frederick and George off to be washed whilst the foreman told the startled parents the whole story.

" Never see nuthin' like it, sir. I see that blasted wall— saving your presence, mam—toppling and was too far away to do a thing. That young woman threw those children out o' harm's way quicker'n lightning. The fastest, bravest bit o' work I ever seen, sir. She knew that she was like to be crushed along wi' the children ! "

Mr. Cobbold gave the man a florin and when he had gone remarked to his wife : " It seems that you've found a real treasure in Margaret, m'dear."

Mrs. Cobbold smiled, happy that the impish Frederick and George were safe, happy that Margaret had been able to justify herself and also her mistress's belief.

" I rather think we have, John, I rather think we have," she answered dreamily.

CHAPTER NINETEEN

I

LAUD lay in his hammock and stared at the huff marks from the vents of the cannon. All the way along the long, low gun-deck the beams overhead were pitted with them : and anyway, there was little else to look at—except, maybe, the ugly, leprous-looking patches of sea-mould on the damp timbers, the long endless line of cannons and the slowly-swinging, wrought-iron battle-lanterns with their panes of horn.

There was nothing to listen to except the snores and mutterings of the sleeping men and the scuttlings of rats, together with the swish of the water that swilled through the closed gun-port doors.

The *Queen Charlotte* was plunging her mighty bow into the heaviest seas he'd ever experienced and life aboard was hell. Many of the crew were down with scurvy and ulcers, and he hadn't had a dry stitch to his back for weeks. All the shifts of clothing he had were sodden ; and rather than endure the agony of climbing warm and dry from his hammock into icy wet clothes, he slept in them wet.

Laud's thoughts were bitter as he lay swinging slowly to and fro, comparing his circumstances aboard the English flagship with those when he was master of the *Alde*.

Here he was nothing but the captain of a cannon with the endless, foul-smelling overcrowded gun-deck to share with several hundred others. The men's hammocks were so crowded that if one unfortunate turned over he disturbed the whole line of men, who cursed sleepily and aimed weary blows at the offender.

Laud cursed Margaret to himself. If she had not carried on so about respectability, he'd have been in his comfortable cabin aboard the *Alde* at this moment, instead of sleeping in the almost unendurable stench of stale salt water, bilge, dirty bodies and wet, foul clothing. The discomfort was appalling : but not so unbearable as the bitter wind that harped in the rigging of the mighty ship as she wallowed in each trough, or the sea-swept upper decks.

Directly beneath him was his gun. It was the same as all the others—an iron, three-and-a-half-ton, forty-two-pounder, as dangerous and unpredictable to its crew as a great wild beast. Christ ! how he'd grown to hate that gun.

They had been standing to with short spells of rest for longer than he could recall and still that damned cunning Frenchman Villaret Joyeuse had clung stubbornly to the weather-gauge. In a bloody great craft like his hundred-and-twenty-gun *Montagne* he could have fought with confidence two like the leaky, foul-bottomed, undermanned *Queen Charlotte*.

What Laud did not know was that a huge American convoy, laden with wheat, was on its way to blood-drenched France. Villaret Joyeuse had been bluntly told by the Convention that at all costs he must decoy the English Channel Fleet away from that precious wheat. If he failed his own head would be forfeit.

To see that this order was carried out to the letter Monsieur Jean Bon St. Andrée, himself a member of the Convention, had sailed aboard the mighty *Montagne*.

In the meantime the English Fleet of twenty-five ships, poor things and unweatherly compared to the mighty French men-o'-war, the most powerful in the world, patiently bided their time—bided their time whilst their crews, pressed men and professional sailors, cursed the ships and the monster guns to whom they were the sorriest slaves. They cursed the food and conditions, but most of all they cursed themselves : and all they had to sustain their cursings was salt horse, so hard and ancient that even the maggots in it had long since died of starvation, foul water, and a taste of the officer's supple jacks if their grumbles became too loud. The petty tally [1] had long since become exhausted and so even those with a little cash of their own could not procure additional food.

Then there were the guns. Never for a moment could they be forgotten.

At all odd hours the master gunner would bawl :

" Guns' crews stand-to ! "

It was " Guns' crews stand-to ! " until Laud wished he was aboard one of the frigates Lord Howe was constantly despatching to keep in touch with the main body of the enemy.

[1] The petty tally was a crude and primitive form of canteen.

Frequently at times the sound of distant gun-fire told that they at least were getting some excitement.

Then there was Laud's gun-crew. Pressed men every one of them, and that bloody cack-handed that they did not know one end of a rammer from the other.

There were the tow-headed twins from Somerset, yokels. One had been caught by the press-gang and the other had volunteered rather than be parted from his twin.

There was Pat the Irish labourer, who had been in Portsmouth on a spree away from his brick-kiln; he too had been caught by the press-gang.

Then there was Jim the little cockney pickpocket, who had volunteered, not from any patriotic motive, but to escape transportation. It was only recently that he had learnt to put the powder in *before* the ball.

One embarrassing day, when Laud had been exercising his gun's crew beneath the eagle gaze of the master gunner, they had done everything they should not do. When he had shouted " Gun's crew number," Pat the Irishman had replied, " One thousand and ten, sor ! "—his number on the ship's books : and one of the Somerset twins had called " A hun'ned and vifty voive "—his number on the watch bill.

Paddy had then proceeded to blacken the eye of a brawny merchant sailor, pressed at sea, with the end of the rammer. To avoid a fight round his gun Laud had bawled, " Awkward Squad . . . still ! " And " Awkward Squad " they had remained throughout the ship.

Laud was sorry afterwards that his exasperation had brought this about and to offset it he had drilled his crew quietly at odd moments in their watch below. Even so he had to watch them, especially the twins, who were very hazy as to their whereabouts and were often found wandering in the wrong parts of the ship. To them one gun-deck was so like another.

The bos'un had kicked them irately off the quarter-deck, and once when the order " Guns' crews muster " had sounded Laud had missed them altogether. At last he had found them on number one gun-deck.

They had taken a mark alongside their own gun to help them remember its position. The mark had been a portable fire-pump, and it had been moved at the last moment, confounding them completely. They had been booted along from one gun to the other by impatient guns' captains until at last Laud had found and claimed them.

When Laud gave the order " Fire ! " they would stand mouths open, eyes closed and thumbs in ears. Ah well, he sighed, they could handle a gun tolerably well now but they were still the " Awkward Squad " to their shipmates.

Laud's thoughts reverted to Margaret, and he was dreaming of the nights in the cottage when he was recovering from the cut across the face, the night when she . . .

" Guns' crews stand-to ! "

The words rattled down the long, dimly-lit gun-deck. Immediately there was furious activity. Hammocks erupted tired, cursing men—men ready for battle nevertheless. Laud jumped down on to the cold, shiny barrel of his cannon directly beneath his hammock. A hoarse murmur of excitement ran down the gun-deck. Had they caught up with Villaret Joyeuse at last ?

No : just another practice with those double-damned guns. There was rancour in Laud's voice when he gave the order, " Out tampion, cast loose your piece." He savagely shouldered one of the men. " You damned lubberly swine, you'll have to move faster than that when we catch the mounseers."

Intolerance and impatience showed in his single eye as he watched the men ease the side-tackles and heave in on the train-tackle fast on the crupper of the gun. He placed his hand on the huge cascable and jumped on to the crupper, thrusting a long wire down the vent of the cannon.

" Gun primed ! "

Then :

" Point your piece," he bellowed. " Traverse left."

Iron-shod hand-spikes were thrust beneath the carriage of the gun and the massive cannon was levered over by sheer muscle. The men on each side-tackle hove with all their might.

When in action it was the side-tackles and the massive ring-bolted breeching which controlled the devilish, leaping recoil. Even with the side-tackles hove taut and the huge breeching secured, the guns behaved like tethered wild beasts. They leapt from side to side and jumped up to strike the beams overhead. Sometimes they even snapped the side-tackles and ripped the breech-rope from its ring-bolts, tearing the stout ring-bolts from the wood. The hotter the gun became, the more unpredictable and dangerous was its behaviour. If more than ten rounds were fired without the guns being sponged with vinegar and water they were liable to recoil with such violence as to crush and maim the guns' crews.

Laud went through the motions of sighting his gun, took the trigger lanyard into his hand, and then bellowed above the din made by the other guns' crews at work.

" To your stations ! "

His crew, with the exception of two who chocked the trucks with hand-spikes against the violent roll of the vessel, lay flat on the deck, clear of the gun.

He jerked the trigger lanyard, noting that a tub of lighted linstocks was handy. He knew from past experience that guns with flintlocks sometimes misfired. In such a case the lin-stocks were used to ignite a firing-tube.

Having gone through the action of firing the gun, he shouted :

" Stop vent, sponge gun ! "

He stopped the vent with his thumb whilst one of the crew ran a sheepskin sponge on a rod down the barrel. Laud ran his wire down the vent to clear it : then, when all the motions of re-loading and securing the gun had been gone through, gave the order :

" Gun's crew . . . still ! "

The whole operation had taken just under a minute.

The master gunner nodded grudgingly. Secretly he was pleased with the speed of the men, but it would never do to show it.

The guns' crews climbed wearily back into their hammocks. The man in the hammock next to Laud's was the pickpocket, a wizened-featured, narrow-shouldered little man. Peering over the edge of his hammock he asked Laud, " D'ye reckon we'll ever catch up wi' these froggies ? "

Laud shrugged. He was tired, uncomfortable and dis-gruntled. " How in hell's name should I know," he muttered. " Better you ask Black Dick [1] ! "

He turned on his side, watched a swaying, dipping, horn battle-lantern for a few moments, and fell asleep.

2

Up to the present the French Battle Fleet had done their work admirably. In keeping the English away from the American wheat convoy they had fulfilled their function.

One morning, however, it seemed that God had grown tired of watching the circling, feinting warships. The wind and the seas fell away leaving a sullen swell and a thick sea fog, which

[1] Lord Howe.

swirled mistily through the now open gun-ports of the *Queen Charlotte*.

The great cannons had been run out and their muzzles were black and dripping like the noses of huge iron hounds, eager to bark and bite.

Linstocks glowed eerily in their tubs, the saltpetre in them occasionally giving a spiteful crackle. Wads of oakum in little net containers with wooden bottoms lay piled by each gun, together with hide-covered budge-barrels holding cartridges. The gun-deck was empty of its swinging hammocks now, for they had been lashed and taken to the upper deck as a precaution against splinters, and the guns' crews had to sleep by their guns.

All wooden bulkheads had been knocked away by the carpenter and his mates to lessen the risk of splinters and fire down below.

Tubs of water holding wet hides were dotted about the deck, to be used to smother any outbreak of fire. The magazine was also draped with wet hides to trap any sparks. Sand had been sprinkled about the gun-decks, whilst the leaden aprons were removed from the vents of the guns and paper firing-tubes inserted. The *Queen Charlotte's* sails had been drenched with a solution of alum to prevent them taking fire, and the carpenter had laid out his sheets of lead and wooden plugs for the stopping of shot holes. The cook and his assistants had put out the fire in the galley and what food there was, was served cold.

Perhaps the grimmest place in the whole ship was the surgeon's cockpit. Here knives, saws, trephines, needles and probes, and all the frighteningly crude implements of the day were being laid out, together with musket-balls for the wounded to bite on and gallon jars of rum, the only known anæsthetic of the times.

For some reason the men on the gun-decks found themselves whispering.

" Do you listen, Jago. Hear anything ? " Laud asked softly of one of his gun's crew, a hulking Cornish merchant seaman.

From the fog came the sound of a distant ship's bell and with it came the cry of the look-outs in the fighting top.

" Enemy vessels to larboard ! "

For an instant they had seen the huge black hulls of the French men-o'-war in a momentary lane in the fog. Then the mist had swirled in again.

The fog hung low, and frequently the look-outs would shout

down to say they could see the masts of the enemy above it.[1]

Two days later the fog lifted and the French Fleet could be seen on the lee bow of the British line.

On the quarter-deck of the *Queen Charlotte* a sad-eyed, red-faced old gentleman in black cravat, blue stiff-collared coat with gold-laced button-holes and gold buttons, white knee-breeches, and stockings thrust into shoes with somewhat tarnished silver buckles, smiled wearily at one of his officers.

" I fancy we have the weather-gauge of them at last," he said. " Pipe all hands to breakfast."

The officer bowed. " Yes, my Lord."

Lord Howe, with none of the fire and inspiration of the man who was yet to come, had at last accomplished his ends by sheer dogged persistence.

Aboard the French battleship *Sans Pareil* the captain turned to Captain Troubridge, an English prisoner of war. " Your countrymen," he sneered, " seem loath to venture down, sir ! "

Troubridge smiled.

" English sailors never like to fight on an empty stomach, monsieur. Be sure that after breakfast Black Dick will pay us a visit."

3

Inexorably the space between the two lines of ships lessened.

Laud, despite his previous experience at sea, felt his mouth dry and his stomach gnawing. Here was none of the excitement of a chase between revenue cutter and smuggling brig. It was all so damnably cold blooded.

Up on the quarter-deck Lord Howe had his glass on H.M.S. *Culloden*.

" What in the devil's name is Molloy up to now ? " he asked irritably.

The *Culloden* had faltered and now lay with her tops'ls aback. Nobody knew that a chance long-distance shot from the French had disabled her rudder.

Slowly the twenty-five smaller British ships with their seventeen thousand men narrowed the gap between themselves and twenty-six of the finest ships afloat, with their complement of twenty thousand men.

[1] The masts of the French vessels were white. The English ships had yellow masts with rope wooldings spaced equally to strengthen them.

The captain of the gun next to Laud's looked across and dashed the sweat from his eyes.

" If you hear tell that these mounseers can't fight," he said, " never believe it. Excitable, but they fight like devils from hell. I know." Then under his breath, " Christ, but I wish we'd start ! "

The French flagship *Montagne* was at that period the biggest and most heavily-armed man-o'-war in the world. She carried one hundred and twenty guns to the *Queen Charlotte's* hundred, and in addition weighed eight hundred tons more. She carried twelve hundred officers and men. To Laud, peering through the narrow opening of his gun-port, she looked a very mountain of guns.

Lord Howe had changed the order of his battle fleet so that each vessel was opposed to a French one of approximately its own size. This was hardly satisfactory, for the fire power and weight of metal of the French were vastly superior. A ninety-eight-gun English vessel threw a nine-hundred-and-fifty-eight-pound broadside ; whereas the blast from an eighty-gun Frenchman weighed one thousand and seventy-nine pounds.

The advantage seemed with the French, more especially as the Convention had gone to great pains to emphasize that captains of surrendering vessels would lose their heads.

Jean Bon St. Andrée, officer of the Convention aboard the *Montagne*, fastidiously took a pinch of snuff, tapped the lid of his box and cast a contemptuous glance at the smaller ships and their weather-worn appearance. He turned to Villaret Joyeuse.

" Is this the vaunted British Fleet ? "

Villaret Joyeuse bowed stiffly. Jean Bon St. Andrée was not loved by the forthright French fighting men. Their dislike for his spying ways made him infinitely more of an enemy than the men in the slowly approaching ships.

" Yes, monsieur," he replied formally, almost coldly, " that is the English Fleet. You have yet to meet their sailors ! "

Aboard the *Queen Charlotte* Lord Howe closed his tired blue eyes and shut his signal book with a snap. Further tactics were unnecessary : it was all in the hands of God now. How utterly weary he was. Endless days of cat-naps in chairs, cold food this last week, and now one of the greatest battles in history before him. It was a ponderous burden indeed for a man nearing seventy.

Down below on the gun-decks the men were talking in a

strange unnatural calm that prevailed. The little London pickpocket turned to Laud, and asked :

" What part of the country do you come from, cap'n ? "

Laud smiled. All rancour and impatience was gone from him now.

" Suffolk, lad. Why ? "

" Oh, I don't know. Yer talk is kind o' queer ; an' yet I like it. What's it like in them parts ? "

Laud glanced with his single eye along the chace sight of his gun. He estimated the distance ; it was a mere six hundred yards between themselves and the towering *Montagne* . . . and still no order to fire on either side. By God, it 'ud be muzzle to muzzle.

" What's it like, Jim lad ? Why it's . . . peaceful. Marshes where feeding geese yelp at night. Long, lonely, curved beaches of sand and shingle and low, sandy cliffs wi' curlews crying over. It's . . . peaceful."

There was a strange rapt look in Jim's pallid, narrow face.

" Funny to be talkin' o' . . . peace now . . ." he said. He gestured to the scar on Laud's face. " How did yer get that ? "

Another time Laud would have resented the outright question. But nothing mattered any more. He smiled and touched the scar gently. Margaret had touched it once.

" That scar, bor," he said quietly. " It happened . . . long ago. Mebbe if we come through this I'll tell you."

Slowly the *Queen Charlotte* came abreast of a heavy French seventy-four-gun ship, the *Vengeur*, which suddenly opened fire.

It seemed to Laud that all the great winds in the heavens were concentrated in his gun-deck and suddenly loosened about his ears, hurricanes of fire and metal. Opposite the next gun there was a sudden, high-pitched, vicious, instantaneous rending. A long gaping rent appeared in the bulwarks, whilst before his horrified gaze half the gun's crew vanished in a fine spray of blood and fragments of splintered bone and torn flesh. Some of it splashed his face warmly.

The three-and-a-half-ton gun lay upside-down. Its trunnions had torn through the cap-squares, and it had leapt clean out of its carriage. Breechings, side- and train-tackles lay in a hideous red raffle.

Beneath the gun's massive barrel a man lay. His mouth was working liked a hooked cod's. The weight of the gun had burst his body and his entrails were wreathed in fantastic festoons around the gun's trucks.

Another man was crying in a dreadful, shrill voice and dashing himself blindly from bulkhead to bulkhead. There was a four-foot-long splinter of oak transfixing him from collarbone to groin.

Suddenly the cries ceased and the figure folded up stiffly from the knees and fell forward. The point of the splinter embedded itself in the deck and kept the figure in a semi-upright position.

The cockney, his face ghastly, turned away and vomited into a corner. The rest of Laud's gun-crew stared in horrified fascination at the macabre scene.

Bloody-gowned surgeons and their mates were soon busy.

Up on deck were other crashings and rendings and cries.

Laud sensed the panic in his pressed crew : he was near to panic himself. This was hell . . . utter bloody hell. A hoarse croaking voice which shocked him as he recognized it as his own, was encouraging his wavering crew.

" Steady there, old pardners. We'll pay the Frenchy bastards for that directly. Steady now ! "

He looked desperately down the tier between the guns. Would the order to fire never come. Human flesh could not stand this tempest of metal and flame.

Then the sister ship to the *Vengeur*, the *Achille*, blasted the still silent *Queen Charlotte*. Laud lost all sense of feeling. Men were being torn to shreds all about him. But the human mind is like a vessel : its capacity is limited.

He stood at his gun awaiting the order to fire, whilst all about him great gaping holes appeared with hideous violence. The air was filled with smoke and the churring of great splinters. The sound of mighty, tearing winds drowned the puny screams of hideously mutilated men.

Suddenly, cutting through the murky turmoil, came the metallic clang of the order.

" *Give Fire !* "

The black hull of the *Achille* was but an oar's length away when Laud jerked his firing lanyard. His gun leaped like a startled horse.

A mighty diapason of smoke, flame and thunder rippled along the side of the English flagship.

When the smoke cleared Laud could see gaping rents in the *Achille*, and the cries and screams coming from the French vessel were like music to him and his gun's crew. He dashed the powder smoke from his eyes, and shouted, " That's started the French frogs croaking . . . Re-load ! "

No time to sponge out. The next vast black hull would soon be abreast their gun-port.

Number two of the crew was shouting, " Cartridge home ! "

Laud tried to moisten his powder-parched lips with a tongue like leather.

" Shot and wad your gun ! "

The man at the gun's muzzle thrust down a wad and hammered it home with his rammer. Another lifted the heavy iron ball and rolled it down the stinking, fuming muzzle ; and a second wad was rammed in and hammered down.

Laud thrust his priming wire down the vent to pierce the cartridge, then cocked his lock.

" Run out your gun ! "

The two men at the gun's muzzle unblocked the trucks by removing the hand-spikes : then lifted the breeching to prevent it fouling the cannon.

The rest of the gun's crew, bodies wet with sweat and blood, huge muscles bunching and sinews and joints cracking, hove away at the side-tackles.

" Square her off . . . heave away on your train-tackle ! "

Laud glanced swiftly along the gun-deck. The choking, stinking clouds of powder smoke had limited the visibility, but even so he could see the furtive shapes of large rats already sniffing round the dead and wounded.

After blasting the *Achille* with one terrible broadside Lord Howe swung the *Queen Charlotte's* head towards a gap in the French line, between the *Montagne* and the next ship in the French line, the *Jacobin*. His aim was to swing up to leeward of the *Montagne* and blast her other side at point-blank range.

The captain of the *Jacobin* and Villaret Joyeuse both tried to prevent this manœuvre. The *Montagne* threw her sails aback and drifted astern whilst the *Jacobin* shook out her tops'ls and forged ahead.

The gap was closing when suddenly the menacing aspect of the *Queen Charlotte's* three tiers of guns broke the nerve of the *Jacobin's* captain.

If those silent guns burst into flame his vessel would be raked fore and aft with a tempest of fire. The *Jacobin's* helm suddenly went over and she fell off to leeward of the *Montagne*.

At that moment Lord Howe ordered the helm of the *Queen Charlotte* to be put over. So close was she to the *Montagne* as she swept round her stern that the fly of the French flagship's ensign brushed the *Queen Charlotte's* shrouds.

At the instant of passing the *Montagne*'s stern came the order, " Fire ! "

For a fraction of a second before he jerked his firing lanyard Laud saw the massive, ornate, gilded stern of the French flagship. Then his gun, together with the others down the vast smoke-shrouded and red-splashed gun-room, leaped and bellowed.

That single broadside into the stern of the *Montagne* was the most destructive blow in the whole engagement. It tore a gaping rent in the stern of the Frenchman as big as a house and smashed over three hundred men into a bloody pulp.

The redoubtable Jean Bon St. Andrée, officer of the Convention, fled to the cockpit, where he remained for the rest of the engagement.

Then the deadly *Queen Charlotte* was around to leeward, locked shroud to shroud, anchor to anchor, channel to channel, with her huge antagonist.

Laud's senses were strained past reception point, or he would have lost his reason. Gun-muzzle blasted into gun-muzzle. Splinters whirred and flew thicker than twigs in an autumn gale. So benumbed was he by the blasts of his own and the *Montagne*'s guns that he was not even conscious of the hideous impact of the shot which burst his gun and turned back the thick metal of the muzzle like fantastic leaves.

Dimly he wondered why he was lying on his back and why he felt no pain. Nothing was left of most of his gun's crew except heaps that reminded him of the offal yard of the slaughter house at Aldeburgh, where he had stood fascinated as a child.

He rubbed the grime and blood from his single eye. Looking at the wreck of his own gun, he saw that the carriage was unharmed.

The blast from the *Montagne*'s guns had blown the trenails from the *Queen Charlotte*'s side with the force of bullets, and the captain of the neighbouring gun lay dead and riddled across the hot barrel of his gun, the carriage of which was a mass of splinters.

Laud found himself giving orders to the remainder of his own and the other gun's crew.

" Get your gun-strops round the trunnions of that gun. Sharp as you like now ! "

He pushed the body of the dead gunner off the cannon. It fell with its shattered and blasted face into the water barrel.

Laud picked up a dipperful of water, then dashed it down as he realized it was bloody.

" Overhaul your train- and side-tackles," he shouted, " and make fast to your carling beam. Then hook on to your gun-strop. We're going to remount that gun on this carriage." He bellowed at a small group of half-stunned survivors of a nearby gun which had also been dismounted. " Double up and bear a hand here ! "

By sheer will and manpower Laud swung the heavy gun into his own vacant carriage, then hammered home the cap-squares over the trunnions.

He did not notice Jacob Bowen, Lord Howe's sailing master, moving swiftly through the gun-deck amid the swirling smoke, and therefore missed the look of swift approval that Bowen gave him. The sailing master was a superb seaman himself and appreciated courage and sailorly qualities in others.

When Laud had finished the task of remounting the gun there was a pause in the firing and it gave him time to look about him.

He failed to recognize any of his gun's crew. They were either dead or so blackened by powder smoke that he did not know them.

Many of the horn battle-lanterns had been shot away, but the sick-berth attendants, old, feeble sailors recruited for the job, were carrying lanterns whose feeble light barely pierced the swirling fog of powder smoke, a fog which mercifully hid many things and from which came sounds of retching coughs and heart-racking groans climbing the scale of unendurable agony.

Laud sagged for a moment against his remounted and reloaded piece, wondering if the sailors aboard the *Montagne* were in as bad a way as himself and his shipmates, or rather what remained of them.

Suddenly the firing commenced again. No time to think. Laud jerked his firing lanyard . . . Misfire ! He swept a linstock from a nearby tub and ignited the firing-tube. The gun thundered, recoiled and bounded up to meet the deck-head, despite the figures straining at the side-tackles.

The *Jacobin* occupied the space which Lord Howe needed and his lordship was about to take the outside position when Jacob Bowen saw the *Jacobin's* rudder going ponderously to port. He touched Lord Howe's sleeve respectfully and indicated the enemy vessel's move off to leeward.

Howe nodded his appreciation. " Hard over ! " he ordered.

At that moment a blast from a brass cohorn in the *Montagne's* mizzen fighting top hurled the helmsman, a bundle of bloody rags, ten feet away.

Bowen dashed to the helm and brought the *Queen Charlotte's* stern round. So close was the English flagship to the *Jacobin* that her jib-boom was drawn across the *Jacobin's* mizzen shrouds.

As the *Queen Charlotte* swung round, her whole three tiers of guns thundered along both sides, one broadside into the *Montagne*, and one into the *Jacobin*.

The *Queen Charlotte* herself was little more than a floating wreck : one-third of her company annihilated ; foremast shot away ; gammoning and bowsprit shot through ; sails in ribbons and her bulwarks a mass of splintered timber, above and below the water-line. The pumps were going, manned by as many men as could be spared from the guns and fighting tops. Nevertheless, she kept up an incessant thunder of fire with a rapidity which utterly confounded the French.

If the *Jacobin* had kept her position, the *Queen Charlotte*, with the hundred and twenty guns of the *Montagne* on the weather side and the eighty guns of the *Jacobin* to leeward, would have been blown to matchwood. But so deadly and rapid were the English flagship's broadsides that the shattered *Jacobin* withdrew, firing spasmodically as she went.

The secret of the British gunners' success was that they elevated and depressed their guns, firing alternately up through the deck and down through the bottom of the bewildered *Jacobin*. The same plan played havoc with the *Montagne*.

In the meantime, the whole battle had resolved itself into a series of isolated duels.

Lord Howe's next in line, the *Brunswick*, was to have cut through the French line behind the *Jacobin*, but the *Vengeur* and the *Achille* moved up and closed the gap. Captain Harvey, commander of the *Brunswick*, became impatient and deliberately rammed the *Vengeur*, the anchors of the British ship hooking into the fore shrouds and channels of the *Vengeur*.

The sailing master of the *Brunswick* glanced across at Captain Harvey.

" Shall I chop her adrift, sir ? "

" Chop her adrift be damned, man. We've got her and we'll keep her."

Both ships paid off before the wind, shrouded in a hurricane of flame and smoke. So closely were they locked that the English gunners could not open their gun-ports and thereafter coolly fired through them.

Up on deck, however, the deadly thirty-six-pound carron-ades of the *Vengeur* were sweeping the *Brunswick's* decks with a storm of shot of every kind from case to langridge, from bar to dismantling shot.[1]

Captain Harvey was hit three times simultaneously and was carried dying from the deck.

Suddenly the hard-pressed crew of the *Brunswick* looked across the smoke-shrouded sea with dismay. They were almost shot to pieces and the great *Achille* was bearing down upon them. Though badly battered by the *Queen Charlotte*, she was still formidable.

There was an uncertain pause on the *Brunswick's* bloody deck.

At that moment a cockerel, released from its coop by a shattered spar, flew up on to the stump of the mainmast, flapped its wings and crowed mightily.

A sudden roar of cheering went along the deck of the *Brunswick*, the firing breaking out again so savagely that the sole remaining mast of the *Achille* came tumbling down in a ruin of cordage and canvas. She fired weakly for a few moments : then the unbelieving English sailors saw the tricolour slowly creep down from the flagstaff.

But so hotly did the *Vengeur* engage the *Brunswick* at that moment that the *Achille* was able to run up a jury mast and creep out of fire with her colours re-hoisted. A little later the swell caused the *Brunswick* and the *Vengeur* to swing apart, still firing sullenly.

An hour passed before the *Vengeur*, blasted by the *Ramillies*, commanded by Captain Harvey's brother, slid with shattered hull and dismounted guns and bloody decks, beneath the surface. As she went the remainder of her crew waved defiantly from her deck and shouted " *Vive la République* " : then she was gone, leaving nought but a red stain and a few shattered spars to mark her going.

In the meantime the hideously battered *Queen Charlotte* was giving all her ferocious attention to the *Montagne*, blasting her with a cyclone of fire and metal.

---

[1] Dismantling shot is several round iron bars whose total circumference is just a little less than the bore of the cannon. They are fastened together at one end by an iron ring which allows them to spread when they leave the muzzle.

Down below on the gun-deck, where Laud was sweating at his gun, many of the guns' crews had been wiped out and many guns dismounted. Now that they were no longer firing at the *Jacobin* Laud took in the situation swiftly.

" Larboard guns' crews double up to starboard ! " he ordered.

Then the mighty orchestration of fire, iron, smoke and blood commenced again.

Despite the size of the *Montagne* she was being rapidly torn to kindling by the devilish speed of the broadsides from the *Queen Charlotte*. It was lucky indeed for the French flagship that the foremast of the English vessel had been shot away so that she was unable to follow when the *Montagne* at last broke off the engagement.

She crept away, her decks a reeking abattoir of fire and iron-blasted human flotsam. Many of her guns were dismounted and her stern frame was blown to atoms. Her starboard quarter and larboard side were a mass of smouldering splinters ; and on her decks lay a tangle of shattered spars and yards, torn and scorched canvas and trailing ropes : whilst the sea around her was tinged with the blood that ran from her fire-blackened scuppers.

As the *Montagne* slowly withdrew the French line disintegrated.

Lord Howe, his hands behind his back and his head thrust forward, gave the terse order, " Signal general chase."

As he spoke a ball hurtled between himself and the sailing master.

Bowen gave a grim smile. " The *Juste*, my Lord, eighty-four guns."

Then the *Queen Charlotte* was at it again, the two vessels hidden in a shroud of flame and smoke and thunder.

Presently the *Juste* ceased firing and, a shattered dismasted wreck, drifted to leeward.

The smoke hung low on the water in dense clouds which seemed loath to dissolve and reveal the hideous evidence of one of the greatest and most sanguine sea battles in history.

Laud looked wearily about the gun-deck. There was about one-quarter of the original number of men left. The others lay about in silent or groaning heaps. Some had been taken to the dreaded cockpit by crimson-garbed surgeon's mates, others had been blasted out of any semblance to humanity, their shattered fragments plastered to bulkhead and deck-head.

Ship's boys were moving about, white-faced and frightened, employed in driving the rats from the wounded.

Blindly, Laud fumbled for the dipper to the drinking water : tainted or not, if he didn't have a drink he'd die.

He picked up the dipper and dashed some of the tepid fluid into his face. He was about to take a drink when he felt a feeble plucking at his leg.

"Save us . . . a drop . . . mate," came a barely audible whisper.

He glanced down, and was hardly able to recognize the figure at his feet as anything human. Its features were just a fire-blackened crisp. He saw with a shudder that the flesh on the fingers of the clawing hand was roasted to the bone and was coming off in strips.

He mastered a desire to turn and run, and bending down, put his arm under the ruin. As he did so the charred clothing fell away in blackened flakes.

He held a dipper to the blackened, blistered lips.

"Who are you, old shipmate ? " he asked gently.

"Don't you recognize me ? " The whisper came back like a sigh. "It's . . . Jim . . ."

"Jim . . . Jim, old pardner . . ."

Laud broke off, not knowing what to say to the poor ruined semblance of a man.

The whisper went on. "You . . . were . . . going to tell . . . me . . . about . . . scar . . . remember ? " The blackened figure took a breath with difficulty. " Better hurry . . . not much . . . time."

Laud tried to make his voice normal. "The scar, Jim ? Long ago, years it seems, I wor a smuggler. A coastguard gi' me this. I thought it wor a terrible injury . . . then."

The sighing whisper broke in again. "You must 'a . . . had . . . exciting life, mate. Mine . . . back streets. Stealing . . . barrers . . . shops . . . cutpurse. When I was . . . nipper, my old man 'ud . . . beat tar out o' me if . . . I didn't."

There was a long pause as the scorched lungs gulped down the foul, smoke-laden air. "Tell me about . . . marshes . . . peaceful beaches . . . birds that cried at night."

The ramblings then became incoherent for a while. Presently the charred form gave a little shudder and a sigh. "Not . . . awkward squad . . . any more . . ."

Laud cradled the dying man's head.

"Have you any folks to tell, Jim bor? They'll be proud to hear of you!" he said softly.

The figure of Jim was still.

Laud looked around for something to cover his one-time shipmate. There was only a wet hide, hardly big enough to cover a child. There was ample room beneath it for the little back-street pickpocket, who, for the first and last time in his life, had gone to sea.

As Laud was bending over the still form he felt a hand on his shoulder and looked up to find Jacob Bowen standing beside him.

"His Lordship wants you on the quarter-deck, Laud," the sailing master said.

CHAPTER TWENTY

I

URING the winter the Cobbolds had moved from Cliff House to a large mansion on St. Margaret's Green, and Margaret of course went with them. She was glad of the flurry and bustle of the move. The excitement of settling in—the explorations, the discoveries, the fresh and unexpected views from the windows ; the thrill, recaptured from childhood, of feeling sufficiently yet not irrevocably lost when out of sight of the house in some corner of the garden—served to fill her mind with impressions, bright and gleaming in their newness, that crowded out her private worries.

The sharpness of these had increased. Now she feared that Will might get wounded or—though she hardly dared open her mind to the thought—killed in a naval action. And as the risk of this was greater than when he was in the free trade—if only because the gentry had avoided as far as possible meeting with the coastguards—her fear for his safety was proportionately increased. But it was a fear of which she could be proud, and she could carry her pride emblazoned on a banner and set it streaming in the wind for all to see. This pride in Will, which was partly pride in her own achievement in persuading him to leave the smugglers, set her head high and lit fires in the depths of her eyes that not even the overlay of anxiety could wholly dim. And the busy days of shifting furniture and keeping the children out of mischief when mischief was everywhere, gave no time for anxiety, but left the fine glow of pride to add radiance to her beauty.

The move itself was an indication that the Cobbold business was prospering. The present house was a superb building standing in pleasant and spacious grounds, and facing the town. The building had mellowed with the passage of years, and was further softened by a fine wistaria which spread across the front elevation and in summer filled the front rooms with its soft fragrance.

A drive swept up to the main entrance from an imposing gateway, and led round the side of the house to the stables. On the other side of the house an extensive and well-kept lawn lay between the formal flower-beds near the house and the wall of the enclosed kitchen garden.

The new garden was a paradise for the children. There were flower-beds to be raced around ; shrubberies in which to play endless and exciting games of hide-and-seek ; trees for the older children to climb amid displays of tearful frustration by the younger ones ; pears and apples that could be seen slowly ripening through the summer months with delightful anticipation—and individual fruits on which ownership claims could be staked and hotly disputed and through whose agency all the emotions from extreme pride to the bitterest jealousy could be fully experienced.

And the pond. Towards the bottom end of the lawn there was a deep ornamental fish pond, with sloping turfed sides, reached by a flight of six stone steps. On its brink grew two beautiful but melancholy weeping willow trees, trailing their sad branches into the water.

It was a fascinating place surrounded by strawberry-beds, and the children were attracted to it like flies to a jam-pot : and the attraction proved almost as fatal.

One morning the cook had to prepare a roast sucking-pig for dinner, and asked Margaret to pick some sage for the stuffing. Margaret took her basket and set off along the path which ran, screened by shrubs, from the kitchen door to the vegetable garden.

Just as she had finished picking what she needed and had closed the garden gate she heard a childish scream, full of panic and coming from the direction of the pond.

She lifted her trailing skirt and dropped her basket all in one motion ; then ran like a frightened hare towards the pond.

On its edge stood a bunch of young Cobbolds, all adding to the confusion with their cries and screams and further distracting the head nursemaid who stood wringing her hands and crying.

Little Henry Cobbold had been chasing his sisters round the grassy edge of the pond. He had slipped and rolled down the steep bank.

Margaret saw it all in an instant. The boy would drown within a few seconds unless somebody acted swiftly.

She seized the nursemaid and shook her hard.

" Run for the stablemen . . . a ladder and a rope ! "

Then she climbed quickly and with great agility along one of the boughs which trailed in the water. Reaching the end of the branch, which sagged dangerously under her weight, she seized the boy's jacket and held him up, speaking soothingly to him all the while.

" Don't you-together be scared now, Master Henry. Margaret has got you. Don't kick. They're . . . coming to . . . pull us out . . . this instant."

The coachman and the gardener came running to the top of the pond. A ladder was slid out and the gardener edged along it and seized Henry, who was almost senseless with fatigue, fright and immersion.

When the boy was safe Margaret called to the coachman to throw the rope. She fastened it round her waist, let go the bough and was hauled to the edge of the pond.

A large crowd, including the master and mistress of the house, was assembled at the pond and as soon as Master Henry was on firm ground Mrs. Cobbold seized him and bore him off, dripping, to the house, followed by the maids, chattering like magpies.

Margaret in the meantime had climbed out and had immediately been caught by Mr. Cobbold, quite overcome with relief that his son was safe—so overcome, in fact, that before the whole assembly he caught Margaret, wet as she was, and kissed her on the cheek.

" Bless you, Margaret, " he cried. " God surely sent you to us."

Margaret blushed and fled away up the path to change her wet clothes.

When she had gone Mr. Cobbold stared thoughtfully at the scene of the accident. Then, deciding with characteristic promptness that the safety of his children was more important than the delights of a fish pond, he told the head gardener to get the pond filled in without delay, and to order as many cartloads of rubble as he might need for the purpose.

Meanwhile, Mrs. Cobbold, having called Doctor Stebbing by a fast messenger, sent for Margaret. Like her husband the good lady spontaneously caught Margaret and kissed her on the cheek.

" Margaret, I don't know what would happen here without

you," she said. " I'm afraid the head nursemaid has been most careless. I've told her to pack her bag and I want you to take her place."

Margaret curtsied.

"Thank you, mam . . . but well . . . I wouldn't feel happy . . ." she began doubtfully.

"Don't worry about that, Margaret. I've given her a reference. You love the children and I know they just adore you. It will be a good thing for everyone." Mrs. Cobbold sighed. " It is a large responsibility . . . so many to watch. You'll get an increase in your wage, my dear." Mrs. Cobbold's face brightened. " By the by, there's dancing and a firework display in the town tonight to celebrate Lord Howe's glorious victory over those dreadful French creatures. You may take the evening off if you wish."

Margaret curtsied and went out.

2

That night she pushed her way through the milling, shouting, jostling, drunken but thoroughly good-humoured crowd in Carr Street. Maroons were thundering and rockets were mounting the sky and bursting in shower after shower of coloured stars which reflected in the black surface of the Orwell.

A dense crowd outside the " Salutation," a public house much patronized by sailors, caught her eye. It was grouped around a young sailor with ginger hair and blue eyes set in a jolly red face, made redder by the enormous quantity of beer he had been drinking all day. He had a slopping beer mug in his hand and was being urged by the crowd.

" Come on there, ' What Cheer.' You wor wi' Black Dick Howe off Ushant. Tell us about the fight and how you lost your leg." " What Cheer," although he had been telling the story all day, was nothing loath. He took a long drink to lubricate his voice and then waggled his wooden leg with pride.

" Ay," he began, " a swab of a French marine in the mizzen top of the *Montagne* did that. B'Gawd, that there was a day, m' hearties. Captain Pearson o' the Queens killed on deck, bless his gallant soul. His red coat made 'm a mark a blind man couldn't 'a missed. We wor starb'd side to when we got alongside the *Montagne*—ah bor, what a ship that wor : but she couldn't stand up to our broadsides for all her weight and size.

" Black Dick gi' the order larboard guns' crews aloft intew the fighting tops—what was left on 'em. The Frenchmen wor using cannister from their thutty-six-pounder carronades : blast they wholly took toll o' our lads on deck.

" Up I went into the maintop wi' a musket. The fight were that sharp and we wor that close it wor like shooting sitting pigeons. I forgot that they wor shooting at us tew— until I spied a French marine sighting at me along a musket bar'l. Then . . . blast if I didn't think some'un had hit me in the leg long of an axe. I managed to catch a'hold o' the main topmast backstay what had been shot through do I'd 'a gone down to the deck. Wholly sick I wor for a bit and then I knew if I didn't do suthin' I'd bleed to death. I put a Spanish windlass round my thigh and arter that I felt better. I'd dropped me musket so I picked up anorther. The marine what had been using of it lay across the fighting top capping wi' a ball in his belly. Ah, but I got the sod what did fer me. Sighted cool as a cuccumber across the dead marine, I did. Took the frog-eating bastard clean through the eye. Blast didn't he haller—just like a frightened woman, on'y wuss. Hulled his musket high in the air and then went down all arms and legs like a scarecrow. Arter that things got a bit hazy-like. I mind thinkin' what a hell o' a mess our rigging wor. You see, the mounseers allus bring their guns to bear on the rigging, using bar and dismantling shot. The main topmast stay and t'gallant stay were shot through and all frapped up wi' the t'gallant backstays. The sails wor like cheesecloths. I dun't remember northen then. Not until I come-to wi' a surgeon's mate sticking a noggin' o' rum under me snout down in the cockpit. ' Here y'are, owd shipmet, you'll need this, owd sawboons is taking your spar off above the knee directly,' he say.

" That half-pint o' rum about saved my life, I reckon. I heard that owd saw going ' rasp, rasp, rasp,' fare shook every tooth in my jaws. When they'd done the surgeon's mate say that I'd chewed a musket-ball flat as a shilling." The narrator sighed. " Ah me, but there wor some right good lads lost limbs and lives that day aboard the *Queen Charlotte.*"

Margaret drew a deep breath and forced her way through the crowd.

" Did . . . did you say *Queen Charlotte* ? " she gasped.

The peg-legged one got politely but unsteadily to his feet. " Ah, I did that, missy."

" Did you know anyone named Laud . . . Will Laud ? "

" Will Laud did you say ?   Are you his sister ? "

" No, his . . . no . . ."

" His sweetheart, eh ? "

Margaret, overcome with embarrassment, flushed a deep red and was hardly able to nod.

The wooden-legged sailor pushed a lane through the crowd with brawny arms.

" Make way there, make way for a brave man's sweetheart."

Then he caught Margaret and, ignoring her protests, swung her up to stand on a table.

" What-cheer " held up his hand for silence.

" A toast, mates," he cried.   " Drink to the lass o' Will Laud, the man Black Dick decorated on the quarter-deck o' the *Charlotte*."

Margaret, though confused and embarrassed, had enough breath to gasp, " Is he safe . . . Will ? "

" What-cheer " nodded his red head vigorously.   " Ay, safe and sound, though by a miracle.   Mawther, you ought to be proud o' your man.   He wor cap'n of a gun on number two tier.   Arter the *Achille*, *Vengeur*, *Jacobin* and *Montagne* had finished wi' the *Charlotte* a lot o' the guns o' number two tier, what got the worst o' the lot, wor dismounted and the gun's crews smashed to pulp.   Laud collected up the survivors and remounted his gun what had been blown off its carriage. Then he carried on blasting at the Frenchie until between us we gave har a bellyful and she drew orf."

Margaret's face was white and her huge eyes blazing with excitement.   Her heart was hammering so that she could barely breathe.

She had been right about Will.   He was as true as steel. She'd known it all along.   It was only his bad companions that had led him astray.

She turned back to " What-cheer."

" You said he . . . wasn't hurt ? "

" Nary a scrat'.   Last I see of him he wor at Portsmouth a'collectin o' his prize money."

Margaret leaped down from the table.   She flung her arms impulsively round " What-cheer's " neck, kissed him full on the lips, and then fled through the cheering crowd.

So excited was she that she failed to see the bulky, squat form of John Luff watching her from a darkened doorway.

As she went past, he gestured towards her and then bent his head and whispered to a companion.

"That's har. Can you bear her face in mind?"

The other man, a nondescript character in seaman's clothes, nodded. "Ay, Cap'n Luff," he agreed, in sharp cockney tones. "And yer say she's in service at St. Margaret's Green?"

"She is. I want you to keep me informed . . . everyone who visits her. I have others on the same tack. Find out all you can about Laud. Cap'n Bargood says he wants me to see that our Will don't come to no harm, like. D'ye follow?"

Used as he was to violence, the little sailor shuddered at the extreme contrast between Luff's mild whisper and the look on his face.

To add emphasis to his words Luff took hold of his minion's lapels and lifted him to his own eye-level as if he were a sack of straw. "And don't let there be any mistakes, my lad," he added. He set the frightened man down and vanished like a shadow into the surging, roaring crowd.

CHAPTER TWENTY-ONE

I

BACK at the Cobbold establishment Margaret was in a
transport of delight. Her Will a hero with prize
money! All her wildest and most cherished imaginings had come true. He had vindicated himself before the
whole world. Now he would soon be back and they could
marry openly and without shame or fear of what people
would say.

She fell to dreaming. Winter nights they'd sit over the
cottage fire, and he would tell her and the children—they'd
have two girls and two boys—the story of that terrible yet
glorious day on the first of June. He'd tell his sons what it
was like to have had a great Admiral pin a medal on your
chest.

Mrs. Cobbold noticed Margaret's face with its glow of
joyous content. She noticed too her servant's sparkling eyes
and the despatch with which she went about her work.

Days passed into weeks, and with their going passed
Margaret's first spontaneous delight.

By turns she became pensive and then peevish, and at
last utterly melancholy. Neither by word of mouth nor
letter was there any news of Will.

From her first joyous imaginings her thoughts turned to
bitterness. Will had deserted her. He had found another
woman on whom to spend his money. He had rejoined his
old companions.

Nevertheless, she crept out at night down to the " Salutation," with her shawl round her head and hope in her heart.

Yet never did she hear a word of her sweetheart. Gradually
she became so despondent that she never left the kitchen fire,
but sat brooding after all the other servants had either gone
to bed or to their nearby homes.

One such night as she sat silently and alone a knock

157

sounded on the door. Opening it quickly, she was disappointed to find that it was not her lover. Nevertheless, it was a sailor ; a thickly-built man with close-set eyes and the air of one who has important news to impart.

"Margaret Catchpole live 'ere ? " he enquired.

"Yes," she answered, " I'm Margaret Catchpole. What do you want ? "

" I'm just up fr'n Portsmouth, mam. A man by the name o' Laud, Will Laud, told me to tell you that he'll be up here in a day or two. He's ben delayed . . . prize money and one thing and another."

Margaret's face lit up and her voice was tremulous with joy.

" Oh, thank you ; thank you. Won't you come in and have a bite and sup ? "

When the man had finished a hearty meal Margaret asked him, " How . . . how is it he has been so long in coming ? "

The man glanced shiftily around the kitchen. When he replied he did not meet her gaze.

" Eh . . . why . . . Oh, he's been standing by his prize. Waitin' to get his discharge. Allus a long job that. I fancy I better get back aboard. Thank 'ee for the meal, miss. Goo'-night." He crammed his monmouth cap over his ears and lurched out into the night.

Notwithstanding the hopeful news, Laud did not arrive. However, other sailors with purported news of him did. As with the first man who had brought news of Laud, they were entertained in the kitchen, and with their going articles began to vanish. One day the housekeeper was forced to report the loss of a ham and a pair of newly-plucked fowls.

Mrs. Cobbold had for a long time been fully aware of what was going on, but had preferred to ignore it. Now, however, she realized that she would have to act. She straightway sent for Margaret.

" I'm sorry to have to say this to you, Margaret my dear. You are one of the family, but so many different stories have come to me of late that I can no longer ignore them. The housekeeper reports that food has been stolen from the larder. I have known for a long time that you have been entertaining sailors, or those who profess themselves sailors, in the kitchen. I have said nothing because I understood why you were doing it." Mrs. Cobbold put her arm in a kindly gesture round the drooping shoulders of her servant. " There's your own character to consider too, my dear. These men have been saying most unpleasant things, utter lies, but at the same time injurious to both your character and to my establishment.

" If you had only come to us at first we would have written to Portsmouth about your sweetheart. Indeed I feel sure that Mr. Cobbold will send a messenger to find him—anything to set your heart at rest, my dear. Now do try and be your old happy self and I feel certain that things will come all right in the end."

Margaret listened to her mistress's kindly rebuke ; then, much to Mrs. Cobbold's dismay, left the room without speaking and without her customary curtsey. The mistress of St. Margaret's Green shook her head sadly.

Margaret returned to the kitchen with a pale face and her lower lip clenched tightly between her teeth. The rest of the staff glanced significantly at each other.

One evening the whole of the staff were sitting down to supper when a knock sounded at the kitchen door. The kitchen maid opened it and called across to Margaret with a sly smile hovering round her mouth.

"Another sailor to see you, Margaret."

Margaret got to her feet with her eyes blazing. She had suffered enough humiliation already and now it was her turn.

" Tell him to go to the devil and take his lies elsewhere ! " she cried. " I've had all I'm ever going to do with thieving, lying seamen."

Hardly were the words out of her mouth than Laud took one step into the kitchen. He glanced at Margaret's pale angry face.

" Well, there's nothing to add to that, Peggy," he said quietly. " You may as well have what I came here to give you."

He unclasped a heavy money-belt from about himself, tossed it on to the table, then went back through the door and vanished into the darkness.

His going seemed to break a spell. Margaret tottered forward. " Oh, Will . . . Will," she wept, " I didn't know it was you. For God's sake stop and let me explain . . ."

Sobbing, she staggered out of the door and along the path, almost colliding with a dark figure as she did so. She clutched it as if she would never let it go.

" Thank God I've found you, Will. Don't . . . don't go before you hear what I've got to say. It has all been a dreadful mistake. There's been all manner of sailors up here, all saying they'd brought messages from you. Lies all of them. Then they stole things and Mrs. Cobbold gave me tongue pie over it. Come back, Will, please come back."

The figure at her side still went striding on saying nothing. By this time they were at the back of the stables, opposite which was a yard with open gates. Margaret and her companion turned in here and closed the gates behind them.

The light from the coachman's cottage fell on the man's face. Margaret nearly fainted. It was not Laud, but John Luff. She was paralysed with fear. The sudden transition from the man she most loved to the man she most feared and loathed almost shattered her sanity.

She backed towards the gates. Luff's teeth gleamed in his swart features.

" You don't seem to be overjoyed at seeing an old friend, Peggy my gal," he whispered. Suddenly the banter was gone from his voice. " Where's Laud ? "

" I . . . I don't know. . . ."

" None o' your damned lies. I had news that he was coming here tonight wi' his prize money. Cap'n Bargood wants Will to skipper a new ship just built." Luff's whisper became mild again. " You wouldn't want him to miss a good chance like that, would you, Peggy ? "

Intuition told Margaret that Luff's story was false. Somehow she sensed that he had one thought in mind : to murder her lover.

" I don't know where Will is. I wish I did. But even if I did," she cried, " I'd never tell you, you bloody-handed murderer."

Luff gave a gentle chuckle and leapt at her. Binding both her arms at her side by encircling her waist, he thrust a knotted rope into her mouth as a gag and commenced to drag her towards the well that stood in the centre of the yard.

Fear doubled Margaret's strength ; and twisting and writhing in that iron grasp she managed to free one arm. In desperation she reached out for the gate to save herself. Her hand caught the heavy iron bar that was used to fasten it, but failed to hold it. It was dragged from her grasp and fell with a ringing crash on the stones of the yard.

The noise brought the coachman to his door. In the dim gleam of light that fell across the yard he saw the situation at a glance, and went straight at Luff. But Luff saw him coming, and with Margaret firmly pinioned by one powerful arm, he drew a heavy pistol and struck brutally at the coachman's head with the heavy barrel. The man crumpled and fell.

Margaret tried to scream, but only a thin trickle of sound escaped past the gag. She felt her knees strike the coping of the well, and fought to free herself with a desperation born of terror. But she could not get free and she felt herself being forced backwards over the low coping and then she was suddenly released and she was falling into nothingness. Clutching frantically in that black slimy shaft her hands encountered the well rope, snatched at it and held it. Then her head struck the side of the shaft and she knew no more : but not even unconsciousness broke her grip on the rope.

This action saved her. Not only did it break her fall, but at the same time it caused the well handle to revolve with such a clatter that it brought the whole kitchen staff out of doors. They heard the splash as Margaret hit the water ; and running into the well yard they discovered the coachman's prostrate body and realized that something was very much amiss.

The coachman groaned, climbed painfully to his feet and stood swaying with the blood running down his face from his gashed scalp. "He . . . he hulled har down the well," he said, and staggered to his cottage to fetch a light.

The gardener and the groom ran for a long ladder which they swiftly placed down the well.

"I'll go down and fasten the rope round the poor mawther," the gardener said, "and ease her up the ladder, if you wind up at the same time."

When they finally got Margaret to the top of the well she was black in the face and the rope gag was still wedged tightly between her jaws. This gag, which had prevented her from drowning, was hastily removed and then she was carried quickly indoors and put between warm blankets, whilst Doctor Stebbing was sent for.

The doctor bled her, and in a little while Margaret opened her eyes and gazed blankly about her. The room was full of people. Her mistress was sitting by the side of the bed, and behind her stood the stalwart figure of John Cobbold, Laud's money-belt in his hands.

The servants had told him what had taken place up to the time when Margaret had run out after her sweetheart.

"Why did he do it, Peggy ? " he asked, under the misapprehension that Laud had attempted to murder her.

"It wasn't him, sir," Margaret said weakly, appalled that

anyone should think her Will capable of such an action. "It was John Luff. Oh, sir "—her voice became shrill with panic—" he's going to murder Will, I know he is. For God's sake stop him ! " And she struggled to get off the bed.

At the mention of Luff the servants glanced at one another uneasily : and, partly to reassure them, John Cobbold called in one of the footmen and gave orders for the male members of the establishment to be armed and for the dogs to be turned loose. He despatched a messenger to inform the authorities that Luff was abroad, and then made a thorough search of the grounds, but without success.

2

During her convalescence Margaret, nearly distraught with anxiety for Laud, told Doctor Stebbing all that had happened.

"I know now that I have driven him away he'll go back with his old companions, sir. I know it. He'll walk unsus-pecting right into Luff . . . and then Luff will murder him, sir. Oh, if I could only get to Will instead of lying helpless here."

She rolled her pale face, with its huge burning eyes, from side to side on the pillow.

Stebbing rubbed his nose thoughtfully.

"You know, it's this worrying that is retarding your recovery, my girl," he said gently. "Now, let's be quite frank about the whole business. It was, of course, quite wrong of Laud to have run off without waiting for an explan-ation. Quite wrong. If he's worthy he'll be back, never fret. I fancy you'll see him in a day or two. And if not—why then he's not worth the tears you are shedding over him. But what puzzles me is why Luff, his old companion, should wish to kill him. What makes you think that ? "

The knowledge had come to Margaret in a flash of intuition on that fateful night, and for some days now she had been attempting to find reasons to support it. The problem had lain within her like a tangled skein of wool, the fingers of her mind picking at it and teasing it in an effort to unravel the knots. At times the thread had seemed free and she had wondered why the matter had ever been a problem at all ; at others, she remained as puzzled as Doctor Stebbing.

Vaguely she realized that before Will had gone away Luff

had needed him, not only for his capabilities as a sailor, but also as a counterweight to his own peculiar and warped personality. Will represented something that Luff lacked, something that he wanted to possess—a way with women, a careless gaiety, an enjoyment of life—and Luff was content to possess these things vicariously. Further, she felt instinctively that his hatred of herself was in part reaction against the dislike that women in general felt for him ; but that in the main it was founded on jealousy, and a fear that he might lose Will completely to her. And she realized that a man of Luff's mentality would not hesitate to kill her if by so doing he could become the sole possessor of Will's friendship.

But a new factor had arisen now that Will had served in the navy and had thereby obtained a pardon for his earlier activities. Luff would now be obsessed by the fear that Will would remain honest and therefore be lost to him ; and Margaret felt sure that Luff would murder Will rather than lose him in this way. She saw too that, given the suspicion that Will might talk, Luff had a still greater incentive for murder.

But if Luff had decided to do away with Will, why had he tried to kill her ? Margaret could only suppose that his bitter hatred of herself had driven him to it. But then suddenly she wondered if this was not further evidence in support of her intuition. If Luff was prepared to alienate Will's affections by murdering his sweetheart, did it not mean that he was out to kill him ? It was all very confusing, and always she arrived back at her intuition. It was something she knew beyond reasonable doubt. But groping for an explanation, she found it only in brief snatches of clarity, never wholly.

Nevertheless, amid sobs, she did her best to make Doctor Stebbing understand why she feared for her lover's safety.

" But poor Will," she cried, near breaking point. " Don't you see, doctor, he'd been saving his money all that time so that we could get married. How happy he must have been thinking of how I'd greet him safely back from that dreadful battle. My words must have cut him to the heart. And . . . and, oh, sir, you don't know John Luff. He's a fiend from hell—the arch fiend of them all. He delights in killing. He'll surely slaughter Will ! "

She turned her head to the wall and started to sob violently. Stebbing shook his head. The sicknesses of the mind, he thought, are more difficult to cure than those of the body.

And opening his bag he gave Margaret a strong sedative to calm her frayed nerves.

" Don't fret about your man, lass," he said kindly. " From what I hear of Laud he is quite capable of looking after himself."

3

One day Mrs. Cobbold came quietly into Margaret's room.

" I think it would be a good thing, my dear," she said, " if you went for a holiday with your father and brother. The magistrates have been here and they desire a statement from you. However, I told them that you would be able to give them a more satisfactory account when you had had a change and a rest." She smiled with a touch of gentle humour. " After all, it's not every girl who gets tossed down a well. The master wishes me to tell you that there are one hundred and thirty guineas in the money-belt. He has put his seal on it and it is in his bank until you desire it. Oh, and I nearly forgot it, here is a letter for you."

It had been sent on from Nacton and was from John Barry. Margaret opened it and read :

SYDNEY COVE,
NEW SOUTH WALES.

MY DEAREST MARGARET,

Although I am so far away I still think of you, hoping that one day I shall receive a letter. None have arrived as yet but I have not given up hope. The supply vessel is more than a month overdue and it would make you laugh to see me. I am as ragged as a gypsy, so are convicts and freemen alike. Each day we go down to the cove to see if there is a topsail in sight. The womenfolk feel their rags worse than the men.

This is a wonderful and terrible country, Peggy. Vast, lonely beyond words. There are great and awful deserts, places where the rocks and soil are blasted to a dust as fine and white as flour by the awful heat of the sun. Places of death where nothing can live except horrid lizards panting in the shade of rocks.

There are gruesome spots, white with the bones of cattle and horses—men, too, who tried to cross the desert without enough water.

Yet there are also great stretches of fertile land, especially around the river Hawkesbury where I have lately been granted five thousand acres of virgin soil by His Excellency the Governor.

It is a great labour, clearing the trees. Some of them are two hundred feet high, handsome cedar and rosewood trees, surrounded by great bushes of castor-oil plant all overrun with wild vine. Clearing the ground is expensive and unsatisfactory. One has to employ time-expired convicts, " emancipists " they call themselves, or ticket-of-leave men who charge £5 per acre and take their time.

If your father and brothers were out here, Peggy, they would make their fortunes. Good stockmen can ask almost any wage they fancy. And the price of good animals is wicked. A farm horse from England costs at least £130, so most of us use oxen ; even these are as much as £60.

Horse theft is rife out here, the thieves being hanged out of hand on the spot where they are caught. When I am ploughing I carry a carbine with me, for the place is infested with blood-thirsty aboriginals who eat human flesh.

The soil itself is very suitable for wheat, maize and barley. The wheat being sown in June and reaped in November.

Imagine how strange I feel, my dear, harvesting in November. Thinking of wet November fogs swirling in from the sea. November in England, getting near Christmas. I picture the light shining from your little cottage on Nacton Heath. I see you so clearly, Margaret, your dear head bent over some household task.

I work hard from dawn to dusk and go back to my hut so tired that I fall asleep over my food. I am grateful for this for I do not lie awake thinking—for I love you as much as ever, Peggy, and to know that I shall never see your dear face again, except in dreams and forever in my mind, is unbearable.

Give my love to my folks at Levington if you see them and ask them to send me all the newspapers, however old.

Always,
JOHN BARRY.

CHAPTER TWENTY-TWO

W ILL LAUD stood on Orford beach, his head bare. The cool breeze from the North Sea ruffled his thick black hair, now, since the ordeal of fire and metal and blood aboard the *Queen Charlotte*, plentifully besprinkled with white. The sky was a pale washed-out blue, liberally smudged with ragged grey rain clouds sweeping in from windward.

He felt utterly burnt out, physically and mentally. Nothing mattered any more since Margaret had told him to go about his business. She had found another man she cared for more than him. Women were like that. Let a man turn his back for a moment. Ha! What a bloody fool he had been. A hero of the first of June! What matter prize money or even the momentary pressure of Black Dick Howe's hand on the quarter-deck of the *Queen Charlotte*?

Like a sick animal Laud had returned to the only place that ever gave him complete peace of mind and body—the North Weir, that strange, mighty shingle bank that swept down the coast from Aldeburgh to Shingle Street.

Peace lapped round him now like a soothing tide. All his life he had been fascinated by the North Weir—" No'th Ear," the locals called it. The utter and complete desolation of the place held a riddle which one day he felt he would solve.

But now he was content to dream, and to listen to the hollow forlorn roar of the swell up the steep shingle, the eerie piping of teal and curlew overhead and the boom of a bittern in the sedges of the Lanthorn Marshes.

He knew the passing moods of this desert of marsh and shingle, home of the mewing fork-tailed terns, the bar-tailed and black-tailed godwits. He loved the primal loneliness of the deadly, sucking mudflats where the brent geese fed and spoke their strange language to each other. For hours he would sit idly watching the stilt-legged black and white

166

oyster-catchers probing the mud, whilst the flights of dunlin flew across the river in their erratic flight.

He knew the moods and seasons of the North Weir better even than his own strange, dark inclinations. In spring it was gentle, the nesting place of countless terns, dotterels and oyster-catchers. The eggs lay in such profusion on the bare shingle it was nigh on impossible to walk.

The outline of the shingle bank was soft then. Sea-plantain, sea-beet, sea-pea and sea-kale shot out thin pale shoots from between the stones. On the river side of the bank, where the stones met the marsh further along towards Aldeburgh, frail yellow-horned sea-poppies bloomed and scattered their yellow petals. Sturdy sea-thistles thrust up through the pebbles.

The marsh itself was a carpet of pale purple sea-lavender, with patches of sea-holly and acre upon acre of samphire. Dotted about the marsh were the small " pulks," little pools left by the Dutch Settlers when they dug the mud for the dyke walls. Some of these little marsh pools held a few inches of stagnant water over slimy mud. Others were dry, caked and cracked and imprinted by hare and waterfowl.

There were old and rotten plank bridges of doubtful strength spanning deep, sinister dykes of clear, slowly moving, iron-tinted water, in which tentacle-like weed of green and yellow swayed gently over ooze which would soon cover a man. Hidden in the marrams and long salt-rank grass were ancient wooden sluices and if your eyes were sharp you might find the short-stemmed, oddly fashioned clay pipes dropped by the Dutch who built the sluices years before.

In high summer there was an elusive quality about the place, a mystery which forever seemed to elude Laud's questing mind ; an elusiveness which tugged at him when the shadows of clouds raced like great galleons across the fantastic loneliness and desolation of North Weir Point.

North Weir Point—with its tide-tormented, nightmarish mounds of shingle, steep as the sides of small cliffs, each pebble miraculously keeping its ordained place until a rare footfall or the distant report of a fowler's gun started a small avalanche of stones. North Weir Point fascinated Laud beyond any other part of the coast. There was an instability about it that was one with the strange instability of his own nature. He was fascinated by the tiers of pebbles one above the other, and the gentle thunder of the surf over the bar on a fine warm day.

Human footsteps rarely, if ever, disturbed the forlorn isolation of the place. Huge pits in the shingle with steep sides and green-slimed bottoms showed where once the tide had eddied before being choked with the endless billions of pebbles.

Along the topmost ridge of shingle lay all the strange things cast aside by the swirling tides of the North Sea— the bleached white skulls of birds and fish, delicately scalloped ear-bones of plaice and cod, seaweed of all species from tangle-weed to carageen moss and bladder-wrack ; the wooden hatch-covers of wrecked ships ; stove-in boats, planks of driftwood by the wagon load. Sea-coal, its contours rounded as the pebbles on which it lay, cast up from foundered collier and undersea seam, was to be found here by the ton. Amber, that fossilized resin of extinct forest giants swallowed up by the flood waters of the melting ice-cap of a million years before, gleamed among the stones. Dead birds and decomposing porpoises lay there, together with long bamboos straight as javelins. Clear pebbles of agate and cornelian, white quartz and chalcedony of every colour glistened like false jewels in the sun.

There was nothing but peace here ; and always the gentle thunder of the surf and the smell of salt-soaked refuse rotting in the sun.

In summer the hot stones were all a-shimmer in the sun and the distant tower of Orfordness lighthouse hung in a mirage upside down against the sky.

Winter brought a different mood : evenings that were melancholy yet with a touch of menace, mornings when the sun came up a fiery ball through the low blanket of marsh mist.

As the winter advanced the melancholy died and North Weir became itself. Roaring winds boomed, howled and thundered across the shingle beds, almost invisible beneath the onslaught of the sea. Great clots of yellow, slimy sea-foam flew like fantastic balls. Blasting easterly gales which rocked the reason and numbed the mind by their sheer ferocity, drove all before them, as the whitened, salt-crusted bones of men sometimes dug from the shingle could tell. Then North Weir gave grudging shelter to myriad wild fowl : grey-lag, teal, wigeon, scaup, pintail, mallard, pochard, shoveller, brent, pinkfoot and even the almost legendary snow goose.

Many a time in winter as a lad Laud had crouched in the

hollows of the shingle with his father's old long-barrelled fowling-piece, an ancient relic with an enormous flint-lock and quaintly carven serpentines. Its barrels were paper-thin at the muzzle, and as often as not it misfired. On the other hand it frequently knocked its handler into a ditch with its recoil.

The North Weir was Laud's own corner of England, the place for which, all unknowing, he had fought the French. It claimed him as a woman might claim a man. He loved it with a love transcending anything in his life, hated it because it had enslaved him body and soul, and was as jealous of it as a man is of his mistress.

As he stood brooding on the beach the shepherd from the old Red Cottage on Havergate Island came along the shingle. He was collecting his flock which was cropping the scant grass of the shingle hollows. His practice was to ferry them across the strip of water known as " The Narrows " and collect them and take them back in the broad, flat-bottomed craft at night. When he saw Laud the tall, wiry old man nodded dourly.

" Evening, my master," he said. " Mind the ghost o' the marsh don't get you."

Laud grinned wryly. He knew the old man had been in league with the smugglers in the past. Apparently the shepherd did not recognize him now. " The marsh ghosts won't hurt me, friend," he said, and watched the old man plod along the shingle to his scattered sheep. Just the same, he thought, North Weir was no place to be alone at night— not that there was anything that might hurt a person, other than perhaps the hobby lanterns or marsh fires which according to local repute led one to doom in the beds of ooze.

Laud gave his boat a shove to refloat it, jumped in and pulled slowly back to Orford.

The evening was cold, and a glass of " bumbo " at the " Jolly Sailor," he told himself, wouldn't come amiss.

The inside of the " Jolly Sailor " was a cosy spot. A bright fire of drift-wood and sea-coal roared up the chimney. A long teak bar ran in a half-circle around one side of the tap-room which was low-ceilinged and half-panelled. The walls were yellow with age and splotched here and there with patches of damp. Around the room in glass cases were stuffed specimens of almost every bird and beast of the district. At the further end of the room three men were drinking : John Luff, Nick Segel and Sam Nye.

Luff went straight over and put his huge hand on Laud's shoulder. "Well met, Will," he said. "Come, have a glass wi' your old shipmets. What's it to be?"

"Bumbo, Jack," Laud said.

When the glass of rum and water was in Laud's hand, Luff gave a cough and asked casually. "Ha' you seen your gal lately, Will lad?"

Laud gave a bitter little laugh and absently drew pictures in little puddles on the bar.

"That's all astern, Jack, all done and finished wi'. A right fine hell of a welcome I got at St. Margaret's Green when I went there. She told me she never wanted to set eyes on another sailor. So I cut my cable, Jack bor, and now I'm back to join the gang again."

Luff ordered another round of drinks, then turned and clapped Laud across the shoulders. "Glad you're come back along o' us, Will. Drink up," he said. He took a long draught, and wiped the back of his hand across his rapacious mouth. "I'm not surprised to hear about your mawther, Will. I heard all manner o' mardle [1] about her. Seemed as if all sorts o' sailors were going up to the house. Then I heard that she was thick wi' one o' Cobbold's brewhouse men. Proper little lorette,[2] if you ask me."

After several more rounds of drinks, for which Luff insisted on paying for old time's sake, he turned to the two other men waiting at the end of the bar.

"You-together wait here for us," he said. "Will and I are going for a stroll to look at some of the old places before dark."

When they had gone Nick Segel stared gloomily into his glass; then shifted his gaze to his companion's face.

"An' that, Sam, is 'good-bye' to our young skipper. Luff's going to put paid to him as sure as Christ."

Sam nodded, equally gloomy. "Ah, I don't like this at all, Nick. A brush wi' the Excise is a different thing to downright murder. Will had no notion o' what wor going on whilst he wor away fighting the mounseers."

Nick Segel drained his glass and thumped it down with a decisive clatter. "I don't know about you, Sam," he said, "I 'int waiting here. I rather fancy I'd like to keep an eye on young Will."

"I'm wi' you, Nick, wi' all my heart. To hell wi' Luff, anyway."

[1] Gossip.   [2] Whore.

The two men nodded to the landlord and went out.

Laud and Luff strolled down Gap Lane and across the marshes, Luff making animated conversation all the while on this subject and that. They came to a deep dyke bridged by a narrow plank. Luff pointed to it with a laugh. "You're lighter'n me, Will," he said. "You go first, then if you fall in I can heave you out."

Laud turned and stepped towards the bridge. He had gone about two paces when Luff drew his heavy pistol and brought the butt down with crushing force on the back of Laud's unsuspecting head, sending him crashing down face first into the slime of the dyke.

With a satisfied gesture Luff thrust the heavy weapon back into his belt and turned and retraced his steps to the "Jolly Sailor," entirely unaware that Segel and Nye had seen what had happened and were racing towards the dyke.

"Hold you on to my coat, Sam," Nick gasped. "Don't let go whatever you do or I'll go over my head. They say there's no bottom to this dyke." He leaned as far out as he could and seized the slowly sinking body of the unconscious man beneath the armpits. Then together the two men dragged the still figure of Laud towards the edge of the dyke.

When they got him safely landed on firm ground they turned him over. His ashen features were covered with slime and blood. Nick Segel shook his head as he hurriedly wiped the injured man's face.

"Little to do for him, I fancy," he said.

A sudden thought struck Sam Nye.

"I've heard Will say in the past," he said, "that he had an uncle at Aldeburgh. The tide'll be with us, Nick."

"Good enough, Sam lad," the rigger of the *Alde* nodded. "We'll get poor Will up there as soon as we can. Wi' a fair tide and wind we ought to do it in an hour."

A little later the small boat with its lugsail set was speeding up river, a bone in its teeth. Nick Segel, who was at the tiller, drew a tarpaulin over the still form in the bottom of the boat.

"We'll soon get him up there, Sam bor, and Whispering Luff can go to hell," he said. "This is the last time I serve under him, the murdering bloody coward."

He luffed the little boat up a trifle to give it all the speed he could.

CHAPTER TWENTY-THREE

I

MRS. COBBOLD had given Margaret permission to stay at her father's cottage at Nacton for as long as she wished. Some days after her arrival her brother Edward said casually to her, " Peggy, did you ever get that letter I sent over to St. Margaret's Green? It was from John Barry wasn't it? "

Margaret nodded in rather a confused way.

" Yes, it was from . . . John. He says he won't ever forget me. He has a government grant of land, five thousand acres. Wonderful wheat land, he says."

Jonathan Catchpole looked across the tiny room. He had greatly aged of late and his seamed and lined face was that of an old man who found the burden of life almost too great to bear.

" Peggy, m'dear," he said, " why don't you give up chasing this wild rip of a smuggler and go out and marry John Barry? He's a fine young man. I hear tell they're running these emigrant ships. The fare is a lot o' money, five pounds, but I dare say we could get it some'ere."

Margaret shook her head decisively.

" I'll never do that, father. All I want to do is find Will. I'll go down on my knees to him after the way I treated him at Ipswich. Besides, he's not a smuggler now. I know that much."

The old man stretched his legs and took a long clay pipe from the iron pipe-cradle near the fire. Carefully he stuffed it with tobacco, taking care not to drop a shred of the precious stuff. Then he picked up a live coal with a pair of ember tongs and lit the pipe. He drew and then puffed out a cloud of smoke.

" That 'int s'easy, to break away fr'n the free traders, my lass," he said, " once you get mixed up wi' 'em. My belief is that Laud'll end his days as a smuggler." He ejected another cloud of smoke and then spat into the fire. He watched the saliva form into a bubble and burst before continuing. "If you're that keen on finding Laud, now you say he's an honest man, why don't you and your brother go down to the coast for a day or two. I'll tend the sheep. The sea air'll do you good, my maid. But for God's sake watch out for Luff. There's rumours of him having been seen at Orford. He tried to do for you once, and if you get into his clutches a second time . . ."

2

The next day Margaret and her brother left by coach for Felixstowe. On the way Edward spoke to his sister as quietly as the jolting, swaying coach would allow.

"Best thing we can do, Peggy, is to see if we can find Laud's old father, the ferryman at Languard Point."

When the coach finally arrived at Felixstowe Edward helped his sister down ; then they went to the ferryman's cottage. Their knocks were answered by an old woman who was manifestly suspicious of them. She opened the door a mere crack.

Margaret spoke first.

"Could we see Mr. Laud, please ? " she asked.

The old woman closed the door still further, until only the tip of her sharp, red nose was showing.

"That you can't, mawther. He's been dead and gone this last two months."

Margaret's face fell.

"Can . . . can you tell me anything about his son William ? "

The door was almost shut now.

"That I can't, that I can't. Do you go away and don't be pestering respectable bodies wi' your questions. Off ye go do I'll set the dog on ye."

The door closed in their faces. Edward smiled wryly at Margaret. "Some obliging old Biddy, that," he said.

3

For a few days Margaret stopped with her brother at Felixstowe, making discreet enquiries about Laud, with no success. From Felixstowe they shifted to the " Sun Inn " at Bawdsey Ferry, where they were equally unsuccessful. At last they left here and went to the old " Beach House " not far from Shingle Street.

The " Beach House "[1] was the last and perhaps the most desolate inn on all of that desolate coast. It was on the opposite side of the river mouth to North Weir Point, a square, clap-board building built flush on the shingle ; a gloomy, desolate place kept by an old retired pilot named Jacob Merrill—not at all the sort of place that Margaret and her brother would have chosen for a long stay. But by its very nature it was as likely a source as any for news of Laud, and for this Margaret was prepared to suffer any discomfort.

Normally the most unfrequented of inns, it was now patronized nightly by crowds of Government surveyors, builders and labourers who were busy erecting Martello towers in the district against the possibility of French invasion. It was just the right type of crowd for Margaret's purpose. Spread out by day along the coastline on the different construction projects, any of the various groups might so easily glean that scrap of fortuitous information which would give Margaret a clue to Laud's whereabouts.

Unfortunately, their stay was cut short by an incident which caused repercussions beyond its immediate importance.

There had been many sly nods and winks in the direction of Edward and his sister, and much lewd talk as to their possible relationship.

Edward was in the bar one night when one of the men, a hulking Irish foreman, voiced his thoughts aloud. " Brother and sister my ——. I wouldn't mind being ' brother ' to that dark-eyed mavoureen for just one night."

Edward Catchpole's tanned face was pale as he slipped through the crowd. Quietly he went up to the Irishman and tossed a pint of beer full in his red face.

" Perhaps that'll wash your dirty mouth out ! " he said.

In an instant the place was in an uproar. Several of the Irishman's comrades held him back whilst he screamed, " Let me get at him, the spalpeen, I'll tear his heart out." Edward Catchpole peeled off his jacket. Ashen faced with controlled rage he handed it across to the innkeeper.

Old Jacob Merrill shook his tousled grey head. He admired the youngster's pluck but he'd get an awful beating from the Irishman. He leaned across the bar and whispered in

[1] Latterly " The Lifeboat " until wrecked by a bomb during the second World War.

Edward's ear, " Watch out for gouging and kicking. He's a dirty fighter."

Just as the crowd, joyous at the thought of something to break the monotony, were jostling through the door, Margaret came down to see what the noise was about. Her eyes widened when she saw her brother with his coat off and his sleeves rolled up.

Edward, however, did not give her the chance to speak.

" Go you upstairs, Margaret," he told her, " and don't come down. Old Jacob'll look after you."

" Oh, Ned, what's happening ? "

" Nothing to worry about. I'll be all right. Now do as you're told."

Outside on the beach in front of the " Beach House " the crowd had formed into a rough ring. The Irishman had removed his shirt, exposing a massive, hairy torso, literally bulging with muscle. Edward also peeled off and his slim, wiry body looked puny by comparison.

" Ten to one on Paddy," a voice in the crowd bawled.

" I'll take that, mister. I like the look o' that little game-cock," came back another voice cheerily. " Paddy's been drinking heavy every night since he's been here, an' that's three months to my knowledge."

Whilst the bets were being made Edward was sizing up his antagonist. The Irishman was big and strong, but Edward fancied he was slow too. He was carrying a lot of blubber and was inclined to have a gut on him.

The crowd was quiet as the two men advanced into the middle of the ring.

The shingle crunched underfoot ; then Edward leaped in with a stinging left to the Irishman's mouth, knocking out a tooth. With a roar of rage the bigger man spat out the tooth and bored in with flailing fists.

Catchpole knew it would never do to mix it. Biding his time, he suddenly jumped in with a rapid left-right to the Irishman's stomach. The sound of the blows was like the muffled boom of a drum. Then they were at close quarters and Edward found his opponent's weight and strength smothering him. One wild blow caught him alongside the head. It was like a blow from a club, and he went down on to the shingle in what seemed to his dazed senses a shower of rockets.

The next instant he realized that if he did not get to his feet he would be kicked to death. Shielding his face he drew his knees up and rolled across the pebbles.

The Irishman followed and launched another kick. Edward seized his foot with both hands and twisted it with all his might. The man went down with a scream. The crowd roared its approval. Edward climbed to his feet, wondering by the pain in his side if his ribs were broken.

His opponent, with a badly twisted ankle, was trying to get to his feet. Edward did not give him a chance. He dealt him a smashing full-arm swing into the face. The Irishman went down, and his second and feebler attempt to get up was met with another haymaker. Edward was merciless, and the fourth time he was hit the Irishman tossed his arms wide and fell with his bloody face buried in the stones.

There was a hearty cheer from the crowd which Edward ignored. He knew that had the other man been the victor they would have cheered him in just the same way.

Up in her room Margaret was waiting, white-faced and anxious, for her brother. When she saw him she ran up to him with a cry.

" Oh, Ned, Ned, are you hurt ? "

" No, I don't think so, Peggy. Ouch ! "

He winced as he tenderly felt his ribs, relieved to find that although they were badly bruised they were not broken. When he had washed his face and tidied himself he turned to Margaret.

" Best we get away from here, Peggy," he said. " We've attracted too much attention, I fancy."

4

Margaret next found lodgings at the " Mariner's Compass " at Orford. Frequently the old innkeeper would put her and her brother across by boat on to the North Weir where they would stroll idly along the shingle together.

One afternoon they were wandering along this desolate wilderness of shingle when they received a surprise.

" Where do you think you're off to ? " a voice bellowed at them, apparently from thin air.

The two young people stared apprehensively about them and just at that moment there was a disturbance in the shingle and a man in the uniform of the Coast Guard stood up, shaking the pebbles from his clothes.

Rubbing his arms to restore the circulation, he stalked up

to them. He looked at the brother and sister and said sternly, " You two have been watched for a spell now. What's your business ? What are you doing over here ? "

" Oh, we're just having a day or two by the sea," Edward answered somewhat lamely. Margaret nodded in support.

The coastguard, a fair, red-faced, blocky man with cold blue eyes, obviously disbelieved them.

" A day or two by the sea, eh ! Well, you were several days at the ' Beach House ' afore you come here. Ay, I know about the fight, young man. You were at the ' Sun Inn,' Bawdsey, before that. And you were making enquiries for Will Laud. Come along o' me. This is a matter for Lieutenant Barry."

Both Margaret and Edward were relieved at this. Lieutenant Barry knew them both.

Back across the river the coastguard marched them both into the Coast Guard station. Barry was sitting at a table writing when they entered.

He looked up with a slight smile on his face. " Well, Miss Catchpole, I hope you are enjoying your stay." He nodded across at the waiting coastguard. " All right, Ward ; you can get back to your station. Keep your eyes lifted."

After the man had saluted and gone out Barry turned and spoke to Edward.

" You and your sister have been under observation ever since you arrived on the coast. What exactly are you doing round here ? "

Margaret drew a deep breath. " Looking for Will Laud, sir," she said.

Barry gave her a keen glance.

" I understand he has received an amnesty and has left the free trade."

" So he has, or at least had . . . but, well, you see . . ." Margaret told Barry of the night when Laud had tossed the money down and vanished.

Barry stared at the table in front of him for a while before speaking. Then he looked up.

" So you think that Laud has returned to his old ways and companions. Well, Margaret, for your sake I hope that he has not. But if you are really minded to find out . . . well, you can."

Margaret looked across the table eagerly. " How ? " she asked.

" I heard about you fighting for your sister at the ' Beach

House,'" he said to Edward. "It seems that you've grown into a man, Ned. If you will, there's man's work that you can do that will serve both your Country and yourself."

"What's that, sir?"

"You have already met my man Ward hidden in the shingle on the North Weir. I have thirty others along the top of the high-water mark, all buried in the shingle up to their necks, poor devils. They are watching. The *Alde* has been sighted backing and filling off Hollesley Bay this last three nights. They are waiting for the clearing signal so that they can land their goods. You may or may not know that since Laud left the gang John Luff has been in command of the brig. There's not one of my lads but would give their right hand to get Luff, dead or alive, after what he did to their mate Last. I suppose you know the story?"

Edward nodded eagerly without speaking, his eyes gleaming with excitement.

"Apart from the fact that my lads are set on vengeance," Barry continued, "the Government have given strict orders that Luff is to be taken, dead or alive. I shall be content to see him dead, without risking any more of my men. Luff is the greatest menace this coast has ever known. Yesterday the Chief Inspecting Commander of East Suffolk, Captain Tyrell, told me that I might have a free hand in the matter. I have the power to swear you in to the service of the Coast Guard for this affair, if you are willing."

Edward Catchpole grasped the offer with both hands. Here was a heaven-sent opportunity to assist in ending the life of that filthy murderer who attempted to kill his beloved sister, and now Lieutenant Barry had asked if he was willing to join in the attack on him! Silently Edward thanked the big Irishman from whose uncouth remark this opportunity had arisen.

"Yes, sir," he said. "That I am."

When Barry had sworn him into the service he explained that from a large number of seemingly unimportant scraps of information he had been able to piece together a general picture of the smugglers' organization and their system of warning which governed the landing of goods. He gave Edward an outline of the system and then detailed his own plan for the capture of the gang.

"When you first arrived here you were suspected of being the person detailed to hoist a white flag on the North Weir, abreast of the old shepherd's cottage on Havergate Island."

Catchpole looked surprised. " Shepherd's cottage, sir ? "

" Yes, it's a half-timbered, ancient place of lath and plaster, barely visible because it lays in a dip. However, it has a small window in the eastern gable from which lights have frequently been seen flashing, lights which have been answered out at sea. The old shepherd who lives there, a fellow named Maud, is suspected of being in the employ of Luff and his gang.

" But back to the business in hand. Because this white flag has not been shown the *Alde* will not land her cargo, neither will that crafty devil Luff come ashore. He smells a rat. Now what I want you to do is this. I want you to take a tall pole and a white sheet over on to the North Weir. When you get the tallest tree in Sudbourne Grove and the old cottage on Havergate in line, plant the flag upright in the shingle. On the way you will pass my men buried in the stones. They will challenge you. You will say ' King George for ever,' and they will answer, ' Hurrah, pass on.' "

Barry went to a cupboard and brought out a gallon jar of rum.

" Take this along with you and give every man a good strong nip. They'll need it. It's a Godless job they have out there, shrammed to the bone. When you have planted the staff and flag take up a position a fair way from the spot. I fancy that Maud will try to remove the signal, for he knows we are here. It's your task to stop him." He went to a case on the wall. " Here are two pistols. Don't use them unless your own life is in danger—the flashes will make the crew of the *Alde* suspicious. If you can get the better of the old man by cunning, so much the better. Here's a whistle. Maud is an old man but he is strong too. If he's too much for you give a blast and someone will come to your help. If and when you get the better of him, lash him up, then ferry him back across the Narrows to the Red Cottage and make him fast to his own bed. You will have to stop with him until it is dark. When dusk has fallen light an oil-lamp— you'll find it under the bed in the cottage—and place it in the little window in the eastern gable. When you have done this, come back across to the North Weir again. Make sure to sink the boat's anchor into the edge of the saltings and shove her off the whole length of the painter, or she'll be high and dry when the tide falls. Then get you up to the high-water mark and bury yourself in the stones like the others.

" It will be cold work the waiting, maybe the worst part

of all. But the smugglers want that boat to get their contraband across to the old cottage, which I believe is the receiving
place. When they see the boat is there they'll start to carry
their goods across. By this time all my men who will have
seen them land will be converging on them. As soon as they
are out of the boat and have the goods on their backs give
two long blasts on your whistle. I won't ask you to join in
the battle ; it'll like to be bloody work while it lasts. I've
given all my men orders to direct their fire at Luff ; if he goes
down the fight'll turn in our favour. When you blow that
whistle keep your head down. There'll be balls as thick as
wasps buzzing tonight, if I'm not mistaken." Barry hesitated
for a fraction of a second. "If I should be . . . unlucky,
there's a letter in my cartridge-box addressed to my brother.
See it is posted, lad."

Barry turned to Margaret, who had been sitting quietly,
saying nothing all the while.

"I trust you will not mind me asking your brother to venture
out with us tonight ? "

Margaret shook her head.

"No—but I wish that I could be with him too ! "

"I'm sorry," Barry said gently, "the North Weir at night
is no place for a young lady, and tonight above all nights."

Back in the "Mariner's Compass" Edward said hesitantly
to his sister, "Supposing . . . Laud is with the others, Peggy ? "

She turned her head away so that her brother could not see
the quivering of her lips.

"If he's there . . . well, I . . ."

Edward put his arm round his sister's shoulders.

"I wish you had married John Barry, Peggy. The Barrys
are fine folk."

5

As dusk fell Catchpole put on his greatcoat and pulled
gently across from Orford to the North Weir, taking with him
the jar of rum, the whistle and the two pistols. He had just
one thing in his mind, to do all that was possible to help Barry
get Luff. For only when Luff was dead would Margaret,
and himself to a lesser degree, be safe.

He shivered as he crunched up the shingle. It was almost
dark and the breeze blowing in from the sea was icy. Breakers
boomed hollowly up the steep shingle to the seaward side of
the North Weir and pebbles dislodged by his passing sounded

oddly like pursuing footsteps. He glanced over his shoulder. Down on Lanthorn Marshes the " hobby lanterns " were flickering balefully. He remembered the tale of one old shepherd who believed that the marsh fires were small lamps carried by supernatural beings. The old man had sworn that one dark night he had taken a lantern down to the marsh to get his flock, and one of the bearers of the " hobby lanterns," incensed at the lantern he was carrying, had dashed it from his hand, leaving him alone and almost terrified out of his wits in the middle of the dangerous marsh.

All manner of tales came to Catchpole's mind as he strode along the eerie beach.

Suddenly a voice startled him. " Halt, who goes there ! "

" King George for ever."

" That's right, m' hearty. Now how about drinking his health. Christ, but I'm clammed wi' cold ! "

Edward poured a stiff tot of rum into the man's can, wished him good-night and then went along the beach from coast-guard to coastguard. Next, he got his bearings as instructed and thrust the long pole and its white flag, as big as a bed-sheet, into the pebbles. The flag streamed out immediately, flapping in ghostly fashion and adding to the eeriness of the scene.

This done, Edward worked himself into the shingle. The pebbles were cold and wet but he wriggled himself in until only his head was visible, glad that he had thought to bring his heavy greatcoat. Even with this the cold soon struck through and the pebbles worked themselves into all manner of uncomfortable places. He found his teeth chattering, partly from cold, partly from excitement.

As he strained his eyes to seaward he fancied that he could see the dark hull of the brig some distance off shore. She had come in about a mile off the beach with her tops'ls brailed up.

For an hour nothing happened. Then the waiting man plainly heard the bleat of sheep and the crunch of their hooves in the stones.

The shepherd, a tall, powerfully built old man, was walking slowly along at the back of his flock. He was whistling softly to himself, but when he saw the treacherous flag he stopped. Glancing swiftly around he caught hold of the staff and started to work it out of its bed.

Catchpole was up and out of the pebbles in an instant.

" Hey there ! " he cried. " Do you let that flag alone."

Maud started violently—he had thought that he was alone on the North Weir—but soon regained his composure and started to walk towards Edward with a long rangy stride.

"Why did you put that flag there, young man?"

"Never you mind. Those were my orders."

"Orders, eh? Now I'm going to take that flag down. It frightens my sheep, a-flappin' about there."

"Leave it alone. You can't take it down."

"Oh, I can't, eh? Who's going to stop me, bor?"

"I am, if I have to."

The shepherd's mahogany features crinkled into a mocking grin in the gloom. He rolled up his sleeves, exposing knotty, muscular fore-arms.

"You! Why, I've et better things'n you afore break'ust."

Edward thought swiftly. This was a time for guile.

"I don't doubt that," he said. "But let's not fight. I tell you; we'll have a friendly trial of strength. Put your crook down on the beach and let's see who can pull the other across it. If you get me over, then you can take the flag down."

Maud sized up the slight frame of his opponent, just visible in the dusk. "Done," he said.

He laughed as he threw the crook down on the shingle; it fell parallel with the sea.

Edward was still playing for time.

"Not that way," he said. "You're down the beach. It would be easier for you to pull me down than me pull you up. Let's have it fair." He stooped down. "Look, I'll show you how . . ."

He seized the crook and suddenly hooking the shepherd's ankle tugged with all his might.

The man went down with a crash, and caught his head on the stones with such force that the senses were knocked clean out of him. Edward hurriedly drew some cords from his pocket and lashed his opponent's wrists and ankles. He then went through Maud's pockets. He found another white flag wrapped round the unconscious man, and a pair of short-barrelled but large-bore pistols.

Whilst Edward was searching him, the old man recovered his senses and started to struggle and bawl for help at the top of his voice. Edward put the muzzle of one of the pistols to his big nose.

"Hold your bloody row, do I'll splatter your brains all

over the stones," he threatened. There was such menace in his voice that the old man's mouth snapped shut like a rat-trap. "What the devil would an honest shepherd want wi' tools like that, eh? Answer me."

Getting no reply, Catchpole thrust the shepherd's crook between the bound man's wrists and started to drag him over the stones towards the waiting boat.

"Wait till John Luff gets his hooks on you, you bastard," snarled the shepherd.

Edward laughed with grim elation.

"After tonight I fancy John Luff won't get his hooks on anyone ever again," he said. He thought of the attempted murder of his sister. Rancour hardened his voice as he continued. "And what is more, if you don't shut your clack I'll drop you in the river just as you are, damn you."

He dragged the bound man nearer the water's edge.

"In fact, if Lieutenant Barry gets hurt tonight that's just what I will do. You had that flag wrapped round you. Is the crew of the *Alde* coming ashore tonight?"

There was no answer. Catchpole drew the shepherd to the very edge of the steep bank that fell away down to the racing tide. One shove and he'd be gone.

"This is your last chance," he said. "Are the smugglers coming ashore tonight?"

The old man's voice was sullen. "They'll be ashore a'right wi' that damned flag flappin' there," he said.

"Who is coming, Will Laud or Whispering Luff?"

"Luff. Laud's dead."

Catchpole squatted down on his haunches beside the bound man.

"Did you say Laud was dead?"

Maud nodded in the light of the rising moon. "Ay, he's dead right enough."

"How do you know? What happened?"

"Loosen these thongs up a bit and I'll tell you," the shepherd said, struggling with his bonds.

"Those cords are all right, if you stop straining against them."

Catchpole dragged the heavy bulk of the shepherd to the waiting boat and laboriously lifted him in.

The boat was a large, flat-bottomed clumsy affair, dung mired and partially filled with water. It was used to ferry the sheep and sometimes cattle backwards and forwards between the mainland and the North Weir. Catchpole had some difficulty in managing the unwieldy craft, but at last he reached Havergate and tied up alongside the little hard leading to the shepherd's cottage.

The moon was brilliant now and lit up forlorn Havergate like daylight from Cuckold's Point to Dove Point.

The island itself was low and marshy. Roughly the shape of a haunch of mutton, it was protected all round by a broad sea-wall. The only habitation on it was the shepherd's cottage, called by some the "Red House" because of its red roof, visible far out to sea.

This strange old place was a timber frame house, its lower half blocked in red brick, fretted and pitted by the salt winds to which it was so pitilessly exposed ; its upper storey built of lath and plaster, criss-crossed with rotting timbers.

Its aspect was southerly, since whoever had built the cottage had realized that it would be impossible for it to face to the east and the ceaseless bitterness of the North Sea. At the western end a chimney stack ran up the outer face of the wall, and against its base stood a large stone trough overhung by a twisted, stunted alder tree. The trough was used for catching rain water ; and this was preferred to the water from the nearby well, which, contaminated by the salt that seeped up through the marshy soil of the island, was quite undrinkable.

At the eastern end, in the apex of the gable, was a small window, no more than two feet square, which gave one of the upstairs rooms a view over the North Weir and the sea. Like the other windows in the house, it was glazed with thick, bottle-green glass.

Here on this desolate island lived the shepherd, together with his charges and a few half-starved rabbits, dark-furred hares and rats. A lonely place where the icy wind hustled across the beds of withered samphire, and stirred the sea-pinks and purple sea-lavender. Havergate was a desert of coarse grass, marrams and dykes ; and here and there miserable gorse bushes overshadowed the patches of shingle that broke like scabs through the vegetation.

When Catchpole had carefully secured the flat-bottomed boat he pulled the shepherd through the little wooden wicket to the threshold of his own cottage.

Edward stood for a while getting his breath before he spoke.

"Where's your key, old 'un ? "

The shepherd was wet and chilled and was anxious to get

inside out of the cold wind. " Under the door sill," he said sullenly.[1]

Catchpole groped in the cavity beneath the door step, and his fingers came into contact with the big key. He thrust it into the lock and turned. The lock functioned with a protesting groan. The salt winds from the sea had not spared it.

Pushing the door open, he dragged Maud inside and lifted him on to a bed. Then he lit the lamp on the table and turned to his captive. " I'm something sharp set," he said. " Is there any food here ? "

The shepherd, realizing that he was completely in Catchpole's power, was tractable.

" Over there in a cupboard," he said, nodding towards the fireplace.

There were many wall cupboards in the strange old place and Catchpole opened several before he found one containing some cold boiled bacon, bread, cheese and a bottle of brandy.

The captive on the bed looked hungrily at the fare.

" I could do wi' a bite and sup m'self, bor."

" So you shall have, do you lay there quiet until I've finished."

When Catchpole had finished his meal he fed the old man, morsel at a time, on the point of his knife, broaching the question of Laud as he did so.

" Did you-together say Will Laud was dead ? "

Maud shrugged.

" Your guess is as good as mine," he said. " I heerd that the pair on 'em set out for a stroll. Only Luff went back to the ' Jolly Sailor.' He say that Will took a boat and went up to Aldeburgh to see his uncle. If you ask me Laud's dead and rotting at the bottom o' some dyke. Some o' them dykes 'int got no bottom. But what made me really think Laud was dead was the way Luff took on one day a while arter.

" I got a hail fr'n the North Weir and it was Luff. He's a right testy one that. I got across as fast as I could but that worn't fast enough for him.

" ' Come on, man, don't be all bloody night,' he whispered, suthen savage.

" Well, when he got over here I say to him, casual-like, ' Where's Cap'n Laud these days, sir ? ' You should 'a

---

[1] Readers might be interested to know that when the ruins of the old cottage on Havergate were searched recently a huge old hand-wrought key was found in that exact position.

seen Luff then. He wor over at me like a great hound ! I'm no weakling but he caught me by the jacket and lifted me up like a babe. Then he fare hissed at me, ' What do you care about Laud ? Have you heard anything about him, then ? ' "

The old shepherd shivered at the memory.

" He glared at me wi' them fiend's eyes o' his'n—fare shrivelled my guts he did. I managed to pass it off do he'd 'a corpsed me on the spot. Said I hadn't seen Laud f' so long I just wondered where he'd got to. After that Luff calmed down and shook his head sorrowful-like. ' No, old man, I don't think you'll see poor Will agen,' he say. ' He vanished that night I saw him at the " Jolly Sailor." Nick and Sam vanished too. The boat were found capsized in Abraham's Bosom two days arter that. The hull lot of us were supposed to have met the rest of the crew at North Weir Point that night. Old Mannel o' Boyton put me aboard after all ! ' "

The old man stopped speaking. Catchpole groped around under the bed and brought out an old oil-lamp.

" Is this your signal lamp ? "

Maud nodded, realizing that the game was up.

Whilst Edward was trimming and lighting the lamp he questioned the shepherd further.

" How many men do you fancy'll land from the *Alde* tonight ? "

" There's a big run. Mebbe twenty or so."

Catchpole climbed the tiny corkscrew stair and placed the lighted lamp in the gable window facing eastwards over the sea. He then returned to his captive.

" I'll have to leave you trussed up, both for my sake and yours," he said. " If Luff gets over here and finds you free he'll think you have betrayed him."

Catchpole went out into the cold moonlight and gently shut and locked the door.

Away in the distance Orfordness light was winking briefly. The cold sea-wind hissed dolefully in the coarse grass as Edward untied the boat and ferried it with some difficulty back across to the North Weir.

The tide was falling, so he anchored it as close to the edge of the shingle as he could and shoved it off. He realized that if the boat was stranded it might cause complications. The white flag was still flapping eerily in the moonlight and casting a wavering shadow on the stones.

A voice hailed him softly. It was Barry.

" I began to think that the old man had the better of you

until I saw the light go up in the gable-end. We can see the *Alde* plain enough. She was waiting for that signal ; the lamp confirms the flag, you see. She's standing in closer now." Barry pointed to the black silhouette of the brig about a mile or less off shore. " Now go you along the beach about a hundred paces and lay down. And when you blow that whistle take care to keep your head down."

Edward walked back along the beach whilst Barry went back to his men, all of whom had crept out of the shingle and were crouching in a little hollow in the pebbles. Barry glanced in the direction of the shepherd's cottage. The light in the gable window shone like a small, yellow star. On the beach the flag flapped ghostly white beneath the pock-faced moon.

Barry addressed his waiting men in a low voice.

" Now you all know what to do. Don't let Luff get to grips or some of us'll lose the number of our mess. It's like broad daylight ; you can't mistake Luff. As soon as he jumps out of the boat give him a volley "—his voice was grim—" a volley for our mate, Jim Last. Don't do anything prematurely. Watch for my signal. Fire when my sword drops. Those that are left aboard the brig are due for an unpleasant surprise too. H.M.S. *Rattlesnake* is waiting in the lee of Orfordness for her."

The wind had freshened and the breakers were roaring up the steep shingle face which lay to seaward, sounding hollow and forlorn. Aboard the silent, unlighted *Alde* standing in close to the shore, Ezra Coffin was saying quietly to John Luff, " Maud took a long time getting that light up, Cap'n Luff."

Luff was peering towards the beach. " Maud won't take chances," he said, and turned towards the silent crew. " Get your boat-slings fast, heave your boat over and load up."

6

On the beach Edward Catchpole watched the brig. He neither blinked nor lowered his eyes and the intensity of his gaze and the cold wind caused tears to run down his cheeks. Suddenly there was a step in the shingle behind him. Not having time to get to his feet he rolled on his side and drew and cocked one of the pistols.

" Who is that ? Come forward or I'll shoot ! "

He thought it was the old shepherd escaped from his bonds. However, it was a woman's voice that answered him.

" It's me, Ned : Peggy ! "

He uncocked the pistol and shook his head. " Well, as you're here," he said, " come and lay quiet. You never ought to have come. There'll be bloodshed directly. How did you get over ? "

" I'm sorry, Ned. I just had to come. I borrowed a boat and rowed myself over."

" Do you be quiet then ! "

Brother and sister lay side by side shivering with cold and excitement. The gulls had long since ceased their mewing and the only sound was the hollow roar of the sea and the harsh murmur of the wind. Edward suddenly caught his sister's arm.

" Do you hear anything, Peggy ? "

They both held their breath so that their breathing would not interfere with their hearing.

The sound grew louder every moment. It was the soft " thud, thud, thud " of heavy oars in wooden thole-pins.

Luff expertly brought the boat broadside-on into the breakers alongshore. She was almost gunwale deep with contraband. He made a gesture with his drawn hanger indicating that the boat was to be hove up as high as possible.

The men worked silently, and as each breaker splintered into flying spray against their boat they used its force to aid them. As soon as the boat was high enough up the beach they started to unload her, each man carrying a sack or anker of spirits on his back. Twice they returned to the boat before it was unloaded. The last two men gathered up the boat's oars and removed the thole-pins.

Catchpole lifted his head and gave two long shrill blasts on the whistle.

The smugglers instantly dropped whatever they were holding and their hands flew to pistols and muskets. Caught all unawares they glanced up the beach. Lieutenant Barry stood there with his men, one rank kneeling, the other standing.

With a roar Luff leaped up the beach, his hanger sparkling in the moonlight. As he did so Barry's sword fell. There was a sudden blast of fire that woke the startled sleepers in Orford village. Disturbed fowl flew screaming overhead. Struck by at least twenty musket-balls Luff went to his knees ; and then was up again, blood splotching his face and clothing in the moonlight.

Then coastguards and smugglers were at it, a hurly-burly of cut and thrust in the moonlight which soon glimmered on wet, red steel.

Suddenly a cry went up from the smugglers. " The cap'n is down. Run for it."

There was a furious mêlée about the boat and the smugglers, unable to float her, ran along the beach, some of them going down before a volley of shots which followed them.

Luff lay face down in the shingle, still alive.

Barry mustered his crew and found two killed and seven wounded, one of them seriously. He pointed to Luff. " Pick him up and bring him with the others over to the shepherd's cottage on Havergate Island."

Those of the smugglers who had not been shot or cut down were herded together under guard.

Edward Catchpole and his sister came running along the shingle. Margaret was shaking from head to foot—the swift bloodiness of the business had unnerved her.

Her first words were addressed to Barry.

" Is Will . . . ? "

Barry shook his head curtly. His voice was grim and uncompromising. " No, young woman, Laud isn't here. He may be aboard the brig. In any case we shall soon know. Listen."

From seaward came the rolling thunder of gunfire where H.M.S. *Rattlesnake* was engaging the smugglers left aboard the *Alde*.

7

Once across the Narrows to Havergate Island the casualties of both sides were laid out in the kitchen of the shepherd's cottage. The shepherd was freed of his bonds and John Luff was laid on his bed. Luff was almost shot to pieces, but still his inhuman vitality strove against death and the striving was a ghastly thing to see. Long shudders ran over him and his powerful hands ripped the bedclothes to ribbons. Looking up he saw Barry and Edward Catchpole, with Margaret peering fearfully over his shoulder. He lifted his dark, blood-matted head, and his voice was the whisper of a whisper, yet still charged with menace.

" I'll be waiting in hell for you, Barry," he said. " Laud's there . . . waiting . . . for me." The mad, flecked eyes turned to Margaret. "Damn you, girl . . . get . . . back . . .

to your . . . well." The sweat was pouring from his face, furrowing the blood ; and for a while the dying man closed his eyes. Suddenly he opened them again and smiled. " I see you there, Last . . . I'm . . . dying a man . . . more'n ever . . . you did."

The coastguard who had been seriously wounded looked up appealingly at Barry.

" Sir, for God's sake shift me to another room. Away from that . . ."

Barry nodded and two of the coastguards carried their wounded comrade into the other room.

Luff stopped his ravings for a while and glared around him, showing no recognition of the appalled watchers ; then he started to rave again.

" You there, Riches . . . did you find a soft bed . . . in the lime-kiln ? "

To the fearful watchers it seemed that the deranged mind of the dying man saw something other than the mere ghosts of his victims.

Suddenly a white form dashed itself against the lighted window of the cottage.

Luff's hands went like claws before his bulging, bloodshot eyes. " The death bird [1] . . . It's come for me . . ."

His body arched in a violent tremor. A trickle of blood ran from the corner of his mouth. The straining body collapsed on the bed. Whispering John Luff was dead.

The silent room in the old shepherd's cottage on Havergate Island seemed to take into the very mouldering plaster of its walls the quality of Luff's passing. The fire fell lower and the crackle of burning sticks seemed as loud as pistol shots.

Outside the window the vagrant gull still dashed itself fruitlessly at the glass, attracted by the light within. Edward Catchpole tightened his arm about the almost fainting form of his sister.

Barry wiped the cold sweat from his forehead. " My God," he said, " what a death. Here, lad, bring your sister into the other room. Then we'll get back to Orford. I'll be glad to get away from this evil place."

Outside the dawn wind sent chilly fingers rummaging harshly through marrams, sueada bushes, sedges and samphire beds. It rippled the surface of the pulks and moaned across dykes and rotting bridges.

[1] An ancient East Anglian belief that a white bird comes to take away the souls of the dying.

It ruffled the feathers of curlew roosting on the river's edge, and made the marsh hare, despite its thick fur, crouch lower in its " squat." It whimpered around the shepherd's cottage and went off to sea.

The ebb tide of the river was gathering weight and speed, clucking and chuckling amid the slimy stones at the base of the sea-wall around Havergate Island. It receded slowly from a million tiny crevices, haunt of the green crabs, and lapped with ever-growing speed around ancient mud and weed-fouled piles protruding from the rapidly appearing mud flats. It swirled in a dozen small but powerful whirlpools around Chantry Point, eddying back upon the main stream so that for half a mile up-river vessels going towards Slaughden Quay had a fair tide, despite the ebb. It swept down Butley River, eddying and rippling louder and louder ; rushed past King's Marshes and around Stonyditch Point in a miniature over-fall, then slid like a steel-grey ribbon past the Quay at Orford out into the " Narrows " abreast of Havergate Island, until finally it sluiced past the steep shingle flanks of the North Weir on its last desperate race to the sea and the thundering maelstrom of the bar at North Weir Point.

Inside the shepherd's cottage one of the coastguards looked at his watch, shivered slightly and gestured towards the silent, shrouded form of Luff.

" That wind, sir. 'Twas a dead man's whisper. Luff went out wi' the first o' the ebb."

As he spoke a rumbling bellow of sound from seaward shook the doors and windows. For a second the brightening eastern horizon was made brighter yet by a brilliant flash of orange light.

Silhouetted against the flash was a mass of flying wreckage.

8

Two days later Margaret and her brother left Orford for Nacton, both of them in fairly good spirits, in spite of the gruesome episode on Havergate Island. Margaret was happy because Laud was not amongst those captured or killed, Edward carefree because the threat of Luff no longer hung over them. It seemed hardly possible that Luff should be dead ; even now he could hardly believe it.

He was less sanguine over Laud's survival than his sister, and he advised her not to hold too much hope of ever seeing him again.

" The old shepherd of Havergate told me that he reckoned Luff killed Laud," he said. " And in any case, the *Alde* was blown to flinders that morning. Lieutenant Barry said that the *Rattlesnake* put a broadside fair into her powder room. She went up like a mine wi' not one man left to tell the tale."

But Margaret would have none of it, and refused to be upset by this almost certain evidence of her lover's death. To accept it would mean the irrevocable step into the void of despair. Death, she felt, would be easier to bear than that living blackness. Every fibre of her being cried out in protest against the assumption of his death, and created within her an iron conviction of his being alive.

" No, Ned," she said, shaking her head. " I'm certain that Will is still living. So many times in the past I have been told that he has either been killed or captured ! I know he never went back to his old crew. If ever he were killed I should feel it here, here "—she clasped her hands fervently over her heart—" I know I would, even if he were at the other end of the earth."

Edward Catchpole, baffled by the peculiar ways of women, shook his head in bewilderment and said no more.

9

So obsessed was Margaret by the need for finding Will that she did not go back to St. Margaret's Green.

In the meantime, Mrs. Cobbold anxiously made enquiries all round the countryside for her servant. She sent a messenger to Brandiston, in case by chance Margaret had gone back to her uncle's house. Another was sent to the cottage on Nacton Heath, only to find it empty—the two men happened to be at their work, whilst Margaret chanced to be at Priory Farm trying to glean some news of Laud there.

But Mrs. Cobbold could not afford to be without a head nursemaid—the under-nursemaid was insufficiently experienced to be in sole charge—and so, no word having been received from Margaret, she was forced to engage another servant.

She took this step with a heavy heart, for she had grown fond of Margaret. She admired her courage and her determination ; and while she thought it misplaced, she marvelled at the steadfastness of her love for Laud. Further, she valued her as a servant, and as a nurse for her children she could not overpraise her.

Now that Margaret had disappeared she feared that some evil had befallen her, either at the hands of the smugglers or as a result of the shock sustained at the time of her attempted murder. Neither did she totally exclude the possibility that Margaret had found Laud and had gone off with him, but she was sure that Margaret would have sent word to her about it.

It was therefore with mixed feelings that she learnt one afternoon that Margaret had returned ; but uppermost in her was a feeling of relief that the girl was safe.

She asked that Margaret be sent into the parlour. When she saw her former servant Mrs. Cobbold was shocked at her altered appearance.

Margaret was still an immensely attractive woman, but constant anxiety and repeated disappointment had etched two deep parallel lines between Margaret's eyes. The eyes themselves once so soft and lustrous had acquired a diamond-like glitter. Mrs. Cobbold stepped forward, both her hands outstretched.

" Oh, Margaret, my child," she said, " why didn't you send me some word ? I tried so hard to find out what had happened to you, but I couldn't ; and so I had to get someone to take your place. I can't send her away just because you have returned." She paused for a moment in thought. " And yet I can fit you in," she continued. " The cook has recently given me notice and I haven't yet engaged another. Would you care to fill her place when she leaves ? "

Margaret's old sparkling eagerness was gone. She seemed indifferent to the splendid opportunity that Elizabeth Cobbold was putting in her way, unappreciative of her employer's kindness and trust in her. Nevertheless, deep inside her Margaret did appreciate it, and wanted desperately to show her gratitude. But the bitter disappointments of the past weeks had built a shell around her from which there was no escaping, no reaching out to touch the hearts of others, no grasping of the hand in friendship.

" Yes, madam. When do you want me to start ? " she asked listlessly.

Mrs. Cobbold was conscious of the alteration in Margaret, conscious of the shell of hardness which she had acquired. Deep in her heart Elizabeth Cobbold felt that Margaret had suffered more than is asked of most women and her kindly nature was prepared to make every allowance for this girl whom she held in such high esteem. She therefore ignored Margaret's apparent lack of courtesy and enthusiasm.

The following week Margaret commenced work as cook of the Cobbold mansion.

There were scullery maids and kitchen maids to attend her slightest wish but Margaret was not the same happy, willing girl that had first entered Mrs. Cobbold's service. Sometimes she neglected her work and even became slovenly in her appearance and careless in her manner. She was harsh to her inferiors until they came to hate and at last even fear her. On one occasion she clouted an unfortunate scullery maid with a saucepan to such effect that the girl was laid senseless.

One day Mrs. Cobbold sent for Margaret and the good lady's voice was unusually severe when she spoke.

" Margaret, since you have returned to work here I find you negligent in your duties and your attire. Furthermore, your attitude towards your fellow servants needs improving. I am aware of the anxiety and misfortune you have suffered in the past. Nevertheless, I wish to remind you that you fill a responsible position and have a duty to discharge towards me as your employer."

Elizabeth suddenly remembered how she had Margaret to thank for the lives of her children on two occasions and the severity of her voice softened.

" Oh, my dear, I know how you must feel. I'm a woman with a woman's heart. Try for your own peace of mind and all our sakes to forget this man Laud. He's not worthy of such devotion. He'll only bring you to ruin. I know that as surely as I know that the sun will rise tomorrow."

This sudden appeal pierced through the hardness which had latterly grown on Margaret. Her lips quivered and her eyes filled with tears. She took a stumbling step forward with half lifted arms, paused and with a sob hurried back to the kitchen.

CHAPTER TWENTY-FOUR

I

WHEN Nick Segel and Sam Nye had arrived at Slaughden Quay with Laud they felt convinced that he was beyond all human aid. Lifting him with a rough tenderness from the bottom of the boat, they carried him along Slaughden Quay to the little inn that stood almost on the beach, the ancient " Three Marianers." Here they explained to the landlord that their mate had had a severe accident, and that he had an uncle living in Aldeburgh who would take care of him. This done the two men put their heads together over two " John Turners."

Nick Segel had a plan.

" Well, Sam old pardner," he said. " I think we have done all we can for Will, poor lad." He took a meditative draught and looked regretfully round at the cosy bar with its huge half-moon shaped oak settle and roaring fire. " I reckon for both our sakes it'd be as well to cut our cables for a spell. Luff'll be arter our soul cases else. We'll lay low here till nightfall, then we'll cast the small boat adrift and make for Ipswich."

It was not long before Will Laud's uncle, a boat-builder at Aldeburgh, got to hear that his nephew was lying seriously hurt in the " Three Marianers." He immediately called in a Mr. Nursey, the most skilful and emancipated surgeon living in Aldeburgh at that time. Together they went into Will's room. Laud was in a coma and when Nursey had made a thorough examination of the injury he turned to the anxiously waiting uncle.

" It is an extremely grave injury," he said. " The blow or fall crushed the skull and is exerting pressure on the brain. This pressure must be removed, otherwise he will never regain his senses. It will be necessary to trepan as soon as possible." He paused and looked gravely at Jack Laud.

" And even so I cannot tell what the results will be. He may die or possibly be—er—deranged for the rest of his life. It is a risk we shall have to take."

Jack Laud, who had more than a little affection for his nephew, nodded slowly.

" Ay, do what you think best, sir. Call in a second opinion if you deem it necessary. Expense is of no moment."

The rest of the day was spent in preparing the unconscious man for the operation and the next morning Mr. Nursey used his trephine.

Despite the fact that he was a busy man Mr. Laud spent a lot of time by the bedside of his nephew, anxiously awaiting for him to regain consciousness and possibly throw some light on the manner in which he received his injury.

Nursey had told him frankly that although his nephew had survived the operation that the outcome was still doubtful. He was brooding on these things when a weak voice from the bed startled him.

" Hullo, uncle Jack. Where the devil have I got to ? "

Jack Laud jumped to his feet, his seamed and weather-beaten face alight with relief.

" Will, my boy," he said, " you've had an accident. But you're all right now. Don't talk. I'll tell you all about it later."

Will smiled sleepily and lay back.

Day by day the injured man gained in strength until at last Mr. Nursey gave permission for him to be moved by carriage to his uncle's small but comfortable house in King Street, Aldeburgh.

Jack Laud lived alone except for a woman who acted as a housekeeper, so although the house was small there was ample room for the two men. The elder man, knowing his nephew's great love of the sea, gave him the front bedroom which looked out over it.

Will spent much of his time gazing seaward. He tried to read but found the effort gave him a severe headache. Headaches in fact worried him frequently. They were not the usual normal dull ache, but something that came like a thunderbolt, as vicious and intense as a summer tempest and of such pain that it set him, head between hands, weeping like a child. Between these attacks he was never free from a sense of deep depression, a feeling of disaster looming in the near future.

One evening his uncle and he were sitting looking out across the sea. " You never told me," he said quietly, " what happened that day at Slaughden, uncle."

Jack Laud took his pipe out of his mouth and wrinkled his kindly, faded blue eyes.

" I wish I knew more about it myself, lad," he said. " All I can tell you is what the tapman at the ' Three Marianers ' told me. He said that two seamen carried you up from Slaughden Quay, saying that you'd had an accident. They vanished the same night. Can't you remember anything at all that passed ? "

Laud wrinkled his forehead with effort.

" Be damned if I can, uncle. All that I can remember is going across from Orford to the North Weir for a breather. After that memory fails."

The elder man got to his feet and closed the window : the breeze from the sea was cold. He took rather longer over this action than seemed necessary. When he had finished fumbling he turned back to his nephew.

" Look'ee, Will "—he paused as if uncertain how to continue—" have you any plans for yourself when your head's mended ? "

" Plans, uncle ? What is there for me to do ? "

" Do, lad ! Why, marry. Beget yourself some children so that you don't suffer loneliness as I have done until you came. Have you had no word of Margaret ? "

Laud got slowly to his feet and turned his gaze towards the sea where the moon was rising, a huge orange sphere.

" Margaret, you say, uncle Jack. Why, she's just a light mawther. Nothing to her. . . ." He told his uncle of the night when he had taken the prize money to Margaret and of his unwelcome reception.

The elder Laud pondered on this for a while. " My belief is that there was something seriously amiss, lad. Say what you like, I've heard some rum yarns o' that girl and it seems to me that whatever else she is she's no loose woman. You ought not to ha' flung off all in a frap as you did that night without waiting for an explanation. When you are yourself again, why not pay her a visit ? "

" That's likely ! Take it from me she's married by now. Mebbe to someone o' the Cobbolds' choosing."

Jack Laud dropped the subject of Margaret for the time being. " What about yourself, Will ? " he asked.

Will shrugged indifferently. " What plans should I have, uncle ? What is there to do ? The Service—I had my bellyful of that. The only thing I can think of is to earn a pittance as master or mate coasting, aboard some dirty little coastal craft carrying coal, tallow or hides or some other stinking cargo. That, or the free trade again."

"Keep your mind off the free trade, Will : it's caused you enough grief already. Look here, lad, I'm a solitary man. When I die there is no one in the place left to carry on the business, except mebbe you !" The elder Laud's voice became earnest. "Why don't you come into the ship-building with me ? It's a pleasant life on the river at Slaughden. And there's many a worse little town to spend one's days in than Aldeburgh. It's quiet—I know that—but even though I've been a solitary man all my days I've been happy here. I've grown to love the old town, more'n I can ever tell. You could too if you lived here." He leaned across the table to his nephew. "Come, what d'ye say, Will ? "

Laud felt a genuine surge of affection towards his uncle. In any case, all the old restless fire seemed gone from him these days. Working away in the ship-building yard at Slaughden would be quiet. Maybe in time he might even find there some measure of peace and forgetfulness. Slaughden was a pleasant enough little hamlet. To be sure the tide sometimes threatened it, but then what place anywhere along this coast from the Wash to Walton wasn't sometimes flooded ? Laud squeezed his uncle's hand. "You're good to me, uncle Jack," he said.

2

For the first week or two, Will did little other than potter around his uncle's shipyard. He found it pleasant. He had always liked the atmosphere of Slaughden—the small, friendly whitewashed cottages, the cosy "Three Marianers " with its excellent ale—and there was always some vessel or the other discharging merchandise on to Slaughden Quay, mostly dairy produce from Holland. In the shipyard there was something soothing in the measured swish of the planes and the leisurely thud of caulking mallets. The smell of newly-cut wood and shavings mingled pleasantly with the odour of the river.

Many times he had sailed a craft all careless as to the hours of love and labour that went into its being, and he now found an increasing interest in watching a fine vessel come to life under his uncle's skilful directions.

He would stand for hours watching a sturdy craft grow from nothing.

He watched the oaken keel laid in two pieces and scarphed and bolted ; then the raising of the carefully chosen stem-piece and apron and the spacing of the vessel's floors. Next the stern-post would be bolted into position and the ribs scarphed along between stem and stern. After that the keelson would be bolted into place to give strength to the vessel. The shelf would then be laid along the ribs and the beams bolted athwartships, all the bolting being done with stout copper bolts. After this stanchions would be bolted between beams and decks—and the skeleton of the vessel was complete.

Then the planking would commence. The hog-strake of elm would be laid first, followed by the rest of the planking of either oak or pine. Next the decks would be laid along the beams, and all seams caulked with oakum and carefully pitched. Lastly the rails would be bolted into their place together with the taffrail. Then the bulwarks would be bolted over all.

Jack Laud's craft were noted the whole length and breadth of the coast for their strength, beauty and seaworthiness. It was instantly obvious even to the most casual idler why the craft built at Slaughden shipyard were of such excellent quality.

Jack Laud personally superintended every step of his vessels' construction, from bolting of deadwood to apron to the stepping of a mast.

Although Will preferred sailing ships to building them, his uncle's enthusiasm soon infected him, and he grew to look forward to each morning, when he saw with new vision the work he had helped complete the night before.

Thoughts of Margaret were faint in his mind. If he was not truly happy the work gave him bodily fatigue and he slept. The violent headaches were not so frequent now that he spent so much of his time in the open air.

As his uncle had said, he grew to love Aldeburgh. Not only was the small straggling town by the sea ; it was *of* the sea.

Saturday was market day in the market square around the old Moot Hall, and on market day there was always some diversion. One day it would be a dishonest butcher in the stocks for selling tainted meat by candlelight : another day it would be a beggar woman at the whipping post. Not so brutal, this, as it might seem, for the constable was a humane man and did little other than curl the lash round the woman's back. After half a dozen easy strokes she and her brats would be fed at the town's expense.

When the last bell of the market had sounded its warning that all stalls should be shut on penalty of fine, Laud would wend his way down the old straggling thoroughfare. This was composed mostly of fishermen's and pilots' cottages, some of them hovels which in any other setting would have been sordid in the extreme. Sprinkled among the houses was a fair number of inns and taverns of all types, from the lordly " White Lion " to the questionable " Boar." Laud, however, preferred to climb the town steps to the " King's Head " ale-house on the low sandy cliff at the back of the town. Why he drank his pot of beer at the " King's Head " Will could never really say, for it was a dismal little place. Perhaps it was because the seafaring fraternity used it. It was more for the company than the beer he went there, at last to go home to supper, a smoke, and bed, with the sound of the sea purring on the pebbles coming through the open window.

CHAPTER TWENTY-FIVE

I

UNCLE and nephew stood on the slip-way at Slaughden admiring the hull of a newly-completed cutter. The vessel had been given its first coat of black paint and the labourers were greasing its keel with rancid mutton fat on wads of oakum.

Jack Laud ran his hand across his grizzled head and smiled. " Well, that's finished her, Will," he said to his nephew. " Her suite of sails is ready in the loft. Get her mast shipped and her deck furniture and ship's chandlery aboard and she's ready to be launched." He turned to a nearby foreman. " Jed, get a strop around that spar and we'll ship it into the tabernacle."

The man did as he was bid, whilst Will climbed aboard the new craft ready to guide the butt of the mast into position. When the strop was fast two men on the lifting derrick hove slowly away.

The heavy spar was rising into the air when suddenly Will called across to his uncle with the urgency of fear in his voice. " That spar . . . the strop's slipping . . . Lower away and get a cat's-paw in it . . . shorten it . . . *look out* ! "

What Will foresaw happened, too late for him to do anything but stand in horrified dismay. Like a giant harpoon the spar tilted and shot from the strop straight at Jack Laud. The butt caught him square in the chest and hurled him over the edge of the slipway into the shallow mud left by the ebbing tide.

Will did not wait to climb the ladder ; he jumped clean from the cutter's deck to his uncle's side. Jack Laud's face was grey-white and a trickle of blood ran from the corner of his mouth as his nephew lifted his head from the mud.

All the work in the shipyard had ceased and the workmen stood around in a dismayed huddle. Will looked up. " One

of you get a horse," he ordered, " and ride to Aldeburgh for
Mr. Nursey as fast as you can."

Jack Laud gasped painfully. " No . . . good, Will . . .
chest crushed . . ." He smiled with such a tremendous
effort of will that his nephew turned his head aside in order to
hide his distress. The elder man's voice fell to a whisper.
" Don't take . . . on, Will. Carry on building ships . . .
keep clear o' the free trade. God bless you . . ."

Jack Laud gave a gentle sigh and died.

They carried his body up to the shop he had known and
loved. There they laid him reverently on a carpenter's bench
and covered him with a piece of canvas. Will sent for the
man who had slung the spar. " There's a week's wages," he
said, his voice controlled and icy. " For your sake and mine
don't let me see you about after today."

2

When Jack Laud's will was read his nephew found himself
the richer by several thousand pounds, several houses, including
the one in King Street, and in addition the thriving ship-
building business.

This good fortune, however, did not make up to Will for the
loss of his uncle, for he had grown genuinely fond of him.
The queer little house of wrecked ship's timbers in King
Street seemed infinitely less cosy without the old man. Sleep
was not as easy to come by as it had been, and the headaches
returned. Each night Will would wander through the tiny
house, gazing pensively at the old beams, iron-clinched and
worm-eaten. He would open cupboards and finger the
clothes of his uncle. Then he would look at the exquisite
model ships which it had been Jack Laud's pleasure to build,
a perfect miniature of every vessel that had been built on the
slipway at Slaughden.

Will knew that common sense dictated he should get rid of
all his uncle's effects, but he could not bring himself to do it.
He had dismissed the housekeeper, and the little house became
neglected and dusty, merely a place to sleep and eat in, no
longer the beloved abode of quiet and comfort it had once
been.

Regularly every night Will visited the " King's Head " ale-
house on the cliff and stayed there till it closed. The " King's
Head " was a mean little place. It did not even boast a bar,
the tapman drawing the ale straight from barrels in the cellar.

One night as Will sat staring at the damp-patched ceiling, a slopping ale-pot carelessly grasped in his hand, an excited voice came from the doorway. "Will ... Will Laud!" The next instant both his hands were grasped by Nick Segel and Sam Nye. Neither of the men made any effort to hide their joy at seeing their one-time skipper.

"God, Will lad," said Nick with genuine emotion, "we never expected to see you alive agen. How are you, man? Hey there, landlord, rum all round."

Will was touched by his former shipmates' joy at seeing him.

"Sam ... Nick! No, I never thought to be around again after that mishap." He put his hand to the silver plate in his head and wrinkled his brows. "That'll always be a mystery to me. I found myself in bed at the 'Three Marianers' at Slaughden."

The other two men exchanged swift glances. Then Nick said, "Mystery, Will? Here's no mystery, bor. Luff laid for you on Orford Heath. He clouted you across the figure-head wi' a pistol bar'l and dropped you in the Deep Dyke. Sam and me here fancied suthin' like that was about due so we follered fr'n the 'Jolly Sailor,' pulled you out and brought you, dying as we thought, to Slaughden."

Laud was still puzzled.

"John Luff did that? But why? Where is he now?"

Nick took a long draught of rum to help him with a difficult explanation.

"Lookee, Will," he said, "after you left the gang and joined the Navy Luff turned agen you. Don't ask me why. No one could follow the workings of *his* mind. He swore he'd do for you. He went up to see Margaret ..."

"Don't talk to me of that mawther!"

"But, Will ..."

"I said I don't want to speak of her, Nick!"

Nick gave Sam a significant glance. The clout with the pistol hadn't improved Will's temper.

"Tell me, Nick," Laud went on in a quieter voice, "where is John and the rest of the gang?"

Nick took another swallow of rum.

"Luff is dead ... and in hell, I hope. The others blown to shreds ..." and he went on to tell Will of all he had heard of Luff's death and the destruction of the *Alde*.

Laud listened in silence. It seemed that the old world of which he had been a part was vanishing—had vanished, leaving him high and dry, a piece of flotsam hurled up by the overwhelming tides of circumstance.

The tale of Luff's treachery and death in the old Red Cottage chilled him. He called for more rum, and listened attentively until Nick had finished.

"So you and Sam here are the only two left of the old gang," he said. "What are you doing now?"

Sam shrugged and smiled somewhat wryly. "Doin', Will?" he said. "Northen except jump fr'n ship to ship. A voyage here, a voyage there. Amsterdam, Rotterdam, Antwerp, the Low Countries. Times 'int so prosperous as they used to be, old pardner. What're you doing?"

Laud told his two old comrades of his rise in the world since the death of his uncle. Suddenly an idea came to him.

"How'd you two like a steady berth along with me?" he asked. "It'd be quiet, but a sight more comfortable than the life you-together are leading now. I've an empty house. There'd be a bed there for the pair on you." The idea seemed to please him and his voice became animated. "You, Sam, you always knew how to dish up a bit of salt hoss and dough-boys. You could cook and keep the place a bit shipshape. God knows it needs it. An' you, Nick," he said, turning to Segel and putting his arm round his shoulder. "I could do wi' a sailmaker of your skill at Slaughden."

That night the three men went back to the little house in King Street and for the first time since the death of his uncle Will was not lonely.

3

Despite the fact that Will was busy from dawn till dusk at the shipyard he could not rid his mind of John Luff. He could not believe that he was dead, he'd seemed so indestructible ; neither could he believe that it was Luff's hand that had dealt the devastating blow that had come so close to causing his own death.

The ghost of John Luff was for ever at Laud's elbow. Aft on the poop of a vessel about to be launched he would turn, half expecting to see Luff lounging on the rail in his nonchalant way, regarding him quizzically with his strange eyes. At times Laud fancied he heard the dead man's sinister, hoarse whisper.

One day in the sail-loft Will mentioned these things to Nick

Segel who was busy stitching a new suite of sails for a vessel lying off at the mooring in mid-river.

Nick laughed, but his laugh had a touch of fear in it.

"You know, Will," he said, "I have a fancy that wherever Luff is he wants you to go back into the free trade." He paused as he drew a length of sailmaker's thread through a piece of beeswax. He settled his sailmaker's palm more comfortably on his hand and then continued. "You remember old Bargood, him that was the owner of the *Alde*? Last I heard of him he wor still alive and thriving. I heard say that he keeps a log of all his ships. When one is captured he strikes its name out, the same wi' his men. It must ha' cut him deep when he had to strike out Luff's name. Oh ah, Luff was a madman sartain but a fine sailor for all that."

Segel lubricated his twine with wax again.

"Bargood was allus my idea of what a free trader really should be," he went on. "The man who gets someone else to do the dirty work whilst he sits back in comfort and safety and shovels in the golden boys." He pulled the sail across his lap and took up another bight of canvas on the sailmaker's hook. "You know, Will, you're in a grand berth for making a bit o' money on the side."

"I don't follow your drift, Nick."

"Simple, Will, simple. Be the same as Bargood."

"I've finished with those capers, Nick. The free trade has brought me enough grief to last a lifetime."

Nick Segel, however, was carried away with his dream. "I can see a craft on the stocks now, Will . . ." Nick's face was alight and there was an almost visionary look in his eyes. ". . . A lovely vessel, same rig as the *Alde*. She'd be longer wi' less beam. More draught, less freeboard, a grand clean entry. Cut-away starn to make less drag. Ay, an' I'd make such a suite o' sails for her, sails the like o' which I've never made afore. All cringles and bolt-holes double-stitched for strength. I can see har now. She'd have hollow ballast and hollow beams. There'd be secret spaces each side o' the keelson. She'd be a flyer, a ghoster. The fastest thing on the coast."

In spite of his determination never to enter the free trade again Laud, who knew Segel for a fine practical sailor, not usually given to visions, was fired by the flame of Nick's enthusiasm.

4

One day a new stem and stern reared skywards in the shipyard at Slaughden, a stem and stern more raking than anything that had ever been built there before. Nick Segel removed his sailmaker's apron and his palm and climbed down from his loft. Will Laud was superintending the bolting of an apron. Nick nodded towards the raking stem and stern. "They're wholly sheer, Will. A new idea?"

Laud nodded and there was an exuberance in his voice that had not been there for a long time. "Ay, Nick. Shall we say it is the 'ghost' of an idea?"

Day by day the *Ghost* became a reality. Day by day planes hissed and caulking mallets thudded—and the three old shipmates were the only ones who were aware of the new vessel's real purpose.

Nick Segel, feeling that the brig was his own child, put every atom of his mastery into the fashioning of her canvas. Instead of the usual seventy to eighty stitches to the yard he put in a hundred. Instead of the usual single last or seam for joining the selvedged edges of the canvas, Nick made them double for strength.

The canvas he used was the best quality obtainable. And even so, before he started to make the sails, Nick carried out rigorous tensile tests on two-foot strips of canvas.

He carefully chose the canvas for each individual sail. The jibs were made of number six canvas : the fore and mains'ls of number four. The lower fore and lower main tops'ls, and lower and upper fore and main topgallant sails were made of the lightest but strongest canvas, number seven.

One day when the planking and caulking of the *Ghost* had been completed and the tall, tapering fore- and mainmasts had been shipped, Will, Nick and Sam stood on the quayside watching.

"She'll be a taunt [1] craft when she's done," Nick said with pride. "There'll be northen on the coast to touch her for speed. You'll be able to show anything a clean pair of heels in her, Will."

Laud looked into Segel's keen blue eyes, set in a hatchet, mahogany-coloured face. "I'm not going to skipper her, Nick," he said.

"Got someone in mind, Will?"

[1] Lofty masted.

" Yes, old shipmate. You as skipper and Sam here as mate."

Segel's mouth fell open. " Why . . . what me, Will ? I'm no navigator like yourself. A plain sailor me, like our Sam here."

Laud put a hand on Nick's shoulder.

" Look, man, stow your jaw for a minute. You know as well as I do that you can find your way anywhere in the North Sea blindfold on a rafty [1] night wi' a lead line. Beside that you know the trade. I'd trust you and Sam anywhere. Why, dammit, if it hadn't been for the pair of you I'd be at the bottom of Deep Dyke. Besides, you hatched the whole matter. You can choose your own crew."

5

So came the day when the *Ghost* left Slaughden Quay and Will Laud was once more in the free trade, this time as master smuggler.

Other keels were swiftly laid and soon there was a small fleet of speedy brigs and brigantines, ostensibly respectable trading craft, but all of them running huge quantities of smuggled goods.

To offset suspicion Laud still lived in the small house in King Street. He still went daily to the shipyard. However, his clothes were of finer quality and in addition he had purchased a stable of thoroughbred horses.

One bright, windy afternoon Laud stood on the quayside at Slaughden watching the *Ghost* being warped alongside. When she was made fast he jumped aboard. Nick Segel was there to greet him.

" Good day to ye, Captain Laud, sir. Would you be pleased to step below," he said formally.

Down in the cabin and away from the crew, however, both men dropped their formal attitude. Segel pulled out a bottle. When they had discussed business and brought it to a conclusion Segel sat looking awkwardly at his captain. It was obvious that he wished to say something but did not know how to begin. He coughed and twirled his rum glass on the polished table, leaving little swirls of wetness on the wood.

Laud sensed Segel's hesitancy. " Come on, Nick man, out with it. What's wrong ? "

" Nothing wrong, master. But . . . this last trip we had
[1] Foggy.

occasion to call at Ipswich. While we were berthed I went for a jar o' beer at the ' Salutation,' the tavern in Carr Street. Just by chance I got yarning with a stranger. He said his name was John Cook, that he knew John Luff and . . . and Margaret Catchpole ; she's . . ."

Laud did not allow his henchman to finish. He was round the table in an instant. Seizing Nick by the neckcloth he ground his knuckles into his throat.

" Damn you ! I thought I told you once that I never wanted to hear her name."

Although Laud was half throttling him Nick Segel made no resistance. He looked steadfastly into his owner's face. " Choke me if you must, Will," he said, " but you can't choke truth. You'll hear it sooner or later, if not by my telling."

Angered as he was, Laud could not but recognize the sincerity in the other man's voice.

" Sorry, Nick. I didn't mean to treat you so roughly. What was it you heard ? "

Segel settled his neckerchief with a wry smile. " Christ, Will, ye've hands like grappling-irons. Well, as I said, I met this fellow Cook. A flash cove he was. Not above drinking a few free glasses though. I primed him well. He told me that Luff used to pay him to go up to St. Margaret's Green— ah, and other sailors too—to find out all they could about you from Margaret. Cook told me that he'd been there himself. He told me that Margaret is still with the Cobbolds. She's not married. He often sees her down at the dockside watching the ships . . ."

Laud, however, was not listening. He looked like a man who had just awoken from a dream. When he spoke his tones held bitter self-condemnation.

" Nick, I've been a perfect bloody fool—ay, a blind, bloody fool. You've done me a greater service than ever you'll know."

He ran up the companion of the *Ghost* two steps at a time. At the top he turned round to the gaping Nick. " I'm going to Ipswich to get Margaret, Nick man. I'll tell you everything when I get back. God bless you," he said ; and putting his hand on the rail of the *Ghost*, leaped over on to the quay and ran for his horse. Vaulting into the saddle, he thundered up the quay splattering shingle right and left.

When he was gone Nick Segel, still scratching his head, said to Sam Nye, " That clout our Will had seems to ha' driven him light, fares to me."

Sam grinned. " Not so light as you might think, Nick. That mawther's a rare fine piece, spite o' the tales Luff spread about her."

" Ay, and talking of Luff, Sam, I fancy in some quare way he loved Will. He wor wholly jealous o' that mawther. Ah, he was a rum un was Luff. I once heard a high larnt un say that in all men there is something of a woman. Luff had that feeling for Will and when he left the gang it drove Luff crazy with jealousy. I've no love for the Excise but that day Barry and his men put a volley into Luff 'twas the best thing they ever did. He worn't . . . well . . . natural, some-how."

Sam was staring out of a window in the port quarter of the *Ghost*.

" Talking o' the Excise, Nick, look ! "

Nick peered out of the window into the waning sunshine of the late afternoon. " Barry and party, by God ! " he exclaimed.

Segel picked up his sword belt and buckled it on.

" Everything clear below, Sam ? "

" Ah, all but several ankers o' brandy on the platform built into the keelson."

" The ballast is over the top o' that, 'int it ? "

" Ah, Barry 'ont find aught amiss here, damn his poking snout."

There was the thump of feet on the deck overhead and a little later a sword hilt rapped on the cabin door. Nick opened it. Barry stood there with another Excise officer, a stranger to the master and mate of the *Ghost*.

Barry came straight to the point. " Can I see your manifest, master."

Segel handed the papers to Barry and the two officers initialled them. Barry then ordered his companion, who was his junior, to conduct a search.

When the other officer had taken his crew of red-shirted, blue-trousered, canvas-skirted ratings below Barry spoke in crisp staccato tones to Nick Segel.

" Are you master of this vessel ? "

" I am, sir."

" Then it is my duty to warn you that information has been laid that this vessel is engaged in running contraband."

Nick looked surprised. " Running contraband ? Smug-gling aboard my vessel ? "

Barry broke in brusquely. " This vessel belongs to

William Laud, master. You know that without my telling. Be so kind as to come below."

Segel shrugged and stepped out of the cabin.

Down in the hold the other preventive officer and his men had just finished thrusting swords into the medley of sacks and piles of odorous hides. The officer saluted. "Everything seems in order here, sir. Nothing to report."

Barry returned the salute of his junior. "Thank you, Mr. Padge," he said.

As they were about to climb the ladder from the hold, Barry paused. "By the way, Mr. Padge," he enquired, "did your men search beneath the ballast?"

The Excise ratings exchanged rueful glances. It would mean hours of slogging labour, moving the pig-iron ballast. Ships' masters insisted that everything was left exactly as it was found, too.

Padge, a beefy youngster with pale blue eyes and hair so fair it was almost white, grew red in the face and blinked in an embarrassed fashion. "Why—er—ah, no, sir," he stammered.

Barry spoke tersely. "Start moving that ballast, men."

Nick Segel gave a swift, desperate glance at Sam. Will was well on the way to Ipswich by now. He'd come back to Aldeburgh with his bride-to-be and walk straight into the arms of the Excise.

With a sudden movement Segel drew two heavy calibre pistols and thrust them into Barry's middle.

"Now get up that ladder, sir. One move from any of your men and I'll blow you in twain. Come on, Sam."

Barry looked coldly at Segel. "So that's the way of it, master. Take no notice, men," he said calmly to his bewildered ratings. "Fire . . . drop him, I say!"

Segel drew back his lips in a snarl. He was, at that moment, as deadly as a viper, and the customs' men sensed it. "Well . . . who's going to fire?"

He laughed. "They show better sense nor you, sir," he said to Barry. "Now get up that ladder!"

Padge looked at his superior with imploring eyes. "For God's sake, sir, do as he says! He'll shoot else." Barry backed up the ladder, Segel following step at a time. Sam Nye had gone up first. The feeble lamp-light glimmered on the brass pistols.

At the top of the ladder Segel made a lightning move. Setting his foot against Barry he thrust him back into the arms of his men below. Together Nick and Sam leaped over the rail of the *Ghost* and ran along Slaughden Quay as fast as they could.

By this time the men in the hold were pouring up on to the deck. They were steadying their long muskets on the vessel's rail. The blast of musketry that followed sent a dropping of mallard, which had been roosting below the partially constructed martello tower, high into the air and out to sea. The red flashes reflected briefly in the strip of water between the brig and the quay.

" We've got to warn Will somehow," Nick Segel said as he ran.

" Ah, that we have, Nick. I . . ." There was a hollow thud as a musket-ball took Sam in the back. Tossing his arms wide he plunged face down into the shingle of the quay, dead before he hit the ground.

" Sam . . . Sam, old shipmet ! " Nick's voice was hoarse with grief as he knelt by the crumpled figure.

Realizing that Sam would never speak to him again, Nick got to his feet. The pause had given the Excise men time to reload. They came along the quay at the double. Several of them knelt, steadied their aim, and fired at Nick's running, dodging figure. He staggered once and then was lost from sight in the gloom of the marshes.

CHAPTER TWENTY-SIX

I

THE late meal was over in the house at St. Margaret's Green and from the scullery came the voice of the scullery maid crooning over the last of the dishes. Margaret sat quietly in the kitchen reading the latest of John Barry's letters :

. . . This year the River Hawkesbury rose ninety-seven feet, fed by heavy rains from the mountains. We had to take boats and save whole families perched atop their floating houses together with pigs, chickens, cats and dogs. An almost laughable sight, Peggy, until one stopped to consider the loss of food and property.

This is a strange land indeed, none of the regularity of the climate at home. This year floods that swept away even the soil from the rock and next year there will likely be a drought that will slay sheep and cattle by the thousand and wither the corn before it is half grown.

Apart from the natural hazards of the climate there are a great many social evils too and the worst of all these, my dear, is the unlimited sale to all and sundry of spirits which are imported in huge quantities.

I have seen men and women, yes, Peggy, and even children, sitting round a bucketful of neat spirit, drinking it with pint mugs.

I cannot hope to tell you of the dread results of these orgies. Madness, murder and rape are common. Theft is an every-day affair. No man goes unarmed.

At home if you caught a thief red-handed he would attempt to escape. Here they shoot to kill.

Another cause for unease is the injudicious granting of free pardons to convicts who immediately set out to corrupt free settlers.

The Governor makes grants of land to " emancipists " or

time-expired convicts. This land is straightway transferred over to wholesale and retail dealers in spirits.

Many of these dealers have grown enormously wealthy and are fast becoming a power to be reckoned with.

Oh, Peggy, when I think of the friendly little inns at home and compare them to the public houses here my heart misgives me. Here they are not only frequently houses of ill fame but receiving houses for stolen goods and lurking-places for bands of desperate men who style themselves as " bushrangers." Free men and convicts alike who have banded themselves together to kill and rob.

Educated convicts have risen to power by unscrupulous means. I have seen the unprecedented situation of a convict attorney, pilloried in London for forgery, serving a writ on an honest man here.

Others of these educated convicts are taken by wealthy settlers as tutors for their children. Some of them have even become editors of newspapers.

You can well imagine the chaos brought about by this sad state of affairs, my dear.

And yet the faults are not always with the convicts, many of them are settling down and becoming good, hard-working citizens and indeed upright and fearless men.

It is sometimes the free settlers who are given convict labour for their farms who are cruel and unjust . . .

Margaret was interrupted by a tap on the door and the scullery maid looked in.

" I've finished the dishes, mam," she said.

Margaret looked up. " All right, Ivy. Get the kindling in for the morning, then you can go."

Not long after the girl had gone and Margaret had settled down to finish the letter, a knock sounded on the kitchen door. Placing the letter on the table Margaret went across and opened the door.

" Can I come in, Peggy ? "

The shock of hearing Will's voice was so great that she staggered to the door jamb and clutched it. Laud stepped into the kitchen. His manner was restrained, as that of a man not sure of his welcome.

For a moment they looked at each other.

Margaret noticed that his clothes were finer than they had ever been before and his manner was rather more sober. Beneath his quietness of manner, however, she sensed that he was labouring under the stress of some emotion. But he was still the same man who had fascinated her as a young girl and almost against her will she felt the old fascination taking hold of her.

To Laud Margaret was no longer a high-spirited girl. She was a remarkably comely, mature woman. The great dark eyes still held their magic.

He took a step forward, arms outstretched. " Margaret . . . Peggy darling . . . that night I cut my cable . . . I'm sorry," he said, and the humiliation and gentleness of his voice completely overwhelmed her. The next instant she was in his arms, sobbing with sheer happiness.

As she brushed swiftly by the table her skirt knocked the letter flying. Its pages lay scattered and unheeded beneath their feet.

2

Some time later Laud was trotting easily along the road from Ipswich, his heart lighter than he could ever remember. Humming a gay little tune under his breath he jogged along giving full rein to his thoughts.

Margaret still cared for him. Had always cared, in spite of his long absence. There had never been anyone else except himself.

He was off back to Aldeburgh now. His lovable little house there would soon have a mistress. He grinned to himself in the darkness : they'd call it " Smuggler's Cottage "—nobody would ever guess the real truth.

They'd be married at Aldeburgh in the old grey stone church on the hill, the church with its " lucomb " or little watch tower on the corner of the square steeple, where watch was kept for the French. He'd have the choir and the organ, flowers and all the pleasant foolish fripperies so dear to women. He had a bit of money now. It would be the most fashionable wedding the old town had seen for many a long day. He laughed aloud as he pictured Sam's face when he heard the news. Sam Nye, the confirmed bachelor.

Laud jogged quietly through the deserted streets of Saxmundham. Some time later he was on the last lap of the road to Aldeburgh. The tower of Snape church was away to his left ; to his right lay the beautiful vale of Slaughden.

The river was shimmering in the moonlight, and there was

a nostalgic mystery about the glistening mud flats that halted him, despite his haste to get home.

Away in the limitless distance across rolling heath land, corn-field, marsh and dyke, Orfordness light gleamed orange against the sky.

A teal gave its phantom whistle overhead, and the night breeze was cool on his cheeks.

In front of him lay the sea, like a great glistening sheet of pewter. The wind bore snatches of its gentle pulsing to his ears.

This was his country. His to marry in, to live in, to raise children in. To grow old and die in, and to lay at last in peace in an old moss-grown churchyard, like the one that lay to his left. He sighed. Such beauty as the night held was not good to gaze upon for too long. It bemused and bewildered the senses.

Then he laughed. Will, he told himself, you're becoming as sentimental as a girl—and all because of a bit of moonlight. He gave the reins a gentle shake and the horse moved forward.

At that moment he caught the sound of other hoof-beats, sharp with urgency, rising discordantly through the peace of the night, ringing with ever-increasing violence on the hard road.

He reined in to one side, and presently horse and rider came into view. The rider was swaying oddly in the saddle.

Laud smiled. Some drunken fool on a runaway. Ah well, better try to stop him. He pulled his horse around ready to give chase. He'd welcome a wild gallop through the moonlight.

As Laud was about to spur his horse into motion the wild rider pulled his mount to so sudden a stop that it reared backwards, throwing the rider into the road.

Laud caught the heaving, lathered horse, noticing as he did so that the saddle was wet and shiny. The figure in the road, its face as pallid as the moon itself, gave a hoarse gasp. " Is that you, Will lad ? "

Laud was on his knees in an instant.

" Is that you, Nick ? For Christ's sake, man, what's amiss ? "

" Everything, Will. Barry came aboard . . . *Ghost* . . . knows everything. Excise and constable waiting for you. I got away, hid in the marshes all last night and until dusk tonight . . . they . . . searched for me . . ."

"Nick, man, you're hurt. And where's Sam?"

"They shot Sam . . . Slaughden Quay. I'm done, Will. Get away and . . . save yourself . . ."

"And leave you here, Nick? Not likely, old shipmate. Here, try and get aboard your horse."

Laud struggled to get Nick to his feet. His efforts wrenched a groan from the injured man.

"Ah, Will . . . for God's sake, man . . . no ! . . . Carry me to the side of the road . . . but little time left . . ."

Laud swung Segel up in his arms as gently as he could, and gritted his teeth as he felt the mess of splintered bone where the heavy musket-ball had torn into Nick's back. It was a miracle he had survived.

Segel made fumbling motions inside his jacket. Presently he brought out a piece of paper, darkly stained in the moonlight.

"Here, Will . . . address of a tavern . . . London," he gasped. "You'll be safe . . . there. Safe till things . . . blow over . . . Hurry now." Nick's mind started to wander then. For a while he mumbled to himself. Then suddenly his voice gained strength and clarity. "All right, Sam, old shipmet. Don't push the boat off wi'out me . . . I'm coming."

Nick Segel's head fell back and his mouth gaped blackly in the moonlight. He had gone to join Sam.

For a moment Laud stood gazing dumbly at the still figure, too shattered by the sudden turn of events even to feel sorrow. Then he turned and unstrapped the saddle from the horse which Nick had ridden. Taking the saddle-blanket he spread it over the lifeless body where it lay on the moon-drenched roadside. He mounted his own horse and gave the shrouded form one last look.

"Nick, old comrade," he said quietly, "they murdered you and Sam for a miserable groat's worth o' goods. But I'll repay them with interest, so help me God !"

He gave a swift glance at the bloodstained slip of paper. On it was an address, barely discernible : "Ned Handshake, 'Prospect of Whitby,' Stepney, East London."

Raking his horse with his spurs Laud clattered off into the moonlight which was no longer beautiful, but held only menace and death.

CHAPTER TWENTY-SEVEN

I

LAUD rode headlong through the night, changing his almost foundered horse at Colchester. At ten o'clock the next morning he reached the " Prospect of Whitby."

The " Prospect " stood by the side of the Thames—indeed, it possessed a gallery which overhung the river—and Laud derived vague comfort from the close proximity to water. It was a strange place, dark by reason of its sombre panelling and full of a multitude of curios brought back from all parts of the world.

On arrival Laud enquired for Ned Handshake, only to learn that he was out. He therefore ordered himself a meal, thinking to await Ned Handshake's return. Whilst waiting for his meal he went to his room and wrote a hasty letter to Margaret.

> " THE PROSPECT OF WHITBY,"
> STEPNEY,
> EAST LONDON.

DEAR MARGARET,

I have had to leave Aldeburgh for business reasons and am stopping for a while at the above address. I cannot explain matters in this letter. You must join me here as soon as possible. Do not tell anyone of this but borrow one of Mr. Cobbold's horses—Crop is the fastest, I believe—and ride all haste to me. Do not wait for the coach. Burn this as soon as you have read it.

> In haste,
> WILL.

Laud folded the letter, sealed and addressed it, then went down to the tap-room and called for the potman.

"This letter is important," he told him. "It must be delivered as soon as possible."

The potman, a pallid, narrow-shouldered man with close-set eyes, glanced up from the pewter he was shining.

"The mail coach don't pass here until midday tomorrer."

"This letter has got to go now. I'll give twenty guineas to the man who delivers it."

The potman read the address doubtfully. "Ips'ich is a tidy ways from here," he remarked. "But I fancy I know someone who'll do it for ye at that price." He called a boy over to him, spoke softly and then gave him a shove to hurry him on his way.

Laud gave the potman a crown and then went in to where a plateful of boiled beef, carrots and potatoes awaited him. After a while he pushed the half-eaten food to one side and called for a bottle of rum.

A little later a bow-legged little man with nondescript clothes and a peaky face came into the room. He touched his cap to Laud. Speaking in harsh East London accents, he asked: "Are you the gent what wanted a letter took'n, sir?"

Laud nodded. "Get it to that address as soon as you can. Here's ten guineas. I'll give you the other ten as soon as you get back. Don't spare the cattle."

The little man touched his forehead and with a furtive motion slipped out of the room.

Laud picked up his bottle and leaving the rest of the food cold and congealing on the table went up to his comfortless room which overlooked the river.

As soon as Margaret arrives, he thought, I'll book two berths to the continent. There are plenty of craft here-about.

He poured himself another glass of rum, and swallowed half of it at a gulp.

2

Down below in the tap-room the potman had finished the last of his pewter and was about to go to the cellar to draw some fresh ale, when suddenly the door opened, and a man entered. He was short and thick-set, with blue jowls below cheeks whose colour matched the brilliant scarlet of his waistcoat. He lifted his curly brimmed hat and mopped his steaming bald head with a huge blue and white check handkerchief.

"Hey there, Tom," he called, "a quart of ale. It's a thirsty world."

The potman drew a quart of ale and handed it to the Bow Street runner who, burying his face in the foam, took a long, gasping draught. Then he blew the froth from his face and sat back with a contented sigh. "Phew, thief-taking is dry work, Tom, my lad."

There was a gleam of interest in the potman's usually lack-lustre eyes.

"Anything o' note, Jem?" he enquired.

"The usual run o' cutpurses, horse-thieves and what-not." Jem drew a sheaf of bills from his pockets and handed them to the potman. "Have a look through them, Tom."

Laboriously the potman spelt out the names of the people, their descriptions and the crimes they had committed. "Jack Pursglove, horse-thief. John Arkwright, Jacobite. Edward Smallbone, cutpurse. All small stuff, Jem. No murder or highway robbery."

The Bow Street runner gave a grim little laugh. "No one seems to fancy a rope collar these days!" he said.

He brought some more bills to light. "Ah, here's one as might interest ye, Tom."

The potman took the handbill casually whilst the runner went on speaking.

"Got that through from Ipswich by the morning coach. Fellow by the name o' William Laud. Two hundred jimmy o' goblins re-ward. De-fraudin' His Majesty's revenoo. In other words a free trader. Little likelihood o' seein' him around these parts. Those gentry stick to the coast "—the Bow Street runner shook his head—" an' a good job too. They're rare wild, desprit coves by all accounts."

The potman was carefully reading out the words: "'Scar on face; black patch over one eye.'" His voice shook with excitement. "Jem, Jem man, there's a rooster upstairs what tallies exact to this bill "—conviction was strong in his voice—"ay, an' . . . by God he's just sent an urgent message to some party at Ips'ich."

The Bow Street runner got to his feet with a purposeful look on his face. "Take me up to his room, Tom: quietly now."

The potman threw off his apron and beckoned to the runner. Together they tiptoed up the stairs. On the first landing the runner whispered, "There's no one moving. He must be asleep." He bent down and peered through the keyhole of Laud's room. "He's sound asleep," he said, and pulled out

220

two pistols. " Get in there and see if you can get your hand under his pillow for his barkers."

Laud awoke and groped, too late, for the pistols which had been beneath his pillow.

The Bow Street runner stood at his bedside, pistols levelled and his voice crackling with menace.

" William Laud, I arrest you in the name of the King." He spoke out of the corner of his mouth to the frightened potman. " There's two o' my mates outside, Tom.. Run and get them whilst I keep an eye on this cove."

The potman clattered down the stairs as fast as he could go.

CHAPTER TWENTY-EIGHT

I

It was the sudden clatter of hooves on the hard road that awoke Margaret with a start. She peered uncertainly around, wondering if she had been awoken by a vivid dream. The moon was low in the sky, sending its brilliance straight through her bedroom window.

Outside she heard footsteps and throwing her cloak over her night attire she opened the window. The slim, short figure of a man was standing peering this way and that in the moonlight, as if wondering what to do.

Margaret called down softly. " Who are you? What do you want? "

" Got a message for a Mistress Catchpole, ma'am. Does she live hereabouts? "

" I'm Margaret Catchpole. Go round the back and for God's sake go quietly! "

Margaret dressed swiftly, her heart thumping with dread. She went swiftly and silently as a ghost down the stairs and noiselessly unbarred the door.

She took the message from the man, read it in the moonlight.

" What was he like . . . the man who gave you this letter? "

" A tall, darkish-featured gent wi' a black patch. Something scarred about the face he was too."

Margaret was anxious in case any other members of the household should awaken. " I'm sorry," she said, " I can't ask you in for a bite and sup."

The courier was equally anxious to be gone.

" That's all right, ma'am. I'm used to riding. I been well paid for my trouble."

Margaret thought furiously.

" Tell him I'll be there as soon as I can," she said.

The messenger nodded, went back to his horse and a little later the rapidly diminishing clatter of hoof-beats sounded in the road.

Up in her room Margaret read and re-read the note. There was something about its urgency which filled her with dread. Unthinkingly she twisted the letter into a tight ball and let it fall to the floor.

What could she do? Will was in trouble of some sort. He needed her. London was a lifetime away. She thought of the words in the note, " Take Crop, he's the fastest horse. . . ." Crop! John Cobbold's strawberry-roan with cropped ears. Her master's favourite horse. A grand, great-hearted horse who could go like the wind, even with his heavy master up. How much faster would he go with only a slight woman in the saddle!

Margaret looked at her clothes. It would never do to be seen riding in those. She blew out her candle and crept down the stairs a second time on her way to the stable. Behind her, in a small patch of moonlight, lay Laud's letter, crumpled and forgotten.

Opening the stable door Margaret spoke softly to the horses in order not to startle them into giving the alarm. The splendid Crop was stabled next to another fine horse, a fiery-spirited grey named Rochford, whom Mr. Cobbold had not long purchased from Lord Rochford. Margaret rubbed their velvety muzzles. " Whoa there, Crop! Whoa, Rochford! "

Luckily for Margaret, old George Teager the stableman who slept above his charges was not only a heavy sleeper but hard of hearing as well.

She trod lightly up the wooden stairs which led to his room. Opening the door she let the feeble rays from a shaded stable lamp shine about the room.

She saw Teager asleep in his bed, one arm above his head, mouth open and snoring loudly. His clothes were in an untidy heap beside the bed. Carefully gathering these up, Margaret tiptoed back down the stairs into the stable where she swiftly changed into the stableman's clothes and donned his cap.

Her long dark hair persisted in falling from beneath the cap. In a very fury of impatience Margaret looked about her. A pair of heavy shears lay on a shelf amid curry combs and bottles of horse medicine. Snatching them down she swiftly and ruthlessly clipped her beautiful tresses.

She threw a saddle-blanket across Crop's back, remembering with thankfulness the times she had ridden a horse as a child,

and the times out of number she had seen her father harness
up horses when he worked for the Denton's.

Hastily searching about the stable she found some old pieces
of sacking, which she bound about Crop's hooves. Gently
opening the stable door she walked out, keeping to the
shadows, leading the horse behind her. Once on to the road
she swiftly removed the sacking and climbed into the saddle.

Then, for the second time that moon-drenched early morning, the urgent clatter of hoof-beats drummed against the
quiet air and swiftly died away.

2

It was Ivy the scullery maid who discovered that Margaret
had gone.

When the cook of the Cobbold household did not appear in
the kitchen, Ivy, thinking that Margaret must have overslept,
went up and found the empty bed and the crumpled letter on
the floor. Even as Elizabeth Cobbold was reading it, George
Teager, clad in an old coat over his night attire, thumped at
the door and asked in a gasping voice for the master.

John Cobbold came down in his dressing-gown. " Get
your breath first, George man," he said. " What's amiss ? "

" It's Crop, sir . . . he's gone. So are my clothes. I
found these in Crop's empty stall ! " He put Margaret's
clothes and the locks of luxuriant black hair on the table.

In utter dismay, Elizabeth Cobbold handed her husband
the letter from Laud which had been found in Margaret's
bedroom. He read it swiftly, then turned back to the shaking
stableman. " Don't take on too much, George. We'll get
the horse back," he said reassuringly. " Dress as quickly as
you can, then come back here."

3

About four miles from Colchester the driver of the Ipswich
mail heard the thunder of hooves rapidly approaching. A
few moments later a snorting strawberry-roan swept past in
choking clouds of dust.

The driver's eyes widened. " Somebody in a pelt, b'God,"
he said to himself.

He drove on for a few moments, trying to think where he
had seen that superb roan before. Suddenly conviction came
to him. " Damme, John Cobbold's Crop ! Wonder who

that groom was ? A stranger to me. Something amiss wi' the family the way that young fellow was going." His eyes narrowed. " Either that or Crop has been stolen." He cracked his long whip over the ears of his six horses. " Hey there, geddap, geddap," he shouted.

The passengers in the coach felt it lurch forward at increased speed and several of them poked enquiring faces from the window.

At Ipswich the driver of the mail leaped down from his seat and without even knocking the dust from his clothes, ran into the coach office.

Leaning across the counter, he spoke swiftly to the Post-master. " I fancy John Cobbold's in some trouble," he said. " Either sickness, or that horse of his, Crop, has been stolen ! "

A messenger was sent to St. Margaret's Green. He arrived just after George Teager had reported the loss of the horse. John Cobbold went to the stable and easily traced the horse's muffled hooves across to the paddock gate and the road.

" George," he said, turning to Teager, " go you up to Spink the horse-dealer and hire the fastest horse he has. I'll take Rochford. Hurry, man, we've got to overtake that unfortunate girl at all costs."

John Cobbold was a God-fearing man and not given to profanity but his anxiety overcame him.

" Good God Almighty, doesn't she realize horse-theft is a capital offence ? "

Whilst Teager was at Spink's and Cobbold was saddling up Rochford a constable came into the yard. He touched his hat.

" It has been reported that a horse has been stolen from these premises, sir."

There was a frown on Cobbold's face as he looked up.

" I'll get the animal back, constable, never fear."

The constable nodded ponderously and brought his authority from his pocket—a short staff capped with a brass crown. His tones were respectful but there was the authority of the law underlying them. " I don't doubt that, sir, but it's my duty to apprehend the thief. Have you any idea who it might be ? "

Cobbold thought swiftly. Thought of his children who might have been lying in the churchyard but for a slim dark girl, who at that very moment was hurtling Londonwards.

" I've no idea, constable. No idea at all."

The man returned his authority to his pocket and gave Cobbold a keen glance, touched his hat and went straight to the offices of the County Press and ordered handbills to be printed in time for the London coach.

When he had gone Cobbold went in to his wife. " Elizabeth, my dear, those things of Margaret's," he said. " Get them out of the way . . . hide them. Better still, burn them."

There was a noise of hooves outside as Teager rode in on a tall, rangy black. A few moments later master and man galloped away down the London road.

At every toll-gate they heard the story of a foam-flecked, thundering strawberry-roan and its slim, dust-covered rider : and they might possibly have overtaken Margaret but for the fact that they were misdirected by persons who said that they thought they had seen the horse and rider galloping along the road to Maldon in the Hundred of Essex.

4

In the meantime Margaret had eased the headlong rush of the mighty animal beneath her and trotted quietly into the village of Marks Tey.

Here she stopped at an inn known as the " Trowel and Hammer." Climbing out of the saddle she beat the dust from her clothes ; and going into the tap-room she called, in a voice as gruff as she could make it, " Hey there, landlord, get somebody to rub my horse down and bait and water it. And I'll have a glass of brandy and some bread and cheese."

The landlord brought her order, which she ate and drank as quickly as she could without attracting attention. At the back of her mind, as insistent as the chirping of a cricket and mingling with the drumming of the hooves which still echoed in her head, came the words, " Horse-thieves hang . . . horse-thieves hang . . . horse-thieves hang . . ."

She glanced about her. Nobody was taking the least notice of her. Even so, their apparent indifference might be a trap. With a mighty effort of will she forced herself to walk casually, and strolled out to see how her mount was faring.

Crop had been watered and was eating the last of his oats. Margaret got into the saddle, tossed the groom a coin and trotted gently off in the direction of Chelmsford. As soon as she was clear of the village she gave Crop his head. Then

with mighty muscles bunching beneath her she once more
thundered Londonwards.

"Horse-thieves hang . . . horse-thieves hang . . . horse-
thieves hang."

At Chelmsford she eased to an amble again. It was not
easy. A horse of Crop's calibre loved nothing better than a
wild headlong gallop. He snorted and shook his massive head
against the restraining pressure of the rein, but once through
the town she gave him his head again.

On she sped, through Ingatestone, Mountnessing, Ilford ;
and behind her the dust rose in rolling, choking clouds.

5

Trotting quietly into the yard of the " Bull " at Aldegate,
Margaret climbed stiffly down and clapped the dust from her
clothes in as masculine a way as she could.

She called to the ostler and told him to rub the horse down.
" Let him cool off, and then give him a bucket of tepid water
with brandy in it," she said. " After that a mouthful or so of
hay—not too much."

The ostler shifted the straw to the other corner of his mouth.
" Have ye come far, young sir ? " he enquired.

" What's that to you ? Get on and rub the horse down."

" He's a grand horse that," he mused, lost in admiration.
" Worth any man's money."

Margaret turned to go into the taproom to order a meal ;
then stopped as an idea came to her. " He's better than he
looks," she said, " and although he's for sale it's not any man's
money that could buy him." Many sales, she knew, were
effected through the agency of ostlers : and so, having cast
out her line, she went in for a meal to give the fish time to
collect.

" The Prospect of Whitby," Stepney. How did she reach
Stepney from here, she wondered. Why was Will there ?
What was the reason for the urgency in his note ? Had
something happened ? Questions seethed in her tired mind.
Had Crop's disappearance been noticed ? Were they after
her already ? She must reach Will as soon as ever she could.
But money. He would need money. Money would be more
useful than Crop. And she mustn't be caught with Crop.
Until now she had not thought what to do with him, but
clearly she must get rid of him. But how much to ask for him,

should the ostler find a buyer? If she asked too much she might not sell him; too little, and they would be suspicious. One hundred and fifty guineas? She had heard Mr. Cobbold say that Crop was worth all of that. But then owners always overpriced their favourite horses. A hundred guineas? That should last Will and her for a bit. Yes, a hundred guineas would be about right. But she mustn't stay long here. She had yet to find Will.

She had just finished her meal when the ostler looked in and beckoned to her. She followed him out into the yard where a man was waiting who was introduced to her as Jack Goodchild, a livery stable keeper. "Knows a bit about horse-flesh," the ostler added. "Maybe he'll be able to make you an offer."

Margaret trotted Crop quietly up and down the yard. "There you are. Did you ever see a better shape?" she asked proudly, trying to remember to keep her voice gruff. "Look at shoulders, fore-end. What a crest! Have you ever seen such a head? Legs as straight and clean as a colt's! Six years old and never done a stroke of hard work in his life. Quiet to ride or drive. There's very few horses in this county have the heels of him, if any."

Jack Goodchild was cautious. There were a lot of stolen horses about these days. It was almost as bad to buy a stolen horse as to steal it.

"Can I have a written warranty with him?" he asked.

"That you can. I'll write you one." Margaret was anxious to get on with the deal, but she could see suspicion rising in the man's face. She thought swiftly. Better take a bold line. "Perhaps you'd like to wait till my master comes. I'm waiting for him now, and maybe you'll strike a better bargain with him."

The bluff seemed to work. The liveryman relaxed visibly. But not completely. "I suppose you are authorized to sell that hoss, young feller?" he enquired, sticking his thumbs into the armpits of his waistcoat.

Margaret thought, Oh, why can't he get on with it? Why must he waste time with all these questions? "D'ye fancy I'd be standing here talking o' selling him if I wasn't?" she said.

"How much d'ye want for him?"

"One hundred guineas."

"Can I take him for a trial run?"

Margaret's grip tightened on Crop's rein. " When you've bought and paid for him, not before." She wasn't as simple as all that !

But the liveryman was hedging. " I want to see his paces. Damme, young man, a feller laying out a hundred clinkers is entitled to see what he's buying, surely ? "

Oh, hurry up, Margaret thought, and make up your mind. But she knew that she had to play to the rules of the bargaining game, or suspicions would be aroused.

" You've seen him trot," she said as calmly as she could. " If you know anything about horses you'd tell from his movements that he is absolutely sound. I'd ridden him hard to get here ahead of my master and there was no trace of bellows to mend—was there ? " she appealed to the ostler. The man shook his head. " Well, a hundred guineas is the price," Margaret said, " and he's not going out of my hands until he's sold."

But Goodchild did not want to be pushed. Once before he had bought a stolen horse and had great difficulty in establishing his innocence. He was determined not to be caught a second time. But Crop was a fine animal, and he was going to have him. Thought he could knock the price down a bit, too.

He called to his head stableman who, having heard that a deal was on, had come across from the stables. " Hey there, Peter, come and look at this nag and tell me what you think on't."

The stableman, a lanky being in shirt sleeves, curry comb in hand, shot Goodchild a swift glance. What was he supposed to say ? Goodchild shook his head. He wanted a genuine opinion. " Take a look at his mouth, Peter," he said.

Margaret controlled her impatience with difficulty. She wondered now if it had been wise to start this business. She was wasting time. She had to get to Will at Stepney. It might take a bit of time to find the inn. Every moment might be bringing pursuers nearer to her. She was a horse-thief. Horse-thieves hang. And the refrain that had been drumming in her ears during her ride suddenly took on a new significance. It was no longer a rhythm, a refrain : but it was as if an outer layer of disguise had been stripped away and the meaning lay startlingly and appallingly bare.

Peter stepped quietly up to Crop and gently prised the powerful jaws apart. The horse objected to this familiarity, snorted and stepped back a pace.

" He's a'right, sir," Peter told his master enthusiastically. " About six year old, I should say."

Peter's judgement was sound, Goodchild knew. It was now merely a question of the price.

" What's the lowest price you'll take for this horse, young feller ? " he asked. No need to pay a price higher than was necessary.

" I've already told you. One hundred guineas." How long was this game of haggling to go on ? How much more time could she afford ?

The liveryman shook his head. " It's a fine animal, I grant you," he stalled, " but not everybody's hoss. Too spirited for a woman for one thing. He'd not be easy to match eether, apart from not being suited to town work. I'll give you fifty guineas for him."

Fifty guineas. Should she accept ? Could she afford the time not to ? Fifty guineas. That would be something at least for her and Will. But would a too ready acceptance make the man suspicious ? " You'll have to come to nigh twice that," she said. Dear God, how much longer must she go on ? Somewhere Will was waiting for her, wondering why she did not come, thinking perhaps she had let him down.

" Well, we won't argue over a guinea or two," said Goodchild jovially. The boy was beginning to crack. He'd come down from his hundred. " Sixty yellow boys ! Come, what d'ye say ? "

" Not enough. I'll take eighty."

" You drive a hard bargain, young feller." Goodchild grinned ruefully as though being pushed to a price higher than he had intended. Yet, had he been forced, he would have paid the full hundred guineas for the incomparable Crop. But he mustn't show this. He turned to the head stableman again. " Well, what d'ye say, Peter ? "

" He's wuth eighty, master."

Margaret's heart leapt with joy. The game was finished. Now only to collect the money and go.

Goodchild was about to enter the house for the money when one of the men came into the yard with a paper in his hand. He made a quick gesture with his head and vanished into the stable. Margaret, her mind full of her approaching meeting with Will, did not notice the incident.

" Hold on a minute, young man. I'll not be long," Goodchild said. And to the stableman he added, " Peter, I want you a moment."

Margaret sighed. "Hold on a minute." What was a minute to him. To her it was an hour, a lifetime. The thought caught at her savagely, gripped her. How much time has my life? she wondered. At any moment she might see—what? Mr. Cobbold? A constable? A Bow Street runner? Would she recognize a runner when she saw one? At any moment they might come into the yard. And Will would be waiting, and would never know. She turned with a feeling of sadness and fondled Crop's velvety nose.

Inside the stable the man thrust a paper excitedly into Goodchild's hand. "Look at that, sir!" he said.

Goodchild looked at the handbill:

TWENTY GUINEAS REWARD

Whereas last night or this morning May 24th a fine strawberry-roan gelding was stolen at the stables of John Cobbold Esquire of St. Margaret's Green, Ipswich, together with a new saddle and bridle and coachman's stable dress.

Whoever shall give information so as to lead to the recovery of the horse and the conviction of the offender shall receive the above reward.

N.B.

The horse is sixteen hands high, has cropped ears, a cut tail and is very strong and fast.

GOD SAVE THE KING

Ipswich, May 24th, 1797.

"By Jiminy," he exclaimed, "that's the animal! I felt there was something wrong there. Peter, you run and fetch a constable. I'll keep that young thief busy until you come back."

The stableman slipped off round the back of the stables. Goodchild sauntered back into the stable yard. Margaret watched him anxiously. Oh, hurry, please, *please* hurry, she begged silently, on the verge of tears.

When Goodchild spoke his tones were as casual as he could make them.

"That's certainly a fine hoss, young man. Ah, and a fine saddle and bridle too. Are they included in the price?"

Should she say yes? Would it appear too eager? Perhaps there was no one after her. It would be foolish to arouse suspicions here unnecessarily. "They are not," she said with an attempt at indignation. "My master told me if I could sell them they would be my perquisites. They'll cost you another five guineas." God, she thought, what a farce, Must I, can I, go on playing it? She felt like screaming. Take the damned things. Take them, take anything, but let me go. And she felt a tide of hysteria rising within her.

At that moment Peter the stableman re-entered the yard. By his side there was a tall man in a long frieze coat and red waistcoat. Margaret saw them coming towards her. Why was everyone suddenly silent? Had they come at last? Was this a runner? Certainly the tall man wore an air of authority. Had he come for her? Her stomach went hollow with fear and her head reeled. They seemed a long way away now, striding towards her with enormous steps. Now they were close to her, teetering on little mincing feet. It was Will they were after. She must warn him, but she was rooted to the spot. She opened her mouth to scream, and a wave of blackness rose up out of the ground and enveloped her in its velvety folds. Margaret crumpled up in a dead faint.

Prepared for an attempted escape the men looked at each other in surprise. The Bow Street runner, squatting down on his heels, undid the coachman's jacket Margaret was wearing. He looked up round-eyed at the others.

"By Goles! . . . it's a wench!"

Whilst the Bow Street runner and the liveryman were getting a trap to drive the unconscious girl to custody the news of a female horse-thief spread rapidly and soon the stable yard was packed with sightseers, milling hither and thither.

Into the midst of them came John Cobbold on the foam-flecked, labouring Rochford. He had long since left George Teager, for the black could not pace the dynamic grey.

Dismounting, he forced his way through the crowd to where Goodchild and his ostlers were talking in the stable. He walked up to them and nodded at Crop, munching hay in a nearby stall.

"That's my horse," he said. "Where is the . . . ah . . . groom who was riding it?"

Goodchild, seeing that he had a man of substance to deal with, spoke respectfully. "The constable took . . . er . . . him . . . away, sir."

Cobbold's fine head sank on to his chest.

"Too late, poor child, too late."

Turning back to Crop he mounted, and, leading Rochford by the reins, rode away.

Goodchild gazed after him in perplexity. Here was odd behaviour from a man whose fine horse had been recovered so quickly. He shrugged and sent his lewdly whispering ostlers about their work.

CHAPTER TWENTY-NINE

I

WHEN Margaret regained her senses she found herself in the corner of a filthy cell occupied by a mass of equally filthy humanity, both male and female. Some of the women amongst the crowd were mothers with children at their tattered skirts ; others were mothers to be.

In one corner was a group of women who, by their degraded looks, were prostitutes. Some of them were planning further evil against the day when they were set at doubtful liberty. Others were telling lewd and obscene tales.

Another group was clustered avidly against the window of the cell watching a crowd that was streaming from Newgate Street, Fleet Street and Smithfield. One of the watchers, a slatternly, pickpocket-prostitute, turned to Margaret and remarked, " So the Jarkman got his daddles on you, luvvy. What was it ? "

Margaret's answer was little more than a whisper, " . . . a horse . . ."

Her interrogator gave a screeching laugh. " Hey, mates," she called to the group by the window, " she prigged a prancer. Gi' her the place o' honour." The speaker pushed Margaret to the window and pointed out with a black-taloned finger. " He prigged a prancer too, luvvy. Watch now."

Margaret, wedged against the window by a press of bodies, could do nothing else.

Somewhere a bell was tolling ; slow-spaced, hideous reverberations across the bright day. The gathering crowd was in a wild, near-savage mood. Pickpockets were busily at work in the very shadow of Newgate Gaol, and louts were pulling off women's hats. Young lads were being hoisted over the heads of the crowd and beaten and pinched until they roared with pain—the crowd needed diversion until the main show started, a show about to be enacted upon a raised wooden platform overshadowed by a wooden structure the shape of an inverted " L." From this structure dangled a rope fashioned into an ugly and curiously knotted loop.

Suddenly a cart appeared, pulled by what seemed to be the skeleton of a horse.

A dreadful roar went up from the crowd, a sound which shocked Margaret as if she had been suddenly drenched with icy water. In the creaking, rocking cart was a man, handsome in a swarthy gypsy fashion. Golden rings danced and glittered in his ears and although his hands were bound he lifted his head and laughed. His laughter had a ringing, courageous quality to it and his white teeth glittered in the sun.

This pleased the crowd : they liked guts. A roar of acclamation went up that drowned even the dirge-like tolling of the bell.

Presently the cart stopped, and the condemned man leaped out on to the scaffold. Because his hands were bound he stumbled. The hangman caught and steadied him.

The doomed man nodded appreciatively.

" Thank ye, mate," he said. " Wish I could do the same for you."

The hangman took out a black cloth to bind the other's eyes. The man about to die seized it in his teeth and with a jerk of his head flicked it to a woman weeping at the foot of the gallows.

" Don't cry, Liz," he said. " A scarf for you to remember Tom Geldart by."

Another roar of appreciation went up from the crowd. It was a long time since they had had such entertainment.

Geldart stepped on to the platform and stood with his legs firmly a-straddle. Then he lifted his head and shouted over the crowd to a glittering-eyed crone who stood on the steps of a nearby tavern, a quart of ale in her hand : " So long, Ma. Don't let the sods have my gold ear-rings ! "

The woman, her yellow-grey hair streaming wildly, raised her ale mug. " So long, Tom lad," she called back. " Your old mother's proud of you. I won't let 'em keep your ear-rings."

Margaret closed her eyes but to her ears came the crash of the released trap-door and the thud of a falling body. For a while the taut rope twanged, quivered and danced over the empty black square in the platform.

The crowd roared and cheered, whilst the wild-eyed woman on the tavern steps went inside to get her mug re-filled.

2

Back at the house on St. Margaret's Green John Cobbold strode, dusty and tired, straight into the room where his wife was at tea. As soon as she saw him she put down her cup and got up anxiously.

Her husband's grim face told the story even before he spoke. " Too late, m'dear. They apprehended her at Aldegate. She's in Newgate. Be so good as to pour me tea."

He sat, legs sprawled in front of him, gazing unseeingly into the fire.

Elizabeth put her hands on his forehead. " Don't fret, dearest," she said. " Go to bed and have a good night's rest. Tomorrow we'll get the coach harnessed up for London."

John Cobbold's tired, dusty face suddenly lit up with an affectionate smile, as if the burden of his distress had been diminished by the justification of his faith in his wife. He had known that she would not leave the unfortunate girl to face her troubles alone, that the goodness that was in her would not let her rest while help could still be given to Margaret.

And so it was that, after an early start, and a struggle through the throng that had collected at Newgate to look at the woman horse-thief, the Cobbolds were let into Margaret's cell, where she sat guarded by two grim-visaged female warders.

Margaret had steeled herself to meet the harsh conditions of prison life and, sitting there, the hardness of her face might have been mistaken for depravity of mind. But the sight of her master and mistress was too much for her ; and in the presence of these loved and kindly people the pitifully thin protective shell Margaret had built up around herself collapsed completely. She stumbled across the stone floor into Mrs. Cobbold's arms and burst into a storm of tears.

Would they ever be able to forgive her ? Yes, John Cobbold told her in his awkward, comforting way, they had already forgiven her. They quite understood why she had done it, and had come to see what they could do for her.

But, he wondered to himself, does she understand the position she is now in ? She did not appear to be worrying about what would happen to her, but rather about the offence she had committed against the Cobbolds.

The taking of the horse was, in the mind of John Cobbold, a minor thing. Crop was safe in his stable and Cobbold would have been quite content to have reprimanded Margaret for borrowing it without permission and . . .

A clerk of the court touched his elbow respectfully. "Would you please to come this way, sir," he said. Cobbold looked at his wife with raised eyebrows and followed the clerk into another room.

Whilst he was gone a statement was taken from Margaret and then re-read to her by the clerk, after which she signed it. An order was then made for her removal to Ipswich Gaol. Just as these formalities were finished John Cobbold came back into the cell. His face was grave but he said nothing until he and his wife had left Margaret.

Once outside the prison he unburdened himself to his wife. "Things are in a bad way, m'dear," he told her. "I refused point-blank to prosecute. Then the magistrates bound me over and constrained me to do so, whether I liked it or not. They explained in no uncertain terms that this business of horse-stealing is rife throughout the country and that they are determined to stamp it out. 'Twas useless for me to tell them that Margaret had merely borrowed the horse without permission. They'd already heard of the unfortunate girl's association with that villain Laud and . . ." Cobbold paused, as if not liking what he was about to say.

Elizabeth looked intently at her husband. "Yes, dear . . . go on," she prompted.

"I'm afraid that they are going to make an example of her !"

Beneath Elizabeth Cobbold's sweet-natured exterior was a broad layer of iron determination. She looked steadfastly at the troubled face of her husband.

"John, whatever she has or has not done, we owe more to Margaret than we could ever possibly repay," she said. "I know she's wilful and reckless. I know of her mad, almost criminal infatuation for Laud. But she'll . . . she'll not suffer the fate of a horse-thief if we have to go personally to every man, woman and child in the whole county of Suffolk !"

A few days after her arrest Margaret was removed to Ipswich Gaol.

Mr. Ripshaw, the Governor of the gaol, was a kindly man for one of his calling. Feeling a trifle embarrassed at having

to deal with a woman horse-thief for the first time in his life
he sought to cover his feelings by assuming a brusque, hearty
manner. When the turnkey unlocked Margaret's cell Ripshaw blinked his deep-set grey eyes and coughed.

" There you are, young woman," he said. " This'll be
your home for a while. Behave yourself and life won't be
difficult—for either of us."

Margaret soon won the heart of Mr. Ripshaw, and a few
days after her confinement to her cell she was permitted to have
pen and paper to write to her mistress.

From her cell window Margaret could see the Cobbolds'
house and the green fields all about it. So great was the
surge of happy memories associated with this spot that tears
welled into her eyes as she started to write.

My Lady,

At last I have arrived at the County Gaol. From my cell
window I can see your house and the fields where I used to
play with the children. It almost breaks my heart when I
think of the happiness I once knew in your service.

Oh, I do beg of you come and see me, I am so frightened.
Many people at Newgate Gaol flattered me, and indeed
called me brave for my act. If the act was brave, why then
do I feel such fear ?

I have so much time in which to think. Every time I hear
footsteps coming down the long stone corridor I feel as if I
shall die. Some of the prisoners act like demented things.
They scream, cry and pray aloud at all hours of the day and
night. Some of them beat their naked hands against the
iron bars of their cells until they bleed. Anything rather than
endure the solitude in which they are forced to live.

For the sake of the old days, my lady, hurry to see
Your most grateful though wretched servant,
MARGARET.

When John Cobbold returned from the brewery Elizabeth
gave him the letter. With a shadowed face he read the badly-
spelt, tear-stained missive, with its ill-formed writing. Poor
Margaret, he thought, how badly she needs comfort. But what
comfort can we give her ? How easy to raise her hopes, and
how unkind to do so.

Horse-stealing had become so common, not only in East
Anglia but all over England, that the full power of the law was
now arrayed against it. Things looked black indeed. Cob-

bold had been round to see some of his friends, including Doctor Stebbing; and they had all agreed to appear at the trial and to testify on Margaret's behalf. But would this be sufficient?

Refolding the letter he spoke softly to his wife.

"Perhaps their testimony will influence the judge. God in his mercy alone knows."

Elizabeth Cobbold, through the good graces of the prison chaplain whom she knew, obtained permission to visit her former servant. She tried to explain to Margaret the seriousness of her position, but was baffled by Margaret's complete refusal to implicate Laud in any way. The girl was determined to say nothing that might endanger her lover's life— she would rather die.

Mrs. Cobbold recounted how, after Margaret's disappearance, Ivy the kitchen maid had found Laud's letter where Margaret had thrown it away. She told how her husband had been forced against his will to prosecute. She explained that Laud's letter was evidence, that they would have to produce it in support of statements as to her character, and that it was a strong point in her defence.

But Margaret would have none of it. She beseeched Mrs. Cobbold not to bring Will into it. She was sure he must have been in great trouble when he wrote the note. "Burn that letter, I beg of you," she pleaded, "for the sake of your children whom we both love, for the sake of the old days, for my sake—oh, *please*!" Margaret was rapidly becoming hysterical.

Mrs. Cobbold sighed. Such single-mindedness and devotion to the man who was the cause of her present danger! If only that greatness of spirit could be diverted into worthier channels. In the meantime Margaret must be saved from her own folly, must be led from the peril in which she now stood.

"Margaret, my dear," she said gently, "your master and I both understand what it was that led you to do this thing. We know that you have been nothing more than the tool of this unscrupulous man." Tool? thought Margaret. Unscrupulous man? Oh, how can you who are so good be so blind? I love him, don't you see, I love him. But she said nothing. "We know these things, but it won't be so easy to convince the judge. The Lord Chief Justice Baron MacDonald, who will try your case, is a man to be feared. He is the sworn enemy of "—Mrs. Cobbold hesitated over

the ugly word—" of horse-thieves.   Oh, I know you are not a
horse-thief, Margaret, but this is the charge you will have to
face.   Did Laud think of this when he asked you to come to
him ?   What has he ever brought but sorrow to you and
yours ?   And now this.   If he really loved you he would
never have placed you in such hideous danger.   Was he not
only thinking of himself ?   Has he not always only thought
of himself ?   Margaret, you must, for your own sake, tell
the judge everything."

Margaret said nothing, but sat with head bowed, her fingers
nervously clasping and unclasping.

Oh, such obstinacy, such blindness to the consequences of
this man's actions !   Mrs. Cobbold was nearly frantic.   She
seized both of Margaret's arms and shook her, speaking with
an intensity of feeling unheard of for a well-bred woman of
those days.   " Dear God, child, don't you—can't you understand ?   Because of this man's villainy, because of his selfishness, you stand with the hangman's noose around your neck.
You *must* tell all you know at the trial ! "

And still Margaret sat.   And was silent.

With a sigh that was almost a sob Mrs. Cobbold got to her
feet and left the cell.

CHAPTER THIRTY

I

NORMALLY Bury St. Edmunds was a dull town, stagnant and cold.

The Assizes however brought colour and excitement to the sleepy old place.

People lined the streets to stare open-mouthed at the splendour of the High Sheriff's gilded coach and richly attired retinue.

A line of splendid coaches congested the narrow streets which echoed and re-echoed to the blast of trumpets and the pealing of bells which announced the arrival of the judges. Great crowds stood around the Angel steps to see the great men in their white wigs, scarlet, ermine-lined cloaks and black silk knee breeches, descend from their various vehicles.

Their coaches were preceded by the gilt sedan chairs of the mace-bearing Sheriff's Officers.

A further multitude of people were gathered about St. James Church where the Lord Chief Justice Baron MacDonald and Mr. Justice Heath were at prayer before entering the court.

Margaret, however, saw nothing of this judicial splendour and pomp. Since leaving Ipswich in the prison van she had been herded with the other felons into the cages beneath the court.

It was striking twelve when the Lord Chief Baron Mac-Donald took his seat with Mr. Justice Heath presiding in the Nisi Prius. On the right hand of the Lord Chief Baron sat the High Sheriff, Chaloner Archdeckne, Esq.

The Proclamation was read and then the names of the Grand Jury for the County and the Liberty. After the names had been called and answered the Lord Chief Baron, remote and dignified, addressed the Grand Jury. His voice was high-pitched with the ringing quality of tempered steel.

" My lords and gentlemen, you are well aware that horse-stealing is rife throughout the country. It is not merely a matter of some misguided individual's taking animals in a moment of temptation, but highly organized gangs of desperate beings who will stop at nothing, nay, not even violence to gain their ends. As you all know, I have sworn . . ." The high-pitched voice acquired such a timbre of deadly purpose that many an upright citizen in that packed court-room felt goose-pimples form on his shrinking flesh. " . . . I have sworn to crush this menace, this abominable form of crime." The judge's slim white fingers closed into a clenched and quivering fist and then slowly unclenched. " An extraordinary case is about to be brought before you, a case unprecedented in the whole of my experience. A woman horse-thief ! "

A loud murmur ran through the court. The Lord Chief Baron rapped with his gavel.

" Because this person is—er—a female, I ask that your sense of duty be not biased in any way and that justice shall take its course, irrespective of the sex of the prisoner ! "

When the Judge had finished his speech the petty jury was sworn in and appointed a Mr. John Bloomfield, auctioneer and farmer, as its foreman.

Every word uttered in that court was audible to the prisoners in the cage beneath. As each name was read out Margaret experienced a dreadful sinking feeling. Would hers never come ?

How tired and faint she was ! No food had passed her lips for twenty-four hours. The kindly gaoler at Ipswich had tried to persuade her to choke down a mouthful before she left, but his efforts had been in vain.

Margaret leant her fevered head against the cold iron bars of the cage.

One of the prisoners, a hardened poacher, put a rough, comforting hand on her shoulder. " Bear up, mawther. They 'ont swing a pretty piece like you. Transportation, I fancy."

Margaret's eyes widened with dread. " Oh God, away from my folks ? I'd sooner die ! "

At that moment a paper was handed from the grand jury to the clerk of the arraigns who called in a clear ringing voice : " A true bill against Margaret Catchpole for horse-stealing."

Two warders led Margaret out of the cage.

The poacher winked and nodded. " Good luck, my gal. Keep a stout heart and a cool head."

A gaoler thrust the speaker away from the door.

" Shut y'r gob. You'll need more'n luck time his lordship's done wi' *you* ! "

The poacher spat coolly on to the floor of the cage and gazed, completely unafraid, into the face of the gaoler.

High above the court-room an oriel window allowed a shaft of dusty sunshine to strike down into the dock. It shone on Margaret's figure, casting shadows in the hollows of her pale face. It glistened on her already growing hair and accentuated the length of her long, black, curling eye-lashes. It revealed to the startled jury the soft femininity of her figure in its plain blue cotton gown.

Margaret's slender fingers grasped the savage iron spikes arrayed around the top of the dock.

Lord Chief Baron MacDonald coughed gently behind his hand and shot a swift sideways glance at the jury. He had been prepared for a bold, hoydenish type of woman ; not for a slim good-looking girl with nothing of a criminal in her appearance. Margaret gazed around the court, wondering if by some impossible chance Laud might be among the crowd. She caught sight of her brother and her father. The latter looked even more feeble and aged than when Margaret had seen him last. His face was working and the tears were running unchecked from his hopeless old eyes.

Edward was at his father's side, holding his arm, almost as if he feared his father might collapse. He waved encouragingly to his sister, and then the Lord Chief Baron was speaking in his high-pitched, icy tones.

" Prisoner at the bar, you stand committed upon your own confession before two of His Majesty's Justices of the Peace, for the County of Middlesex.

" On the night of May 23rd last you stole from the stable of your late master, John Cobbold, Esquire, of St. Margaret's Green, Ipswich, a strawberry-roan gelding. You rode the same from Ipswich to London and were in the act of selling the horse when you were taken into custody.

" Do you plead guilty or not guilty ? "

A great silence settled on the court. Margaret gazed abstractedly at the great man. He seemed too remote and dignified to be feared.

She answered in a low voice, that nevertheless carried to every corner of that packed court-room.

" I plead guilty, my lord."

A sigh went through the court and there was a restless stirring amongst the listeners.

Lord Chief Baron MacDonald leaned forward, peered intently at the prisoner and then resumed.

" Prisoner at the bar, although you have made this confession you are at liberty to retract it and plead ' not guilty ' if you wish and so take your trial. Your plea of ' guilty ! ' will avail you nothing in the sentence which must follow. Consider your answer carefully ! "

Margaret spoke in the same low but clear tones as before.

" I . . . am guilty, my lord."

Lord Chief Baron MacDonald coughed as if to clear his voice and when he spoke again his high-pitched voice was a shade less icy than before and a careful listener might have detected in it a troubled note.

" Prisoner at the bar, it is the first time in my long experience that I have had the painful task of addressing one of your sex in such a situation. I cannot judge of your motive in committing such a foolhardy crime. There are no motives in your confession. I am at a loss to conceive what can have induced you to commit it." He paused ; and when he resumed his voice was cold once more. " The sentence to which you have subjected yourself is . . . death ! Have you anything to say why this sentence should not be passed upon you ? "

Margaret stood with bowed head, silent.

Lord Chief Baron MacDonald glanced around the silent court.

" Have you any friends in court who could testify to your character ? "

At these words there was a considerable movement among the crowd as several people pushed their way forward, all crowding round the witness box.

John Cobbold was called first and his voice was hoarse with emotion when he spoke.

" My lord, in this unfortunate girl you see no hardened criminal. I know, and many others will, no doubt, bear witness to what I say. She has been the victim of circumstances in a way which, thank God, rarely befalls the human race. She has been in my service ; and I can say without hesitation, that, although unfortunate in her own affairs, she has brought nothing but good fortune to myself and mine."

Cobbold went on to tell the judge how Margaret had twice,

at the risk of her own life, saved his children from death : and then concluded, " The greatest crime of this girl, m'lord, is that she has lavished a great and splendid devotion upon a rogue utterly unworthy of her.   Indeed, it is through him that she stands accused today."

Cobbold handed Laud's letter to the clerk of the court, who passed it on to his Lordship.

The Lord Chief Baron read it in silence and looked across to Cobbold.

" May I conclude, my lord ? "

The judge inclined his head.

Cobbold took a deep breath.   " All I wish to say, my lord, is this.   I did not wish to prosecute but was constrained to do so.   If and when the prisoner is released, then I shall be very happy to have her back in my service."   Cobbold climbed down from the witness box, giving Margaret a swift smile of encouragement as he did so.

The next witness was Doctor George Stebbing, his rubicund face even redder.   He climbed up into the box, pulled out a voluminous handkerchief and trumpeted loudly into it.   Then he spoke jerkily.

" As m' friend Cobbold says, m'lud, Margaret's a good girl, good girl.   Dupe of a villain, sir.   I, ahem, believe her a worthy subject for Royal Clemency, m'lud.   Trust you will find some mitigating circumstances.   Give the lass the benefit of the doubt, m'lud."   He trumpeted into his handkerchief again and tiptoed noisily down the steps.   At the bottom he paused and then returned to the box.   " Glad to take her into m'service when she's at liberty, m'lud."

One after another, witnesses poured in to the witness box to testify on the behalf of Margaret.

Even Jack Leader, stuttering and frightened, informed the judge of Margaret's beneficial influence on his fortunes and his children : strangely enough, supported valiantly by his wife.

Mr. Wake, the tenant of Priory Farm, also gave Margaret a good character, mentioning her unfortunate connection with Will Laud.

So earnest and sincere were the witnesses on the behalf of the prisoner that a feeling of hope pervaded the whole court. When the last of the witnesses had left the box the Lord Chief Baron addressed the packed room.

" Can anybody in the court give information as to the whereabouts of this William Laud ? "

Edward Catchpole pushed through the crowd and going into the witness box told the judge all he knew of the seizing of Laud's property at Aldeburgh, the killing of Segel and Nye by the Coast Guard and the disappearance of Laud.

The judge deliberated for a long time and was in deep conference with the High Sheriff for a further period. Hopes began to run high. The longer judgement was delayed the more likely it seemed that Margaret would be dealt with gently.

" I believe the girl'll be acquitted yet, m'love," John Cobbold whispered jubilantly to his wife.

Edward Catchpole had his arm around his father's shaking shoulders. It seemed as if the old man had the ague, and his eyes were glazed. Edward looked at his father in alarm.

" Bear up, dad. I think our Peggy'll be let off."

As he spoke the judge turned back from his low-toned conversation with the High Sheriff and looked steadfastly at the pale-faced girl in the dock.

Every eye in the court was fastened upon the austere face beneath the massive wig.

Lord Chief Baron MacDonald groped beneath the desk and produced a small square of black velvet which he placed slowly upon his head.

A shuddering sigh swept through the court. Somewhere a woman's screams were cut short as she was swiftly carried out. Elizabeth Cobbold turned her face and hid it in the broad chest of her husband. Edward Catchpole, ashen faced, supported his father, who was almost unconscious.

And then the judge's voice was ringing through the huge room, high-pitched and icy once more.

" Prisoner at the bar, I have considered your case in all its aspects, including the testimony of the witnesses on your behalf. It seems that you are by no means ignorant of your duties as a member of society and that you are possessed of common sense and good feeling." His voice became merci-less. " Therefore your conduct is the more inexcusable. I will not aggravate the feelings of remorse which I am sure you must feel. In all my judicial career I have never met a person who so well knew right from wrong—and who so perverted that gift. I must also add that I have never met a person who received so good a character at such a moment as the present. The representations that have been made on your behalf shall be forwarded immediately to the King, with whom the prerogative of mercy in your case alone exists. It would be cruelty, however, if I did not tell you candidly that the crime for which you are to suffer is of such bold and desperate commission as flagrantly to defy the law. Persons brought to justice as you are stand little hope of mercy. It is not within my power to give you any hope of escaping the full punishment of the law."

The Lord Chief Baron paused and coughed.

"Nevertheless, this night, before I sleep, I will represent your case to the only quarter whence any alteration on your behalf can be obtained."

A shadow passed over the almost inhuman features. The Lord Chief Baron, despite his reputation as a terrible upholder of the law, was finding this task distasteful in the extreme. His voice, utterly devoid of feeling and as cruel as the east wind, continued : " It only remains for me to fulfill the sentence of this court upon you. It is this. That you be taken back to the place whence you came and thence to the place of execution and there be hanged by the neck until you are dead. And may God have mercy on your soul."

Margaret, pale of face and strangely composed, curtsied in the dock : and then toppled forward in a dead faint. Sounds of muffled weeping came from all over the court-room. Even men were wet eyed.

John Cobbold, his own face stark, led his wife out, sobbing bitterly, to their carriage.

Old Jonathan Catchpole stood for a moment and then swayed like a lightning-smitten oak. His son caught him and carried him into a little anteroom off the court.

Doctor Stebbing had seen old Catchpole's face and pushed urgently through the crowd. He felt the recumbent man's pulse, lifted his eyelids and then looked straight into the eyes of Edward Catchpole and slowly and gently shook his head.

2

Not long after Margaret was sentenced a letter arrived from the Home Office for the Lord Baron MacDonald. He sent for the High Sheriff and Mr. Cobbold at once, and put the letter before them.

There was relief and even joy in the judge's normally icy voice. " Thank God for this mercy, gentlemen " he said. " His Majesty has given me full powers to exercise the prerogative of mercy in the case of that unfortunate young woman." He fingered his long chin. " However, I am afraid I shall have to punish her in some way. This business of horse-stealing is widespread all over the country. I propose to sentence her to the shortest possible term of transportation—seven years."

Noticing how Cobbold's face darkened MacDonald smiled. " I wouldn't worry too much about the hulks, Cobbold. There are very great difficulties arising just at present over this business of transportation. No ships for one thing. She will serve the whole of her sentence in Ipswich Gaol." The judge's voice became almost congenial. " I must say privately that I greatly admired the general demeanour and conduct of that young woman during the trial. If she is as sensible as she appears to be her sentence may be shortened considerably."

John Cobbold took his leave of His Lordship and hastened back to St. Margaret's Green with the news.

CHAPTER THIRTY-ONE

I

WHEN Margaret heard that her sentence had been commuted she experienced a feeling of revulsion so deep that she burst into tears. She had firmly made up her mind that she was to die, and the prospect of death was no longer bitter.

After a while, however, she adjusted herself, and through her industry and trustworthiness became the personal maid of Mrs. Ripshaw, the Governor's wife. So exemplary was her conduct that she exercised more good influence over the rest of the prisoners than any matron could have done.

Besides the Cobbolds and Dr. Stebbing Margaret was occasionally permitted to see her brother. One day he came in with a big harvest cake, something which had always pleased Margaret. After he had given it to his sister she sat for a while fumbling with the wrapping. Then she lifted her dark, long-lashed eyes.

" Ned, have you heard or seen anything more of . . . Will lately ? " she asked.

In the face of this direct question Edward Catchpole felt that he could no longer prevaricate. When he spoke it was through clenched teeth. " Yes, Peggy, he was taken at London and I hope to God Jack Ketch gets his hands on him. I didn't want to tell you this but I can keep it to myself no longer. The day you were sentenced—the moment after the judge had finished speaking—father was stricken down. He died in the anteroom of the court whilst you were still in the dock."

Catchpole's voice was gaining in bitterness. " Laud is a murderer. Our brothers ; father as surely as if he'd shot him through the head ; you in a felon's cell—and you still ask after him ! "

Afraid to say any more, Margaret's brother turned and

rattled the cell door for the turnkey to come and let him out. As he went he tossed a letter on to Margaret's narrow bed.

When the echo of his footsteps had died in the long stone corridor Margaret lay down on the narrow board that did duty as her bed. Long, desolate sobs shook her from head to foot. The turnkey peered at her through the iron grill of the door, and shaking his head slowly he walked away to the next cell.

The next day Margaret had recovered some of her self-possession and although still numbed by the news of her father's death, sat down and wrote a letter to her brother.

IPSWICH GAOL.

DEAREST EDWARD,

I do not know what to say about the sad news you brought yesterday. One thing stands out above all others. I am responsible for our dear father's death. Oh, Edward, how dreary it will be for you all alone. If only I could come home and look after you. I have given up all thought of Will now and only long for the day when you can come again to see

Your loving sister,

PEGGY.

When she had written the letter and passed it, unsealed, for the turnkey to deliver to Mrs. Ripshaw for postage, she remembered the letter Edward had given her, which she had thrust beneath her pillow and forgotten. She fumbled for it and sitting beneath the sun-lit window of her cell she opened it. The letter was from John Barry.

SYDNEY COVE,
NEW SOUTH WALES.

MY DEAREST MARGARET,

Since my last letter there has been a mutiny amongst the convicts. A sad affair and several lives lost. On the next settlement to mine one of the convicts, a quiet, oldish man named Ward, broke a plough.

The settler, a harsh man named Tully, swore it was done a purpose and called in the district scourger and had Ward flogged. Being an elderly man Ward died and his mates, waiting until dusk, blackened their faces and stole up on Tully, murdered him, fired the house and corn-stacks and took the best horses and arms.

Then they rode from settlement to settlement calling on

other convicts to join them. Many did and there were men killed both among the settlers and convicts. Houses and barns were fired and horses and cattle stolen.

For some reason they left me in peace. Why I do not know, unless it be that my small dwelling did not hold promise of much plunder. His Excellency the Governor turned out the military immediately and the convicts straightway took to the bush and lived as bush rangers, coming down at night to pillage for food. For months folk have been going to bed in fear and trembling, but one by one the mutineers have been hunted down by bands of settlers, or murdered horribly by blacks. A few weeks back the last of them, almost at starvation point, marched in and gave themselves up and were forthwith hanged out of hand.

The great pity being that it was all due to Tully's harsh treatment in the first instance.

Left alone with normal supervision the convicts are mostly quiet enough, for their lot is not a hard one. In point of fact convicts fare better here than free labourers do at home. Although they get no pay they receive ample food and other items to make their lives more comfortable. Their weekly rations are ten and a half pounds of flour, seven pounds of beef, four and a half pounds of pork, all the tea, sugar, butter and milk they need, together with free clothes and ample smoking tobacco.

The settlers pay one pound a head for the convicts and lodge them in split timber huts with straw rooves. The convicts are allowed their own vegetable gardens and are aroused by the overseer at daybreak.

At breakfast-time a bell rings and they go to their food, being allowed an hour for this meal. They then return to work until one o'clock, getting one hour for dinner. Then they labour until sunset.

I think you will agree with me, my dear, when I say these conditions compare favourably with those your father and brothers worked under.

Life is by no means dull here. We have our amusements in the form of regattas on the Hawkesbury River, cricket matches and horse races are greatly in favour too. Even convicts being allowed to attend.

The mock fights and kangaroo dances of the aboriginals are greatly diverting, although they are a depraved people and do not hesitate to plunder and fire a lonely settlement and slaughter and devour the settlers.

The weapons of the natives are fearful things. Barbed spears, bows and arrows with poisoned tips. Clubs studded with sharks teeth and queer implements called boomerangs. These are pieces of heavy, curved, sharp wood which can be thrown to knock a man insensible or completely sever his head, according to the wish of the user. If the mark is missed then this odd weapon returns to the hand of the thrower in a fashion almost approaching witchcraft.

We have our settlement dances too, Peggy, and then—oh my dear—how I wish you were here. In my mind's eye I see us dancing together. How I envy the men who are lucky enough to have their sweethearts, even though the majority of them are female convicts from the Parramatta Gaol.

As I write the night is warm and clear and the moon, larger than ever you see it in England, is shining on the land I am clearing. This is a vast and lonely land, but rich too, Margaret, and destined to be one of the Mother Country's greatest colonies, for strange as it may seem, even the most hardened convicts are loyal at heart and still love the land where they were born.

One of the most touching sights I have yet seen here was a group of huge, bearded convicts clustered about an English blackbird in a cage, brought out by a supply vessel. The bird was whistling softly, glad to see some green bush after the long days at sea. As I watched I saw several of the felons turn aside, the tears running down their cheeks.

It is strange too, hearing the men, their daily labour over, sitting round the fire talking lovingly of the old country. A country where their lives were nothing else but misery.

There is little stigma attached to convicts here. In fact many wealthy free settlers are taking better type female convicts as their wives.

Oh, my dear, how my heart would sing if you were at my side. How much lighter would be my daily tasks if I could come back to my solitary dwelling and find you there and hear your dear Suffolk voice which I love so much.

Whenever a convict or trading vessel calls I always go down to the quayside to see if by chance anyone has come from near Ipswich. Sometimes I wonder what I would do if you suddenly came walking down the gangplank. The joy of it would drive me out of my mind, I think.

Although I know this can never be, I never forget you, Margaret.   Yours always,

JOHN BARRY.

Margaret lowered her head on her arms and wept a little.
How futile life seemed. She could never forget Laud, never,
never . . . and yet?

If only things could have been different If she had never
met Laud . . . what then?

2

As time passed Margaret found the only way to keep her
mind quiet was to work until she was so tired that even the
narrow board and single blanket of her cell was welcome.

Her most tiring task was on washing day when she helped
with the prison laundry, and the heaviest part of this task was
the moving of the weighty drying-horses into the drying
ground and back.

When Margaret did this she had to pass down a narrow
passage lined on each side by oaken palisades topped with
sharp tenter-hooks. This passage ran between the male and
female prisoners' compounds. One afternoon she was moving
the last of the drying-horses when a voice came through to her
from the men's compound. It was only a whisper but it held
all the urgency in the world. " Psssst ! Margaret . . . Peggy
lass ! "

Not daring to make any commotion she put the drying-
horse down and leaned, her breasts heaving and her eyes
dilated, against the palisades.

Glancing swiftly from side to side she saw that there was no
one about. She swung back to Laud. Her face was ashen
and she clung to the rough wood savagely, deliberately hurting
her face and hands so that she would not faint.

" Will . . . my God, is it you ? What are you doing here ? "

Laud thrust a hand through and squeezed her trembling
fingers. " Ay, Peggy, it's me. What I'm doing here is a long
story that'll keep." He glanced swiftly around and saw that
there was no one listening. He spoke quickly, almost
savagely. " Look, mawther, this place, nor any other I
don't want, 'int holding me. I've planned to break gaol—
with you. Two nights from now a Dutch ship will be laying
off Sudbourne beach on the North Weir. They're sending a
boat ashore for me. We can go to Holland and get married.
What d'ye say ? Are ye game ? "

The immense magnetism of Laud once again held her in
its grip. Gone were all thoughts of misery, gone too were all

thoughts of the hard-won good name she was throwing away.

"Oh God, yes, Will," she cried. "Anything to get away with you—anything."

Laud glanced swiftly about again with his single, glittering eye. "The woman in the next cell to you died last night," he hissed. "There's an empty cell next to yours. Tomorrow the Governor is going to Bury with prisoners." He pulled her closer to the palisades and spoke in low, incisive tones. When he had finished Margaret's pale cheeks and magnificent eyes were ablaze.

"Yes, Will, I'll do it. But how about you?"

Laud's scarred face puckered in a lop-sided smile that boded ill for some unsuspecting person.

"Never you worry about me, girl," he said. "I'll be there."

"But, Will, where do we go when—if—we get out?"

"My sister, Lucy Keely, at Sudbourne is expecting us. Now go you about your work until tomorrow as if nothing has happened."

That night Margaret managed to get a stump of candle under the pretence of working late.

3

The next morning Mr. Ripshaw left for Bury with seven prisoners; and in the evening Margaret prolonged her task of washing until after dark. When she had finished she casually left one of the tall clothes-horses against the outer wall at a place where Laud had pointed out that one of the revolving *cheveaux de frise* was broken off.

She then swiftly removed the long clothes-line, and instead of taking it to its appointed place she wound it round her body.

She went into her cell and lit the stub of candle. Then she slipped into the next cell and crouched under the empty bed.

Hardly had she done so when she heard the footsteps of the turnkey as he came along the passage, challenging the inmates of each cell as was his custom when locking the cells for the night.

When he got to her cell Margaret thought she would choke from sheer suspense.

"Margaret, are you there?"

Putting her lips to the thin partition between the cells she spoke as if she were half asleep.

" Yes, Mr. Jennings."

The turnkey, thinking that, by her muffled tones, Margaret had her head under the blankets, turned the key in the lock.

" Blow your candle out before you go to sleep, won't you," he said.

" All right, Mr. Jennings."

Now was the moment. Would he lock the " empty " cell ?

Margaret's heart was beating so violently that she clasped her bosom with both hands as if she feared the turnkey might hear its hollow thumping. Crouching beneath the bed she heard the massive door creak open. Heard the turnkey's voice, " Poor Sarah, you won't sleep in this bed again."

Would he lock the door as he went out ?

The suspense was so great that the hiding girl had to bite her lip until it bled to stop herself from screaming. The huge iron key did not grate in the lock. The turnkey's footsteps died away down the passage.

Overcome with relief, she lay there trembling in every limb. Now an even greater ordeal was ahead. Laud had planned their escape for midnight. Three whole hours to lie, cramped and uncomfortable, counting the chimes of the prison clock.

Supposing Laud failed in his attempt. The turnkey would find her there the next morning. How would she explain why she was not in her own cell ? They'd know that she'd tried to escape and failed.

After ten, and then eleven, o'clock had slowly chimed away she began to suffer agonies of cramp. The coldness of the stone floor was striking through her thin prison dress. She stifled a moan and with infinite care stretched her numbed limbs, stiffening and holding her breath as she heard the footsteps of the returning turnkey. He passed her cell without speaking, and she knew that her plan had succeeded and that the short stump of candle she had lit had guttered out. Out in the clear, warm night the prison clock sounded half-past eleven.

At a quarter to twelve she carefully eased herself out from under the empty bed and removed her shoes. These she tied together and slung round her neck, and tiptoed swiftly and silently out into the compound.

The ponderous drying-horse still stood on its side beneath the broken *cheveaux de frise*.

Then she heard Laud's voice from the other side of the palisade. "The rope, Peggy, quickly!"

Swiftly untying the rope from about herself she made a loop and thrust it over one of the iron tenter-hooks with a clothes prop. She tossed the other end over to Laud. He swarmed up the rope sailor-fashion and dropped in the compound by the side of Margaret.

From that point Laud took charge. Flipping the wide noose expertly off the tenter-hooks he tossed it with equal dexterity over the shoulder of the broken *cheveaux de frise* of the outer wall. He pulled himself up, hand over hand, and squatting on the wall swiftly fashioned a bowline on a bight which he threw down to Margaret.

"Sit in that, mawther," he whispered. "Climb as high as you can on the drying-horse. I'll haul you the rest of the way."

Margaret did as she was bid and Laud, with a few powerful heaves, pulled her up beside him.

"Careful of those spikes, Peggy. Watch what I do and then follow me. I'll be underneath to catch you."

He threw the clothes line over the prison wall, then fitting his lean, powerful body into the space left by the broken spike, revolved the roller. Going head over heels he grasped the rope and slid down it with a true sailor's agility. At the bottom of the wall he looked up.

"Come on, Peggy girl, quick as you like!"

Margaret eased her body over the roller as Will had done and then slid willy nilly down the rope into Laud's waiting arms. At the bottom she felt his coat was wet and sticky. "Oh, Will—blood. You're hurt."

His laugh was little more than a bark. "Don't worry about that, girl. It's not mine."

They ran swiftly down the steep slope leading from the prison walls, crossed a dry ditch and entered a lane near St. Helen's Church. From there they made their way to the Woodbridge Road.

At last Laud stopped at a cart-shed.

"There's some clothes for you and a couple of nags inside," he said. "It won't be long now."

Margaret turned and gazed at him for a breathless moment. Then she was in his arms and they were lip to lip for a few seconds.

It was Laud who first disengaged himself.

"Time for kissing when we're safe, Peggy."

Nobody took much notice of the two sailors galloping head-long towards the coast in the dawn. The only people to see them were farm labourers and fishermen. Sailors on horse-back were a common enough sight.

They arrived at Woodbridge Ferry just as dawn broke, their intention being to cross and make their way over the lonely stretches of Sutton Hoo Walks to the even more lonely wastes of Butley Heath ; and thence to Sudbourne and the North Weir.

Cantering slowly down to the ferry, Margaret suddenly grasped Laud's arm. " Oh God, Will—old Coulson the fisherman. He'll recognize me ! "

Laud laughed exultantly. " He's too mazed in the wits to recognize anybody except mebbe his fiends and witches. Leave it to me."

As they passed the fisherman, his rags all a-dangle with his gruesome charms and relics, Laud lifted a hand in greeting. " Ha, Robin. Seen your foul fiend lately ? "

The old man grinned, exposing blackened stumps of teeth.

" No, that I 'int, Master Will. That is, not until this marnin'. He's a settin' on your crupper and a-pointin' at your good-looking young messmate there ! "

Laud half swung to look, then he laughed. " Ah well, Robin, he's giving you a holiday if he's along o' us. Come on, Tom, we've got to catch the tide."

He shook the reins and he and Margaret went slowly down to the broad flat punt which would ferry them and their mounts over to the lonely heathland which was the last lap of their journey to Sudbourne Beach.

Now that they seemed comparatively safe Margaret glanced about her. Never had the world seemed so fresh and lovely. The sun was gaining power and the grass beneath their horses' hooves was afloat with sparkling beads of dew. In a nearby hawthorn bush a blackbird was giving his bright whistle to the new day. Overhead a leisurely heron gave a harsh " Fra-a-aank ! " The salt smell of the sea was strong and ahead of them over the eastern horizon the sky was a light blue, fading to a blue-white.

Margaret took a deep breath and gave Laud a happy glance.

Behind them on the other side of the Deben old Coulson the fisherman was tittering to himself.

" So that rake-hell Laud thought old Robin wouldn't know

his piece all dolled up in sailor's clothes . . . heh . . . heh . . . heh ! "

Then he picked up his basket of fish and lengthened his stride towards Woodbridge.

CHAPTER THIRTY-TWO

I

THERE was confusion in Ipswich Gaol. The turnkey on the men's side was found with his head battered in with his own key; and a little later Margaret's cell was found locked but empty. This second event caused even more alarm than the murder of the turnkey and Laud's escape.

Some of the other prisoners swore that Margaret was in league with the devil, who had spirited her away. The dangling rope and the drying-horse showed the way by which the desperate couple had escaped, but how Margaret had managed to get out of her locked cell was still a mystery.

Mrs. Ripshaw, the Governor's wife, was greatly agitated. Her husband stood to lose a thousand pounds—five hundred pounds surety for each prisoner. She sent a fast messenger to Mr. and Mrs. Cobbold right away.

John Cobbold and his wife were horrified at the news, knowing full well that Margaret's life was in the greatest jeopardy. She could be shot on sight; and death would most certainly be her portion if she were recaptured, as she most surely would be. The Cobbolds went straight to Ipswich Gaol and into conference with the Governor's wife.

Outside the prison a huge crowd was milling around the spot where the getaway had been made. Armed constables were sent hot-foot to every place where Margaret and Laud might be in hiding: to Nacton Heath, Priory Farm, Brandiston.

When the Governor arrived back from Bury St. Edmunds he found the Magistrates at the gaol questioning the turnkey. The poor man was almost weeping, for he had been accused outright of conniving with Margaret and for accepting a bribe from a person or persons unknown.

In the meantime handbills were being struck off and circulated as rapidly as possible.

£500 REWARD

Whereas on Tuesday night the 25th of March or early on Wednesday morning William Laud and Margaret Catchpole, felons confined in Ipswich Gaol, did make their escape by scaling the prison wall.

This is to give notice that the above reward will be given to any person or persons who will bring the said fugitives to Mr. Ripshaw the Governor of Ipswich Gaol. And one half of the said sum to any person or persons furnishing information such as shall lead to their apprehension.

And notice is hereby given that any person or persons concealing the said felons shall, after this notice, if detected, be, by order of the Magistrates, punished as the law directs.

N.B.—The man William Laud is known to be desperate and will be bearing arms.

Ipswich Gaol,
    March 28th.

On the morning of Margaret's escape old Coulson had navigated his crazy, patchwork craft up as far as Levington Creek and from there had trudged to the Cobbold establishment, where he had a regular order for his fish.

The cook who had taken Margaret's place was a gossip and as soon as she saw the old man her tongue started to wag.

" Well, Robin, I suppose you heard of Margaret's escape from gaol last night ? "

Colson lifted his uncouth head and the cook involuntarily shrank back from the mad eyes gleaming through the tangle of hair.

" No, I 'int hard northen. But I fare to think I seen her at dawn o' day, do the foul fiend ha' played me one o' his tricks."

The cook's pale blue, rather porcine eyes, widened.

" Seen her, Robin ? Where ? Softly, man, softly ! "

" I seen that rum 'un Laud and someone wholly like our Peggy, dressed in sailor's gear, go across Sutton Ferry together. Heh . . . heh . . . heh, she'd ha' deceived anyone else but not Robin. The foul fiend were wi' 'em you see. I told your mistress long since that no good would come o' that mawther."

He swung his basket up and strode down the path, his bone charms and relics clicking like gruesome castanets.

Breathlessly the cook tidied herself and hurried to the parlour. She was gratified to find that her employers had not heard the news, but disappointed that she was not encouraged to give her own views on the escape. This disappointment was immediately swallowed up in the pleasurable prospect of imparting the information—with suitable embellishments—to the kitchen staff; and she hastened away to indulge in an orgy of gossip.

Meanwhile Elizabeth and her husband looked at each other, and saw their own thoughts mirrored in the other's eyes. Everything they had done on Margaret's behalf—the petitions they had asked people to sign—had been of no avail. The good name Margaret had earned by her conduct in gaol had been erased by this one last, mad act. She was in the company of a proven murderer, the most deadly and most desperate man in the whole of the Eastern Counties.

For a while John Cobbold gazed in mute enquiry at his wife, and reading the answer in her face turned to the hall where his riding clothes hung.

His wife heard him ride away, and sat staring bleakly into the fire.

Margaret had put herself beyond the pale.

2

At Ipswich Gaol John Cobbold told Ripshaw all he knew, and a few minutes later three men thundered off at a stretched gallop in the direction of Sutton Ferry. At the Deben the ferryman's story bore out Coulson's statement. In addition he informed the pursuers that the couple had been seen making for a lonely shepherd's cottage in the desolate heathland of Sudbourne, which rolled gently down to the sullen River Alde.

A little later they galloped up to the cottage. It was a typical shepherd's dwelling of the period and district. Its ragged, moss-patched thatch of reeds looked as disreputable as the lichen and damp-stained walls.

Lucy Keely, the wife of the shepherd and Laud's sister, came to the door.

She was a tall, strongly-built woman whose black eyes and lank black hair bespoke the gypsy blood in her. She was wiping a long butcher's knife on an old piece of sacking. Her expression was so menacing that Ripshaw, powerful man and armed as he was, involuntarily drew back a pace. Then he asked sharply, " Where's your husband, my good woman ? "

Lucy Keely gave him a long, unfriendly look.

" Out along o' his sheep. Where else should he be ? "

" We're Law Officers," Ripshaw explained. " Two fugitives from Ipswich Gaol are known to be in the district. Have you any knowledge of them ? "

Mrs. Keely shut the door another three inches.

"What would I be doing wi' fugitives. Now do you be off and leave honest bodies to their own affairs!"

Ripshaw, Cobbold and the constable were staring at a closed door from behind which came the thud of a falling bar. The constable scratched his ginger head.

"Well what do we do now, sir? Break down the door?"

Ripshaw shrugged. "We've no warrant to search the place," he said, "and that woman looks to me as if she'd try to use that knife. Let's see if we can find her husband."

They cantered away along the salting of the river.

Some way from the cottage they found Keely and his flock. He was a fitting partner for his dangerous-looking spouse. He had a thick thatch of tangled black hair and hawk features tanned the colour of mahogany; whilst through his tattered clothes one could see his spare, iron-hard limbs. He carried a heavy copper shepherd's crook and at his heels were two vicious, droop-tailed, mongrel sheep-dogs.

Ripshaw tried another kind of approach. Pointing at Keely he spoke with the voice of authority.

"Constable, arrest that man!"

Keely gave a sneering laugh, exposing strong yellow teeth. He sprang back, lithe as a panther, his crook at the ready.

"Where's your warrant, Mr. Ripshaw. You don't catch old birds wi' chaff. Come, your warrant!" There was menace in every line of the shepherd's formidable figure. "Do you lift a finger to me wi'out one and I lay you'll live to regret it."

The two dogs were rumbling nastily in their shaggy throats, their eyes flashing green fire.

Keely stood alert, the wind whistling unheeded through his rags. Then, knowing that Ripshaw had no warrant, Keely gave his dogs a whistle, deliberately turned his back, and drove his flock along the saltings.

"If what I think is true, Mr. Keely," Ripshaw called after him, "it won't be long before I have that warrant!"

Keely spat backwards over his shoulder.

Suddenly the constable caught Mr. Ripshaw's arm excitedly. "Look, sir. Look—there's the topmasts of a vessel laying off Sudbourne Beach!"

The three men searched frantically up and down for a boat, for anything that would carry them across the river to the North Weir and Sudbourne Beach.

Just as they were deciding upon the somewhat desperate measure of swimming across the swiftly swirling, muddy stream they heard the splash of oars. A boat was coming round the saltings, rowing close in to the land to cheat the force of the tide. It was the revenue boat with Edward Barry at the tiller and Margaret's brother and five other men at the oars.

The three men on the bank hailed the boat with all their might. "Boat ahoy . . . boat ahoy . . . hurry!"

Edward Barry, startled by the urgency of the cry, put the tiller over and told his men to pull up. He recognized the Governor of Ipswich Gaol.

"What is it, Mr. Ripshaw? Anything wrong?"

Ripshaw was breathing heavily. Without speaking he thrust one of the handbills into Barry's hand and pointed to seawards, in the direction of the vessel at anchor.

Barry gave a quick glance at Edward Catchpole.

"Up together on your oars men," he ordered. "Up together!"

Over on the shingle of Sudbourne Beach, at the very edge of the breakers, Margaret Catchpole and Will Laud were standing. Hand in hand they stood watching a small boat that had just left the anchored vessel and was proceeding in their direction.

Laud half turned and smiled at the slight figure by his side. "That sailor's gear doesn't hide the fact that you're a woman, my little dunlin."

Margaret flushed and then smiled. "Oh, Will."

He squeezed her hand. "Pity Lucy never had any clothes your size. Never mind, we'll get you rigged out when we get t'other side. It won't be long now."

Laud turned for a last long look about him. This would be his last sight of England: his last sight of his beloved North Weir, the mighty shingle desert which had repelled and fascinated him ever since he could remember.

The mystery of the place was strong on this bright morning. Never had he felt it draw so much. It would haunt him all his life.

He looked around, absorbing every detail. The steep fulls of stones going up and up in tiers of pebbly steps to the high water mark hid himself and Margaret from prying eyes to shoreward. He shivered and his face looked strangely drawn as he swung back to watch the approaching boat.

Margaret sensed something of his mood. "What's the

matter, Will?" she asked. "Aren't you well? Don't you want to go with me?"

He kissed her on the cheek. "Don't talk squit, Peggy. It's——"

Suddenly footsteps crunched in the shingle above them. Edward Barry and Margaret's brother, being the youngest and fleetest of foot, were over the top of the shingle bank first.

Margaret's eyes widened, and it seemed to her that her heart stopped beating, that she was dead and yet had power to see all the frustrated years, the bitter grief and tears, the longing, the hoping, the laughter and the dreams accumulated into a single instant of time. Was it for this instant she had lived, knowing no man's arms or lips save Will's? And then came the knowledge that it was so, and the revelation tore a shriek from her contracted throat.

A sound as desolate as the keening of Deirdre over the headless sons of Usnach went echoing away down the long pebbly corridors of the North Weir. Then she threw herself headlong into the breakers.

She would have been swept to sea in the powerful undertow had not Laud caught her and dragged her back, unconscious, to his feet.

He stood astride of her and as if by legerdemain a heavy double-barrelled pistol appeared in each hand.

"Hey there, Barry," he shouted, "if you want us, do you come and get us. Remember Nick Segel and Sam Nye. There's payment due!"

There was a deadly, flat, metallic ring to Laud's voice and his single eye was glazed. It seemed that he had forgotten the unconscious girl at his feet.

For an instant the two men looked into each other's faces. As floating objects are drawn together and flung apart only to be drawn together again, so had they been, each knowing in his heart that they were but flotsam in the tide of circumstance.

Even as they stood Laud's fingers were taking up the last fraction of trigger slack.

Suddenly his heavy weapons crashed and jumped.

Barry's pistols exploded but their charges only tossed a shower of pebbles around Laud's feet. He took a step towards Laud, the empty weapons dangling laxly from his hands.

"Laud, I——" he gasped. Then he collapsed and fell face downwards on the pebbles.

Thrusting his empty weapons into his belt, Laud swung

the limp form of Margaret up into his arms and as he turned to seawards and the approaching boat, another explosion splintered the bright morning and slapped flatly back across the desolation of the pebble beds and Lanthorn Marshes.

Overhead a huge " corpse eater " gull, which had been revoltingly busy on the decomposing body of a puffin, wheeled, indignant at the noisy interruption of his meal. " Agh . . . agh . . . agh . . . agh . . ." he barked, swinging his wicked, flat, predatory head this way and that. He peered with his savage yellow eyes, and clicked his powerful, curved, orange beak angrily at the figures below, some still, some violently in motion.

A thick white cloud of powder smoke lifted lazily on the air. The boat which had been pulling for the shore from the anchored vessel, hastily back-watered and returned to where the sounds of shouted orders and the clanking of a swiftly moving capstan came floating over the water.

Barry lay dead on the shingle, his blood staining the sun-bleached whiteness of the pebbles.

Edward Catchpole was staring unbelievingly at the smoking carbine in his hands. He was unharmed, while Laud, who had concentrated his fire on Barry and had forgotten about Margaret's brother, was kneeling dazedly on the wet pebbles at the water's edge.

Laud lifted his head and stared short-sightedly about him. It was growing dark and cold and the hollow roar of the breakers seemed louder than he had ever heard them before. He focused his wavering gaze upon Catchpole, then, gasping painfully, he dragged himself over the shingle to where the unconscious Margaret lay. Propping himself across her he fumblingly drew a short barrelled flintlock pistol from inside his coat. His hand was red and wet as he withdrew it.

He steadied himself across the recumbent figure of the girl, and by an immense effort of will pointed the pistol at the slowly advancing Catchpole.

" Back, Ned, back—do I'll shoot . . . not even you . . . taking her back."

He peered seawards. Strange how long the boat was getting to them. It was getting so dark ; and cold.

Soon Margaret and himself would be safe. He could hold them off until the boat arrived. This damned darkness and cold. He patted the cheek of the unconscious girl, leaving red wet smears where his fingers touched.

" They're coming, Peggy. I can hear the oars. They're

. . ." Edward Catchpole took a step forward. Laud pulled the trigger. There was nothing but a click.

Suddenly the roaring of the breakers grew into a mighty surge of sound that swept over Laud in waves of darkness. He crumpled across the girl's limp body.

Will Laud had solved the mystery of the North Weir at last.

The rest of the party, who had not dared to move for fear of endangering Catchpole's life, closed around the still figures on the shingle.

One of the revenue boatmen bent and picked up the pistol which had misfired in Laud's hand. Throwing open the priming-pan he gave it a queer look and then handed the weapon across to Edward Catchpole.

" See what saved your life, Ned ! "

Margaret's brother glanced into the open pan. The priming powder was wet with Laud's blood.

With a gesture of repugnance Edward tossed the weapon on to the beach. He stooped and picked up the unconscious form of his sister : then turned, stony eyed, up the shingle towards the river and the boat. The rest of the party followed with the bodies of Barry and Laud.

Overhead the " corpse eater " circled, still snapping his beak. " Agh . . . agh . . . agh . . . agh." When the men had gone he curved his wings forward and dropped back on the shingle to resume his interrupted meal.

A gaggle of startled brent-geese, interrupted by the gun-fire in their search for zostera, wheeled above the mud flats. They drew together in a dense black cloud, thinned like a wavering pencil line against the blue-white sky, and were gone.

A ninth breaker, greater than its fellows, reached up the beach. As it withdrew the whiteness of its foam was tinged for a brief instant with pink.

A sailor's straw hat went bobbing seaward like a tiny boat.

CHAPTER THIRTY-THREE

I

MARGARET's first conscious impression was the small, barred window of her cell.

Lifting her head up from the hard board of her prison bed she gazed about her. A grim figure of a woman warder sat near, her hands folded in her lap. For a moment she fancied it was just another day in the prison.

The savage shock of capture and the brief instant she had regained consciousness to recognize Laud's dead body beside her in the boat had completely numbed her mind. Slowly there came to her the knowledge that the venture had failed and that Laud was dead.

Nothing mattered now. Her dreams were shattered when she saw Laud's waxen face beside her in the bottom of the boat. She closed her eyes and a great peace washed over her. All stress and strain was gone. There was nothing left to worry over.

It seemed to Margaret that she was being shaken from a sleep from which she had no desire to wake. It was the female warder. Beside her stood a tall, dark man.

"Wake up, Margaret, wake up. This is Mr. Gibson, the visiting Magistrate."

Gibson nodded quietly to the warder, who left the cell and stood on the alert outside the cell door. Female convicts were worse than men in many ways : potentially violent both to themselves and to anyone who might cross them. Not that the slim, silent, white-faced girl inside would give any trouble ; she seemed half-dead already.

Gibson coughed gently.

"I'm sorry you did this, Margaret. Apart from Laud killing the turnkey and being shot himself, you have betrayed the confidence that Mr. and Mrs. Ripshaw had in you. If he had not recaptured you he would have lost £1,000. In addition to that you nearly ruined the turnkey. Why did you do it?"

The stricken girl lay back on the bed, her great eyes with their purple shadows beneath staring into nothing. It seemed that she had not even heard him speak. Gibson was an intelligent, humane man. He was aware of the great shock she must have suffered and decided not to worry her for a while.

Outside he spoke quietly to the warder.

"Keep a strict watch on that prisoner. See she has nothing in her cell with which she could do herself any mischief."

Nobody could get Margaret to speak, and at last in sheer desperation Ripshaw sent a messenger to Mrs. Cobbold, begging her to come to the prison.

As soon as Margaret saw the gentle, kindly face of her one time mistress she burst into tears and flew into Elizabeth's comforting arms, like a child.

"Oh, my lady," she said through her sobs. "I never thought to see you again. Tell me, have you seen anything of Ned? Why, oh why doesn't he come to see me?"

Elizabeth Cobbold was silent for a moment. But there was no other way. It had to be done.

"I'm afraid this will add to your sorrow, Peggy, but—your brother Edward has left the district. You see, it was he who . . . shot your . . . Will."

Margaret did not speak. There were no tears in her eyes now. Only an alarming glitter.

Mrs. Cobbold affected to ignore it, although inwardly she wondered if Margaret's sanity were leaving her. She took the girl's pale, clenched hand in her own.

"Oh my dear, why did you allow all the respect and love you had won for yourself to be swept away in one mad act of folly? Couldn't you see what the consequences would be? If you had only confided in me I could have prevented you throwing your life away—as you surely have done!"

There were tears on Elizabeth Cobbold's cheeks as the turnkey respectfully opened the door.

2

Between the time of Margaret's recapture and her second trial Mrs. Cobbold was a constant visitor to Ipswich Gaol ; but other than Doctor Stebbing, who came in a professional capacity, nobody else saw her.

When the day arrived for Margaret to go to Bury St. Edmunds for the second time she was much calmer than on the first occasion. Then she had been in doubt. Now she was in no doubt whatever. She knew that Lord Chief Baron MacDonald would have no mercy. For the second time she had passed beyond the bitterness of death and her mind was perfectly at rest. She had no desire to live. Will was dead. Her only living brother, sickened and shocked at having killed his sister's sweetheart, had gone.

She was fully aware of all these things as she stepped into the dock, clad in the same blue cotton dress as she had worn on the previous occasion. This time her head was up and her gaze did not waver as she eyed the packed assembly coolly and without a tremor.

There was no one to speak for her.

A tremendous quiet hung over the court room, so packed that it was difficult to breathe.

Outside a huge throng swayed this way and that.

When the indictment had been read, the clerk of the court, a tall, pale man with the appearance and manner of an undertaker, spoke in a nasal voice.

" How say you, prisoner at the bar ? Are you guilty or not guilty of these charges ? "

Margaret ignored the speaker and addressed the Lord Chief Baron MacDonald. As crisp as the tinkle of a broken icicle came her answer, " Guilty, my Lord ! "

When the judge spoke his voice lacked the faintest inflection of humanity.

" Prisoner at the bar, I cannot address you in the same strain as I did formerly. You have proved yourself to be hardened in iniquity. I pitied you once for your sex. I considered that given the opportunity you would reform. I see that I was mistaken. I look upon you as one dangerous to the morals of others. Besides this you have been responsible, indirectly or directly, it matters not, for the deaths of three men : the man who was your lover and the men who tried to circumvent his escape. So bold a woman as yourself would make bad company for any man. You are, in my opinion, too dangerous to live. You may say anything you have to say. Nevertheless, I feel that whatever it is, it cannot be good, neither can it mitigate the severest penalty of the law which you have so justly incurred."

Margaret stood silent for a moment, calmly but without the least trace of boldness or insolence in her manner. Every person in that packed court, from those present out of mere curiosity to the barristers and the judge himself, had their eyes intently upon the pale, calm face of the woman in the dock.

When she spoke there was not the slightest tremor in her voice.

" My lord, I fully expected that you would condemn me for my offences. But I did not expect to receive the language of judgement without justice from one who had treated me with such kindness formerly.

" I know that before the last assizes your lordship received a petition for my release signed by all the visiting Magistrates to Ipswich Gaol. It was because of Mr. Ripshaw's account of my exemplary behaviour. If your lordship had opened your heart to that petition I would have been a free woman and the life of the man whom it has been my fault to love would have been spared, as would that of the unfortunate turnkey, and Lieutenant Barry. I feel that if I had not seen Laud he would have made no attempt to escape from captivity."

Margaret's voice quivered very slightly.

" And now, my lord, I have nothing left in life, so I beg of you pass sentence and give me that liberty where the laws of man cannot trouble me."

All heads were turned towards the judge, who sat with his fingers locked and his head bowed to hide his troubled features.

There was a murmur through the court and the judge heard a muttering from the barristers.

" Sensible speech."

" Brave girl."

Lord Chief Baron MacDonald looked across at Margaret with cold eyes.

" Prisoner at the bar, no one is sadder at heart than myself, that the petition on your behalf was not sooner complied with. This does not, however, excuse your crime. You have very artfully tried to divert the blame, which rests entirely on your shoulders, upon me as your judge." The deadly rasp was in his voice. " I shall not blame myself again. I was far too lenient at your first trial. I shall add no more to the judgement of this court, which is : that you be taken from here to the place whence you came and upon an appointed day be hanged by the neck until you are dead. May God have mercy on your soul."

MacDonald removed the black cap, almost snatched it, from his wig.

Margaret's dead-white face did not alter by so much as a quiver. Her head still up she curtsied to the judge and stepped firmly from the dock towards her escort.

As the court filed out a young barrister tore his wig from his head, threw it down and stamped on it.

" By God, what a woman, what a woman. I'd willingly sacrifice my career at the bar to keep her from the gallows ! "

That night at his chambers Lord Chief Baron MacDonald was entertaining some of the magistrates, among them Sir Beaumont Hotham, Lord Viscount Broome and the High Sheriff. Usually after a trial MacDonald was able to thrust the days proceedings into the back of his mind. Tonight he found it impossible. Margaret's pale, composed face was before him constantly.

He paced irritably about the room, speaking to his guests in monosyllabic, preoccupied tones.

Sir Beaumont Hotham, an old friend of the judge, clapped his host on the back.

" Come along, Archie man, what's the matter ? You're like somebody hag-ridden. Liven up. Here, let me offer you a glass of your excellent port."

MacDonald swung round and looked his friend candidly in the eyes. Without his regalia the great judge looked like a quietly dressed gentleman of private means or possibly the secretary of a cabinet member.

" It's that girl, Beau old man," he said. " I must admit she's baffled me all along. Where does she get such powers of speech, such simplicity of manner. Obviously she is an uneducated country girl, but her ability of mind is quite remarkable. She's been well instructed, too."

Sir Beaumont coughed.

" Well, Archie, I must tell you that we all hoped, in the light of our previous recommendation that you would have . . ." He glanced around at the other guests and received nods of support. Seeing that he had the whole-hearted approval of the others, Sir Beaumont spoke with feeling.

" Gad, Archie, that wench deserves to live for her sheer

271

courage and ability alone—apart from the fact that, to me anyway, she seems more sinned against than sinning."

Before the Lord Chief Baron had left Bury St. Edmunds Margaret's death sentence had again been commuted; this time to transportation for life.

CHAPTER THIRTY-FOUR

THE transport vessel *Nile* was fifty days out and had been becalmed now for nearly two weeks of that time.

Margaret Catchpole sat in her cell, thinking of the days that had finally led up to her going aboard the *Nile* at Portsmouth. Never would she forget the brutal, degrading riot of it all. The yelling, roaring crowds at the dockside shouting obscenities and throwing filth. That last drive to the convicts' wharf, between high walls that shut out the sun.

Margaret's cell was one of a series that ran in two rows the whole length of the ship. There was a narrow passage between the two rows, along which the warders came every day on inspection and to distribute food and drink. Within the cells the sanitation was primitive in the extreme, consisting of large, open wooden tubs, which were emptied once a day by a gang of heavily guarded convicts ; while very occasionally lime was burnt between the cells as a crude measure of disinfection.

There were a dozen other prisoners in Margaret's cell, among them Elizabeth Killett and Elizabeth Barker, also from Ipswich.

The cell itself was a small, box-like space about twelve feet square. In fact it was nothing more than a cage with iron bars on three sides and the ship's side on the fourth. Margaret could see the prisoners in the cages on each side of her and the brutal, depraved look of some of them frightened her.

Some of the women convicts had their children with them —frightened-eyed, wan-faced mites, wondering at the bedlam, pallid from long confinement with their unfortunate parents.

There were men convicts too. Machine breakers, strike leaders, bread rioters ; those who had expressed sympathy with Revolutionary France ; Irish rebels. Educated offenders, men who had defrauded creditors. Poachers, pick-pockets and men forced to steal by hunger.

But it was the women she had noticed, and one woman in particular : a poor mad creature, who had on several occasions either attempted to destroy herself or attack the turnkey. She was so heavily ironed that she had difficulty in walking. An iron hoop was locked about her waist and chained to iron hoops above her knees, and from these hoops were further chains which were attached to her ankles. At night her hands were locked to the iron hoop about her waist.

All day long aboard the vessel the convicts played with cards or dice, which they hid in their rags as soon as a warder approached.

Sometimes the prisoners would fight among themselves and make an ugly scene even more hideous and brutal by their blows, clawings and cursings.

One woman in Margaret's cell was pregnant and not far from her time. She already had a child in the cage with her, a sickly infant which, despite the united efforts of Margaret and the woman Elizabeth Killett, a tall, blonde, haggard-featured prostitute, seemed determined to die.

Elizabeth Killett swept a lock of matted hair out of her eyes with one hand whilst she nursed the sick babe with the other arm. She looked up. " If they don't let this babe go up in the open her's going to die," she said to Margaret.

Margaret eyed the gasping infant, got to her feet and loudly rattled the door of the cell. One of the warders came along bearing a smoky lantern.

" Well, what d'ye want ? " he enquired roughly.

Margaret spoke quietly. " This child—can't something be done ? If it has to stay below here it'll die."

The warder shrugged his thick shoulders.

" Nothing I can do about it. You know the master'll only have convicts on deck during the exercise hour. Who'd look after it ? Better it were dead anyway."

He went back up the ladder to the deck amid a chorus of groans, cat-calls and hisses from all along the cells.

Already the death-rate was high. Burials were taking place with increasing frequency, and for the last ten days or so a giant fin, rigid as grey slate, had hung in the vicinity of the *Nile*.

Margaret went over and took the infant from Elizabeth Killett. Its tiny face was shrunken and yellow like a wizened little monkey's. It was in the grip of diarrhœa and Margaret was almost naked, having torn up most of her underclothes for the sick child. She cradled it in her arms and bowed her head over its tiny, wasted form. She knew that there was nothing she could do other than nurse it gently until kindly death took it.

Early the next morning the child died and was taken on deck, sewn in canvas and slid overboard. There was a tiny splash ahead of the giant, grey fin which immediately disappeared in a swirl of water.

The same night the baby was buried the mother started labour.

Knowing the futility of asking the morose warder for help Margaret appealed to some sailors who were passing through. " For pity's sake get me some hot water and clean rags. Anything to help. You can't let a woman have a child in a place like this without some aid."

The sailors looked sheepishly at one another. It was their task to haul on halliards and topping lifts, not to help convict brats into the world. One of them said cheerily, " All right, my chicken. I'll see what I can get in the cook's galley." A little later he came back with two wooden deck buckets of greasy but hot water.

Margaret and Elizabeth Killett then set to work and helped deliver the child, whilst the rest of their cell mates sat in an opposite corner of the cell and cursed the labouring woman because her cries interrupted their endless games of cards and dice.

Elizabeth Barker, the other Ipswich woman, a wild gypsy-looking creature, peered through her hair across at Margaret.

" Better she were to die, my chav. How do you fancy us women'll live when we get to Van Diemen's Land ? "

She swept her hair from her face with one, long-taloned hand—talons more than one sailor had felt when he had tried to be over-familiar.

Despite her rags and filth Elizabeth Barker was a fine figure of a woman. Her arms were bare and her breast showed through her split bodice.

Dominated by her voice the card and dice players stopped and stared at her. She glanced swiftly at them with her blazing, black eyes.

" Yes, I said how do you think we'll live in Van Diemen's Land ! I've been there before, this is my second time out. I said too much at home in the old country. Ah, I know a thing or two, I do ! " She shook her wild head so that the golden rings in her ears flung back small bale-fires from the sullenly smoking oil-lamps. " Ah hah, there's only one way the likes o' us can live. Wi' our bodies ! First we'll all go to the Female Factory at Paramatta. We'll make ' Paramatta Cloth ' there for a while. Then mebbe some on us'll be lucky enough to get taken into ' service ' with free settlers. ' Service ' they call it ! Mebbe some of us won't get taken. Then, if you want a roof over your head you'll have to go and live wi' a man as his mort—that or give up what few wittles you get as a ration, for a lodging. Then you'll have to earn more food an' there's only one way to do that for a woman convict in Van Diemen's Land.

" I'll tell you something else. John Marshall, agent of the Female Emigration Board, God rot him, encourages vice and evil. Why ? Because it's lining his pockets, that's why ! " Elizabeth Barker nodded at the woman and her new-born babe. " What future is there for them ? None, I tell you, none. Better for them to die, better for us all to die." She threw back her head and howled with hysterical laughter.

The other convicts, quickly catching her mood, started weeping, howling and laughing in sympathy.

Elizabeth Killett, still retaining some vestige of sense, went across to the hysterical Barker and slapped both her cheeks and shook her.

" Stop that. Stop that ! You'll have the warders down, then it'll be the dark cells for all on us. Stop it, I say ! "

All the way along the cells hysteria was spreading like a forest fire. The cell doors were rattled to the accompaniment of shrieks, screams and curses. Elizabeth Barker and Killett, both powerful women, were struggling in one corner. The rest were clawing or tugging at the first head that came within reach. Margaret crouched over the mother and the new-born babe, trying to protect them from the hurly-burly.

Suddenly like a wild cat she flew into the battle, kicking, slapping and tugging impartially.

" Get up, you stupid fools, get up I say. Here come the warders. It'll be the dark cells and the lash for us all ! "

Elizabeth Killett had temporarily silenced the hysterical Barker by winding her with a thrust of the knee. Between them Margaret and Killett sorted out the combatants and shook or slapped them into silence.

The uproar died. A little later the tramp of warders'

boots sounded along the ill-lit, foul-smelling passage between the cells.

"Parties one to five for exercise!" came the order.

Killett, tenderly touching a groove on her cheek made by a sharp finger-nail, looked across at Margaret.

"Thank God for that!" she said.

CHAPTER THIRTY-FIVE

I

THE convicts were divided up for their periods of exercise into groups of about thirty, and were chained together to prevent them jumping overboard. They were under the supervision of a warder and two assistants armed with whips, and were watched by whichever part of the ship's company was working nearby.

Up from the airless dark of the cells they would come, out into the heat of the day. As they emerged on deck they would momentarily turn their faces to the sun and take deep breaths of air, glad for a brief instant to be alive. Then they would shuffle off, dragging after the felon immediately in front, round and round the deck until the monotony and the heat bit into them and reduced them once more to a subhuman acceptance of their miserable lot.

But Margaret in that allotted hour never quite lost the lift of spirit occasioned by the comparative freedom of the open deck and the fresh touch of the breeze on her cheek. And where others moved dully and listlessly and empty-minded, she walked with her head held high and with a grace that distinguished her from her fellow convicts.

Now, after the fight down below, the very sounds of a ship under sail were soothing, the creak of the rigging and the rattle of the blocks, and the perambulation was doubly welcome. The sun was fierce and Margaret shut her eyes tightly against the violence of it, the pull of the chains on her wrists being a sufficient guide as she followed Elizabeth Barker around the parched deck.

Confinement below decks had accentuated her pallor ; but in spite of this, in spite of her rags and the dreadful food, she still remained an attractive woman, and this attraction was heightened by her brief spell of liberty in God's clean air.

The master of the *Nile*, a huge black-browed Londoner

with the Irish name of Hogan, had noticed on previous occasions that here was an unusual type of female convict; and now he called down from his quarter-deck :

"Warder, come up here a minute."

The warder slowly climbed the companion. When he was at the top Hogan pointed to Margaret. "That pale-faced one : who is she?"

"Name's Catchpole. Margaret. Hoity-toity piece. Different to the others."

Hogan grunted.

"Could do with someone like her to look after the cabin," he said. "Bring her along after exercise."

The warder nodded non-committally. If the master wanted a female convict—for whatever reason—all well and good. One less for him to worry about.

When the hour allotted to exercise was over and Margaret was about to return to her cell with the others, the warder swiftly unlocked the chain about her waist and told her to come with him.

Margaret turned startled eyes towards Elizabeth Killett, who merely shrugged her half-naked shoulders.

When they had run the gauntlet down the long alleyway of hissing, screaming felons the warder gruffly told her that the captain wanted her.

He marched Margaret through the waist of the ship, where the sailors were at work overhauling running gear against the day when the *Nile* should get under weigh again.

One of the sailors had stuck a knife in the mast, haft pointing in the direction of the longed-for wind. He was whistling between his teeth for a breeze and when he saw Margaret he stopped. "Hey there, m'hearties, Hogan's got a cabin-boy."

Margaret reddened to the roots of her hair and half turned to go back to her cell. The warder caught her arm and thrust her in the direction of Hogan's cabin, a roar of coarse laughter from the sailors speeding her on her way.

Inside his cabin Hogan sat, his sleeves rolled up, exposing huge, black-haired forearms which were sprawled across a dog-eared chart.

As the warder entered, Hogan looked up, a worried expression on his rough-hewn face.

"We'll have to reduce the water ration below. We're running short and no signs of a breeze."

The warder looked askance and for the moment Margaret was forgotten.

" We can't reduce it much more, sir. The convicts are only getting a pint a day as 'tis."

" Can't be helped. That's all my lads are getting—all I'm getting." Hogan turned to Margaret. " I want you to clean this cabin up a bit, girl. You can start now. Get things a bit shipshape. I shall want you to lay the table and get m'food from the cook's galley meal times."

Margaret looked around the roomy cabin. It was untidy and not over clean. She went aft and threw the huge windows wide. Hogan's bed was a huddle of bedclothes and the table was a litter of dirty dishes from the previous night. There were splotches of candle-grease visible on the part of the table that Hogan had cleared for his chart. Margaret set about moving the debris from the table. Then she made the bed and picked up the filthy rope mats and took them out on deck.

Some time later Hogan looked around with an appreciative eye. " That's better, me girl. Now run along to the cook and get m'dinner." He eyed Margaret's bare shoulders poking through her dress. " Wait a moment," he said. He went and rummaged in a clothes closet, pulling out a small size sailor's jacket. " Here, better put that on."

The sight of the jacket awoke in Margaret bitter memories and she blenched and took a step back ; then, seizing the jacket, she fled from the cabin.

Hogan shrugged. No accounting for these women.

A little later when he had finished his meal of boiled salt pork, dumplings and water diluted with rum he called Margaret over and nodded to what remained on the table.

" There you are, m'girl, eat hearty."

Too embarrassed to eat in front of Hogan she cleared the table and made a hurried meal when he had left the cabin, carefully wrapping up the remnants for her cell mates down below.

2

Hogan was kind to Margaret in his rough, seaman's fashion. The dread that had been with her when she had first entered his cabin soon disappeared. In any case the master of the transport *Nile* was too preoccupied to think of anything but the predicament of his vessel.

The mate was already down with scurvy and the crew was unreliable—almost as bad, in fact, as the scourings down below. And Malliss the bos'un was an ugly customer if ever there was one.

Overhead the sun blazed down, a white-hot disc in a cloudless sky. Beneath the *Nile's* keel the water, oleaginous in the heat, was as clear as crystal and in it were revealed lazily sliding sharks, twisting and turning with a flash of pallid bellies—green-eyed brutes impatient for the grisly meals which were occasionally flung to them, lately without even the usual canvas shroud.

All around the vessel's water-line grew festoons of hideously waving weed, aswarm with huge sea-lice. The decks exuded boiling pitch and the bulwarks shrank and gaped with the heat until Hogan gave orders for the primitive pumps to be manned and the decks flushed in order to close the cracks and cool the ship. But the water was as warm as milk and did very little towards cooling anything.

On deck it was airless, but below decks it was even worse. The convicts lay sprawled about gasping for breath, without even the energy to play their endless games of chance, without even the breath to curse and slobber their obscenities.

From time to time one would become hysterical and scream and batter the cell bars until he or she fell exhausted with bleeding hands.

Hogan increased the time for exercise so as to keep the wretched creatures longer in the open. It was not only from a humanitarian viewpoint that he did this, but also because he was afraid that a sudden and malignant outbreak of pestilence might scourge his becalmed vessel. Lime was now being burned every day below decks and the allowance of tepid, slimy water was further decreased.

Forward the temper of the crew was becoming ugly. Nothing had been said, but Hogan, wise in the ways of ships and men, sensed it as surely as he was able to sense a change of wind.

One morning the cook stumbled panting into Hogan's cabin, his frightened face a mess of pork-fat.

Hogan looked at him with furrowed brows.

" Well, what is it ? "

" It's . . . it's the men, sir. Malliss the bos'un came into the galley with some of the others and complained about the food. When I told him that you got no better aft here, sir, he called me a bloody liar and pushed me face into a cooking-pot ! "

Another time the situation would have been funny, but there was no smile on Hogan's face. " Yes," he said, " go on."

The cook cast a frightened glance over his shoulder. " It's Malliss, sir. He's coming aft here with the men." The cook vanished as the slap of bare feet on the deck and the babel of hoarse voices sounded louder and louder.

Hogan turned to Margaret, who was about her usual duties. " Get inside that clothes closet, girl. The men mustn't see you ! " Hardly had she done so when the cabin door burst open and Malliss, a hulking, scowling Tynesider, came in, followed by several others of the crew. They were a formidable looking lot, burnt almost black, and clad for the most part in filthy tattered shirts and trousers cut off at the knees.

Stepping up to the table, Malliss pounded it with a huge, knotted fist.

" Me and the lads here ha' had enough o' stinking water and salt hoss that'd make a pig spew," he shouted. " What're you going to do about it, eh ? What're you going to do ? "

Hogan looked straight into the shifty, muddy eyes with their yellowed whites. When he spoke his voice was edged.

" Who gave you permission to come bursting into the master's cabin like this, Malliss ? It'll be the lash for you, my lad, fifty of them. Now get forrard, the whole bunch of you, before I change my mind and make it a hundred ! "

The leader of the deputation threw back his ugly head and laughed. " Listen to him, mates, talking about giving the lash. Him that's been aft here gettin' the best o' the wittles and hugglin' with that black-haired convict wench."

Like lightning Malliss seized the edge of the table and hurled it over. It caught Hogan unawares and he fell with Malliss and the rest of the crew on top of him.

Hogan was a powerful man and fought like a tiger. One of the mutineers went down like a pole-axed bullock with Hogan's heavy sea-boot beneath his chin. Another reeled away, moaning, from iron fingers that had gouged an eye. Hogan was desperate and fought with any means at hand.

Malliss, after his initial onslaught, left the dirty work to his shipmates, and stood to one side with an empty rum bottle. Then, as Hogan's head came clear of the press for a second, he brought the bottle crashing down in a shower of splintered glass.

Blinded with blood, Hogan gave a groan and collapsed. Malliss, with the neck of the bottle, still an ugly weapon, in his hand, gave an exultant laugh baring his black, jagged stumps of teeth.

" The ship's ours now, lads. We'll find that black-haired doxy, then we'll string Hogan up and gi' him some of his own medicine—a hundred of 'em."

He picked up a bottle of rum and took a long swig at it, snorting with satisfaction. " Here, lads," he said, passing the bottle round, " sluice your ivories, then we'll get to work and find that wench. She's not far away."

Suddenly a soft voice startled the mutineers.

" Are you looking for me, gentlemen ? "

Margaret had stepped out of the clothes closet with the captain's watch-coat across her arms.

Malliss stared at her open mouthed for a moment, then laughed. " B'God, you're a cool one. I likes a wench wi' spunk ! "

As he lunged at her, Margaret shot him in the face at a foot range with one of Hogan's pistols, concealed beneath the coat. The ball from the heavy weapon tore Malliss' face to a red pulp, scattering his brains from a hole in the back of his head as big as a man's fist. He crashed backwards, and clawed once at the deck ; his feet drummed spasmodically for a moment and were still.

Throwing the coat from her arms, Margaret exhibited the other weapon. " You damned fools," she said. " How do you fancy you'd fare without Captain Hogan. Can any one of you navigate a ship ? What would happen when the wind *does* come ? You'd pile us on a rock and we'd all perish ! "

The mutineers, their leader very suddenly and very hideously dead, shrank back from the slim, pale girl.

Margaret gestured with the still smoking pistol at the body of Malliss.

" Go on, get him out of here : he's dirtying the floor. Two of you bring back buckets and swabs."

A shaky, but authoritative voice broke in.

" Well done, lass, well done. Here, you can let me have that pistol now." Hogan came round the table rubbing the blood out of his eyes. " Yes, go on, do as you're told, ye scum. Get that damned carrion out of here and heave it to the sharks. Hurry, unless some of you want to join him."

When the thoroughly cowed would-be mutineers had gone, dragging their dead leader, Margaret suddenly dashed to the open cabin window and leaning out, was very, very sick.

Pale faced and trembling she came back and suddenly sat down on a chair. Her legs would no longer bear her. Hogan, who was a great believer in rum as a panacea for everything, gave her half a mugful.

"There you are, sweetheart, drink that. It'll settle your little chitterlings."

Margaret took a small sip and shuddered at its strength.

Hogan covered her small hand with his big one. "Good girl, good girl," he said gruffly. "You saved a very ugly situation. God knows what would have happened to us, ay and those poor wretches below, if that lewd, bloody-minded rogue Malliss had taken charge."

Hogan went to a closet and brought out some rags and a bowl. "Be a good girl," he said, "and slip along to the sailmaker. Tell him to bring his palm, needles, a couple o' fathom o' sail twine and a bucket o' salt water."

When Margaret came back with the old, bowed, white-headed sail-maker Hogan took an immense draught of rum, sat back for a while and then gestured to the five-inch gash in his scalp. "All right, Sails, get to work!"

Margaret, fascinated despite herself, watched the sailmaker sew Hogan's scalp together with sail twine. When the job was finished and the sailmaker, also fortified with rum, had gone for'rard, Hogan turned to Margaret, speaking somewhat thickly. Even a man of his calibre could hardly have his scalp stitched with sail twine and drink best part of a pint of neat rum with no effect. "I'm proud of you, gal, proud of you. As soon as we berth I'm taking you straight to the Governor. If you hadn't done what you did the ship and everything in it would ha' been lost."

He bent and like a big, clumsy, embarrassed boy, kissed Margaret on the cheek. Suddenly he leaped to his feet and dashed towards the open window in the after part of the cabin. There was a mad exultation in his voice.

"Wind! Wind! By God, the wind has come at last! Come here, lass."

Together the massive captain of the *Nile* and the slim girl stood side by side. Hogan pointed to where dark shadows were rippling across the oily surface of the sea. " Praise God for his mercy," he said piously. " A breeze at last."

Out on deck the crew, their recent grievances forgotten, were cheering and shouting. One of them went below and returned with an old, battered fiddle. Sitting on a capstan he started to play a lively air.

Hogan lifted up his speaking trumpet.

" Shake out your tops'ls. Then get your wind chutes on the breeze ! "

From a dead, inert hulk the *Nile* came slowly to life. The limp sails filled and tugged at their sheets. Blocks squealed and ropes creaked taut against belaying pin and cleat. Behind the vessel a tiny swirl showed in the water and grew larger and larger as the *Nile* gathered weigh. Soon she was churning along with a bone in her teeth.

An hour or so later black rain clouds, with ragged streaming edges of light-grey, swept across the hitherto cloudless sky. Then, as if God had sent a second Deluge, the flood gates of the sky were opened.

The rain came down with such violence that only half the ship was visible. For'rard she was hidden by steam from the thirsty decks and a billion loudly drumming raindrops roared on the sails, the decks and the surface of the sea with a violence that numbed the brain.

Every available utensil was set out to catch the water.

The crew took off their clothes and danced joyously, naked as the day they were born. They knelt on the deck with the warm deluge drumming on their bare backs, scrubbing their clothes on the steaming, streaming wood.

When the rain had passed the *Nile* was a different ship. Bone-dry cordage had sucked up the water until every rope in the ship, running and standing, had to be eased off. The sails had taken up the moisture too. They stood out as rigid as curved sheets of metal. The crusted salt on deck and bulwark had gone and the ship smelt sweet and clean.

Now that there was water in abundance the convicts were brought up on deck to cleanse their stinking bodies and rags. A further working-party was given mops and buckets and set to work cleaning the appallingly dirty cells. Wind chutes were turned in the direction of the wind so that a torrent of clean air searched every foul nook and cranny of the gloomy 'tween-decks.

CHAPTER THIRTY-SIX

I

Days passed, days of rain and sun, during which the *Nile*, now clear of the doldrums, steadily drew nearer to the Cape of Good Hope.

The convicts diced, played cards, brawled, and now and again broke out in spasms of hysterical protest against their fate. Many suffered from scurvy ; all suffered from thirst, although the water ration had been increased following those few blessed days of rain. Hogan, too, extended their periods of exercise, and by this means kept the more serious illnesses at bay. Deaths among them, though still frequent, occurred far less often than during the early weeks of the voyage.

Margaret's health had improved, due partly to Hogan's sympathetic treatment, but mainly to the fact that she was able to escape from the sights, sounds and stench of the cell for an hour or two each day. Since the mutiny she had been treated with far greater respect by the crew, who no longer jeered at her when she went to Hogan's cabin. Hogan himself had become greatly attached to her, while she in turn respected him for his courage and straightforwardness.

One day, as they were nearing the Cape, Hogan called to Margaret from the quarter-deck. " Come out here a moment, Margaret."

She went out into the cool sunny day. Hogan pointed to a grey blur just visible on the port bow.

" There she is, lass. The Cape of Good Hope. We'll soon be round the corner."

He glanced overboard at the heaving gentle swell. Margaret watched the shoals of purple and silver flying fish flitting from wave to wave. A huge manta ray lay basking lazily on the surface—a monstrous carpet of a fish, weighing several tons and alive with sea-lice and remoras.

For'rard at the bow large porpoises frolicked and skipped around the vessel's rushing forefoot. From time to time they rubbed their shiny bodies on the wood, ridding themselves of vermin. They would glance up every now and again with their small, wise eyes and then with a flick of a powerful tail they'd shoot away ; only to come cleaving back the next moment, slicing like swords through the clear, deep-blue water. They leaped and tumbled over each other like children released from school.

Hogan, however, was not interested in the frolicking sea-pigs. He was gazing at the swell with a little frown on his face. Speaking half to himself and half to Margaret he peered towards the distant Cape and then at the swell again.

" There's something about these swells I don't like. They don't mean fog or wind. Every now and then one is larger than t'others, and they're getting heavier all the time. The last time I saw this was in the South Pacific. But never mind that now. Go down and tell Hardy the acting mate I want him. Then get the warder here, too. Hurry now."

Jack Hardy, a tall gingery young man, second mate of the *Nile*, now promoted during the first mate's sickness, was a capable sailor with great faith in his skipper. When Margaret told him that Hogan wanted him he was up the companion in a matter of seconds. A little while afterwards the warder also vanished into the cabin. The three men were in conference for a short time and when they came out there was urgency in all their actions. The warder went down to his assistants and his charges whilst Hardy went for'rard and spoke to the man who had taken the place of Malliss.

" All right, Vowles," Hardy said. " Get all hands out and secure everything. Batten down the hatches and rig life-lines fore and aft. See the boats are well lashed."

Vowles, a short, thickset, fair-headed west-countryman, touched his forehead. "Ay, ay, Mr. Hardy, zur. What is it ? Dirty weather ? "

" If Cap'n Hogan is right—and I've never known him wrong on the weather—something worse, I fancy. Get it done as quickly as you can."

Hardy noticed that the sullen, slow-heaving, irregular swells were getting heavier and heavier. For a moment he stood sniffing the air and as he did so his nose wrinkled in disgust. The *Nile* was rolling almost to her beam-ends.

Hogan went into the cabin where Margaret was busy with some of his clothes.

" Drop those for a while, Margaret," he said. " Close all your closets and then put up the shutters over those windows."

Looking out through the bow windows of the cabin Margaret saw the sullen swells; the giant shoulders of the sea heaving up from the ocean abyss for the assault. The sight appalled her. Pale-faced she turned back to Hogan.

" What—what is it, sir ? "

Hogan's head popped through his oiled canvas jerkin. " God knows, child. If it's what I think it is, you—never mind." He finished dressing and went out on deck.

His massive fists grasped the taffrail almost convulsively as he gazed bleak-eyed and without hope across the water, horrified at what he saw.

A vast wall of water, foam-capped and greyish-green, was roaring down on the *Nile*.

The speed of its coming was faster than galloping horses and it moved with a soul-shaking roar that caused Hogan's face to blench, despite his years of sea experience. Here was complete and utter destruction of his ship and every soul aboard her.

If he gave the order to release the convicts to give them a chance for their lives, there would be panic. No time now. Better they should stop below in ignorance of the dreadful visitation about to overwhelm them. Their end would be mercifully swift.

He jumped to the wheel and helped the helmsman bring the *Nile's* sluggish head round to meet the terror. Then he seized the end of a nearby halliard and lashed himself and the helmsman to the wheel, muttering a prayer as he did so.

Now the air was filled with the stench of millions of dead creatures, annihilated by the undersea volcanic explosion which had caused the giant wave.

Inside the darkened cabin, with its securely shuttered windows, Margaret stood, back to the bulkhead, listening. The *Nile* was scending heavily and Margaret could hear the confused roaring of the approaching wave.

Never in all her life had she heard such a noise. The confusion of sound was too vast for the mind to cope with, too gigantic even for terror.

Then it seemed to her that she was overwhelmed in a thunderous green twilight and that giant hands were bearing down on the ship, thrusting her to the ocean bed. The cabin door burst in with a crash and it seemed to the bewildered girl that God had allowed the flood gates of the ocean to burst open into the little cabin.

Green water, solid as a ram, picked up the stout oak table

and shattered it to flinders against the bulkhead. Had Margaret been in the direct path of the water she would have been crushed to pulp, every bone in her body broken. As it was the cabin was instantly filled from deck to deck-head and Margaret was aware only of the fact that she was drowning— that her lungs were bursting—that the sea was thrusting itself down her strangling throat—that she was being battered to death. She struggled bitterly for a while and then grew calmer.

What was the use of struggling back to life, a life destined to be dragged out in Van Diemen's Land? Suddenly the savage water seemed kindly and she abandoned herself to it as if it had been a lover's arms. Agonized life was behind her and was replaced by a great peace.

It was then that the sea, like a capricious lover in the very act of consummation, left her limp, unconscious body in a corner and swirled back through the shattered door, whence it had come.

By some miracle the antiquated *Nile*, instead of broaching-to and capsizing, had burst through the tidal wave. Tons of water fell on and about her and, tearing away her topmasts and securely-lashed boats, ring-bolts and all, filled her decks to rail level but did not stave in the hatches.

And then the wave was gone, leaving her a loguey half-wreck, dismasted and decks swept clear even to the last of the livestock—a lean, morose pig in a coop which had gone as a meal for some roving shark.

The battered vessel rolled sluggishly from side to side, sluicing great volumes of water through her gaping bulwarks. Hogan found himself on his back still lashed to the splintered remains of the steering-wheel. Of the helmsman there was no trace. Groping for his sheath-knife the master of the *Nile* cut himself adrift and squelching for'rard mustered the crew. Most of them were unhurt with the exception of minor knocks and cuts.

Down below in the cells things were more serious. There were several convicts with broken limbs where they had been flung violently against the bulkheads. From below came a chorus of groans and screams and blasphemous demands to know what had happened.

Luckily, owing to Hogan's excellent seamanship, no water had got below, so, leaving the injured felons to the warder and his assistants, he started to repair the damage done to his ship. Sprung masts were fished.[1] Jury topmasts were rigged

[1] Strengthened by lashing stout timbers on each side.

and the sailmaker set to work making sails to replace those lost. The steering-wheel was repaired and shipped back into position.

Right in the middle of the work Hogan suddenly thumped himself on his broad chest.

" My God, the girl ! "

He almost ran back to the cabin where he found Margaret, still unconscious, her black hair falling damply across her face, amidst a chaos of bottles, plates, sodden charts and equally sodden carpets.

Hogan went down on his knees and ran his hands swiftly over her. Then he drew a deep breath of relief. Margaret was half-drowned and badly bruised, but she was still alive.

2

Under Hogan's sympathetic treatment Margaret soon recovered. Her bruises healed, and although the shock of her terrible experience left her weak for some time, she fared immeasurably better than many of the convicts who had been injured by the wave. These, unable to take their place in the exercise parties, suffered tortures of thirst in the fetid atmosphere of the cells ; some, their broken limbs becoming gangrenous, lived days of agony before their wasted bodies were thrown to the sharks.

One evening, when his meal was over and Margaret was clearing the table, Hogan stretched his legs and looked quizzically at his cabin boy.

" You've never yet told me how you came to . . . to be aboard this craft, Margaret." He lit a pipe and drew deeply. " What happened to ye, lass ? You haven't got the same look as those cattle down below."

Somewhat hesitantly she told him of all the events which had led up to her deportation. Hogan listened attentively and when she came to the episode of the ride from Ipswich to London he thumped the table with an appreciative fist.

" By God, girl, that took guts."

Margaret shrugged. " So many others said ; but that didn't stop the judge from giving me this. I was sentenced to hang but the sentence was commuted. Would to God it had never been."

Hogan rubbed his face and glanced up at the girl. " Margaret, you've had a rough passage," he said, and his voice grew softer. " Look, girl, you're a lonely soul. So'm I. What say we get spliced ? Married, d'ye see. I have a cosy little place in London. You'd want for nothing. I'll get you a pardon from the Governor and we'll get married at Sydney. Then I'll bring you back with me. What d'ye say ? "

He was so carried away with the idea that he failed to notice Margaret's drooping head, and the tears that were gathering in her eyes.

" Oh, sir, Captain Hogan, don't ask me that."

Every man that she had ever cared for or who had cared for her had died or gone. Will Laud, her brothers, her father. Even poor bullying Will Riches, who had been harmless really. She was accursed. As the Lord Chief Baron MacDonald had told her, she was unfit to live, unfit to live . . . unfit to live . . . unfit to live ! With the words echoing in her mind she clasped her hands over her ears and giving a stifled sob, fled from the cabin.

She leant on the teak rail and wept. She knew now that she had no right, nor wish, to live. Captain Hogan had made her an honourable proposal, and she a convict. It had opened her eyes to what perhaps she had known all along— that the shadow of her past lay too heavily upon her for happiness to be possible. And as through her tears she looked down at the sea, she recalled that moment of release just before she had lost consciousness when the tidal wave had engulfed the ship. The slow heaving of the sea beneath her spoke to her of peace. A soft, gentle death, she thought. A soft and gentle death.

" Margaret ! "

The cry made her pause involuntarily, and before she could make a further movement Hogan's powerful hands caught her and dragged her back to safety.

" I'm sorry, Margaret," he said, mistaking the reasons for her action. " I didn't know that . . . that life wi' me would have been so distasteful to ye. Never mind, girl. Forget what I said."

Margaret, sobbing with released tension, did not reply. Hogan led her gently back to the cabin and tiptoed quietly away.

CHAPTER THIRTY-SEVEN

I

WITH her jury-rig the half-wrecked *Nile*, now lacking a bos'un and a quartermaster and with her chief mate sick with scurvy, ploughed her way across the vast spaces of the Indian Ocean. Through fair weather and foul, through days of torrid heat and nights of suffocating airlessness, Hogan sailed his battered ship.

Margaret, though her feelings seemed to grow ever more numb as they neared their destination, continued to perform her duties for Captain Hogan with exemplary efficiency. The memory of his blundering though honourable proposal had receded and he now treated her like a daughter whom, in his own rough way, he loved dearly. But Margaret was sick to death of the *Nile*, with its appalling sights and sounds, its rats and its foul smells ; and the memory of green and pleasant England was almost wiped out. Still more, however, did she dread the thought of Van Diemen's Land, which was now perilously near. She remembered Elizabeth Barker's frenzied words : "What future is there ? . . . Better for us all to die." What future indeed for her, Margaret Catchpole, horse-thief !

It was on the vessel's one hundred and thirtieth day at sea that Hogan called Margaret to his side. There was a look of relief on his strained, black-bearded face. There was relief in his voice when he spoke. He was deathly tired of navigating this half-wreck of a vessel with its freight of human wrecks. He pointed to two blue blurs on the horizon, all a-shimmer with heat.

"Landfall, Margaret, thank God. Journey's end for us at last. We go between those two points into Sydney Cove."

As the *Nile* neared the shore Margaret felt a lump come into her throat. This strange unknown land looked so like the banks of her own beloved Orwell.

Below, the warders were preparing the convicts for landing. The more desperate felons were to be marched ashore chained to each other.

The chief warder came up to Hogan. "What about Catchpole, sir, shall I take her ashore with the others?"

"No." Hogan shook his head. "I'm taking her to the Governor's residence myself. If ever anyone has earned a pardon, she has."

2

Margaret stood looking fearfully over the ship's rail at the roaring crowd of ticket-of-leave men, free settlers, emancipists and natives surging to and fro on King's Wharf. She was appalled at their condition: they were nearly as ragged as the convicts aboard the *Nile*.

One huge red-bearded emancipist roared in a bull-like voice, "Any good-looking wenches aboard there? Ask for Luke Jaggers, he'll look after you!"

Another man nearly as big bawled in a voice equally as loud. "We know how Luke looks after his women, don't we, mates?"

There was a roar of savage laughter at this sally.

These huge, ragged, muscular, work-toughened men with their twanging speech were woman-starved. In fact, so short of women was the colony at that period that the Governor had written to the Secretary of State at home requesting that more female convicts, and if possible free settlers, be sent out.

3

The warders of the *Nile* were shepherding the convicts through the crowd amid the shouts of, "Anyone there from London?" . . . "Aldegate?" . . . "The West Country?" . . . "Kent?" . . .

The convicts from the *Nile* were overwhelmed by the sudden change from the endless monotony of the voyage out. Some staggered around like drunken beings. Others wept. Others acted idiotically, one or two even falling down in convulsions.

When the Superintendent of Parramatta gaol had taken charge of the women convicts, Hogan gave Margaret a seaman's cloak to cover her rags. "Come along, Margaret," he said, "we'll go and see his Excellency." Margaret hung back. She did not feel equal to seeing the great man in such a hideous array of rags and patches.

Hogan laughed her fears away. " Never mind, we'll rig you out a bit respectable when we get ashore."

On King's Wharf was a small log shack which sold everything from dresses to shoes and buttons. Margaret was unlucky, for the store was empty and had been for months. It was in fact awaiting part of the cargo that was even then being broken out of the hold of the *Nile*.

Hogan shrugged humorously. " Ah well, it can't be helped. We'll have to go as we are."

Most of the crowd had dispersed, but Luke Jaggers was still standing at the bottom of the gangway. He lounged up to Margaret, who, despite herself, shrunk away from him. He was less a man than a big, evil-smelling animal with a red beard. He leered at Margaret.

" You'll be needing a man to look after you, sweetheart."

He caught her wrist with a big, ginger-haired, freckled hand. There was lust in his eyes with their light-blue, glassy centres.

Hogan's voice came from behind them.

" She won't be needing your sort of man, Jaggers. Keep your hands off."

Jaggers turned swiftly, baring his yellow, stained teeth in a snarl. " Who says she won't ? "

Hogan, used to dealing with men like Jaggers, wasted no more time with words. He leaped in at the red-bearded man behind a driving fist as big as a ham, hard as a maul and with the power of a cannon-ball behind it. Notwithstanding his size, weight and strength Jaggers was flung off his feet. He lay on his back with blood on his beard, snoring unseeingly at the sky.

Hogan blew on his raw knuckles and turned back to his wide-eyed charge.

" I know my Jaggers of old. He won't be worrying anyone else for an hour or two ! "

They pushed through a crowd of free settlers, ticket-of-leave men, emancipists and natives.

The natives frightened Margaret. They were armed with spears and boomerangs. Their grotesque adornments were frightening too : hair festooned with dogs' teeth and lobster claws, kept in place by gum. She noticed that all the males had a single tooth missing in the front upper row whilst the native women had the first and second finger joints missing.

These disfigurements were common to all and appeared to be some sort of tribal mark. In addition to this both men and women were further disfigured by strange ridged scars on body and face. They were poor specimens physically and wore little clothing.

Hogan nodded to them. " Ugly devils, aren't they? Treacherous as snakes. They won't hesitate to murder a white if they catch him alone in the bush. Murder him *and* eat him ! "

Along the sandy street to the Governor's residence Margaret noticed that the place seemed alive with mangy curs of all descriptions, snapping at each other and at the heels of all and sundry. Hogan kicked one particularly vicious brute from under his feet and it ran yelping and snarling down the street. " There's a plague o' curs in this place," he explained. " The first dogs ever brought out ran wild and mated wi' dingoes."

4

The Governor's residence was a large split-log building reached by wooden steps. At the foot of them Hogan paused and looked at Margaret.

" You won't be afraid to meet his Excellency, will you, Margaret ? "

She shook her head a trifle uncertainly. " No, but I wish I had some clothes."

" Don't worry about that. His Excellency has been a sailor himself. He won't expect to see a woman con—a woman who has just done one hundred and thirty days at sea, looking like a mutton [1]."

Hogan rapped heavily on the door which, much to his surprise, was opened by a bewigged, powdered and breeched footman who asked in an affected, high-pitched voice if he had an appointment.

Hogan regarded the footman with an unfriendly eye. " Appointment be damned, we've only just arrived from England. Tell the Governor it's Captain Hogan of the transport *Nile* ! " The footman sniffed and gave a disparaging glance at Hogan's and Margaret's clothes. " His Excellency is in conference. Possibly his Excellency's private secretary will see you."

When Hogan answered his voice carried a rasp to it. " Well, stir your stumps, my lad. I haven't all day."

[1] Fancy woman.

The footman's broad, tightly trousered bottom quivered with indignation as he turned and walked majestically away. Hogan's lips tightened and he felt the almost overwhelming urge to plant a heavy sea-boot against that offending portion of the footman's anatomy.

After a while the footman stalked back to the door. " His Excellency's secretary will see you in a few moments. Will you step this way ? "

Hogan and Margaret were left in a large room which showed the Governor's nostalgia for all things English. Prints of English country scenes hung on the walls. The furniture had been imported from England, as had the carpets on the roughly boarded floor. In one corner a huge grand-father clock swung its ponderous pendulum and gave out the half-hour in mellow chimes.

A little later the footman reappeared and beckoned.

Hogan said softly, " Better let me go in first, lass."

5

The old clock in the corner was chiming the hour when Hogan reappeared. There was a look of satisfaction on his face as he beckoned Margaret to the door. As she entered the secretary's office the secretary got to his feet so suddenly that ink, quills and documents were scattered unheeded.

Hogan gave a startled glance at Margaret, whom he thought was going to faint. He instinctively put an arm round her waist. The Governor's secretary came swiftly round the table and relieved him of the burden.

At the door the scandalized footman saw his Excellency's private secretary, Mr. John Barry, with a female convict in his arms. The dreadful person was crying and laughing hysterically in turns on the secretary's only white shirt.

Hogan, with surprising tact and delicacy of feeling, even though he did not know what it was all about, shouldered the gaping flunkey from the door.

" Cut your cable, you lubber. Can't you see we're not wanted ! " The captain of the *Nile* quietly closed the door.

APPENDIX

TO THE READER

I F you would care to see a portrait of the heroine of this story pay a visit to Christchurch Mansion, Ipswich.

Priory Farm, just outside Ipswich, on the bank of the Orwell is much the same now as when Margaret was in service there.

The old Cat House still stands on the opposite side of the river. The original white cat has gone and the window is bricked in with a white cat painted on the brickwork.

That strange and fascinating old inn, " The Butt and Oyster," still stands at Pinmill.

Sudbourne beach is still as desolate and draws me as much as it did Will Laud the day he died there.

The old Shepherd's hut, on lonely Havergate Island, is a ruin. It has collapsed with sheer old age, but the ruin yet retains much of the terror of that grim night when John Luff died raving there.

The cottage where Margaret once lived still stands on Nacton Heath. It is called " Halfway House " and belongs to Dr. and Mrs. Swinstead, who were kind enough to show me over their charming home.

The " Three Marianers " inn at Slaughden, where Laud was taken after Luff had left him for dead, has been washed away this thirty years.

My old friend of happy Aldeburgh schooldays, Basil Tiffin, lives with his charming wife in "Smuggler's Cottage," Aldeburgh, a quaint and lovely little dwelling, where, according to local tradition, Will Laud lived for a while when he was ship-building at Slaughden with his uncle.

Lastly I suggest that if you enjoyed this book you one day pay a visit to Aldeburgh.

You may not like it but you will never forget it.

GEORGE GOLDSMITH CARTER.

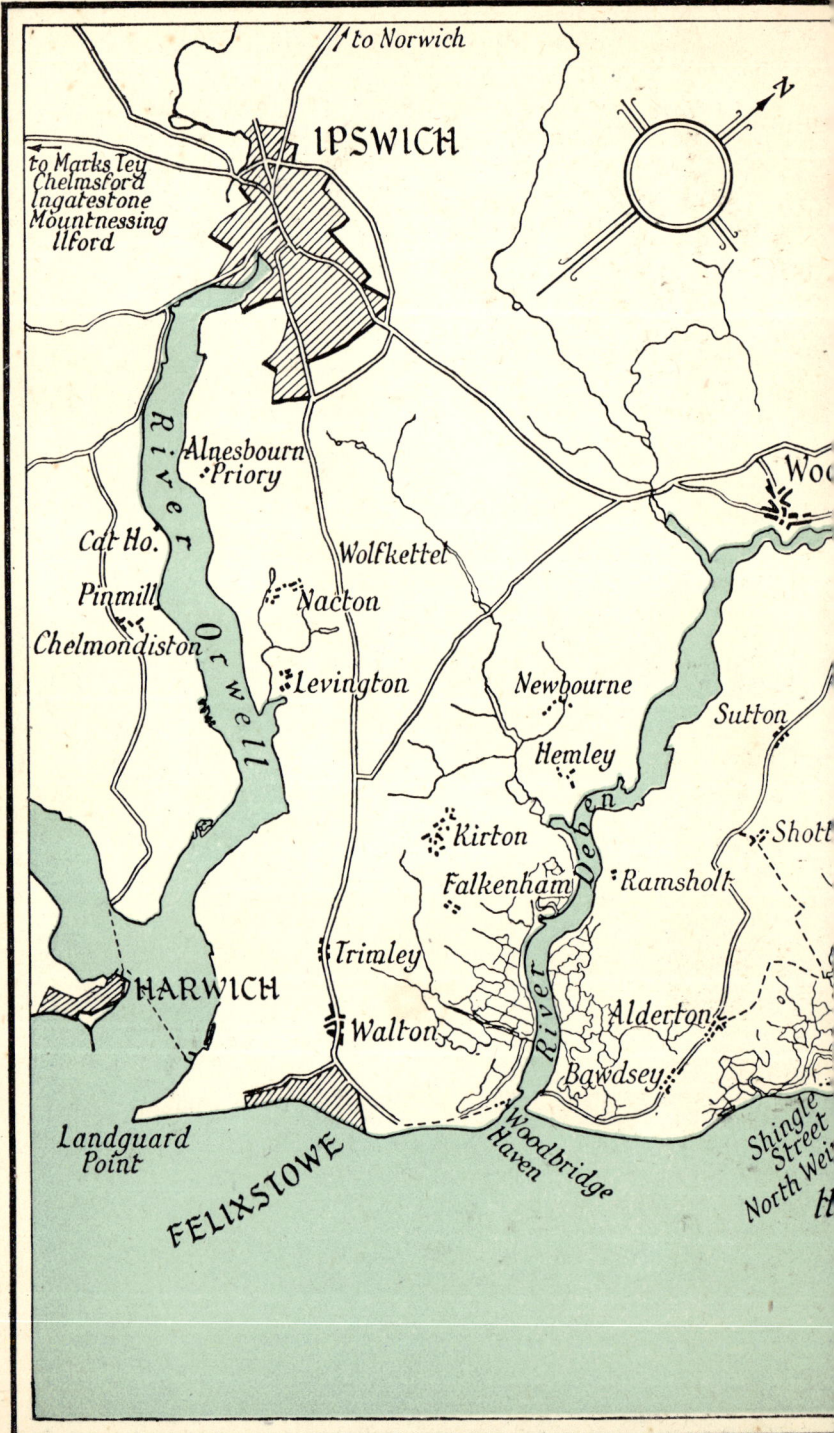

to Norwich

IPSWICH

to Marks Tey
Chelmsford
Ingatestone
Mountnessing
Ilford

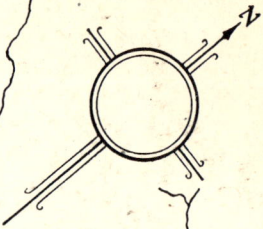

Woo

River Orwell

Alnesbourn
Priory

Cat Ho.

Pinmill

Chelmondiston

Wolfkettel

Nacton

Levington

Newbourne

Sutton

Hemley

River Deben

Kirton

Shott

Falkenham

Ramsholt

Trimley

HARWICH

Walton

River Deben

Alderton

Bawdsey

Landguard
Point

FELIXSTOWE

Woodbridge
Haven

Shingle
Street
North Wei